DEAD AMERICA
THE NORTHWEST INVASION COLLECTION
PART 2
BOOKS 7 - 12
BY: DEREK SLATON
© 2020

BOOKS:

FOLLOW NEW RELEASES AT:

www.DeadAmericaBooks.com

DEAD AMERICA
THE NORTHWEST INVASION
BOOK 7
SEATTLE PART 5
BY DEREK SLATON
© 2020

CHAPTER ONE

Day Zero +25

"Watch that window, watch that window!" the wounded soldier screamed, and began to fire his pistol as fast as he could with his good arm. His left dangled to the side, an angry bite sound at the bicep. His heart pounded, spreading the sickness through him faster and faster.

His panic fire didn't do much to stem the tide, as the entire front window of the big box store had been shattered, crushed under the pressure of hundreds of zombies now pouring into the building. Several of his teammates pressed shopping carts against the horde in an attempt to hold them back.

"We need more guns on the line!" he yelled, but it fell on deaf ears. Nobody could do anything but react, try to survive.

Private Janey Watts ducked down behind a register, completely overwhelmed, clutching her rifle with white knuckles. Gunfire erupted from every direction of the store as her unit was totally overwhelmed by zombies. Glass shattered on the other side, and dozens more creatures poured in, swallowing a couple of troops who had stood their ground to try to stem the tide.

"Oh god they're in the aisles!" somebody screamed from the back of the store, and several shots rang out, followed by agonized screams.

Watts blinked rapidly, her breath catching in her throat at the terror in the man's voice as he succumbed to death.

"Watch the flank!" somebody yelled from her right, much closer. "They're coming around the other side!"

Sustained fire followed, but soon stopped. Watts zoned out, her mind having a hard time processing everything that was happening. They were going to die here. She was going to get eaten alive by undead monsters. She could already feel them tearing at her flesh, ripping her meat from her bones and smacking their lips at the taste of her blood.

"Watts!" somebody cried, shaking her from her reverie. "To your feet, soldier!"

She tried to shake her fear, getting to her feet on trembling legs. Four soldiers struggled against the carts as the horde pushed against them, and a ghoul managed to grab a hold of an arm, pulling it in for a snack.

Blood splattered across the carts as the man screamed, jerking back, his leg tangling in the carts as he fell to the ground. He tried to flip himself over, but the zombies overwhelmed him within seconds.

"Let's get out of here!" somebody cried, and the other three cart soldiers broke rank, moving away from the window.

The wounded soldier with the dead arm barked orders, reloading his handgun and firing again, hitting several creatures at point blank range. A few of the zombies on the pile peeled off, moving towards a new target. He kicked one in the chest, sending it tumbling to the ground. This gave him enough of an opening to point his gun at his fallen comrade and shoot him in the head.

Watts watched in horror. Watching someone she'd just spoken to hours before be put down like a dog, to avoid being reanimated as an even more brutal undead corpse… she clutched her assault rifle tightly, unable to raise it as if her arms were made of lead. Her only defense was to remain motionless in the shadows, hoping that the ghouls would pass by.

A few did just that, wandering further into the store, but one caught a glimpse of a fresh meal and turned towards her, mouth opening. Watts screamed as the decrepit ghoul in tattered sweat pants staggered towards her. She froze, unable to fight, unable to do anything, and then the zombie's head exploded, sending rotted brain matter everywhere.

She stayed still, stunned, blinking at the now unmoving corpse.

"If you want to live, you have to fight!" the wounded soldier barked, and she looked up at him as he raised his handgun and fired a few more times. He glanced back at her, and then turned, slamming his gun on the register counter and grabbing her by the shirt collar.

He jerked her forward, grabbing the barrel of her assault rifle and aiming it towards the mass of zombies less than ten yards from them.

"Either you pull that trigger, or we both die right now!" he yelled.

Watts stared at him, terrified, noticing that he wasn't picking up his gun to fight anymore. His arm was covered in blood, hanging dead, the bite wound starting to coagulate. He was dead no matter what, which put her dire situation into perspective.

She finally raised her gun, squeezing the trigger and putting a single round into a zombie near the shopping carts. It ripped through the ghoul's chest, sending it stumbling back over the other bodies.

"There you go!" the soldier said, waving to her. "Now come on, let's get to the back."

He picked up his gun and fired a few more times towards the window, the zombies struggling to move past the mass that had clustered over the dead soldier to feast.

He led her down the checkout line, deeper into the store. Watts raised her assault rifle, steeled herself, and followed. It was large, a giant grocery plus department store. Outside of the light coming from the few skylights and the front windows, it was very dim inside, making it difficult to see very far.

The two ran parallel with the front of the building, trying to make it to a cross aisle. As they went, there was yelling and gunfire coming from various points in the store, but it was far less than it had been just a few minutes prior.

The soldier led Watts to the first cross aisle, which led to the back of the store. As they came around the corner of the shelving unit, the soldier ducked back behind cover, grabbing her and pulling her to safety.

They peered around the edge, seeing a feeding frenzy in the center about fifteen yards down. There were a dozen or so ghouls hunched over a body, tearing and ripping and chewing.

The soldier leaned into Watts and whispered, "We have to fight through them. At least enough to get by."

"What about another aisle?" she whispered back.

He shook his head. "We had forty men when we came in here," he said quietly, and pointed up. "Listen. Do you hear much gunfire or screams? Or anything?"

Watts strained her ears, only hearing a single sustained gunfire coming from the other side of the store. She swallowed hard, knowing that their situation had gone from dire to desperate. She nodded jerkily.

"Good," the soldier replied, "come on. We're going to make it."

They came around the corner, guns aimed at the zombie buffet. They inched forwards, ready to open fire as soon as the ghouls noticed them. A few aisles down, moans erupted from the right, and the wounded soldier whipped in that direction, quickly squeezing the trigger a few times while backing up.

Two zombies in military fatigues came tearing towards them, sprinting. His panic fire hit the lead one in the torso several times, and one managed to find a forehead, dropping the second one.

The lead runner reached him with a shriek, latching onto his shoulder. He let out a bloodcurdling scream before putting the barrel of his gun against its head, pulling the trigger at point blank range.

He slumped to one knee, handgun clattering to the floor as he pressed his good hand against the fresh wound. He pulled it back and stared at his slimy crimson palm, letting out a frustrated yell.

Before he could get up, Watts opened fire on the feeding pile. Some of them had broken off from the noise, heading for the wounded soldier. Her shots were off target, mostly hitting them in the chest, but it was enough to force them to stagger back a bit. She rushed over to her fallen comrade, grabbing him under the arm and pulling him up.

"Come on, we're good, we're good!" she urged, and he nodded, even managing a slight smile.

They raced down the aisle to the left, moving away from the lumbering group now giving chase. As they approached the far end, which led to the outer wall of the store, several more ghouls staggered around the corner, one of which was in military gear.

At the sight of a potential runner, both Watts and the sounded soldier raised their weapons and fired, concentrating their attention on the fresh corpse. Several direct hits exploded its head in a spectacular fashion, enraging the other three zombies next to it.

The duo moved toward, getting within
a few yards to maximize their aim before
pulling the trigger. Within seconds, the
path was clear.

They reached the aisle on the outer
edge of the store, with a relatively clear
path to the back, only a few zombies
staggering about. They moved at a quick
pace, with Watts aiming downrange while
the wounded soldier cleared each aisle as
they passed.

She focused, taking better care in
her aim before firing, hitting the next
two targets in the head.

"There you go," the wounded soldier
said shakily, "let your training take
over."

She nodded, her confidence building
with each step.

When they reached twenty yards of the
back wall, they took each aisle carefully,
clearing it. The final three were free of
zombies, but the back wall was a mess.
They ducked behind cover, using the final
shelving unit, and looked out at the dozen
creatures, half of which were in military
gear.

The ghouls were fighting over scraps
of a corpse on the floor, blocking the
double doors to the loading dock behind
them.

Watts glanced behind them, seeing that their followers were still about thirty yards back, giving them a few moments to figure out their plan.

"How do we do this?" she whispered.

The wounded soldier dropped the mag in his handgun and struggled to reload it with one hand. Watts grabbed the gun and helped him out, handing it back when it was fresh.

"Thanks," he gasped.

She nodded firmly. "Sure thing."

"It's far too narrow for us to fight our way through," the soldier said quietly, "we're going to have to go around."

Watts pursed her lips. "What about those runners, though?" she asked. "There's too many of them by the door."

He looked again and then faced her. "How fast are you?"

"I'm not going to win any medals," she admitted, "but I wouldn't finish dead last, either."

"Okay, this is what we're doing," the soldier said, wincing as he raised his gun. "I'm going to start shooting and pull them this way. We go down this aisle and sneak into the back before they can circle around."

Watts was a little concerned about the plan, but nodded, as it was the best they could come up with in the next sixty seconds, which was all the time they would have. The soldier rounded the corner, aiming his gun at the horde.

"Go, now!" he yelled.

Watts took off as he opened fire, shooting five times almost blindly into the pack, unconcerned with headshots. Within seconds, the runners in the group pushed past the slow ones, making a beeline for him.

Watts looked back over her shoulder, watching her companion follow her as quickly as he could, wincing with pain as he pumped his bite-infested arms.

She reached the end of the aisle, doing a quick sweep in either direction. As she looked to the right towards the front of the store, there was a group of zombies, one of which wore military fatigues. It let out a scream and ran for her.

Watts raised her assault rifle and began firing, pulling the trigger as fast as she could. The bullets ripped into the torso of the running ghoul, doing little to slow it down. She adjusted her aim higher, hitting it in the throat just before it tackled her.

She tumbled to the ground; her rifle crushed against her. She pushed up with it, acting as a barrier between her face and the gnashing teeth above. She strained to keep the zombie away, snapping within a hair of her face.

As she struggled, several shots came out of the aisle, hitting the creature in the back. This distracted the zombie momentarily, and it whipped over to look at the new threat. The wounded soldier fired into its face, dropping it on top of Watts.

She struggled to shove the unmoving corpse on top of her, smearing blood all over herself in the process.

"Move move move!" the soldier barked as he turned, firing down the aisle at the runners still in pursuit of them.

Watts thrashed, finally managing to free herself from the weight of the ghoul, and leapt to her feet. She tore for the double doors and into the back loading dock, realizing too late that she'd forgotten her rifle in her panic.

The wounded soldier broke from his firing position, running after her with the zombies still in hot pursuit. Watts rushed through the door, looking around and noting the back area was mostly clear with only a half dozen slow-movers near the back wall.

Her companion burst in through the double doors, quickly followed by a couple of runners. One of them grabbed his bad arm, jerking him back towards the door. It sunk its teeth into his hand, claiming a couple of fingers.

The soldier screamed in pain before shooting the munching monster in the face. The other one tackled him, sending him to the ground, giving it a chance to bite into his chest. He fired several shots at point blank range, killing it.

"Oh god," Watts groaned as she rushed over, "come on, we're almost there." She grabbed him by the collar, pulling him towards the small office at the back, about ten yards away. S she pulled, another runner burst in and the soldier fired a few more shots, missing the head badly.

The zombie sprinted for them, but Watts managed to pull her companion inside the office, slamming the door shut just before the runner smacked into it.

There was a single large window inside with the blinds shut, and another window on the door. She stood up, looking the dead soldier in the eyes, seeing nothing resembling human left in their milky depths. As it banged on the door, desperate to get in to eat her, she closed the blinds, shielding them from the outside.

The wounded soldier let out a cough, rolling to spit blood onto the linoleum.

Watts knelt and helped him sit up, leaning him against the wood-panelled wall. She sat down on the floor, across from the lone desk, as the runner continued to slam against the other side.

"Well…" the soldier said hoarsely, "it's not the comfiest spot I've ever taken a woman to." He coughed. "But it will keep you safe."

Watts blinked rapidly, her chest tightening. "I… I can't thank you enough." She swallowed hard. "And I… I feel so ashamed to say this, but I don't even know your name."

He cracked a smile, coughing a little more, the life quickly leaving his pallid face. "It's Larry," he said weakly. "And if it's any consolation, I didn't know your name until yesterday. That was only because another soldier was talking about how good your ass looked and pointed you out."

They shared a small laugh, and her cheeks pinked a bit.

"Well Larry," Watts said, lacing and unlacing her fingers in front of her, "it's good to know I made an impression on you."

He managed a weak smirk. "Your ass did look good," he admitted, "I'm just saying."

They laughed again, but Watts' quickly dissolved into tears as the weight of her situation came crashing down on her all at once.

"Hey now," Larry said, "save those tears. Don't you dare waste them on me. I'm just a grunt doing what a grunt does." He coughed again. "Knew this going in." He paused. "Granted, I thought it would be an IED or an ambush that got me, not zombies. But it is what it is."

She took a deep breath to compose herself, wanting to honor his last wish. She could easily see that the life was seeping out of him quickly, the blood pool beneath him growing larger. She drew her handgun slowly, setting it in her lap, her lips pressed into a thin line.

She didn't want to have to do this. But she knew she had to. He wouldn't want to be a zombie, and she didn't need another runner in here with her. The thought of putting a bullet in this man's brain made her stomach tighten. He'd saved her life, and how was she going to repay him? By shooting him like a dog? Her mouth went dry.

Larry held up his good hand. "No, put that away," he rasped. "It was my dumb ass that got bit, I'll handle it."

"But…" Watts trailed off, chewing her lip. Part of her was relieved, because she didn't want to have to do it. But to make the man take his own life? That felt so callous.

"Stop," he said. "Only thing I want you to focus on is surviving. We radioed in our position before things went to shit, so somebody should be here in a couple of hours for you."

She lowered her gaze. "And if they're not?"

"Then do me proud by surviving any way you can," he replied.

She looked at him, steeling her gaze. "You have my promise, Larry," she said as firmly as she could muster.

He forced a smile and then waved his hand for her to look away. "It's about that time," he said, "and I don't think you're going to want to see this."

She nodded jerkily. "Thank you," she whispered.

"Anytime," he said.

She turned her head away, and out of the corner of her eye, she saw the muzzle flash light up the side of the small room. The deafening *BOOM* was like a nail in a coffin, followed by the clatter of metal as the gun hit the floor.

The sound seemed to echo inside of her head, and it was as if she couldn't control her eyes, turning back to look at him. Normal dead bodies looked so peaceful in sleep. Maybe if he wasn't covered in gory wounds and blood, he would have looked peaceful. His eyes were closed, but the carnage was sickening.

Several more zombies joined the runner at the door and window, the pounding growing louder and louder.

Watts curled her legs up to her chest, letting the tears flow as she stared at her dead friend. She hoped he'd found peace, away from the pain, away from the exhaustion of fighting a losing battle and then using his last moments to save her life.

She hoped he'd forgive her for weeping for him now. There was nothing else she could do in that moment.

Watts checked her watch. Eleven thirty-seven A.M. It had been three and a half hours being stuck in the small office with Larry's unmoving corpse.

They should have come by now, she thought, scrubbing her hands down her face.

There was nothing. No rescue, no gunshots in the distance, only the shuffling feet and occasional moan from zombies in the loading dock. The only positive thing going for her at the moment was that the zombie runners had given up on having her for brunch and wandered away.

I don't think they're coming. The thought was terrifying, and she wanted nothing more than to just curl up in a ball. But she couldn't stay here. If nobody was coming for her, she'd die of dehydration in here. Or the zombies would succeed in breaking down the door and get at her and what used to be Larry.

Her heart rate tripled at the thought. She couldn't just sit here. She had to get out and find a unit, any unit, to get her back to safety. Or as much safety as could be guaranteed in the apocalypse.

She sat and contemplated for a few moments before digging into her back pocket, pulling out a folded up satellite image of the area. She studied it, placing her finger on a circled shopping center.

The suburb of Kenmore was nestled at the northern tip of Lake Washington, right on the highway that led straight to the interstate. Their breakaway group of five hundred had pushed forward from the town of Redmond that had been cleared out the day before, with the intention of making this place a diversion point.

While Watts didn't have the full details of the mission, rumor had it that there was a huge group of zombies coming up from downtown, attracted by the intense fighting to the north. Some sort of blockade had been tried and failed, which was why they'd been sent pushing ahead.

"Not sure what they were thinking," she muttered under her breath, "but whatever it was, they didn't put much thought into it."

She tapped the circled store at the north end of the suburb, a good three-quarters of a mile away from the highway, and the last major store before the massive residential area started up. It was hard to tell where Kenmore ended and the next subdivision suburb began, but it really didn't matter since her only goal was to get back to the command center.

She traced her finger down the main road to the highway, then to the east half a mile or so, finally stopping on a building a couple blocks to the north of it. She stared at the roof of the building, a large warehouse that they'd taken pretty easily upon their arrival just before dawn.

That's where I have to get to, she thought. *No more than a mile or so. Come on Janey, you can do this. It'll be just like playing hide and seek with the other kids in the neighborhood… only if you get tagged, you die.* She couldn't help but chuckle. *Okay, so it's an extreme version of the game, but the concept is still the same. Move quick and don't get touched.*

Her attempt at a pep talk to herself fell flat, and she let out a deep sigh. She took out her handgun and inspected it.

If something does get close, this should help. She removed the mag, seeing it was mostly full. She patted her side, feeling one additional magazine for it before putting her hand on the knife sheathed on her belt.

Really wish I hadn't left that rifle behind, she thought bitterly. *But if you hadn't, you'd probably be like poor Larry over there… or every other member of your squad.*

Watts pulled herself off of the ground, stretching a bit to work out some of the cramps from sitting for so long. She moved over to the door, carefully pulling back the blinds so she could see out into the darkened loading dock.

There were a few zombies milling about, none of whom wore military gear.

Well, at least there aren't any runners, she thought. *That I can see, at any rate.* She holstered her handgun and drew her knife, wanting to save every precious round she could.

She glanced back at Larry, jaw clenched as she took in the back of his head blown out. She took a moment to silently thank him before turning back to the door.

Okay, just have to run across, throw open the door, and get outside, she thought. *Nothing to it.*

She readied herself, taking a few deep breaths to calm her nerves before making the move. She carefully unlatched the lock and opened it as slowly and quietly as she could. A third of the way open, the hinge started to creak a little, and she seized up. Two zombies in the loading dock turned towards the noise.

Watts remained motionless, hoping
that they'd forget what they'd heard.
Several tense moments passed before they
decided there was nothing there, and
turned back around, shuffling into the
darkness.

She let out a deep breath and
steadied herself, focusing on the locked
door across the dock, about twenty yards
away. She took a deep breath, pushed the
door open, the creak alerting the same two
ghouls.

This time however, she didn't
hesitate, darting out from cover and
tearing for the loading door.

The duo of monsters moaned loudly and
began to shamble towards her. The noise
they made attracted the attention of
several other ghouls down the way, who
made excited noises and ambled after them.

Watts rushed the door, grabbing the
large bolt-style lock and throwing it
open. She turned the knob and pushed, but
the door was still locked. Panic-stricken,
she searched the door, finding an
additional deadbolt underneath the handle.

As she fumbled with it, rapid
footsteps pounded from the far end of the
dock, echoing on the concrete.

She grunted as she finally freed the
deadbolt, gripping the knob. She made the
mistake of looking over her shoulder to

see a runner pushing through the slower moving creatures, knocking them this way and that and closing fast.

Watts quickly turned the knob, relieved when the door freed itself, sunlight pouring through the crack as she pushed it open. She quickly darted to the other side, slamming the door shut behind her as the runner smacked into it. She threw her weight into the door, even though it was solidly shut, more of an instinctual reaction than a rational one. The creature thrashed violently on the other side, desperate to get to her.

Moans erupted from outside, and Watts snapped back into the moment to see the area behind the building was littered with zombies. A dozen, maybe a few more, scattered all about and coming her way.

She let instinct take over, hopping down from the top of the small stairs and hitting the pavement, running away. A quarter of the way down the building, a thought hit her. She didn't know where she was going.

There was an eight-foot high chain-link fence to her right, keeping her in an alley with no idea what was on the other side. And she had no way to know what was standing in her way to get to the command center.

Watts whirled around, staring at the zombies shambling her way before spotting a lone truck backed up against the building. It was close enough to the stairs that she could climb on top and pull herself up to the roof.

I need to know what I'm getting into, she thought, and squeezed her knife tightly before running back to the stairs.

There were three zombies spread out across the back alley between her and the stairs, with the rest not far behind. She ducked around them with relative ease, making the turn for the stairs.

Before jumping over to the truck, she turned and took in the congregation forming at the base of the stairs. She shook it off, ignoring it and leaping over to the truck, struggling to pull herself to the top of it.

Finally, after a tense moment, she rolled on top of it, laying on her back for a moment to let the sun baked metal warm her skin.

"That feels nice," she breathed, and enjoyed being alive for a beat before sitting up. She looked down at the stairs, ten zombies reaching and clamoring for her. She glared at them, and then turned on her heel, heading for the roof and pulling herself up the last few feet.

Watts held her breath as she crossed the roof, battling the dread at what she would see. Her heart sank as she came within twenty yards of the edge, already seeing zombies flooding the parking lot despite it being far back from the entrance.

The rest of the walk sunk her spirit. When she finally reached the edge, she looked out over a sea of thousands of zombies, all crammed against the front of the building even though the treats inside had been long devoured.

At least the diversion kind of worked, she thought bitterly, and sat down. She pulled out her map, making sure she was looking to the south, and found some landmarks so she could plot her course to the command center.

She looked out, but every landmark was surrounded by an ocean of zombies. Thousands, maybe even tens of thousands. Nothing but rotted flesh, waiting on the smallest hint of life to chase after.

"That's disheartening," she muttered.

She strained her ears, struggling to hear anything over the constant moaning. No gunshots, no vehicles, no nothing. Just moans from the damned.

Watts turned around and headed to the north end of the roof. On the other side of the chain-link fence was a residential area covered in trees. She tried to look through the trees to see any movement, but it was difficult to tell.

"Well, can't be any worse than what's out front," she said with a sigh.

She shook her head, knowing she'd have to go north and take the long way around to the command center. Glancing down, the zombies by the truck had increased their numbers to around twenty, most of them still near the stairs but several spread out as well.

She studied the area, trying to figure out how to get over the tall fence, as well as how to get back to the ground safely. She'd been hoping there was something that could cause a noise on the ground to distract them, but nothing was viable.

The only option she had was to hop down off of the front of the truck and use the momentum to get to the fence. There were a few zombies within ten yards of the front, so she'd have to land perfectly.

Watts carefully climbed down onto the back of the truck, staying low and moving quietly so that the ones at the front wouldn't pay her any attention. When she reached the front, she looked down and saw one of the creatures had wandered mighty close.

She debated with herself for a moment about whether or not to use her handgun, but ultimately decided on the silent approach. She slid down the front windshield of the truck, squeaking on it and drawing the attention of the ghoul in front.

She went for it, leapt down off of the front of the truck, thrusting her knife downwards. The force of the impact jammed the blade into the top of the creature's head up to the hilt as they both tumbled to the ground.

The noise attracted the other zombies, who immediately began wandering towards her. She quickly put her foot on the dead creature's shoulder and pushed so she could free her blade. After a few tense seconds, it finally came free.

She didn't have time to sheath it, so she tossed it over the fence and raced towards it. She leapt up and began climbing, reaching several feet off of the ground as the first creature hit the chain link. It reached up and grabbed the bottom of her boot, but she kicked it free and kept climbing.

She got to the top and flipped over, falling down the other side and landing on her feet. She quickly scrambled for the knife, grabbing it and hopping into a crouched position, chest heaving. She

frantically looked around, finding herself
in an empty fenced-in backyard. Moans and
smacking and rattling came from the chain-
link fence behind her, but she was
relatively safe for the moment, and took a
beat to collect herself.

     She leaned over, hands on her knees,
taking in a few deep breaths, and then
straightened, squaring her shoulders.

     "Okay Janey, get moving."

Watts rummaged through the pantry in the quiet two-bedroom family home. She was relieved to find some bottled water and gulped it down to moisten her parched throat. She used a little from the bottom to wash away some residual blood caked on her face, and then tossed the empty plastic aside.

She grabbed another and cracked it open, sitting at the kitchen table. She pulled out the satellite image of the area and sipped a lot slower at the water as she plotted her course.

"Okay, I'm a few blocks north from where I started," she murmured to herself, tracing her fingers along the map as she spoke. "If I go due east, I'll get to the woods in half a mile or so, then it's a straight shot south."

She tapped her finger on the wooded area, large in scale, looking like it was about the same size as the entire residential area she was currently in. "Just hope there are some trails through here," she said, chewing her bottom lip.

She took another sip of water and then folded up the map, carefully pocketing it. She headed for the front window, peering out at a handful of zombies wandering around in yards across the street.

She shook her head. *Like a hot girl on the dance floor, I just can't stop attracting attention,* she thought with a sigh. She moved towards the front door, but paused at the sight of a deer head mounted above the fireplace.

"Wonder if you were a hunter," she murmured, and then headed for the closet, opening it up. There was nothing but jackets and a vacuum cleaner, so she moved through the house, checking every closet in every room, finally coming to the master bedroom.

She opened the door and it looked like a budget safari. Several animal heads adorned the walls. Deer, bears, even a large tiger skin blanket on the bed. She wrinkled her nose at the tackiness, almost too much for her to bear.

"Guessing you didn't do much entertaining," she said, and stepped into the room. She checked the closet. "Bingo," she said as she revealed a large rack full of hunting rifles.

She inspected a couple of them before picking the one at the top, a jet black model with a high end scope and a detachable magazine.

"Yeah," she said as she ran her hand down the barrel, "you'll do nicely." She raised the rifle and looked through the scope, satisfied with the clarity. She slung the gun over her back and then knelt to dig through the ammo box on the floor, pulling out two additional magazines already loaded. "Fifteen shots," she said. "Might even be able to hit the target on half of those."

Watts knew her limits. She wasn't the greatest marksman, finishing near the middle of the pack for her unit back in basic, but at a close enough range she felt confident she could at least do a little damage.

She made her way back to the front of the house, looking out at the zombies in the neighboring yards, only a couple of them on the street. She readied her knife, wanting to stay as quiet as she could.

Okay, half a mile and I'm in the woods, she thought. *Just gotta get there and I'll be good.*

She exited the front door, moving at a deliberate pace but not much faster than a mall walker. When her feet hit the pavement, the noise was enough to attract the attention of zombies in the yards, which turned and began moaning, shambling in her direction.

Her pace was faster than theirs, so it was a simple walk down the road. She kept glancing over her shoulder to make sure a runner wasn't mixed in with the bunch. After a few blocks, she'd attracted quite the crowd, fifty to sixty based on her quick estimate.

The tree-lined street was quaint. She looked over the small single-story houses and let her mind wander. *What kind of people had lived here? New husbands and wives, maybe some new families?* On its face, the neighborhood looked like the perfect place for people to move in and get their start in life.

At least… it had been, a month ago. Her idyllic view of the area was broken as she passed the next house. The front bay window was partially shattered, bloodstains coating the inside, and a lone hand laying across the bottom will, reaching for safety that had never come.

Watts quickly turned away from it, swallowing hard, and focusing her attention straight ahead. How many new families had perished here? How many children? She clenched her jaw.

The path to the edge of the woods was clear, only another block to go. She sped up a little to put some distance between her and the pack, now a hundred strong, giving her a few moments to study her next move.

Well… this looks uninviting, she thought as she stared at the entrance to

the woods. It was densely packed with a
lot of underbrush, with no discernible
path through. She checked the left and
right, seeing no pathway, or at least any
that she could see from where she stood.

*Looks like this is as good as it
gets,* she thought bitterly, and let out a
deep sigh. She stepped over a large fallen
branch into the woods, pushing her way
through the dense brush into a bit of an
opening on the other side. The thickness
of the trees cast a shadow over the
entirety of the forest, and she readied
her knife.

She checked her watch, that
thankfully had a small compass at the top
of it, and found southeast. She squared
her shoulders and began her hike.

CHAPTER FOUR

Watts ducked cautiously through the woods, rays of sun piercing through the branches above, the shadows creating dark pockets along her path. She stopped at each shadowy area, making sure nothing was going to pop out at her.

She couldn't slow too much, however, as the zombies from the neighborhood continued their pursuit. Their numbers had dwindled in the woods after about a mile, so she wasn't too worried, but she still didn't want to have to deal with them. The forest was easy for her to navigate, but the trees posed a significant challenge to the directionally impaired zombies.

She reached a sun-drenched mini-clearing, and pulled out the map, consulting her compass. She focused on a small opening in the trees towards the south-easternmost point on the map.

Well, I'm getting closer… she thought. *I think.* She looked around, still not seeing anything resembling a trail. *Was this place a wildlife preserve? How can there be no trails or anything?* As she contemplated, there was shuffling and some light moaning from ahead. She pocketed the map and readied her knife, moving up to a tree on the edge of the clearing.

She peeked out from cover, trying to get a read on where the sound was coming from. It took a moment, but she spotted a few creatures emerging from a darkened area of the woods across the way, directly in the path she needed to take.

She tried to plot her course around them, but her stomach sank at the sight of more zombies coming into view, some out of the shadows, and others from around trees. Her heart began to race as dozens of ghouls appeared, blocking her way.

What do I do? Her mouth went dry as she thought. *Do I fight? Do I run?*

She looked up at some low-hanging branches and thought about climbing up. After a beat, she shook her head. She knew if one of them spotted her, she'd be stuck up there, and being treed by a horde of zombies would be significantly harder to navigate than being on the ground, spread out.

She turned back to the growing threat in front of her and gripped the handle of her knife tightly. *Okay Janey, you gotta suck it up girl;* she thought firmly.

She scanned the area, honing in on what had once been a teenage female, with a slight build and matted blonde hair drenched in blood. It was twenty yards away, and clear by several yards of any other zombies.

You can take her, she tried to convince herself. *Just hit her and run. That clearing can't be too much further ahead, and then you're nearly home free.*

She psyched herself up, bouncing a little, and then finally darted out from cover, pumping her legs as hard as she could. The noise attracted the attention of dozens of zombies nearby, all turning towards her with arms outstretched.

Watts ignored them, focused solely on the teenage corpse in front of her. When she came within a few yards, she raised her knife, jamming it straight into the eye socket. As it fell backwards, one of its flailing arms caught her ankle, and she stumbled forward.

She hit the ground hard, sliding in the dirt into a tree. She leapt to her feet, the moans and shuffling getting closer every second. She slid on the dirt floor of the woods, struggling for traction. Finally she was able to find her footing, dashing away and barely escaping the outstretched claws of the dead.

She darted around trees, moving nimbly and hoping to hell that there was nothing else ahead of her. After several minutes of running, she slowed, panting heavily. The sounds of moaning behind her were lower and farther away, but it seemed like the hum was growing in strength.

Watts braced herself against a tree, catching her breath before looking up. There was a clearing up ahead, no more than a hundred yards away. She forced herself to keep moving, although slower than her earlier sprint. She knew she'd have to pace herself, otherwise she'd burn out.

It took a minute, but she finally made it to the clearing, stopping just before stepping into it. Her mouth fell open at the sight of the entire hundred yard radius full of carnage.

My god... she thought as she blinked in horror. *Did people try to escape the city by coming here to camp?*

Dozens of tents and various campsites spread out, all of which were torn and bloody, showing signs of struggles. Several were knocked right over, many laying in fire pits half melted and burnt. Blood splashed everywhere, mostly eaten corpses rotting in the sunlight.

There were a few zombies still standing, milling about, but most of the former campers had long since wandered off, it seemed.

The moans at her rear continued to get stronger, so Watts forced herself out into the open. She moved lightly and cautiously through the makeshift campground, making sure to steer clear of

tents and other debris, in case something
was waiting to pop out and catch her by
surprise.

She looked over the landscape, coming
to the conclusion that straight through
the center was the best way to go. She
moved quickly and quietly, stepping over
debris and pools of coagulated blood. A
quarter of the way through, some of the
zombies on the edge spotted her movement
and groaned hungrily, heading her way.

The zombies were less careful in
their pursuit, stumbling over tents,
falling, and making a general racket. As
this happened, more ghouls in the woods up
ahead moaned and emerged from the trees.

Watts glanced over her shoulder,
seeing the first wave of creatures in
pursuit of her were coming out as well.

Your cover is blown, she thought
bitterly. *Might as well go for broke.* She
sheathed her knife and drew her handgun,
readying it before picking up the pace to
the other side of the clearing. Just
before she reached it, a small army of
ghouls poured out of the woods, forcing
her to adjust course.

She ran to the right, down an alley
between tents, straight at a pair of
creatures. She stopped just short of them,
aiming, and taking both of their heads off
with clean shots.

She glanced to either side, seeing that the walls were closing in on her, and sped up even more, leaping over the fallen corpses and darting past them.

Luckily, the number of zombies in her path by the woods were less substantial than the other direction, with only half a dozen blocking her path. She stopped several yards short, took careful aim and fired twice, hitting two on the left in the head. She took aim at the next one, but decided to save her ammo and take her window.

She broke out running, aiming for the area to the right of the still-standing creatures, ducking to avoid an outstretched arm. She hopped over the limp corpses, reaching the edge of the woods and disappearing into it.

A few trees deep, an arm shot out from behind a tree, latching onto her right bicep. The sudden force caused her to whirl around, sliding on the dirt floor and slipping down to one knee.

The ghoul lunged forward, still with a death grip on her arm, trying to take a bite out of her. Watts instinctively threw the handgun forward, putting it to the zombie's chest and pulling the trigger. The bullet ripped through the decrepit flesh, and the ghoul didn't react, snapping its teeth closer and closer to her face.

The weight forced her to fall back, twisting her knee as they fell. She let out a scream and rolled to the side to prevent more pain, the two of them crashing onto the ground on their sides. The impact sent the ghoul sliding a few feet away from her, allowing her to raise her weapon.

Watts aimed directly for the nose and fired, taking the back of the corpse's skull out. She let out a sigh before hauling herself to her feet, hissing as soon as she put weight on her twisted right knee.

She fell against a tree trunk, using it to brace herself. She gingerly put some pressure on her leg, grimacing at the sting. Moans and shuffles grew in volume behind her, and she grunted, pushing herself away from the support to keep moving.

She hobbled along at a much reduced pace, not much faster than the ambling zombies behind her.

"Come on Janey, play through the pain," she huffed as she moved. "You're almost home."

Watts pushed through the rest of the woods, approaching the edge of it into the developed portion of town. She continued to rub her injured knee, hoping that would help the pain. It had gone down a bit, but still smarted.

Finally, she thought, hope soaring in her chest at the sight of the treeline. The moans and footsteps behind her had subsided for the most part, at least falling behind her and becoming faint, so she took a moment to recoup.

When she reached the edge of the woods, she leaned up against a tree and looked out, taking in her surroundings. About fifty yards from where she stood was an apartment complex, and across from that a warehouse. She pulled out her map and studied it, trying to get her bearings.

She traced her finger around, and finally deduced that she was about half a mile to the west of the command center. She looked out over the complex, noting about a hundred zombies spread out, but beyond that it was difficult to see. She pulled out the hunting rifle, aiming it south and scanning the area.

The scope allowed her to see more of the warehouse complex, and the throng of zombies there as well. Pasts that, she could just make out the highway. It was too far away to really see it clearly, but close enough that she could tell it was jam packed with the dead.

So now what? She shook her head as she thought. *Definitely not hitting the highway, that's for sure.*

She continued to stare out, mentally plotting different courses around the immediate threat, noting smaller buildings and other obstacles as cover. As they did this, something began to niggle at the back of her mind, and her blood ran cold.

I'm less than half a mile from the command center, she thought, heart rate picking up in a panic. *Why isn't there gunfire? Why are there so many zombies out in the open if I'm this close? My god, is the command center even still there?*

The realization turned her stomach into a rock hard knot. If the command center wasn't there, then she was well and truly screwed. She had no radio to contact anyone, and no idea where a safe place would even be. The last safe place she'd been in was Redmond, but that was fifteen miles or so away.

Watts gave her head a vigorous shake, as if to forcefully remove the negative thoughts from it. Even if the command center had fallen, it didn't change what she had to do. She pulled herself together, pocketing the map and slinging the rifle back over her shoulder, and took a deep breath before pushing off of the tree.

She rushed forward a couple hundred yards to a small building to the east of the apartment complex. When she reached the back of the building, she turned and peeked out towards the horde. Relief flooded her than none of them had paid her any attention, giving her another moment to catch her breath and give her knee a chance to recoup.

She walked to the other side of the building, glancing down the alley between the structures that ran fifty yards or so. There was a lone zombie staggering around a dumpster, seemingly fascinated by it.

Watts watched as the ghoul smacked against it, then moaning at the resonating echo it made. She waited for it to smack again before moving across to the next building, hoping the noise would keep it from noticing her.

To her disdain, the creature moaned and began shambling her way. She contemplated for a moment, knowing that she could outrun it—or out-hobble it with her knee—but decided on taking it out instead.

If there's trouble up ahead, I'll have enough to deal with, she thought, and

readied her knife. She waited patiently
for the creature to get within striking
distance. As it reached the corner of the
building, she lunged forward, jamming the
blade into the top of its skull and
dropping it.

Now free of zombies, she worked her
way to the east, along the back side of a
long building. About halfway up was a
window, which she peered into. It was dark
inside, but there was plenty of movement
in the warehouse-type structure. She shook
her head and kept moving.

*As long as they're inside, it's not
my business,* she thought to herself.

As she reached the edge of the
building, she noticed that the next
stretch of cover was a mini-mall across
the street. The problem was that there
were a few dozen zombies in the road, near
the front of the building.

*Gonna have to push through the pain
to get across,* she thought, chewing her
bottom lip. *They're going to see me, not
much I can do about that. Just going to
have to hope I get enough distance between
us to make it through.*

Before she moved, she pulled out her
rifle and looked down towards the other
end of the mini-mall. There were a few
zombies at the far end, but not much past

that before it got to a small residential street.

Okay, run across, take those three out and then get to the neighborhood, she thought, taking a deep breath. She pulled out the satellite image printout and took a quick glance before stuffing it back into her pocket. *Three more blocks after that, then I'll be at the command center.*

She grabbed her knife in her off-hand, and drew her handgun in the other, prepared for whatever was to come. She did a silent countdown and then broke from cover, moving as quickly as her knee would allow across the street.

When she got halfway across, her hobbled footsteps attracted the attention of some of the ghouls on the road.

Immediately they moaned and shuffled towards her, gnashing their teeth in excitement. Watts picked up the pace to make sure she beat them to the corner of the building, making it about ten seconds before they did.

She pushed hard, trying her best to put distance between herself and the horde. Halfway down the building, she glanced back, the wall of rotted flesh no more than fifteen yards away. Her knee screamed, but she kept pushing. It was pain or death.

A trio of zombies ahead moved towards her, and five more came into view from the corner of the building. Her heart pounded in her ears.

Please don't let there be any more! She didn't know who she was praying to, but it worked, as the eight zombies ahead were all that stood in her way to reach the neighborhood.

Watts moved away from the rear of the mini-mall, stepping out into an overgrown field, but not too much as the grass was too thick to allow for speedy movement. She took aim, firing several times at the ghouls ahead of her, hitting a few in the head and dropping them to the ground.

She walked another few steps before stopping to aim again, firing rapidly at the five remaining zombies. She finished off her magazine, eight shots, but only killed three of the corpses. She aimed at the next one, ten yards away, and pulled the trigger, only hearing a sick metallic *click.*

"Damn," she muttered, holstering her gun and moving her knife to her dominant hand before moving forward. She reached out, grabbed the nearest creature by the shirt collar and stabbed, jamming the blade into the bridge of the zombie's nose.

The final ghoul, a young and frail looking thing, continued to shamble towards her. Watts lowered her shoulder and bowled right into her, moving quickly past without looking back. She pushed herself, building up some speed, the adrenaline spiking and overpowering the throbbing in her knee.

The residential area was small and run down, with single story homes that would have looked frightening even during non-apocalyptic times. Watts reached the first street, looking ahead and only seeing a smattering of zombies.

Her knee protested as she put weight on her leg, reminding her she was still injured, and she winced hard.

Gotta find some way to distract these things, she thought, and inched forward, moving about as quickly as the zombies behind her, which were twenty yards away at most. A few houses up, she spotted a newer looking sedan in the driveway of a rundown house. She rushed up to it as fast as she could, seeing a small blinking red light on the dash.

"Alarm system, thank god," she huffed, and checked the side of the house, peering into the backyard and finding it empty. She limped back to the car and pounded on the hood, smacking it as hard as she could. "Come on, go off!"

Finally, after a couple more shoves, the alarm blared. She moved as quickly as she could to the side of the house, reaching the backyard. She rushed over to the house on the next block, going up to the back door and smashing out the small window with the hilt of her knife, reaching in to unlock it.

When she got inside, she locked it behind her and did a quick sweep of the small house. In the living room there was a lone recliner and a large flatscreen with a video game system surrounded by empty beer cans.

"Gotta love bachelors," she muttered, and then jumped at the sound of a thump on the back bedroom door.

Watts moved to the top of the hallway and aimed her gun down, but saw the door closed tight. She steadied herself and moved to the front of the house, looking through the window to the street.

A few dozen zombies emerged from between houses, attracted to the car alarm noise in the distance. They got to the street, all moving in one direction, and then the alarm cut out. Without the noise drawing them in, their interest waned, some of them stopping dead in their tracks.

"Son of a…" Watts grumbled. "Just want one thing to go right today."

She knew she couldn't stay put, so she reloaded her gun with her last mag and drew her knife in her off-hand again.

"Here goes nothing," she whispered, and then threw open the front door and darted out into the yard. She moved as quickly as she could, despite her knee, and two zombies lunged for her. Rather than attack, she shoved the closest one back, knocking it into its partner and sending them both to the ground.

Several other ghouls in the vicinity came her way, but she pushed on, hobbling to the next row of houses, relieved to find a fenced-in yard.

"Finally," she huffed, and threw herself over the waist-high chain-link fence. She struggled with her injury, but managed to land on her good leg without falling on her ass. She darted out of sight from the pursuing zombies, hoping that once they hit the fence they'd give up.

At the back of the yard was a small line of trees, with the command center on the other side. She couldn't help the creeping doubt in the back of her mind that it had been abandoned, especially with the lack of any noise. But she had to push on.

She reached the trees, darting through the fifteen yards or so to the other side, hoping to see an army of troops waiting to greet her.

Watts stopped short at the edge of the trees and her heart sank, her worst fears realized. The command center was a war zone.

The makeshift sandbag barricades at the outer rim of the warehouse still mostly stood, but there were several breach points. Just beyond them was a collection of blood, limbs, and a few mostly eaten corpses. The mangled bodies twitched and struggled to move, but at least there wasn't enough left of them to get up and run around.

In the parking lot, within the perimeter, were a few dozen slow-moving zombies. Once that had found their way in, but couldn't find their way out again, it seemed. Several of them pushed up against the sandbags, unable to figure out how to break free.

Now what? Watts' mind reeled, and she put away her weapons, grabbing her rifle and looking towards the building. Through the scope, she could see that the front of it was closed up. The door was coated in blood, evidence of zombies banging away on it for quite some time.

If they were able to get the door shut, she thought, hope blooming in her chest, *maybe there are still some survivors inside!* She tried not to talk herself down, rolling with the situation so she couldn't talk herself out of doing what she needed to do.

She scanned the outer edge of the building, seeing a loading bay door near the back that was partially opened. While it was no more than a couple feet open, she figured it was large enough for her to squeeze through.

But what if the survivors inside used that as their escape? What if there's nobody inside? Doubt crept in, despite how hard she tried not to let it, and she clenched a fist, chewing her lip. *Even so, I have to get in there,* she thought firmly. *If the post has been abandoned, maybe there is still a comm station still set up. I can let them know I'm here, and they can come get me.*

Watts slung her rifle back over her shoulder and moved out, jogging just inside the treeline for cover. Finally she was parallel with the loading dock door in the back. She checked both ways, making sure the coast was clear. And it was.

She walked over, not wanting to put extra strain on her knee, before sliding underneath the door. She quickly stood up, drawing her weapons once again and straining her senses.

The warehouse didn't allow in much natural light, with only the skylights around the top of the building. There were several artificial lights set up still, however, making the room nice and bright.

She reached the edge of the loading dock door, looking out into the main area. The place was totally abandoned, at least from the living. There were several zombies still roaming about, most of them near the front door, a few near the lights. She continued to scan, finally laying eyes on the communications table.

She pulled out her rifle, looking over at the table through her scope, seeing trouble. The laptop with the satellite uplink had a cracked screen and was lying on its side, several wires strewn about.

Shit, she thought. Most likely, that computer wasn't going to work. She lowered the rifle, unsure of her next move. *So now what? Come on Janey, you gotta figure this out. Think.*

She took in a deep breath and then squinted when she noticed one of the zombies was wearing military gear. Her blood rushed in her ears at the sight of a runner, but then her brain tuned in, remembering that some of the promoted men were issued walkie-talkies that could stretch for several miles.

Watts raised the rifle again, looking at each zombie through the scope. The first few runners had nothing on them, except for tattered bloodied fatigues. She kept looking, heart rate spiking with each count of yet another fast zombie, and then finally found one near the front door wearing a packed utility vest. On the front of it was a walkie-talkie, clear as day.

Unfortunately, the creature was surrounded by a dozen other ghouls, as well as two runners between her and it.

How the hell are you doing this one, Janey? She chewed her lip. *Those things are runners! If I can hit the two closest to me, it will clear the way for the other one to get to me. Those shamblers will take time to get here, and I can be gone before they do…* She nodded to herself, though fear pumped through her like a rushing river.

It was risky, and dangerous, and crazy. But it was the only idea she had. She raised the rifle and took aim at the runner closest to her.

Just like when you were hunting, she thought to herself. *Deep breath, squeeze the trigger. You got this.*

She lined up her shot at the temple of the former soldier and squeezed the trigger. The resounding *BOOM* echoed throughout the cavernous warehouse, sending the zombies inside into a rage. The bullet found its target, however, eviscerating the runner's skull.

She quickly adjusted her aim towards the other one, which was now sprinting towards her. It was hard to get a read on it as it was close, within thirty yards, and moving quickly. She abandoned the plan to snipe it and instead hopped up off of the ground and braced herself.

As it got closer, she drew her handgun and fired rapidly. The third shot found its target, and the zombie flopped forward, sliding along the ground to a stop just a few yards from her.

Rapid footsteps echoed, along with a rabid moan. The other runner, the one with the radio, was closing in. She waited until it was within ten yards to fire, not wanting to risk a bad shot striking the radio.

The first bullet missed low, hitting it in the throat. She screamed as it got closer, firing again, and this time hit it in the eye. Watts darted forward to catch it, breaking its fall so that it didn't crush the walkie-talkie, whimpering at the strain on her knee in the process.

She set it down and rolled it over, grabbing the radio and pocketing it. She patted down the rest of him, finding another magazine for her handgun. She wanted to keep looking, check the other bodies, but the rest of the slow ghouls were getting too close for comfort.

Watts broke from her position and made her way back to the open door on the dock, sliding back out into the open area. She moved away from the building, pausing in the field beside it to consult the satellite image. The command center was at the far end of it, with only a tiny bit of space just to the east of it visible. It appeared to be wooded, but there were two roads going into it.

"Gotta be a residential area," she muttered, heart still pounding. She glanced back at the warehouse, seeing zombie feet at the dock. Past that, towards the front, were several more ghouls outside of the barrier that were starting to come her way. "Anyplace is better than here," she huffed, shaking her head. "Get moving, Janey."

She turned and hobbled off towards the residential area, hoping for the best, deep in disbelief that she'd killed three runners and secured her radio.

Watts broke into a nearby house a few blocks east of the command center, stepping over the busted *For Sale* sign on the front lawn. Inside, it was completely empty, devoid of all furniture, but she did a quick sweep just in case of stray deceased real estate agents shambling around.

Once clear, she sat on the floor in the living room with her back to the wall, sighing with relief and easing the pressure on her leg, and pulled out the walkie-talkie. She flicked it on, turning the channel dial to the first one and raising the device to her lips.

"This is Private Watts," she said clearly, "I need help, can anybody hear me?"

She waited a few moments for a response and then switched to the next channel.

"This is Private Watts," she repeated, "I need help, can anybody hear me?"

After six channels with no response, despair began to knot in her belly. This had been her last hope, her last-ditch attempt at surviving, getting out of here.

What if there's been a full retreat? Or worse… what if they've been overwhelmed? The dark thoughts swirled in her mind, and she shook her head hard, as if to knock them loose. She continued through the channels, firmly repeating her message.

"This is Private Watts, I need help, can anybody hear me?" She pressed the radio to her forehead, closing her eyes, silently praying for someone, anyone.

"Private Watts," a firm voice snapped, "this is a command channel. Please get off this line and switch to your designated unit channel."

She nearly dropped the walkie talkie as she fumbled to get it to her mouth. "Please wait!" she cried, the words gushing out of her like vomit. "My unit, they're all gone. I need an evac. Please, this is an emergency!"

There was a moment of silence, and then the soldier replied, "Please hold."

Watts trembled as she stared at the radio, shellshocked at having heard another human voice, willing herself not to panic. *Please, please let them help me,* she prayed, hoping that they could—or would—do something for her.

"Private Watts," a no-nonsense voice barked, "this is Captain O'Neil. Would you mind telling me why the hell you are on my channel?"

She immediately pressed the button, steadying her voice. "Captain, my unit was completely overwhelmed this morning," she explained quickly. "We had a runner outbreak and… and I was the only survivor. I need an evac."

"What's your position, Private?" O'Neil asked sharply.

Watts staggered to her feet, looking around frantically, and then noticed a stack of real estate fliers on the kitchen counter. "I'm at seven forty-two Greenbrook Lane," she replied.

To her surprise, the Captain chuckled. "My GPS is in the shop," he said, sounding amused. "Why don't you walk me through your day, and we'll see if we can't figure out where you are."

Her heart soared with hope. This man seemed to really want to help her.

"Okay, Captain," she said. "My unit was in the northern part of Kenmore when we were hit. Once I escaped, I tried going back to the command center, but it was abandoned and-"

"Command center?" he cut in. "Soldier, where are you?"

Watts blinked a few times, and then replied, "Sir, I am a few blocks to the east of the Kenmore command center."

"Soldier, you need to get out of there right now," O'Neil said rapidly, his tone panicked.

She shook her head. "Captain, there are zombies everywhere," she replied.

"Not for long there isn't," the Captain replied gravely.

Watts swallowed hard, cold dread sinking over her. "Captain," she said hoarsely, "what's going on?"

"No time to talk now," O'Neil snapped. "You need to get south of the highway and do it *now*! There is an airstrike coming in minutes!"

She gaped at the radio, eyes wide as saucers. "But I… where… where do I go?"

"Keep it together, Private!" the Captain barked. "You get south of the highway into the residential area. There is a golf course half a mile to the south, southwest of the command center. Get there and I'll fill you in further. Now move!"

Watts shook, taking in a deep, ragged breath and trying to push the panic out of her body. "Yes, sir," she replied, and shoved the walkie talkie into her pocket. She hobbled over to the front window of the house, seeing a handful of zombies on the road.

Scanning the area, she spotted a side street running south towards the highway. She nodded firmly to herself, and slung her rifle over her shoulder, readying her hand weapons.

I'd been looking forward to a rest, but looks like it's gonna have to wait, she thought to herself. *Come on Janey, you're almost there.*

She burst out the front door and ran as hard as she could. Her knee screamed, and every once in a while she had to do a bit of a hop when she just couldn't take the spike of pain shooting up her thigh like lightning.

But she pushed through it. *Pain or die, pain or die,* she reminded herself, the words in time with her strides.

The zombies on the road immediately began their pursuit, but she didn't have time to worry about them. She made it to the side street and began heading south, seeing even more zombies in front of her leading up to the highway half a mile or so ahead.

She looked down the side streets as she moved, and ghouls were everywhere. Picking a different path wasn't a viable option. The zombies, while numerous, were somewhat spread out, with a couple of yards in between packs.

It's either risk getting eaten or for sure get blown up, she urged herself. *Keep moving, Janey!*

Watts kept pushing, getting close to the first few zombies on the road. She looked past them towards the highway, and the slight incline up to it was jam-packed with creatures. She swallowed hard, chest heaving, seriously doubting about how she was going to make it across.

The first few monsters were facing the other way and didn't see her until she blew past them. As soon as she did, however, they moaned and reached for her, alerting other nearby zombies.

She kept moving, knee singing, darting between groups, and trying to keep her distance from the rotted hands clawing for her.

She made it through a block of them, only three blocks from the highway, and encountered a line of ghouls blocking her path.

She did the only thing that she could do. She raised her handgun and fired, hitting a zombie in the face and knocking it to the ground. She picked up as much steam as she could and burst through the line, clearing the ghouls with her body, but not her rifle.

A zombie gripped her rifle barrel with a death grip, and she struggled with it for a moment, trying to wrench the gun free. With the others closing in quickly, she grunted and slipped out of the strap, leaving the weapon behind and continuing to move forward.

When Watts was within a block of the highway, she saw there was absolutely no way she was going to be able to make it across. The road was a sea of corpses, shoulder-to-shoulder.

Think, girl, she thought frantically, *there has to be a way to get across.*

She put a hand to her forehead, leaning on her good leg to give her bad knee a brief rest as she contemplated.

Underpass! But which way? She looked back and forth, chewing her bottom lip. *I have to backtrack to the west anyway… might as well make it one trip.*

Watts ran up the final side street before the highway frontage road, relieved to see that the zombie population was manageable there. She got up to the next intersection and looked towards the highway, relieved to see that there was an underpass leading to the southern portion of town. She was less relieved to see that there were numerous zombies standing between her and her destination.

She didn't pause, didn't think, just pumped her tired, pain-filled legs. The frontage road had several packs of ghouls, but a narrow path through them.

The underpass was another story.

Running forty yards and shrouded in shadow, there were easily a hundred zombies packed in there. The road was buried under a sea of rotted flesh, and her heart rate tripled just looking at it.

On the left side, she spotted a narrow elevated pedestrian walkway, presumably put there due to the underpass being a drainage location. There were only a few zombies dotting it, given that stairs were their natural enemy.

Watts made her way to the stairs, quickly hopping up as several grey arms reached for her, narrowly missing her arm. The first ghoul on the walkway was ten yards away and immediately turned towards her as she crested the staircase.

Due to the narrow walkway, the creatures were in single file, which would make it easy for them to be dealt with. The first one received a decisive blow to the face with her knife. She shoved it aside, flipping it over the railing to the zombies below, turning it into an undead crowd surfer.

The next two fell just as easily, however during the battle the entirety of the zombie population in the underpass had been drawn to her side. She quickly moved to the end of the walkway, seeing a few ghouls standing at the bottom of the stairwell, with the others just to the side and well within reach.

Watts paused at the top of the stairs, aiming down with her handgun and opening fire. She pulled the trigger as quickly as she could, sending several rounds into multiple monsters, clearing her a narrow pathway back to the daylight.

She pinned herself as close to the wall as she could while racing down the stairs, skipping a few as she went, trying to use mostly her good leg for landing. The arms reaching through the handrails grazed her arm as she went by, but she managed to hit the ground and move away.

A few steps later she was out of the nightmare tunnel and to the south of the highway, a symphony of moans coming from inside as well as above. Across from the highway was another small stretch of houses, as well as a small waterway.

When she reached the houses, she slowed right down, cautiously moving between them, and she let out a sigh of relief when she saw there were no creatures between her and the water.

No time to try and find a bridge, she thought quickly, *I have to get across now!*

She raced to the water, pushing through thick tall grass and reaching the river. While still in knee-deep current, she looked to either side, hoping to find some sort of boat, but there was nothing, not even an inflatable inner tube.

"Guess I'm swimming," she grunted, and then dove forward into the water. She began to paddle, but after a moment, the weight of her gear combined with the pain and exhaustion of the day began to set in, so she flipped over onto her back.

She floated gently, using her arms to propel her backwards across the water. Thankfully, the current was minimal, so she wasn't going too far to the west.

She couldn't help but enjoy the coolness of the water combined with the warm sun on her face, a rare moment of peace and almost relaxation.

This was broken, however, by splashes coming from the other bank.

Watts quickly flipped back over, seeing she was ten yards from the shore. There were two zombies in the water, falling face first into it as they struggled to navigate the mud to get to their floating meal.

She pulled her gun, struggling to stay afloat while still inching herself forward. Five yards from the first zombie, she tried to aim while bobbing in the water, and pulled the trigger. Much to her surprise, her aim was on point, striking the creature in the head and sending it splashing to a watery grave.

The other zombie continued to push out into the water, and she continued her aim, waiting until it was within two yards to pull the trigger. The near point-blank shot found its target, sending the second threat washing away in the river.

Watts managed to pull herself out, breathing heavily on the southern bank. The break was short-lived as high-pitched humming rose in the distance, getting louder and louder.

"The attack!" she gasped, and hauled herself to her feet, racing south as fast as her legs would allow. The sound continued to grow in volume even as she reached a block away from the water.

She knew she only had seconds, and found the first house she could, shooting out the back patio door and rushing inside. There was a zombie in the living room, but she ran past it, straight to a back bedroom and slamming the door behind her.

It was thankfully free of ghouls, and she dove for the closet, shutting herself inside it for cover.

The sound of the missiles whistled overhead as they passed, and a moment later there was a cacophony of explosions to the north. Half a dozen, maybe more. It was too difficult to tell, but it was more than enough to shake the foundation of the house, shattering the windows in the bedroom.

As quickly as it had begun, the bombardment ended, filling the area with an eerie silence.

She sat there in the closet, almost in shock, staring at a horrible leopard-print gown hanging in front of her.

Banging on the closet door startled her, and she couldn't help but laugh, shaking her head.

"Okay," she said shakily, relief flooding her, "going to take this thing out, and then find out what the hell is going on."

Watts staggered to her feet, drew her knife, and then did a silent countdown before shoving the closet door open, throwing the zombie back onto the bed. It flailed around, tangling itself up in the flower-print bedspread, and she lunged forward, stabbing at its face.

It flailed away, and she stabbed the mattress instead, cursing under her breath. It lashed out and grabbed her thigh on her bad leg, and she howled in pain at the death grip so close to her injury. She fell to her knees, and her eyes widened at the putrid face gnashing so close to her own. She instinctively stabbed upwards, the blade catching the ghoul in its cheek and coming out the other side.

The knife missed its brain, as it continued to try to get to her, moans gurgled around metal. She grunted and put a hand on its forehead, holding it back as she tore the knife free and then jammed it forward into the zombie's eye socket.

It finally fell limp, and she reached down to pry its death grip from her thigh. Her chest heaved, and she whimpered as she got back to her feet. She wiped the blade on the ugly comforter and sheathed it, leaving the corpse in a down-filled burrito.

Watts limped out into the living room to escape the thick smell of the dead ghoul. She stayed out of sight from the windows, but could see through the sheer curtains to outside. Zombies moved north towards the explosions, marching to see their blasted brethren.

She pulled out the walkie talkie and leaned back, putting her feet up and resting her leg. "Captain O'Neil, do you copy?" she asked.

"Good to hear from you, soldier," he replied immediately. "Have you made it to the golf course?"

Watts shook her head. "No sir, not yet," she replied. "Took everything I had just to make it across the river. Got to cover just before the bombing run."

"Well, you're still alive and kicking, so that's half the battle right there," O'Neil declared. "Are you in a safe spot now?"

She rubbed her knee, staring out the window at the stream of ghouls. "Yes sir, I'm holed up in a house a couple blocks south of the river," she explained. "I was out of the blast zone, but it was close enough that it took out the windows."

"Yeah, those missiles can pack quite a punch," the Captain replied. "How's your zombie situation looking?"

Watts tilted her head back and forth. "Moderate, but nothing like it was on the other side of the river," she said. "Looks like they're all headed towards the blast zone. Gonna have to stay put for just a bit until they get cleared out."

"Understood," O'Neil replied.

She took a deep breath and sat back, hugging her torso with one arm. "Sir, may I ask what happened in Kenmore?" she asked. "I thought we were being ordered up there because they didn't want to risk the infrastructure… yet they just bombed the hell out of it."

"That's not really information we're passing down the line, Private," the Captain replied, a chill in his voice.

Watts bristled. "Sir, with all due respect, I just lost my entire unit because they didn't want to risk the highway," she said firmly. "Now they just bombed it. Don't I deserve to know why?"

"Under normal circumstances, I would tell you to fuck off," O'Neil admitted with a sigh. "But these are far from normal times, aren't they?"

She wrinkled her nose. "Understatement, sir."

"We had orders to push north to Kenmore to set up a command center and a roadblock for zombies coming up and east from the downtown area," he explained. "There was a mission to block the interstate coming up from Seattle, but it was mostly a failure. The higher ups thought we could secure it, but they were wrong. I'm sorry to say that your unit was part of the roadblock force."

Her heart skipped a beat, and she hugged herself tighter. "Did any other units make it out okay?" she asked.

"We sent two thousand troops up there," he replied, "and at last count only a hundred and forty-five made it back to Redmond."

Watts' eyes widened. "We've had to pull all the way back to Redmond?" she gasped.

"We're a little bit outside of Redmond, but honestly not much further," the Captain said. "After this failure, command wants to take the push nice and slow, not going more than a mile away from the front lines with the diversion points." He paused. "Which I'm sad to say is bad news for you."

She chewed her bottom lip. "How bad is it, Captain?" she asked, not sure she wanted to know the answer.

"With where you are, it's too far away to send rescue," O'Neil admitted. "So you're going to have to help me help you. Are you up for it?"

Watts straightened her shoulders and nodded firmly. "Just tell me what I need to do, Captain."

"We're making a push into the Totem Lake suburb," he replied, "which is about seven miles southeast of your current position."

Her stomach sank. "Seven miles?" she asked, shaking her head. "No way I can make that."

"I figured as much, given the amount of zombie infestation in the area," the Captain agreed. "We're estimating tens of thousands of them in that area, and that's just what we can see between the trees. Which is why we're going to set up a rally point a few miles away from where you are."

She chewed her lip for a moment. "I think I can do that."

"Good," O'Neil replied. "To the southeast of your position is a high school. This is going to be your pickup point. Now, I'm guessing you don't have a map?"

She pulled out her wrinkled satellite image. "Only one I have is of Kenmore, which might need some updating," she said.

"You have a compass though, right?" he asked.

"Yes, sir," she replied.

"Okay, you're going to have to take an indirect route," the Captain explained. "But it's really the only way. You need to get to the golf course, fight your way to the southernmost hole, then go due east for a couple of miles. As long as you stay to the east, you'll run smack dab into the school."

Watts nodded, swallowing hard. "Thank you, sir," she said hoarsely.

"Don't thank me yet, because we're going to be on a timetable," O'Neil countered. "Due to my orders, I'm going to have to sneak a transport off to pick you up. They'll be there in two hours, and won't be able to stay. So if you don't make it, you're going to be on your own for a while. I'm also not going to be able to answer any more calls from you, because if it gets back to a higher up, this rescue mission will be quashed."

She wrinkled her nose. "Sounds like I'm expendable," she said dryly.

"In the grand scheme of things, we all are, Private," the Captain replied with a sigh. "But I've been in your position before, and let's just say I'm not a fan of leaving soldiers to hang out to dry."

She nodded, stuffing her map back into her pocket. "I appreciate that, Captain," she said. "More than you know."

"You can thank me by making it back alive," O'Neil said firmly. "Now get a move on Private, you're on the clock. Good luck."

She looked at the ceiling for a moment to compose herself. "Thank you, Captain."

She stared at the radio for a moment and then pocketed it. She checked her watch and set a two-hour countdown before swinging her legs down to the floor.

"Golf course is to the southwest," she said as she got to her feet. "Time to get moving, Janey."

Watts finally reached the golf course, her injured leg on the verge of giving out entirely. She'd thought that resting it would help, but if anything it had made it more stiff and hard to navigate with. She dragged it across the parking lot of the clubhouse, looking like one of the zombies she was moving closer to.

Come on leg, don't fail me, she thought frantically. *Just a few more steps…*

She stabbed a ghoul in the eye socket before shoving it violently to the ground in frustration. Her fear had steadily been giving way to anger at her situation.

Just a few more steps, and we can rest for a few minutes, she silently told her leg.

There were two more creatures in the parking lot, both of which started coming towards her. She summoned the strength to hit them both in the head with her knife before throwing their corpses to the ground. She let out a satisfied grunt at her handiwork.

She finally reached the front door of the clubhouse, pulling on it but finding it locked.

"Of course," she snapped under her breath.

She drew her handgun and smashed the butt of it against the small glass panels to either side of the door, peeking inside to make sure there wasn't anything waiting for her. She reached in and unlocked it, throwing it open and then locking it behind her.

The clubhouse was large, with a bar/restaurant down the left hallway, and the main golfing store on the right. Directly in front of her was a reception area, which was elegant, but thankfully deserted.

Watts stood at the crossroads, looking towards the eatery and the store, chest heaving and leg throbbing. She threw her head back and let out a loud scream, partially to vent her pent-up frustration, but also thinking it would be better for the zombies to come to her than to go hunting for them.

She stood motionless for nearly a minute, relief sinking over her when nothing came out of the woodwork.

She hobbled over to the reception desk, pulling out a map of the golf course and tracing her finger along the holes before stopping on the southeastern most one. "Fifteenth hole, I can make that," she murmured, and then pocketed the map.

She checked her ammo, noting two
rounds in her mag, and another full one of
fifteen. She looked around and saw that
the clubhouse store had a wide variety of
clubs on sale. She hobbled in and found a
titanium driver, picking it off of the
wall and giving it a few experimental
swings.

Out of the corner of her eye, she
spotted a mannequin, and turned towards
it, lining up a shot as if she were aiming
for a t-ball. She took the head clean off
of it, and then inspected the club,
finding no damage.

"Well, that will help things out,"
she said, resting the club on her
shoulder. "Now, let's do something about
this knee."

Watts walked across into the bar and
restaurant, heading straight for the back
wall. At first she picked up a bottle of
vodka before setting it back down.

"This really feels like a job for
bourbon," she said, and reached for a
brown bottle before her eyes flicked up to
the top shelf. "Gonna splurge," she
declared. "I'm worth it." She pulled down
a bottle of bourbon that probably would
have cost her yearly paycheck back before
the apocalypse.

She found a glass from underneath and
poured three fingers of booze into it. She

stood there for a few minutes, swirling the amber liquid and taking ample sips. The warmth coursed through her body, and the pain in her knee began to subside. She picked up the bottle again, contemplating whether she should pour another glass.

She shook her head. "Settle down Janey," she quipped. "This isn't a frat party. Gotta keep your head about you."

She walked to the back door that overlooked the golf course. There were some zombies dotted along the landscape, but they were spread out and in no bigger groups than four.

She chuckled to herself. "Even during the apocalypse, they're still enforcing golf party size," she said, and then rubbed her forehead for a moment, realizing just how much she'd been talking to herself. Was this how people went insane?

She clutched her trusty golf club and exited the bar out onto the course, readying her metallic driver. She didn't have to wait long to test it out, as a zombie came stumbling around the corner of the building.

Watts stepped up, positioned herself like a softball batter, and waited for the pitch. With a forceful swing, the entire side of the ghoul's head collapsed in on itself, sending it to the ground in a bloody heap with a caved-in face.

She inspected the weapon, pleased with its performance before giving it a few light swings to clear off some of the blood. "Next stop, fifteenth hole," she declared, and sauntered off.

The walk through the golf course was surprisingly pleasant for the most part. The sun still shone down on her, with only a few lazy clouds in the sky. Even though the rough was looking overgrown, the fairways were still in pretty decent shape.

The zombies for the most part stayed to themselves, not picking up on her since her limping in the grass didn't make much noise. The only exception were a couple of creatures on the sixteenth green who had become tangled up in some plastic fencing off to the side where they were doing some major landscaping.

Watts headed closer to them, making sure that they were indeed stuck before moving on. "No sense in wasting a hit on you guys if you aren't a threat," she said, waving them off.

The fifteenth green was a different story from the rest. There was a golf cart on it, with a flailing corpse trapped beneath the front wheel. The still-short green grass had numerous dead patches from being soaked in blood.

"What happened here?" she wondered, peering around. "Nothing good, that's for sure." She scanned the area, making sure that the only threat was the zombie pinned beneath the cart. Whatever had killed it and left the bloody patches had long since moved on, it seemed.

She looked at her compass, finding east. Looking in that direction, all she could see was a large, wooded residential area.

"Okay," she said, taking a deep breath. "Here goes nothing."

CHAPTER NINE

Watts checked her watch before stepping onto the first street of a heavily tree-lined neighborhood. One hour and twenty-two minutes were left until her pickup arrived. The bourbon from earlier had begun to wear off, and her swollen knee began to whimper at her once again.

She looked down the street, as much as she could with the numerous shady spots, noting the smattering of zombies bumbling around.

Doesn't look too bad, she thought. *At least on the road. God only knows how many are hiding between the houses.*

She paused for a moment to motivate herself, before finally stepping forward. Her feet echoed on the pavement, gaining the attention of a few ghouls in a nearby yard. She debated which ones she should try to fight, because she knew that there was no way she could take them all.

Only the ones that make it to the road, she decided, and wound up her swing.

She didn't have to wait long to strike, as a zombie shambled up from the yard into the street, coming straight for her. She adjusted her course from the center of the road, moving to the side and giving a hearty swing, catching it in the side of the head and swiftly dropping it.

Watts stepped over the unmoving creature, glancing behind her to see she was attracting a crowd now a couple dozen strong from the back. The first intersection created a new set of problems as she hobbled into it, seeing dozens of zombies in both directions.

Oh god, these roads are packed, she thought frantically, chewing her lip. She kept hobbling along to the east, trying to put as much distance between her and the pursuing pack as she could. The growing horde behind her began to moan loud enough that ghouls ahead began to turn around ahead of her.

The next intersection started to close as a viable avenue of escape as packs of zombies came out from both sides. She clenched her jaw, sucking up the pain and breaking into a near-run to get across the intersection as the two sides began to converge into one horde.

She barely made it with only a few yards to spare, her knee screaming now as she ran and skipped and pushed herself to put some distance between them. The sea of zombies had grown to well over a hundred, or probably more, but she didn't have time to count, trying to focus on what was ahead.

Realistically, it didn't matter, because she knew just a few dozen would be more than enough to do her in. What was a couple hundred more?

I have to do something, she thought, panicked as she continued to push forward. *No way I can make it to the rendezvous with this much noise behind me.*

Her mind raced as she desperately tried to figure out some way to lose the horde. She reached the next intersection and was surprised to see that there were only a handful of ghouls to the right. Without batting an eye, she headed that way.

A couple of zombies were close to the intersection, so she quickly swung and smacked one in the face as it turned. The impact unfortunately didn't kill it, but did but forced it back into the other one, staggering them both enough that they got swallowed up by the horde following her.

When she got halfway down the street, she noticed a fenced-in yard to the east. She hobbled over, tossing her golf club over the top and clambering up. She grunted as she put most of her weight on her arms, scrabbling with her good leg.

The zombies clustered around the bottom, and one swiped at her boot, causing her to panic and flail up over the top. She lost her grip and instinctively kicked off of the fence with her good leg so she would fall on the empty side.

She landed hard on her side, her shoulder exploding in pain, and the wind knocked right out of her. She rolled onto her knees, gasping for air, panic gripping her chest and not helping the situation. She knew she had to get up, had to sweep the area, something could be on her in seconds.

She dug a hand into the grass, focusing on her breathing, finally able to take in a few ragged gasps, her vision coming back into focus. She glanced over her shoulder at the zombies behind her, and they pressed up against the fence, moaning and gnashing and trying to break through.

At the *ping* of a metal post beginning to fail, Watts' eyes widened, and soon a few more sounded, and the edges of the fence began to buckle. She scrambled to her feet, grabbing her club, and hobbled across the yard, chest heaving.

Halfway across, the fence completely gave out on one side, and zombies began to pour into the yard. It was fairly large, about forty yards from fence to fence. When she reached the other side, she tossed the club over and began climbing once again. Adrenaline fueled her ascent, and at the top, she noticed that three ghouls had come around the outside towards her.

"Give me a break!" she snarled, and threw herself over, this time landing on her feet, trying to absorb most of the impact with her good leg. She pulled her handgun with her sore arm, rubbing the shoulder as she took quick aim. She fired two shots, hitting the targets dead on, despite the recoil from the gun making her wince at the pain in her joint.

For the final zombie, she pulled her knife, using her good arm to stab it in the eye socket, dropping the corpse.

The horde in the yard had reached the fencing, but thankfully the numbers weren't as severe yet since they were still filtering in from the other side, so the fence wasn't in peril just yet.

"Well…" she huffed as she checked her weapons, "that's four blocks down." She shook her head. It was going to be a struggle getting to her destination in one piece, and her situation was growing more bleak by the minute.

Watts walked the rest of the way through the yards to the next street, dragging her leg and club behind her. Her knee was almost unbearable, and her arm was only comfortable if it was limp. She sighed heavily when she reached the next street, finding a couple dozen ghouls roaming about.

There's no way I'm going to be able to make it to the high school like this… she thought, ready to just give in and lay down. *No… no, Janey. Keep moving.* She steeled herself and pushed on, reaching the other side of the street with only attracting a few creatures.

The next few yards were empty, with another fence looming ahead. She moved as quickly as she could, hopping over it and landing with a thud, her good leg quickly becoming exhausted from the extra use.

When she reached the middle of the yard, her wounded knee gave out completely, and she fell to the grass, hissing in pain. She rubbed it frantically, willing it to work, just to get her a few more miles. She glanced at her watch. Just under an hour, just a couple more miles.

Watts grunted deeply as she willed herself back to her feet, limping to the house. She tried the back patio door, finding it surprisingly unlocked. She slid it open silently, readying her handgun just in case of any close encounters. She locked it behind her and swept the house, finding it gloriously empty.

She crept into the front room, peeking out the window at the street. Dozens of zombies shambled about, looking around for their next meal. Most of the driveways were empty, without even a car.

She perked up at the sight of a lone house at the end of the block, six houses away, across the street. A lone car sat in the driveway, a clunker of a sedan easily twenty years old.

That's your ticket out, Janey, she thought, taking a deep breath. *Now just have to hope it runs… and that the keys are in the house… and that the gas hasn't gone bad…*

She blinked back tears. The hopelessness of her situation threatened to overcome her, but she shook her head violently, clenching a fist. She had to buy herself some time if she was going to be able to get over to the house, get inside, and find the keys.

She scanned up and down the road, trying to think of an idea, but nothing came to her.

What can I use as a distraction? She chewed her bottom lip as she studied the area. *The only car on the block is the one I'm going to… uh… borrow. And it's unlikely that a clunker like that has an alarm. How am I going to get those zombies away from it?*

She contemplated for a moment, and then an idea hit her, but her blood ran cold at the thought.

You have got to be out of your mind, Janey! She berated herself. *That's really the best idea you can come up with? Seriously?!*

She closed her eyes, letting out a deep breath, but knowing that this was the only option she had. She pushed away from the wall and walked to the back door, looking out to make sure the coast was clear, which it thankfully was.

Watts headed back for the front of the house, and threw open the door, stepping out onto the porch. She took a deep breath and then let out a sharp scream.

"Come and get me!" she bellowed. "Yeah you, over by the street! Don't tell me you don't want a piece of this!"

The zombies in the street perked up and moaned, immediately moving in her direction.

"That's it!" she yelled as they grew closer. "Come and get me!"

As they stumbled towards her, she backed into the house, leaving the door open. Once inside, she moved to the back of the house, still yelling and whistling as loudly as she could. She kept an eye on the backyard, making sure it remained empty despite the noise.

She quickly whirled around when she heard the first zombie enter the house.

She let out a few more yells and taunts before stepping onto the back patio, still hollering. As the lead zombie reached the patio door, she slid it shut, trapping the ghouls inside.

Watts turned and spotted a zombie coming around the side of the house, so she stepped over and swung the slub, hitting it in the dist of the head and dropping it.

The head of the club flew off with a *crack,* and she groaned, but then held up the newly sharp tip. "Not ideal," she muttered, "but still could be useful."

Watts moved over a couple of houses, staying in the backyards and checking for zombies around every corner. As she looked to the road, she saw it was mostly clear of zombies as they moved towards the house.

Finally, she made it across the street from the house with the car, moving up to the corner of the building. She glanced down the street to see most of the zombies still focused on trying to get into the diversion house. There were only a few ghouls within twenty yards of her target, and she took a deep breath.

Come on, leg. She didn't wait any longer, and hobbled towards the house, taking care to walk as softly as she could on the pavement. Much to her surprise, she made it across without attracting any attention.

She walked around to the back, wanting to stay out of sight as much as she could. The back door was ajar, which caused her some concern. She readied her golf club spike and quietly pushed inside.

The kitchen was very dark, across from the front room which had blackout curtains. She moved into the living room, and a set of bloodied hands reached out to grab her by the collar.

Watts pulled back, but the creature's grip remained strong. They tumbled into the kitchen, the ghoul pinning her against the wall. She pushed against its chest with the spike, unable to maneuver it to be useful in such close quarters. She reached for her knife with the other hand as another zombie staggered from the back hallway, moaning loudly with excitement.

She quickly abandoned her plan for the knife, and readied the club, pushing against her current attacker with her hand. When the new zombie came within range, she thrust forward with the spike, getting it through the eye and dropping it.

She dropped the spike and grabbed her knife, slamming the blade into the ghoul's temple and shoving the corpse aside. With both enemies down, she shuffled back over to the kitchen door and shut it, turning the deadbolt. She hissed as she knelt down to pick up the spike, but there was another weak point in the shaft, so she decided to leave it, tightening her grip on her knife.

She took a quick breather before looking at her watch. Forty-five minutes to go. She took a deep breath and hobbled into the living room, looking at every wall and table, hoping to find the keys to the clunker outside.

She tore back into the kitchen as fast as she could, and relief washed over her at the sight of a set of keys hanging by the door.

"All right, I'm in business," she said, and snatched the keyring from the hook, wincing at the pain in her shoulder.

Watts hobbled to the front door, peering through the window to see that the coast was clear. She didn't waste any time, rushing outside and over to the car, unlocking it and hopping in. She put the keys in the ignition and paused.

"Oh please, sweet baby Jesus," she prayed, "let this thing start up."

She squeezed her eyes shut and turned the key. The car struggled to start up, revving several times but refusing to turn over.

"Come on, come *on*!" she urged, trying again and hitting the gas pedal a few times, hoping that would do the trick.

The car finally turned over, but struggled to stay running. She hit the gas a couple more times, revving the engine up further, and finally it hummed steadily.

"Got it!" she cried, and threw the car into drive, tearing out of the driveway. She headed east, past a cluster of zombies that had approached the noise, and left them in the dust.

The road went on for nearly a mile, with only a handful of ghouls in her direct path, but lots of them stretched down side streets and into yards. She reached the end of the road, forced to make a left before turning to the right to continue in the proper direction.

Another mile later, she knew she was close to the destination with time to spare, just over a half hour on the clock. On the right side of the road was a big sign boasting *Stream High School – NEXT RIGHT*.

"Gonna make it!" she cried, smacking the steering wheel. "I'm gonna make it!"

Watts took the next right and then slammed on the brakes, her heart sinking.

There was a wall of zombies ahead, easily in the dozens but probably in the hundreds.

She rested her forehead on the steering wheel. "So close, yet so far away," she groaned, shaking her head back and forth.

She sat back against the headrest, staring daggers at the wall of rotted flesh. She contemplated ramming through them, but knew that she would more-than-likely get stuck in the center of the mob.

Reluctantly, she put the car in reverse, doing a three-point turn to head back to the previous road. She looked down it, seeing another impressive collection of ghouls.

Two roads back, she found a road that looks passable. She made the turn and picked up some speed, smacking a few zombies as she wove in and around clusters of monsters. As she travelled several more blocks, she continually looked down the side streets in hopes of finding the school, but all she could see were zombies packed shoulder-to-shoulder.

Hope drained out of her at an alarming rate, especially after she spotted the high school proper. Throngs of ghouls surrounded the building, bleeding out onto the road.

"What if they see that and don't come?" she babbled to herself, panic rising in her throat. "Can this car even make it to Redmond? Or Totem Lake?"

She hit the gas, moving forward to the intersection and seeing that the zombies were a little more thinned out. "Okay… might be clearing out…"

When she reached the next intersection, there was a smattering of creatures, but then another noise, like music to her ears.

Machine gun fire popped in the distance, which drew the attention of the ghouls ahead. They started walking away from the school, and Watts' heart soared.

"The rescue team!" she cried and waited for them to appear in the intersection.

Moments passed, and nobody came. Her heart rate doubled, pounding harder and harder. And then the gunfire ceased.

"No, no, no," she moaned, and slammed on the accelerator, tearing up the road towards the main one before doing a hard right turn. She could see the rescue transport about five blocks up, starting to drive away.

Her eyes watered at the hundreds of zombies between her and her rescue. "I'm here, I'm here!" she screamed, and laid on the horn as she punched the gas again, driving as fast as she could towards them. She wove around zombies when she could, but soon it got too thick for her to avoid them.

Corpses smacked against the front of the car, several flipping right over the vehicle, slamming into the windshield and creating multiple shatter points. There was so much blood that she could barely see, especially with the spider web of glass zigzagging across.

But she pressed on, flooring it and continuing to honk the horn over and over again.

All she could see was blood and zombies, crimson and gray. She couldn't pick up any speed as shit hit a thick wall of ghouls, pushing through several layers of bodies. The car bounced up and down as she rolled over them, the engine straining as it climbed.

She managed to push through the bulk, a little bit of daylight peeking through as the car gave out.

"No, no, come on!" she yelled. "Please, start back up!" She tried to restart the stalled vehicle, but it was to no avail. Soon even the starter didn't make a sound, just an empty, dull *click*, like a nail in a coffin.

Watts sat in despair, the little bit of light through the blood growing dimmer as zombies converged on the car, pounding at all sides. Just rotted, putrid bodies smacking against what had quickly become her mausoleum.

Her heart sank. This was the end.

"Well, Janey, you gave it a heck of a go," she said hoarsely, swiping at her eyes. "You made it a lot further than you thought you would, and you gave it your all. Can't do anything more." Her leg throbbed. Her shoulder ached. Her body slumped against the seat as if all of the exhaustion of the day suddenly caught up with her. All she could do was await her fate now.

She looked down at her handgun. She didn't want to be a zombie. Though with a horde this size, there wouldn't be much of her left to become anything. At least they'd chew her up enough that she couldn't be a runner, putting people in danger.

She fingered the butt of the gun, but didn't pull it out of its holster. A bullet to the brain would be far preferable to getting torn apart by hungry corpses. She shuddered as she imagined what that would feel like, putrid, nasty, rotten teeth tearing at her flesh.

She thought of Larry, covered in zombie bites, leaning against the wall of that tiny office, telling her to look away so that she wouldn't have to watch him kill himself. How nice he was, how he'd saved her life, how he'd pushed on even though he was doomed to die. She thought of his blood splattered across the wall, blood pooling beneath his limp body, and then she realized she'd unholstered her gun.

She looked down at it, in her hand, her small but strong hand. Could she do it?

"This isn't how I thought I'd go out," she murmured, echoing Larry's sentiment before he died. Nobody ever thought they'd have to kill themselves to avoid getting eaten by undead humans.

She raised the gun. Her hand shook as she put the barrel to her temple. She thought of her family. Her friends. Her unit. She closed her eyes.

Gunshots suddenly peppered the air, muffled through the horde, and zombies suddenly started to drop.

Watts blinked at the windshield, almost in a daze, as someone leapt up onto the hood of the car, driving a crowbar through the glass and jerking it out.

The entire front glass came off in a single piece, and a soldier tossed it aside into the horde. Watts stared up at him dumbly, unable to believe someone was standing there, reaching in to rescue her.

"We have to go *now*!" the soldier cried, snapping her back into reality.

Watts clambered out of the opening, taking his arm. It felt like a million years since another living being had touched her, and the contact gave her a surge of adrenaline she hadn't thought possible.

To either side were two troops each, laying down suppressing fire. The soldier helped her down from the hood.

"Can you walk?" he asked.

She nodded jerkily, putting her weight on her good leg. "I'll manage."

"We're moving!" he barked, and motioned for her to stay close as the group backed up, covering the rear as they moved to the armored vehicle.

When they reached the truck, the soldier helped Watts into the front passenger seat, slamming the door. Her mind reeled as the soldiers all jumped in, unable to believe that just seconds ago she'd written off her life as over.

"Let's roll!" the soldier barked, and they took off, the vehicle picking up speed quickly down the road to Totem Lake.

One of the passengers in the back reached forward, grabbing a radio from the front. "Captain O'Neil, we have the package," he said. "Returning to base."

"Good job," came the reply. "Put her on, please."

The soldier held out the radio to Watts, and she took it with a shaking hand. "Thank you, Captain," she said, voice thick with emotion.

"You did good, Private," O'Neil replied. "Even made it early. I'm impressed."

She let out an exasperated laugh, rubbing her forehead. "My mother always taught me that if you aren't fifteen minutes early, then you're late," she said.

"Sounds like a wise woman," the Captain said, chuckling. "Now you take it easy. I'll come check up on you in the med bay when I get a chance."

"Thank you, Captain," Watts repeated, swallowing hard. "So much."

The line went dead, and she set down the receiver, leaning her head back against the headrest and closing her eyes. After a moment, she opened them, rubbing her knee as she looked out the window, staring at street after street of zombies and devastation.

Her chest swelled, images flooding her of her dead unit members, of the soldier who'd saved her life in the store, all the pain and suffering she'd had to endure just to make it to this moment.

Watts burst into tears, unable to control herself anymore.

The rest of the soldiers stayed quiet, letting her grieve and deal with

the day she'd just been through. One of
them reached forward, patting her on the
shoulder, and she turned to look at him,
cheeks shining with tears.

He smiled and held out a bottle of
water. "Drink up, it'll help."

She blinked rapidly, unable to stop a
wet laugh from bubbling out of her throat.
"I think the only drink that will help me
will need to be a little stronger than
this."

The soldier snorted, prompting a
ripple of laughter from the rest of the
crew. He reached into his pocket and
pulled out a flask, holding that out
instead.

"Let's test that theory," he said.

She flashed him a genuine smile and
then took a long sip. She passed it back,
relishing in the burning in her throat—the
fact that she was still alive to feel such
a thing. She took a deep breath and closed
her eyes in an attempt to shut out
everything.

Watts had survived the day. But the
day would never leave her.

END

Up Next: As the eastern force
pushes towards downtown Seattle, a major
threat emerges from the south in Seattle
Pt. 6

DEAD AMERICA
THE NORTHWEST INVASION
BOOK 8
SEATTLE PART 6
BY DEREK SLATON
© 2020

CHAPTER ONE

Day Zero +26

"This looks like another fun one," Sergeant Farley declared as he looked out over the high school ahead.

Located on the southernmost tip of Lake Washington, the suburb of Renton played a strategic role for the invasion of Seattle. The 405 interstate came up from Tacoma, through the densely populated suburbs to the south of the city, leading straight up towards the eastern front of the war.

Initially, the fifteen thousand troops that had been sent around Tiger Mountain State Forest were being sent further south to Tacoma to create a blockade so that the eastern troops could do their thing. The mission had changed on the previous day, when the order came down to divert thousands of troops back to the north towards Renton.

The push had been difficult, with the streets jam-packed with zombies. Four miles to the east of Renton was the East Renton Highlands suburb, a densely packed residential area that they were having a difficult time pacifying. The fighting had been brutal, street to street, with many of the troops having to resort to hand to

hand combat due to the bullets running
out.

"Two stories, looks like it stretches
for the entire block," Private Santos
muttered as he appraised the Hanzen High
School, "and with our luck it'll be
another one of those *'safe zones'* that
they set up when things were going to
shit."

"What's wrong, buddy?" Private Sawyer
asked, clapping his companion on the
shoulder. "You aren't in the mood to wipe
out a couple hundred of those things?"

Santos just grunted in reply. Their
supply lines had all but been cut, as the
aid had been sent to the larger southern
force, leaving these troops short handed.
They'd begun using vehicles, dumpsters,
and even furniture to block off roads and
give themselves a fighting chance against
the ever-growing ranks of the undead.

Santos bent over to pick up a five-
foot tall metal post that looked like it
had been ripped away from a chain-link
fence. On one end, there was grey duct
tape that had been wrapped around for a
handle, the other end crudely filed down
into a spike. The first two feet of the
tip was already stained a dark crimson
color.

"Even if I was properly equipped, it
would suck," Santos said. "But being

forced to use discount brand fencing just…" He sighed heavily. This was his first time seeing any action, either before or after the apocalypse, and he'd never in his wildest dreams thought he'd be caught in a zombie battle in the middle of a bullet shortage.

Sergeant Farley squared his shoulders. "Santos, do you hear that?" he asked calmly.

The Private furrowed his brow. "Hear wh-"

Farley interrupted him, reaching out and covering his teammate's mouth with his palm. "Shh," he said. "Don't talk, just listen for a moment."

Santos listened as the Sergeant lowered his hand. All he could hear was the smattering of gunfire in the distance, as well as faint yelling. The main part of the battle still raged, this rag tag cleanup crew sweeping buildings on the outskirts.

"I… I don't know…" he stammered.

"You don't know what you're hearing?" Farley asked, voice cold. "Let me tell you." He fixed his steel gaze on the young Private. "What you're hearing are the front-line troops fighting far more of those things than we're going to face in here, and they're just as poorly equipped as we are." He jerked a thumb over his shoulder. "Now, if you like, I can have you transferred over to them, because from the sounds of it, they could use the help. Or, you can stay here, fighting in controlled conditions with people you trust." He raised his chin. "What's it going to be?"

Santos took a deep breath and schooled his expression. "I'm with you, Sergeant."

"Good," Farley replied, clapping his hands together. "Have you figured out an incursion point yet?"

The Private's brow furrowed. "I thought that was Sawyer's job?"

"We're in the middle of a war," the Sergeant said. "One slip up, one bite, and Sawyer isn't around anymore."

Sawyer barked a laugh. "That's a comforting thought," he quipped.

"When that happens, it's the next man up," Farley continued, unfazed. "So you'd better know how to do his job after he's gone."

Sawyer raised his hand. "Again, comforting thought," he drawled. "Can just feel your confidence in me oozing out of you, Sarge."

Farley didn't react, knowing the Private was more amused than upset as his demise being casually tossed around.

"Okay," Santos said slowly. "Well, we checked the classrooms on the south side of the building, and they were pretty jam packed. Like they were housing survivors before they knew about the blood type thing. We couldn't see into the gym, but heard some moaning and smacking at the door, so that's no good. A few of the classrooms on the north side had minimal resistance, but the most viable entry point was the front office."

"Okay, why's that?" Farley asked, crossing his arms.

Santos held up a finger. "Well, no enemies inside for one," he replied. "Easy access to the main hallway."

"Good," the Sergeant said, nodding. "What else?"

"There's an interior door at the office," the Private continued, "so if we get inside and get overwhelmed, we would have a viable escape route."

Farley cocked his head. "But why not go in through the broken back door we put a makeshift blockade on?" he asked.

"Well sir, we don't know where that leads to, as there are no windows nearby," Santos pointed out. "We also don't know how long it's been open, so there could be a ton of those creatures in there. It's safer to go in through the office."

The Sergeant nodded. "Good job," he declared, and then turned to Sawyer. "What do you think?"

The Private scoffed playfully. "Oh, sorry, I wasn't aware I was back to the land of the living just yet," he teased, but then nodded. "But yeah, Santos nailed it pretty good."

"All right then," Farley said. "When the others get here, we'll get to clearing."

Sawyer looked past his Sergeant, nodding to the area behind him. "Speak of the devil," he said.

Farley turned around to see the rest of his team casually walking up, carrying a wide assortment of melee weaponry. Corporal Barnes led the way, with Privates Burton, Graves, Logan, and Wilcox following behind. Wilcox and Logan were both coated in blood, but it wasn't bothering them.

"How did the clearing go?" the Sergeant asked.

Barnes shrugged. "Routine."

"Routine my ass!" Graves barked. "There were twelve of those fuckers jam packed into a two-bedroom house!"

Logan nodded vigorously. "It was like a slumber party of the dead."

Sawyer appraised Wilcox and Logan, who were coated in blood from head to toe.

"Looks like you two drew the short straw,"
he drawled. "Red's a good color on you
though."

Logan wrinkled his nose and dropped a
pile of material on the ground. Wilcox
just grinned and spread his arms.

"Don't you do it," Sawyer warned,
holding out a hand.

Wilcox took a step forward. "Oh come
on, big guy, you know you want a hug!" he
teased.

"No, no, no," Sawyer demanded, both
palms out now, "I swear to god!"

"Look around," his companion said,
cocking his head, "god can't help you." He
darted forward, and Sawyer leapt away, his
blood-soaked friend chasing him around to
give him a bear hug.

After a few moments of tearing
around, Wilcox finally caught him and gave
him a good squeeze, picking him up off of
the ground.

Sawyer groaned in disgust as the
others laughed. "I hate you so much," he
whined as his friend put him back down on
the ground.

Wilcox grinned and gave him a playful
wet smack on the forehead. "Love you too,
buddy," he drawled. "Love you, too."

Farley stared down at the pile of
materials on the ground. It was a wide
variety of stuff, shovels, a pitchfork,

and a six-foot wide section of chain link fencing amongst the pile.

"You… you brought a fence," the Sergeant said, raising an eyebrow.

Barnes shrugged. "I thought it might be good to block off the door with," he explained. "It'll take two people, but I figure one on each side pressing against it should be enough to hold it in place. I mean, as long as there aren't too many of those things in there."

"All right, we'll give it a shot," Farley agreed.

"You got us an entry point?" Barnes asked.

The Sergeant jerked a thumb over his shoulder. "Other side of the building," he explained, "going in through the front office."

"Then what?" the Private asked. "Standard room by room clear?"

Farley tilted his head back and forth. "On the north side it will be," he replied. "South side and the gym will be another story as they are packed to the tits with ghouls."

"That works for me," Barnes agreed.

The Sergeant waved a hand above his head. "All right, let's get saddled up," he said. "We got us a building to clear."

CHAPTER TWO

Barnes stepped up to the office with a crowbar in his hand. He studied it for a moment, investigating the lock and the edges. He shrugged, reared back, and then smashed out the glass, cleaning up the edges.

"That's some fine work there, Corporal," Wilcox declared.

Barnes shook his head. "Please don't reward me with a hug, Private."

Wilcox blew him a raspberry. "You're no fun." He hooked his hands over the windowsill and pulled himself up, hopping into the empty office. He gave the area a more thorough sweep than they'd done peeking in as the rest of the team joined him, carrying spears. Logan and Santos brought up the rear, carrying the fence.

Barnes led the way to the door, cracking it open a touch and peering down the hallway. There were a few ghouls on the far end, but they weren't paying attention. The stairwell door behind them was closed, signaling the top floor was contained for the time being.

He checked the other end, where the gymnasium lay, the doors also closed.

He ducked back into the office. "Okay, we go in groups of two, check each room all the way down," he said quietly.

"We'll do the gym last, together, and then move up to the second level. Questions?"

Nobody said anything, so he slipped out the door, motioning to Burton to join him. She nodded and followed, and as soon as their bootfalls hit the linoleum, the trio of zombies at the end of the hall turned towards them, moaning.

The duo raised their makeshift spears and moved up, leaving a few doors accessible behind them for the others to take. Quiet countdowns and doors breaching sounded behind them, but they trusted their team and focused on the task at hand.

The zombies were dressed in bloody button-down shirts and khakis, the business casual attire of school workers. One even still wore a pair of busted glasses, hanging low on its half-eaten nose.

"Not all that different from my high school teachers," Burton quipped, and lunged forward, stabbing her spike into the middle of the ghoul's face. She wrenched it back, and it didn't come out as cleanly or quickly as they would have liked, but they had to work with what they had.

Barnes chuckled as he speared the second one through the eye socket. "Not sure if you mean the brainlessness or the blood."

"Both," she replied as she took out the third and last hallway creature. "Lots of fights at our school. They tried metal detectors one year to try to curb the knife wars, but then kids just started making plastic shivs."

The Corporal shook his head as he stepped over the corpses to double check the stairwell door. "Damn, girl, no wonder you're so badass."

She peered into the first dim classroom on the left, seeing no movement, and wrapped her hand around the handle. He readied his weapon and nodded, and she threw open the door. Nothing came rushing out at them, so Barnes carefully stepped inside, sweeping the area.

Burton followed and moved up the far row of desks. They'd seen horrific things in the past twenty-six days, and she was fairly desensitized to the ghouls at this point. But the younger they were, the more unsettling it was, the more sad. None of them were looking forward to finding young teenage zombies lurking around the school.

"Clear," Barnes announced, and they went back out into the hallway.

"Clear!" Wilcox called from two doors down, and the duo crossed to the other side.

"Movement inside," Burton said, and readied the door.

Barnes nodded, and she did a quiet countdown before throwing it open.

Two zombies appeared almost immediately, each receiving a vicious strike to the face. Burton kicked hers in the chest to dislodge it from the spear, knocking it back into another shorter ghoul behind. Barnes slipped in, stabbing another creature through the forehead and flinging it back and forth to knock the remaining two around.

Burton jumped up onto the teacher's desk, stabbing down with her spear like a fisher, taking out two ghouls in quick succession. Barnes smacked one behind him with the blunt end, and then stomped one on the ground with his boot before slinging the spear at the remaining zombie that struggled to get to its feet.

They waited a moment to see if anything else was going to come out of the shadows.

"Clear," Burton announced, and they retrieved their weapons, heading back out into the hallway. Wilcox and Logan emerged from the next room down.

"This end's good," Wilcox said with a thumbs up.

"Okay, let's head down and see how the others are doing," Barnes instructed. "Hopefully the gym is empty."

Wilcox rolled his eyes. "Way to jinx us, Corporal," he drawled.

"Afraid to have a little hope?" Burton asked, raising an eyebrow as they walked.

"Has anything in the last three weeks given the impression that hope is warranted in any situation?" Wilcox quipped.

Sawyer gave him a playful shove as they caught up to them. "Way to be depressing as fuck, bud."

Farley and Santos emerged from the last door on the left before the gym, spikes gleaming with blood. "Clear," the Sergeant declared, and then headed for the gym doors.

The two of them peered inside as the team caught up to them.

Santos murmured something in Spanish and then backed away from the door.

"That's never good," Wilcox muttered, and Sawyer rolled his eyes, leaning against the wall where they'd set down the chunk of fencing.

"Looks like you were right about the safe zone setup," Farley said as he scanned the inside. "There's beds and supplies, and at least five dozen of those things."

Wilcox shook his head. "Nothing like using a school gymnasium as a bloodbath."

"How are we playing this, Sarge?" Barnes asked.

Farley pointed to the fence. "Let's try your fence idea," he said. "The doors open inwards and auto close, so hopefully it can stem the tide so they'll come in smaller groups. Graves, Logan, you hold the chain link on either side. Barnes, you take the center, in case we need to brace it."

The soldiers got into position, and the Corporal reached over the fence, resting his hand over the latch bar. He did a countdown, and everyone readied their spears.

At the end, Barnes shoved each door open in turn mightily, giving them good momentum to swing open. Zombies immediately flooded the gap, pressing into the fence, snapping and snarling.

The Corporal stabbed one in the center, but already Logan and Graves struggled to hold the fence in place. He ducked down and threw his weight into the bottom center of the chain link, hoping to relieve the pressure and create an effective barrier for the ghouls.

The doors couldn't shut again from the tide of zombies clustering around the entrance to the gym, all of them coming towards the noise and pushing forward like a mosh pit of rotted flesh.

The soldiers sprung to action, stabbing and lunging forward as best they could. Bodies fell to the floor, creating a bit of an added barrier to the fence. It acted like a battering ram for a time, until the unmoving corpses were so thick that the ghouls clambered up on top of their dead brethren.

"Raise the fence!" Farley barked, as the zombies had a higher floor to fight against the chain link barrier.

Barnes rolled away, as rotted claws began to reach through the holes at him, the ghouls clamoring over each other at different heights to get at their meal.

Logan and Graves grunted with the effort of holding the fence in place, but the spikes were too thick to fit through the holes of the chain link.

"Ideas?" the Corporal barked as he turned his spear around to try to hold the fence in with the blunt end. The doors were stuck open on the horde, and at this point the fence covered the entire doorway to keep the ghouls from vaulting over the ramp of bodies beneath them.

Before the Sergeant could answer, Graves slipped to one knee, and the ghouls pushed through. Burton and Sawyer darted forward to try to push the fence back into place, throwing their weight against the fallen soldier, and Santos stabbed wildly with his spear above their heads, trying to protect them against the flailing arms.

Shouts filled the hallway, echoing and unintelligible in the panic. Graves' blood ran cold as a tight grip wrapped around his wrist, and he thrashed, putting his boot against the wall and throwing his body backwards.

Burton and Sawyer staggered back from the movement, and the fence buckled, zombies pouring out of the hole.

"Fall back!" Farley screamed. "To the office!"

"Corporal!" Burton yelled as the horde consumed Graves, the fence falling down on top of Barnes as the zombies slid down into the hallway. Logan darted back, narrowly missing the outstretched arms, and the soldiers tore for the office.

The majority of the ghouls stopped to feast on Graves, whose screams died down into gurgles and then nothing as they tore out his throat. As Logan reached the office last, he looked back one last time and saw Barnes underneath the chain link

ramp, pressed up against the pile of
bodies.

Logan slammed the office door behind him in the nick of time as the hallway zombies smacked into it, slapping their hands wetly on the glass.

"Corporal's still alive, he's trapped under the fence," he huffed.

Santos shook his head, eyes wide. "He'll never survive under there."

Logan clenched a fist. "We still have to try."

"Whatever we're trying, we still have to clear all the zombies," Burton snapped. "What's the plan, Sarge?"

Farley didn't answer, simply flipping his spear around and smashing the blunt end into the glass window of the office door. Snarls and moans filled the air, and he turned the spear around again, stabbing at any head that came into view.

Sawyer grabbed a chair and swung hard at the waist-high window along the wall to the hallway, cracking the glass. The others joined in, and soon packs of ghouls lined up against it, clawing at them over the jagged edges of the sill.

The soldiers formed a stabbing line, taking down ghoul after ghoul after ghoul, until the hallway was littered with bodies.

Farley opened the door and stuck his head out, just in time to see Graves sit up and scream. To his surprise, the dead soldier tore into the gym instead of his way, and that was when he realized Barnes was no longer beneath the chunk of fence.

"To the gym!" he barked and drew his handgun. Ammo was scarce, but a runner was a bigger threat than a horde and they'd need to take it out quickly lest they risk a second one in the form of an undead Corporal.

As the soldiers filed into the gym, fanning out, they laid eyes on Barnes, dancing along the seats of the bleachers, occasionally stabbing down at a zombie head. Graves was almost to the bleachers, tearing towards the cluster of two dozen or so ghouls trying to get to the Corporal.

Farley took aim and fired, the bullet tearing through the dead Private's head just before it reached its murderers. The noise alerted the horde, and they abandoned their quest of the difficult-to-navigate bleachers in favor of the fresh soldiers approaching in a spread-out line.

Barnes took the opportunity to jog down the seats, stabbing a few ghouls in the back of their heads in quick succession. Farley holstered his gun and he and his team spread out further, surrounding the zombies in a wide semicircle.

The free-for-all began, spears flying, skulls crunching, bodies falling, and coagulated blood splattering everywhere. In a matter of moments, the horde was no more, festering in a wet putrid pile in the center of the gymnasium.

The soldiers stood in silence for a moment, their eyes trailing to their dead companion laying facedown on the shiny floor, body half-eaten.

Logan scrubbed his hands down his face, shaking his head and storming away from the rest, growling under his breath.

"You all right, Corporal?" Farley asked.

Barnes nodded. "Yes, sir," he replied. "Managed to get out behind them and run in here."

The Sergeant returned the nod. "We need to clear the top floor," he said.

Burton glanced at Logan and then back to her superior. "Sarge… shouldn't we-"

"We don't have time, Private," Farley cut in. "Move out, we have to scope out the stairwell." He turned on his heel and started back towards the hallway. "Santos, Wilcox, sweep the storage and locker rooms and then join up with the rest of us."

"Yes, sir," the men said in unison, and headed over to the far side of the gym.

Burton stared at Barnes, raising her eyebrows.

He shook his head and clapped her on the shoulder. "Sarge is right," he murmured, and walked past her to follow Farley.

Logan pushed off of the wall, gripping his spear with white knuckles, jaw set tight. Burton offered him a sympathetic smile, but he ignored it and stalked after the Sergeant.

Farley cracked the fire door as gently as he could, listening for any movement inside, or to see if a horde pressed back against it. There was nothing, so he pushed it open farther, shining his flashlight up the stairs.

A moan echoed, and then a ghoul fell over the top railing, sailing down and cracking its skull upon impact at the bottom. It was silent after that.

"Well, that took care of itself," the Sergeant muttered.

Santos and Wilcox sauntered up the hallway, having found nothing in the extra gymnasium rooms.

Farley led his team up the stairwell slowly, keeping their footfalls as light as possible. The top door had a small rectangular window and he peered through it, pursing his lips at the sheer amount of movement in the hallway. All the doors were open all the way down, giving no break in the amount of corpses shambling around.

He turned around and waved for the team to huddle in so they could hear him. "At least three dozen, maybe more, I can't get a read on the far end of the hallway," he murmured. "All the classrooms I can see are wide open. Thoughts?"

The group contemplated for a moment, and then Santos raised his hand. "What if we try to break them up?" he asked. "Kick 'em into the rooms and shut the doors so we can try to thin out the rest?"

"I think that would only work for one or two rooms before we're overwhelmed," Sawyer whispered. "As soon as they hear us and start pushing for us, we're boned."

"Did any of them have big windows?" Burton asked. "If we could get into one, or even two across the hall from each other, we could do like we did from the office."

Farley shook his head. "They're all classrooms, with tiny windows in the doors."

Santos raised his hand reluctantly. "This door opens inward…" he began, and paused, scratching the back of his head. "Maybe the fence would work better here–"

"No," Logan growled, shaking his head. "We're not using that thing again."

"This is way less of those things than the gym," Santos argued, though he winced away from the death glare he was receiving from his teammate. "And we could get a stronger angle here."

Logan crossed his arms firmly. "Until they push just enough to knock us down the stairs," he hissed. "We'd be fucked with them falling on top of us."

"How far down are they?" Barnes asked, turning to the Sergeant. "Could we make it to one of the classrooms?"

Farley nodded. "Could probably make it two down."

"What if half of us made for a classroom, and then we ping-ponged them back and forth?" Barnes suggested. "Switch off being the distraction while the other team takes them out from behind?"

There was a moment of silence as everyone contemplated the idea.

"Best we got," Sawyer said with a shrug.

Farley nodded. "Sawyer, Logan, Wilcox, on me," he said. "We go for the second classroom on the left. Logan and Wilcox, bring up the rear and secure the door. Sawyer, we clear the room. Once we're in, Barnes, your team starts making a ruckus. Once those things have passed, we'll start taking them out until they focus on us. Then it's your turn."

"Got it, Sarge," Barnes replied with a nod.

Farley cracked the door and peered through to make sure they could make it to the target classroom. He held up a hand, doing a silent countdown from three, and then darted out into the hallway, three soldiers hot on his heels.

He stabbed a zombie through the chest and used it as a battering ram for the few ghouls in their path, and when they reached the classroom, he put his foot against it to tear the spike free, giving it a mighty shove backwards. His chest heaved as he rushed into the classroom behind Sawyer, who was already stabbing at zombies inside.

"I don't know if we thought this one through, Sarge!" Sawyer cried as he leapt up onto a desk, using his spike as a club and playing whack-a-mole with the numerous creatures below.

"Too late now!" Farley barked and hoped to hell that Wilcox and Logan could quickly secure the door and back them up.

He stabbed a zombie in the head and flung it sideways to knock over two more. Sawyer leapt down from his desk, drawing his knife and dropping his spear in the close quarters, stabbing skulls in quick succession. A zombie latched onto the back of his shirt, and he screamed, arms flailing, as he lost his balance and fell to the floor.

As a rotted face came into view, lunging for his face, he pushed up, but the zombie stilled, a spike emerging from its mouth. Logan shoved the body aside and held out his hand to help Sawyer to his feet.

The quartet looked around at the bodies strewn across the classroom. Wilcox stood against the door, which was latched tight, but zombie hands smacked against the outside.

"Clear," Sawyer muttered, and gave Logan a nod for saving his neck.

"Stay away from the window," Farley instructed, and the soldiers ducked down to wait for the other team to draw the ghouls' attention.

After a few tense moments, there was a racket in the hallway, clangs and yells and hollers. The smacking stopped, and Wilcox popped up to peer out the small window. He stayed stock still, watching as the horde filtered by, and then lowered down again, turning to Farley.

"I think there's too many of them," he hissed. "I don't know if they'll get

far enough down that we can get behind
them."

The Sergeant nodded firmly. "If they
don't, we'll open the door and pick 'em
off while they're distracted. If there's
enough of an opening, we can head down to
a further classroom."

Logan took a deep breath, muttering
something under his breath that sounded
like it had something to do with the word
fence.

Sawyer bit back a smart remark,
knowing better than to pester his grieving
friend.

"I think that's it," Wilcox murmured
from the window. "They're all packed in
tight, pushing for the stairwell. They're
only a few feet past the door."

"We take out as many as we can, while
backing up to another classroom," Farley
said, readying his spear.

Sawyer loosened up his shoulders,
hopping from foot to foot. "An empty one
this time, preferably," he quipped.

"Beggars can't be choosers," Wilcox
shot back, and then held up his hand to do
a countdown for the door. When he pulled
it quietly open, the four soldiers crept
out and created a line across the hallway.
It was just wide enough for them all to
comfortably stand next to each other.

The zombies were very interested in the stairwell door, which was now closed but still clanged and banged from the inside.

Logan made the first move, stabbing a ghoul in the back of the skull. The soldiers moved in turn, two lunging forward as two picked targets, so that they worked tandem. As bodies fell, the back of the pack began to notice them, and began to turn and reach for the more accessible meal.

As more and more shuffled towards the soldiers, they backed up, but continued to strike, spearing ghoul after ghoul like fish in a barrel. When they were halfway down the hallway, the stairwell door opened, and Barnes' crew emerged, creeping quietly with their own weapons. At this point there were only a dozen or so left shambling.

"Fuck the classroom, we got this," Logan declared, and jammed the blunt end of his pole into the stomach of a ghoul, shoving it back into the group and knocking a few over like bowling pins.

From the other side, Barnes dropped zombies easily, Burton and Santos clearing classrooms as they went. Soon, the two teams met in the middle, and the Corporal clapped Logan on the shoulder. He nodded,

but turned away brusquely to clear
classrooms on the far end.

Before long, the floor was cleared,
and the team made their way back down to
the first floor to make sure the doors
were secure so no stragglers could get
inside after they left.

"Take five," Farley instructed as
they emerged into the schoolyard. His team
sat down in the grass to take a well-
deserved break.

As Farley studied his map, working out their route through more of the nearby buildings, Burton sat down next to Logan, who'd parked himself further away from the group. She held out a chocolate-covered granola bar that she'd liberated from the community center.

He stared at it for a moment and then took it, peeling it open.

"At the risk of sounding like a total girl," she said as she tore open her own, "chocolate always makes me feel better."

He managed a chuckle and took a bite, shaking his head. "Thanks," he said through a mouthful of granola.

"Sorry, about Graves," she finally said, unscrewing the cap on her water bottle. "I didn't know him very well, we met just a few days ago, but he was a good guy."

Logan lowered his gaze. "The best." He chewed his lip for a moment. "Brave idiot. He volunteered for this mission. I followed him to keep him safe." He clenched a fist, eyes darkening.

"It wasn't your fault," she said. "This war is… like nothing anyone can predict, try as we might."

He nodded. "I know. Shit happens, and all that." He took another thoughtful bite and swallowed. "Troops are dying constantly, becoming those things, killing more troops. Our life expectancy is a lot less than it was three weeks ago. Doesn't make it any easier knowing that."

"No, it doesn't," she agreed with a sigh. "You guys been together long?"

He nodded. "Been friends since we were kids, but the relationship is… was… new," he admitted. "We were stupid for waiting so long. Wasted so much time."

Burton reached over and gave his shoulder a reassuring squeeze, and opened her mouth to say more, but a squad of soldiers approached Farley. "What's this?" she muttered and got to her feet.

"Sergeant Farley?" the Captain asked as they reached him.

Farley furrowed his brow. "Yes?"

"I'm Captain Rocha," the burly man introduced, holding out his hand.

The Sergeant shook it, but still looked confused. "What's going on?"

"We sent a team out at dawn to scout out the 405," the Captain explained. "We lost touch with them, and we can't make any assumptions about whether or not they completed the mission. We need to send another team, and I'd like it to be yours."

Farley shook his head. "With all due respect," he said, crossing his arms, "why did you come out here to ask the aging Sergeant stuck on cleanup duty?"

"I asked around," Rocha said, a smile curling the corner of his lip. "I said I was looking for someone with lots of recon experience, and, well, your name came up enough times that I couldn't ignore it." He tapped the radio attached to his hip. "I got a bit of background information on you, and I've gotta say, I'm impressed. Multiple tours, and discharged with severe injuries, yet here you are, back in action."

The Sergeant avoided his gaze. "On cleanup duty." He resisted the urge to pat his belly, given the fact that he'd been off duty for long enough he wasn't in the same shape he'd been in before he'd been discharged. "Just doing my part to try to save what's left of the world, Captain." He tried to school the sarcasm in his voice. He did believe in the mission, and doing his job, but he couldn't deny that he'd be supremely happy to be off of cleanup duty.

"Admirable, Sergeant, and now I need you to play a different part," Rocha said, pulling a folded-up piece of paper from his pocket. He unfolded it and held it up so Farley could see while he pointed at different areas. "I need you and your team to get to the 405 and scout it out, and then if possible, push forward to the Renton Municipal Airport and secure it, so we can start bringing in troops from the water. The ultimate goal is to secure the 405 to prevent those things from moving up to the northern area flanks, and be ready to move when the groups push down from the north. I've got hundreds of soldiers prepared to come in once there is a safe landing zone."

Farley studied the map, rubbing his chin. "What's this area here?" He pointed to a cluster of buildings.

"That's a retail center, Whitman Court," Rocha said.

The Sergeant nodded. "It's probably safer to hit the 405 south of that."

"Good call," the Captain agreed. "I have men pushing through there now, so it should be relatively safe to get to the highway."

Farley turned to his team and held up his hands, palms out. "What do you think?" he asked. "Want to go running off into danger?"

"And skive off shit cleanup duty?" Sawyer grinned and held up his spear. "Hell yeah, Sarge."

CHAPTER FIVE

"Jesus," Wilcox breathed as they reached Whitman Court.

A battle raged in the parking lot, zombies shambling out from everywhere and soldiers smacking them down with everything they could find. The whole front of one of the stores was blown out, shattered glass everywhere, and ghouls poured out of it into the lot.

"Let's go!" Farley barked, holding up his spike, and the team rushed down onto the asphalt, stepping up to help stem the tide.

Burton tore up next to a soldier swinging a two-by-four back and forth, trying to keep zombies from swarming him. She stabbed one through the head, skewering a second like an undead kebab, and then kicked them off, sending a few more tumbling to the ground.

Sawyer took the left flank, using his post like a battering ram to knock a cluster of ghouls to the pavement. He set to stabbing them all in quick succession with the spike, blood flying everywhere.

"Runner!" somebody screamed, and everyone perked up, on high alert.

Logan whipped around from a burly zombie he'd managed to crush with his bare hands, just in time to see a ghoul in bloody army fatigues tearing across the wheelchair parking. He lowered his shoulder and caught it in the middle, flipping it over his head.

The zombie hit the ground on its back, and Wilcox lunged forward, stabbing at it. The ghoul was fast and flailed out of the way, darting towards Santos with its mouth open for blood. The young Private froze in fear, eyes wide as saucers, but Logan threw his body into the dead soldier, pressing down on its throat with his hands, struggling to hold it down.

"Kill it!" he bellowed, but before Santos could react, Sawyer flew in and stabbed the ghoul in the top of the skull.

When it fell limp, Logan leapt to his feet and turned to Santos. "You can't choke like that!" he snapped. "Do you want to die?"

"I… I…" the kid stammered.

"What are you like a year younger than me? Two?" Logan demanded, pointing his finger in his face. "You need to get your shit together or you're not going to make it through this war."

"Stand down, soldier," Farley said firmly.

Logan huffed and backed off, then looked around at the pile of bodies in front of them. There were still a few

zombies staggering out of the store, but
the original team seemed to have it under
control.

"Let's go," the Sergeant inclined his
head to the south. "We need to get to the
highway."

"Sergeant," somebody called from the
fray, and approached him. "I need your
team to help us clear out these stores."

Farley shook his head. "Sir, I have
my orders from Captain Rocha, we're to
head up the 405 and-"

"You have new orders," the Captain
said haughtily, raising his chin.

"Captain Monroe!" one of the soldiers
called from the front of the store. "I
can't find Rey!"

Sawyer motioned to the dead runner
behind him. "Is that Rey?"

Monroe cocked his head and pursed his
lips. "No, it's not."

"So more potential runners, great,"
Farley growled, and waved to his team.
"Come on, let's get this shit locked
down."

Barnes motioned to the cart corral.
"What about those?" he asked. "We could
make a barricade across the doors and just
kill everything that comes up to it."

"Works for me," Farley replied, and
led his team over. They started pulling

carts out and linking them together in a long line.

"Hurry up," Monroe urged, waving his hand above his head.

The Sergeant reared on him, eyes blazing. "Corporal," he said, voice low and calm, "let's move out. I think the Captain is good here." The soldiers dutifully stepped away from the carts, turning away from the store.

"No, no, fuck," Monroe said, holding up his hands. "Do it your way. Just do it, Sergeant," he huffed. "But know I'll be filing a report against you for your sass." He turned on his heel and strode back to his team.

"He's a peach," Sawyer muttered.

Farley shook his head and rolled his eyes. "Let's get this done, so we can get on with our mission."

They headed for the doors with the longest line of shopping carts they could make, and maneuvered it across the broken windows. It reached all the way across, and both teams spread out across it, melee weapons at the ready.

Barnes banged his metal pole on the carts in front of him, whistling. "Come on out!" he yelled.

"Come get a nice long spear in your face!" Sawyer bellowed, and zombies came flooding out of the aisles of the store.

In the center, a fast-moving ghoul burst through, tearing for them.

Barnes lined up his shot and jabbed out at just the right moment to spear it through the face. "That Rey?" he asked the soldier to his left.

She shook her head. "No. I've never seen that guy before."

The Corporal furrowed his brow. Not only did that mean there was still another runner in the store, but that somebody else had died here recently enough to still be fast moving. Could it have been the scout team from the morning? They'd have to be careful.

The mini-horde hit the melee zone, and the soldiers got to stabbing and smacking and shoving. The sound of skewering flesh and cracking skulls echoed as they took down their foes.

"Runner!" Burton barked, and Monroe shoved her aside, pulling his rifle from his back.

"What the fuck is he doing?" Farley muttered under his breath, and then sighed as the Captain unloaded automatic fire into the fresh zombie.

It fell, one of the bullets finding its mark, and the Captain stepped back from the shopping carts as the last of the ghouls dropped to join it.

Burton turned to the Sergeant, eyebrows in her hairline, her gaze clearly conveying *what the fuck?*

Farley nodded and stepped away from the carts to approach the Captain. "All right, we need to be getting on with our original mission," he said firmly.

"No, I don't think so," Monroe replied, putting his hands on his hips and puffing out his chest. "I think you're gonna stay here and help clear out the rest of these stores."

The Sergeant shook his head. "No, we're going to complete the mission that Captain Rocha sent us on," he declared. "You're welcome for the help."

Monroe pointed a firm finger at him. "You have a duty-"

"If you really want to push the issue, have at it," Farley cut in. "I'll have my own report to file at your incompetence."

The Captain scowled and waved him off, turning back to his team.

"Let's go," the Sergeant said, and ushered his team towards the south.

"Hey, Sergeant," one of the soldiers from the line said, approaching timidly. "Thank you. That was a good idea, with the carts."

Farley nodded. "No sweat," he replied. "Be safe."

"Yes, sir," the kid replied, saluted, and then ran off to join his asshole Captain.

The Sergeant led his team back across the lot at a quick pace. "Let's get the fuck outta here."

"That Captain is a piece of work," Burton muttered as they approached the road that led to the 405.

"Glad we're working with you, Sarge," Wilcox said. "I didn't know you'd been discharged before all this."

Farley grunted. "Yeah, I was really enjoying retirement when the fucking apocalypse happened."

"Maybe once we get rid of all these brain-suckers, you can go back to sipping margaritas by the pool," Sawyer said with a grin.

The Sergeant rolled his eyes. "I'd settle for a good night's sleep in a proper bed."

"With fresh pancakes in the morning," Burton added, smacking her lips.

"Getting woken up with a blowy from a gorgeous woman," Wilcox added, waggling his eyebrows.

Burton scoffed. "I mean, if you want your dick eaten off by a zombie, by all means," she retorted.

"That's cold." Wilcox put a hand to his chest. "Ice cold."

"Quiet," Farley hissed as they reached the highway, and crouched down behind a row of bushes.

Sawyer sighed. "Of course there's a horde," he said. "There's always a horde."

"There's only a few hundred," Wilcox said, tilting his head back and forth. "No biggie."

Burton raised her eyebrow at him. "Your soulmate in there?"

He smirked at her. "You know it," he said.

She rolled her eyes.

"We need to figure out a plan of action," Barnes said, and looked around. Across the highway was a small apartment complex that looked devoid of ghouls from the outside. "What if we regroup over there? Looks like the horde sucked up all the stragglers."

Farley nodded. "Good call," he agreed. "Come on, and stay quiet." He crept out of the bushes and led them silently across the asphalt. The zombies were headed in the other direction, the way they needed to go, but it was slow moving.

The team headed across the parking lot of the apartment complex and peered into the busted front glass doors of the lobby. There were a few benches there, but no zombie activity. The soldiers took seats on either side of the wood-paneled room, and Farley leaned forward, leaning his elbows on his knees.

"Thoughts?" he asked.

Santos raised his hand. "Couldn't we just go around them?" he asked. "Go through the woods? We can move way faster."

"That would be ideal," Barnes replied, leaning back against the wall. "Except if we're to face significant opposition ahead, we don't want a few hundred zombies pressing up against our asses."

Logan pointed out the broken door, off to the side of the parking lot. "We could squash 'em."

Farley turned and stuck his head out the door, raising his eyebrow at a large cherry red four-wheel-drive truck. "That could work, for a few of them," he agreed. "But not for all."

The team headed outside, keeping their eyes peeled for any stragglers as they approached the truck.

Wilcox let out a low whistle. "Look at this puppy," he said appreciatively, running a hand along the hood. "Not even a scratch on it, even with all this."

"It's about to get a workout," Sawyer declared.

"So what's the plan, Sarge?" Barnes asked. "If we can't take them all out with this?"

"We punch through as far as we can, and then shoot the fuckers," Logan cut in. "Two of us drive out there, and cause a giant ruckus from the truck bed, while the rest of you pick them off from behind while we hold their attention."

The others looked to Farley for confirmation, and he rubbed his chin. Finally, he sighed. "I guess it's our only option." He turned to Logan. "I suppose that you want to be on the truck team, since you said 'us' and 'we'?"

The soldier nodded. "Just need someone to hot-wire it."

"On it," Burton said, and approached the driver's side door.

Barnes grabbed the handle and tried it, finding it open. "Let me guess," he drawled as he opened it for her and waved her in like a car salesman, "high school?"

"Middle school, actually," she replied with a wink, and then slid in under the steering column.

The Corporal laughed and shook his head.

"I'd like to go with Logan," Santos said, raising his hand.

The burly Private glowered down at him. "No, you should stay with the others."

"I can do this," Santos said firmly, straightening his shoulders.

"You don't have to prove yourself to me by being stupid," Logan snapped.

"Enough," Farley cut in, tired of the back-and-forth between the two. "Sawyer will go. He's got the sniper rifle so he can keep an eye on things and scout ahead from the top of the truck."

As if on cue, the beastly vehicle sprang to life, and Burton got out, swiping her palms against each other. "Your chariot, gentlemen," she said.

Logan climbed into the driver's seat, and Sawyer jogged around to jump into the passenger side.

"Be safe," Barnes said, and smacked the side of the truck.

Logan peeled out and headed for the road that would circle around to the highway.

"Let's move," Farley said, and they headed across the lot to wait on the grassy bank for their turn to take on the horde.

"You okay, man?" Wilcox asked, bringing up the rear with Santos.

The young Private shook his head. "I don't know what I did to piss Logan off," he muttered. "I may not have seen any action before the apocalypse, but I've been living with zombies just as long as you guys have."

"He's not pissed off at you," Wilcox assured him, clapping him on the shoulder. "He's really torn up about Graves, and doesn't want to lose anyone else."

Santos lowered his gaze. "I get it," he admitted. "I just… I want to be able to pull my weight. I don't want to let anyone down."

"Then stop worrying about it and just do it, bud," Wilcox said with a grin. "We all have a job to do. Kill zombies and stay alive. Easy peasy."

Santos chuckled and shook his head. "Sure man, easy peasy."

"Good chat," Wilcox said, and clapped his shoulder again.

The team reached the grass and crouched down, just as the truck turned onto the highway to their right. Logan revved the engine a few times, and then punched the gas, screaming towards the horde on their left.

As the truck passed, they heard Sawyer's "Whooooo!", and the soldiers laughed, shaking their heads.

"Brace yourself!" Logan yelled, and then the grill hit the back of the horde. They lurched forward in their seats, but still moved forward at a decent clip, *cha-thunking* over bodies and crunching skulls beneath the fat tires.

The ghouls all turned towards the shiny red vehicle, now splattered in different shades of crimson, smacking at it as it went by, limbs flying everywhere.

About two-thirds of the way across, the vehicle slowed to a stop, the tires unable to move anymore, likely due to corpses wedged too thick into the wheel wells.

"Showtime," Sawyer said, and opened the back window. He shoved his gun through and slithered out onto the bed. "You gonna be able to get those thick-ass shoulders through there?"

Logan shoved his assault rifle through the hole and then gave his companion the finger.

"Gotcha," Sawyer replied, and raised the gun while he waited for his partner to squeeze through the window. He scanned the horizon on the far side, where they were going, but was unable to see too far around the bend with all the trees in the way.

All of a sudden something brushed his leg and gave a sharp shriek. Sawyer instinctively kicked out, but an impossibly strong hand grabbed his ankle and he yelled as he fell onto his back.

A single booming shot rang out, and he looked up to see Logan standing over

him, aiming his rifle at a limp corpse in
military fatigues.

"What do you want to bet he was on
the scouting team?" Logan asked, and
Sawyer shook his head emphatically.

He got to his feet, brushing himself
off, and then readied his assault rifle,
leaving the scoped gun on the floor of the
truck bed. "Thanks, man."

"Good thing I could fit through the
window," Logan replied dryly.

"We have to warn them somehow that
there's runners," Sawyer said, searching
frantically through the moaning crowd for
more military gear or fast moving bodies.

Logan inclined his head to the sniper
rifle. "What if you got on top of the
truck and picked them off?" he asked. "You
should be able to see them, right?"

"Good call," Sawyer agreed, and
swapped guns, clambering on top of the
rack attached to the top of the truck.

He steadied his stance and peered
down at the horde through the scope,
scanning. He moved up at movement from the
back, and saw his team coming out of the
grass, approaching with guns at the ready.

He held up a hand to wave, and it
appeared that Barnes saw him, because he
raised his hand back. Sawyer turned and
did an exaggerated running on the spot,

lifting his knees high, hoping they would
understand what he was trying to say.

"There's one!" Logan cried, pointing.
"It's heading their way!"

Sawyer immediately raised his rifle
again, focusing on the path, and saw a
bald head moving jerkily through the thick
crowd. He fired, and the bullet hit it in
the shoulder, not slowing it down in the
slightest.

As it grew close to the back of the
horde, he didn't want to shoot it again,
for fear of accidentally hitting one of
his teammates, but it appeared they'd
figured out what he was shooting at,
because they took up defensive positions
and waited for the runner to clear the
shamblers.

He sighed with relief as Farley took
it out with a well-placed bullet to the
face.

"Okay, you keep hunting runners, I'm
gonna start taking out these bastards,"
Logan declared, and began to fire rapid
precise shots, hitting zombie after zombie
in the forehead.

Meanwhile, Farley's gunshot attracted
the back half of the horde, despite the
rapid fire happening in the truck.

"Single burst, make every bullet
count!" the Sergeant barked, and raised
his gun. His team did so as well, and they

fanned out, creating a semicircle across the highway and shoulders to fire into the horde.

Bodies fell, the bullets finding their marks, and Logan's shots continued to crack from the other side.

"Runner!" Burton yelled from the far left side and backed up as she fired at a fast-moving ghoul. She hit it in the stomach, and then backed up farther than she'd meant to, losing her balance and falling ass over teakettle down the grassy hill.

Santos screamed from beside her as the runner went skidding down for its tumbling meal. He leapt down after it without even thinking, and a group of zombies from the now-weak left side went tumbling down after him.

"Sarge!" Barnes cried helplessly as he watched the two disappear over the edge.

Farley moved over to cover the hole, still firing. "They can take care of themselves, keep going!" he barked. "And watch out for more runners!"

Sawyer took out the last runner he'd been able to spot, and then did a double take when he saw Burton and Santos disappearing into the trees, the latter clearly limping as at least a dozen zombies followed after them, led by one in bloody fatigues. He turned and managed to take out a few ghouls, unfortunately not the runner, before they gave chase into the forest.

"Fuck!" he cursed. "A runner just chased Burton and Santos into the trees!"

"Can't do anything about it right now, man," Logan snapped. "If there's no more runners you'd better start killing some of these corpses here."

Sawyer slid down off of the roof and took up his assault rifle, standing at Logan's back and picking off ghoul after ghoul. On the far side from where the two soldiers had run off, more zombies shambled out of the woods, heading towards the noise of the gunfire. He looked at the way they needed to go and was relieved to see that at least there wasn't anything coming around the bend.

When his mag was empty, he reached down and picked up a chunk of rebar from the floor and began cracking skulls, bodies piling up around the truck as they thinned the horde.

Soon, Farley and the rest of the team were closing in, stepping over bodies and taking out ghouls from the other side. As the last few fell, leaving a rotted battlefield of carnage, all the soldiers turned to the last few stragglers emerging from the trees, save for Sawyer, who picked up his rifle to try to search for Burton and Santos.

He couldn't see through the thick brush, and it didn't seem like any ghouls were coming out of the woodwork either. "Fuck," he muttered under his breath.

"See anything?" Logan asked.

"We have to go get them," Sawyer said, lowering the gun.

Farley shook his head. "We can't risk it," he said, though there was a note of sadness in his voice. "We have to secure the airport."

Sawyer swallowed hard. "But-"

"They know where they're going," the Sergeant cut in. "Once they've taken care of the danger, they'll meet us either on the highway or at the airport."

Barnes shook his head. "It's only us that can do this," he added. "The last scout team didn't make it through here."

Sawyer sighed and looked helplessly at Logan, but his companion avoided his gaze, simply jumping down from the truck, boots squelching in rotted guts as he hit the ground.

                    CHAPTER SEVEN

     The team of five soldiers walked up
the road towards the 405. As they came
around the bend, they stopped short, eyes
wide.

     "Well, fuck," Sawyer blurted.

     The 405 was jam-packed with zombies.
Shoulder to shoulder, not really moving,
just covering the highway like an undead
carpet as far as they could see in either
direction.

     "How the hell are we going to get
across?" Wilcox threw his hands up.
"Should have saved the truck for this!"

     Barnes shook his head. "No, if we'd
have tried to punch through with the
truck, we would just draw them all to the
airport." He cocked his head. "We need to
get past them without disturbing them."

     Sawyer raised his rifle, scoping the
area. "There's a river over there."

     Farley pulled out his map, running
his finger along the water. "Cedar River,"
he murmured. "It runs right under it, and
right alongside the airport on the far
side."

     "Fancy a swim?" Wilcox asked, in his
best British accent.

     Sawyer rolled his eyes. "There are
boats, dingus." He pointed, and when the
rest of the team squinted, they could see

a cluster of bright yellow canoes bobbing
against a dock on the water.

"Even better!" Wilcox exclaimed and
slid down the embankment to make the trek
to the water.

The soldiers made their way through
the grass, staying quiet as they didn't
want to risk drawing any attention from
the highway zombies. There were a few
ghouls scattered about in the grass, but
they were easily dispatched by Sawyer's
rebar and his companion's knives.

When they reached the dock, Wilcox
leaned into one of the canoes and held up
a metal paddle, holding it high over his
head like a trophy. "Sometimes we *can* get
lucky!" he said with a grin and gave it an
experimental swing. The resounding *whoosh*
made his grin even bigger, and he brushed
past Sawyer to walk straight up to a
zombie ambling along the riverbank.

He swung hard, like a baseball
player, and the wide part of the paddle
thwacked against the ghoul's head,
severing it from its body. The head sailed
through the air and landed with a *plonk* in
the water.

Wilcox gave a mighty bow with a
flourish, as his teammates shook their
heads in various states of amusement.

"I'm not riding with him," Logan quipped, and stepped down into one of the boats.

Barnes got down after him, sitting in the middle seat. "Sawyer, you're with us, Wilcox, ride with Sarge," he instructed. "We'll leave the third just in case the others come this way."

There was an awkward moment of silence as they all thought of Burton and Santos, and then they pushed off from the dock and began quietly paddling towards the zombie-covered bridge.

There was a *splash* ahead, and Sawyer muttered obscenities under his breath as a zombie from the bridge above tumbled over the railing and plunged into the water below. It was sporadic, but concerning.

"It's raining death, hallelujah!" Wilcox sang quietly, paddling away.

Farley took a deep breath. "Keep an eye up," he instructed."

"Not like we can fast maneuver these things," Logan replied, as another ghoul went *splash* up ahead.

"No, but maybe we can bat 'em out of the air," Sawyer suggested.

The soldiers held their breath as they grew closer and closer to the bridge, watching the ambling and writhing bodies moving against the railing above. A few seemed to notice the bright canoes below, and reached out, the combined movement and pressure from the horde sending a few sailing down into the current.

"Go!" Farley hissed, and Wilcox and Barnes paddled as hard as they could to get through the danger zone without incident. A few creatures fell just after them, but *plonked* into the water behind the boats.

Wilcox looked down, seeing a rotted corpse get stuck on the bottom of the river. "At least they can't swim," he pointed out.

"We still don't want to be in that water," Farley replied. "It's not like they can drown."

The team went silent again as they approached the other side, more on edge considering they couldn't see what was coming from beneath the bridge.

"Now!" the Sergeant whisper-yelled again, as they reached the fall zone, and the soldiers paddled mightily to propel themselves out of danger.

A ghoul fell, arms flailing, and clipped Logan's back on the way down. He threw himself around, nearly knocking the canoe over, and both Sawyer and Barnes gripped the sides tightly, trying to overcorrect for the sudden dip in balance.

"You good?" Barnes demanded, looking at the back of the boat, and Logan relaxed, nodding jerkily as the creature sunk to the bottom of the river.

"Yeah, fuck," he replied. "That was close." He looked up at the highway again, jutting out his chin at the corpses squirming about. *You'll get what's fuckin' coming,* he thought bitterly, and turned around to face front as they continued their ride to the airport.

"You gotta let go of me!" Santos begged as Burton practically dragged him through the woods, his ankle screaming at him. "Just run!"

"Shut the fuck up," she snapped, and then something hit her in the back like a battering ram.

Burton went face-first into the dirt, a shrieking and snarling animal on her back. *Not an animal,* she thought frantically. *The runner.*

She flailed, bringing her elbow up instinctively to punt it in the face, regardless of the fact that if her elbow went into its mouth she was done for. Thankfully, it connected with the ghoul's nose, caving in part of its face though not deterring it from lunging for her throat.

She managed to wedge her arm into the crook of its neck, and it was so intent on her face that it didn't think to just bite her arm. But it was strong, the strength of a newly dead body that never grew tired. Her biceps threatened to buckle under the sheer power of it.

And then it went limp.

Burton blinked in surprise as the runner collapsed onto her. And then Santos was there, withdrawing his knife from the back of its skull. She shoved the corpse off of her and stared up at him in shock.

There was no time for small talk, however, as three shambling ghouls appeared behind him.

"Move!" she barked and scrambled to her feet, shoving him out of the way. She lowered her shoulder and barreled into the lead zombie, shoving it back into one of its friends. The third she kicked in the chest, and then drew her knife, lunging down to stab it in the forehead.

She snatched up a thick broken stick from the ground, and swung it like a golf club at the next zombie struggling to get to its feet, snapping its neck in the process. With the third pinned beneath the second, she stabbed it in the eye socket, and then whipped around to make sure nothing else was coming out of the woodwork.

"We gotta move," she said, and dropped the stick, heading over to help Santos to his feet. Or, rather, his one foot.

"No, no, you gotta leave me," he hissed as she forced him up from the forest floor. "I'm slowing you down."

Burton glared at him. "You just saved my life, idiot," she snapped. "Come on." She hooked his arm over her shoulder, and

kept her knife at the ready in her free
hand, as did he.

"I can't believe I did this to
myself," he grunted.

She shook her head. "What, twisted
your ankle, diving down a hill to try to
save me from a runner?" she asked. "Could
have been far worse. You're not going to
die from an ankle sprain."

"When there's flesh-eating monsters
chasing me, I can totally die from an
ankle sprain," he pointed out.

Burton couldn't help but laugh. "I
mean, I guess so," she agreed. "But I'm
not going to let that happen."

"Why?" he asked, swallowing hard.
"I'm not good at being a soldier."

"How are you missing the part where
you saved my life?" she repeated firmly.
"I know you're all self-conscious because
you froze up in front of that runner at
Whitman Court, but this time you didn't
freeze, you stabbed it in the head before
it could eat me." She offered him a smile.
"Thanks, by the way."

He shook his head. "You're welcome,"
he replied. "I'm still slowing you down
now, though."

"Slow or fast, you can rest assured
that I would rather have someone to talk
to while I catch up to the others," she

said. "So, you're not allowed to die, at least until then."

He chuckled, loosening up a little. "They probably didn't wait for us, huh?"

"No, I wouldn't expect them to," she admitted. "The gunfire stopped long enough ago that they should be well on their way past the 405 by now, barring any issues. But the lack of more gunfire is hopefully a good sign."

"Should we try to come back out on the road?" Santos asked.

She nodded. "That's what I was thinking," she replied. "At least we know for sure it's clear."

"That is, if they made it through the horde," he pointed out, though he regretted the words as soon as they left his mouth.

Burton raised an eyebrow. "You are a depressing little dude, you know that?"

"I'm taller than you," he shot back before he could even think, and to his surprise, she laughed, shaking her head.

"Point made," she agreed, and then put a finger to her lips as she spotted a break in the trees ahead. They crept quietly to the treeline and peered out.

To the right, they saw the red truck, surrounded by hundreds of corpses, splayed everywhere in an impressive display of carnage.

"They did it," Santos breathed, staring in awe at the bodies.

"Of course they did," Burton replied. "Come on, let's have a look at that truck."

He patted her shoulder and removed his arm, testing out his ankle a little. "I think I'm okay," he said, putting a light amount of weight on it to limp along on his own. He waited at the bottom of the embankment as she climbed up to have a look.

Burton scanned the area to make sure there were no stragglers and then knelt down to look at the wheel wells. "Damn," she muttered, and then straightened up, turning around. "Well, we should probably take the quiet route anyway. You sure you're okay to walk?"

"As long as I don't have to go up there, I should be good," he replied.

She slid down the grass and gave him a thumbs up. "We'll be following the road towards the 405," she explained. "I haven't heard any gunfire, so they shouldn't be fighting swaths of flesh-eating monsters to get to the airport."

"I like your optimism," Santos said, and they began to hobble towards the 405.

The soldiers got out of their canoes at the southernmost tip of the airport. Armed with metal paddles and rebar, they crept through the grass and crouched behind a row of pushes to have a look at what they were dealing with.

"Fuck," Sawyer breathed.

The airport was covered in ghouls.

"Up shit creek once again," Wilcox said, "but at least we have paddles!"

"How do you want to play this, Sarge?" Barnes asked, ignoring the quipping Private.

Farley pursed his lips for a moment, surveying the area. A fence ran around the long thin property, buildings surrounding the long runway and stretching all the way up to Lake Washington, where the river mouth was.

"We'll need a distraction," the Sergeant said. "Draw out all of those things into the center, and then pick them off from varying cover around the outside."

Wilcox held up his paddle. "I bet one of these puppies could make a lot of noise, smacked against the right thing," he said.

"Good," Farley replied, pointing at him. "You and Barnes run up through the

center, there, and make a ruckus. When
they're all good and clustered, make a run
for it up the runway and circle back
around to help us take them out."

The Corporal chuckled and shook his
head, holding his hand out for Farley's
paddle so he'd have two. Wilcox took
Logan's.

"How's everyone doing for ammo?"
Farley asked.

The soldiers checked their mags, and
while the bullet situation was dismal, if
they were precise it should be enough to
take out the horde.

The Sergeant approached the fence
quietly, and they moved along it until
they found a loose bit of chain link they
could peel back. Logan held it up so they
could squeeze through and then popped
through himself.

Farley silently pointed at each of
them, motioning which way to go, and the
team all nodded, darting off in their
respective directions.

Wilcox and Barnes pressed themselves
against a little outbuilding, peering out
at the smattering of small planes from the
aviation school. There were ghouls
staggering about aimlessly, but none too
clustered together.

"Okay, we run in on the right there,"
the Corporal instructed quietly, "and

smack the paddles against the planes as we
go. If we can get to the line of cars over
there, maybe we can get some alarms
going."

Wilcox nodded, holding his paddles up
like dual death dealers. "Let's make some
noise," he said.

The duo took off like a shot, tearing
out onto the asphalt, legs pumping. Their
bootfalls alerted the zombies in the area,
and they turned, mouths open and arms
outstretched. But they were slow, and the
soldiers were fast.

"Whoooo!" Wilcox hollered and held up
one of his paddles as he ran underneath
the row of small planes. The metal clanged
off of the wings overhead, the noise
echoing loudly.

Barnes swung like a baseball player
to get one zombie out of the way, not
breaking stride, and banged his paddles
together before reaching the wings and
smacking them. Metal on metal. The
distraction was working, the zombies
excited for their loud meals.

When they reached the other side,
there was a line of ghouls waiting for
them, and Wilcox grabbed the paddles
together by the handles, holding them out
in front of him like a double-ended sword.
He barrelled into the line, knocking back

four ghouls, and leapt over their fallen
forms, tearing for the line of cars.

Barnes was close enough behind him
that he could jump over the writhing
corpses, but skidded to a stop as a group
of creatures poured out from between two
vans. He dropped one of his paddles and
swung the other, dislodging the head of
the closest zombie.

Wilcox whipped around and attacked
from behind, jabbing forward with one of
the wide ends, the flat part sinking into
a particularly rotted throat and severing
its spinal column. He kicked the ghoul in
the back, sending the corpse tumbling into
its brethren.

Barnes smacked another, and then
grabbed his knife, stabbing a third in the
head and throwing it into the few left
standing to knock them over.

"The cars!" he cried as the ghouls
struggled to get to their feet. He glanced
over his shoulder as the ones they'd
attracted from the earlier noise began to
catch up.

The duo brandished their metal
weapons, and began smacking the cars as
hard as they could, all the way down the
line. Their stomachs clenched as no alarms
bleated, but they kept at it, running
along the row. Wilcox ducked between two
cars to hit them from the front, and

Barnes whacked them from the back as hard as he could.

A silver ritzy-looking sedan second to last finally erupted into noise, the lights flashing and alarm blaring.

"Go!" Barnes cried, looking back at the thickening horde catching up to them.

The duo tore away from the cars, pumping their legs hard out onto the runway. They skidded to a stop at the sight of ghouls dotting the landscape, all wandering towards them and the source of the noise.

"Over there!" Wilcox yelled, pointing at a hangar across the way. At a quick glance, it looked like it wasn't infested, and they sprinted for the area, knocking over a few ghouls in the process.

Barnes ducked behind a big metal toolbox, pressing his back up against it to catch his breath. Seconds later, his companion joined him, and their chests heaved as they waited.

Wilcox peeked out as the alarm continued to blare and saw the runway zombies shambling towards the cars.

"Thank fuck," he huffed, and set down his paddles, unslinging his rifle from his back. "Good thinking with the alarm."

Barnes nodded and checked his own gun. "Once the rest of the runway zombies get over there, we'll head back out and

start going from behind," he said, and as
if on cue, gunfire erupted from the
distance. It seemed the rest of their team
had begun their assault.

"Left, left!" Burton hissed, and a zombie *plonked* into the water, narrowly missing their boat.

Santos grunted. "You know I don't have a steering wheel, right?" he snapped.

She turned around to growl something at him, but a grey blur plummeted between them as a body smacked into the center seat of the canoe. It wasn't even fazed by the impact, flailing around and clawing for Santos, mouth open in hunger.

He instinctively swung the paddle, hitting it in the shoulder, causing it to fly off of the boat. The momentum swung the canoe wildly, and both of them wavered, leaning in different directions to try to steady it.

"Fucking hell," Burton breathed as they settled, finally floating under the bridge to relative safety. As ghouls hit the water up ahead from the other side, she took a deep breath. "They must be really moshing up there."

Santos chewed his lip for a moment. "Should we go to one side?" he asked. "They seem to be falling more in the middle."

"It's shallower on the sides," she replied, shaking her head. "At least this way we can float over 'em."

He nodded, but inside his heart hammered. If one of those things fell in just the right spot… it wouldn't matter if it was deep or whether the boat survived or what. A bite meant death.

"Okay, we'll float until just before, and then paddle like hell," Burton said, holding her oar up for emphasis.

"Deal," Santos replied. "On your go."

They held their breaths, floating lazily, closer and closer to the other side of the bridge. If they weren't in such a fucked-up situation, it would have been a nice relaxing trip. As it was, breaths held, stress pulsing through their veins… this boat ride was the farthest thing from relaxing.

Plonk, plonk, splash.

"Go!" Burton hissed, and they paddled like mad.

Santos' heart leapt as they made it out the other side and then plummeted as something hit him like a ton of bricks. He barely registered Burton's yell before he flew backwards into the river, the cold water enveloping him with a roar.

The ghoul had him by the throat, and he kicked and tried to hold his breath, lungs screaming at the fact he hadn't taken a big one before he'd fallen. He pushed against the zombie, hoping that it would hit something, dislodge, somehow.

Santos' back scraped up against something hard, and he tried to orient himself. If that was the bottom, he curled himself up and kicked off, trying to account for the current. He wanted to draw his knife, wanted to stab at the creature, but he needed air.

As stars exploded behind his vision, his mouth threatening to open and breathe water, his attacker suddenly went limp.

He broke the surface of the river, gasping deep lungfuls of air, and whipped around to see Burton jerking her knife out of the ghoul's head.

"Are you okay?" she sputtered, shoving the corpse away before swimming towards him.

Santos nodded. "Yeah, yeah, thank you," he stammered.

"You're not bit?" she demanded.

"No," he replied, reaching up to touch his throat where the thing had pulled at him. He didn't feel any scratches, but he was sure there'd be a bruise there. "Where's the boat?" He looked back and forth, and she pointed behind him.

Downriver, the yellow canoe bobbed away from them.

"We can swim up and catch it, but the oars are farther ahead," she explained.

Santos nodded. "I don't know about you, but I could use a rest," he admitted. "Probably safer in the boat."

"Fair enough," she replied. "You okay to swim with your leg?"

He nodded again. "Yeah, the water actually feels good," he said. "Don't need to put weight on it to swim."

"All right, let's go," Burton said, swimming downriver.

Santos looked up at the bridge behind them, the zombies against the railing reaching down to them with hunger in their glassy eyes. He shuddered, touching his throat one more time, and then swam after his companion.

CHAPTER ELEVEN

As the car alarm began to shriek, Farley nodded in approval. "Good job, soldiers," he said under his breath, and peeked out from behind the outbuilding he stood behind. Zombies poured out of everywhere, staggering towards the screaming car.

When it seemed like the cluster had ceased to grow, he emerged from his spot, creeping along the wall and taking careful aim. Every bullet would count.

As soon as he fired, two more shots rang out on either side of him, his team having waited for him to give them the go-ahead. Ghouls began dropping like flies, but the group didn't seem to care about the gunfire, far more interested in the blaring car.

The Sergeant moved up, standing behind a waist-high chunk of engine that had been left out for some reason or another. He fired bullet after bullet, taking out creature after creature, and then the alarm stopped.

The ghouls seemed to shiver as one, almost as if in confusion, but quickly realized that the car wasn't the interesting thing anymore. They began to writhe around, facing outwards into the sporadic gunfire. More shots joined from the far side, as Barnes and Wilcox rejoined the fray from the runway.

The cluster of ghouls began to disperse, wandering in all directions towards the shooting soldiers.

"Fuck, there are a lot of them," Farley muttered to himself. He wasn't sure if they'd be able to take them all out before any of them reached the perimeter. He began to walk backwards, still firing, at least fifty of the ghouls heading in his direction of the zombie star.

He headed back down the building and sprinted around the back, darting down the alleyway between two buildings to pop out on the other side. He began to fire again, into the thinner stream of ghouls that wandered where he'd been standing before.

They quickly turned track and headed towards him.

"Sarge!" Logan cried from across the asphalt, and Farley whipped around as a quartet of zombies approached him from behind.

He leapt back into the alleyway, firing as he went, and ghouls staggered into the bottleneck, shambling over their fallen brethren to get to him.

The Sergeant finally turned and ran for the other end of the alley, but as he rounded the corner, he came face to face

with a cluster of zombies that had come
all the way around the back.

*How the fuck did you get back here so
fast?* He wondered frantically and used the
butt of his rifle to smack the first one
in the face. The alley zombies were almost
to the opening. With the close proximity,
he knew he should flip to rapid fire, but
he didn't want to waste the bullets. They
were already short as it was, without the
full force of their team.

He backed against the fence, still
shooting one at a time, hoping for a hole
or something he could duck through and
then circle around to their original point
of entry. Zombies fell, but it wasn't
enough, and the alley zombies quickly
filled the space between the building and
the fence.

Fuck it, he finally thought, flipping
his gun into rapid-fire, but before he
could shoot, bullets began flying from
beside him, on the other side of the
fence.

He whipped around, eyes wide, to see
Santos and Burton standing there, firing
through the chain link.

Farley grinned and flipped his gun
back to single burst, and with the
combined force of the three of them, they
took out the group of ghouls.

"You made it," he said breathlessly as the last one fell.

Burton smirked. "Thanks for leaving us a canoe, Sarge," she said with a little salute.

"We had a good swim, anyway," Santos added, running a hand through his slick hair.

"There's a break in the fence just up there," Farley said, pointing. "We tried to cluster those things in the middle of the aviation academy area, but they're all over the place now."

"Gotcha," Burton replied, and waved to Santos, who limped along after her.

The Sergeant shook his head and took off back down the alley to help his team, thankful that he hadn't lost two more.

"You good, Sarge?" Logan bellowed as Farley emerged from the alleyway.

The Sergeant nodded and aimed at a lineup of zombies staggering towards him on the right.

Wilcox and Barnes had climbed up on top of the cars, and were each standing atop their own tall van, shooting down into the ghouls below. Sawyer was nowhere to be found, but Farley knew he had to trust his team, and focused on his own task.

Burton peeled back the loose section of chain link and all but shoved Santos through it. "When we get out there, find cover, and make sure you're leaning while you're shooting," she instructed. "I'm going to find some high ground and keep them from being able to flank you."

"I'm not an invalid," the kid mumbled.

"You will be, if you don't take care of that ankle as much as you can," she shot back, and clapped him on the shoulder. "Come on."

Santos managed a limping skip after her as they approached the same path Wilcox and Barnes had taken earlier. As soon as they came around the outbuilding, a pack of zombies greeted them, and Burton immediately opened fire, her rapid bullets finding their targets.

They stepped over the fallen corpses and scurried forward to take stock of the carnage. There was a pile of crates just ahead, and Burton led him over to it, motioning for him to take his post there.

"Make those bullets count," she said, and clapped him on the shoulder one more time before darting off behind the row of small planes, knife at the ready.

Santos raised his assault rifle, trying not to think about the sheer number of ghouls all over the airport. Most of them were facing away, heading towards the others, so he took his opportunity and began to blast them in the back of the head.

After a few moments of shooting, ghouls honed in on his location. His mouth went dry, but he steeled himself. He remembered how he'd frozen when he'd seen that first runner. He remembered *not* freezing the second time when he'd saved Burton. He couldn't let his team down.

He fired shot after shot, once or twice hitting a ghoul in the throat or shoulder instead of the head, but kept up the pace, trying not to count the yards closing in on him. He glanced over at the planes, and saw Burton ducking in and around the machinery, leaping forward to stab a ghoul here and there, stealthing her way around.

As she wrapped her hands around one of the wings and pulled her body on top of one of the small planes, he shook his head in amusement.

Feeling better that she was up out of the way, Santos turned back to his targets. A snarl from the left startled him, and he let out a surprised yell at a cluster of ghouls approaching from behind him.

He staggered away from the crates, not wanting to turn his back to the ghouls approaching from the airport proper. He backed away as he continued to fire, taking down as many ghouls as he could, but it didn't seem like enough.

His heart pounded in his ears as he limped backwards, and then he put weight on his bad ankle at just the wrong angle, and fell down onto his ass.

"Fuck!" he yelled, but continued to fire, trying to push himself backwards across the ground with his good leg. There were too many, and for every one he dropped, two took its place. He looked frantically towards Burton, but he'd backed his way out of her sight.

When his gun clicked empty, he grunted and dropped it, drawing his handgun and aiming. His hands shook, but he managed to hit three zombies in quick succession. But they were faster on their feet than he was on his ass, and he couldn't believe that this could be the end.

All of a sudden, two ghouls right next to each other fell, their heads exploding simultaneously. More zombies' heads blew apart, and Santos blinked in shock, but didn't stop firing until his handgun ran out of bullets. He drew his knife, struggling to get up onto one knee, but Farley and Logan came around the side, firing into the horde and expertly dropping zombie after zombie.

When there was nothing left but a pile of corpses, Santos sat back down on his ass, chest heaving with relief.

"Good to see you made it," Logan said, and offered his hand.

Santos smiled up at him and let him help him up. "Are we clear?" he asked hoarsely.

The Sergeant turned towards the airport proper, littered with bodies, as the others came down from their perches. Sawyer waved from atop one of the outbuildings, and then crossed to the side to climb down a ladder attached to the outside.

The soldiers met in the center of the aviation academy lot, looking around at their handiwork.

"Well, I hope the troops are still coming, after all that," Wilcox said, and gave Burton a playful punch on the arm. "Did you guys enjoy your romantic getaway?"

She rolled her eyes. "Yeah, wine, cheese, and zombies," she retorted, running a hand through her wet ponytail and flicking water at him. "Jealous?"

"Secure the buildings," Farley
instructed. "I'll find the radio tower and
call in the troops."

There was a chorus of *yes, sir*, and
the soldiers headed off in groups of two
to check all the buildings. Thankfully,
everything was shut up tight, and they
congregated outside of the radio tower.

"Captain Beltran, this is Sergeant
Farley, from the Renton Airport," he said
into the mouthpiece.

After a tense moment, the line sprang
to life, and a gruff voice replied, "Read
you, Sergeant Farley. Status?"

"The airport is secure," Farley said.
"You're clear to land."

"Cheers, Sergeant," the Captain
replied. "Stand by."

"Yes, sir," Farley replied, and the
line went dead. He headed back outside to
join his team, where Wilcox was chasing
Sawyer around in a circle.

"Come on, I'm not all gooey this
time!" Wilcox cried, arms outstretched.

Sawyer ducked around Burton, trying
to use her as a human shield. "No, the goo
is rotting and you smell like shit!"

"You don't smell like roses either,
and I still love you enough to hug you!"
Wilcox said, much to the mirth of everyone
else. He ended up wrapping his arms all

the way around Burton, gripping her in a sandwich between him and Sawyer.

"Ugh, you *are* rank," she said with an exaggerated gag, and slid down out of the embrace, allowing Wilcox to wrap his companion in a bear hug.

Farley shook his head and chuckled as Sawyer whined and moaned. He leaned against the door of the radio tower, crossing his arms and watching his team have a well-deserved break.

It didn't take long for the boats to arrive from Lake Washington, troops swarming the airport. Beltran approaches the rag tag team by the radio tower and nodded to them.

"Great work here," he said, inclining his head to the bodies strewn everywhere. "How was everything on the way in?"

"We had to come in by canoe up the river," Farley explained. "The 405 is so packed with those things we wouldn't have been able to punch through."

The Captain smirked and raised his walkie talkie to his lips. "Bit crowded on the 405," he said.

"Ten-four," came the only reply, and Beltran put the radio back in his pocket.

"So, I hear that you're not the original team that was supposed to come out here," the Captain said, cocking his head.

Farley nodded. "You heard correctly," he replied. "There was a scout team at dawn, but Captain Rocha lost contact with them, so he pulled us out of cleanup duty."

"Oh, I bet you were mighty disappointed by that," Beltran said, a mischievous twinkle in his eye.

Laughter rippled through the group, and the Sergeant shook his head. "Absolutely," he agreed, sarcasm dripping from his tone. "We can't wait to go back."

"Did you find the other team?" Beltran asked.

Farley frowned. "Yes," he replied, "seems they got caught by a horde on the road leading to the 405. We took it out and found runners."

"Shame," the Captain replied, shaking his head. "However, impressive that this is your second horde today."

Before the Sergeant could respond, helicopter blades cut through the air, and a chopper roared overhead. The *whir* of a mini gun buzzed as it fired on the 405 zombies, clearing out a big space for them to work.

As this happened, another fleet of boats arrived, and the soldiers followed the Captain as he barked out orders. Troops ran every which way, carrying giant bags of ammunition and heavy machine guns, as well as other supplies.

A soldier noticed Santos limping and approached him. "What happened to your leg, Private?" he asked, eyebrow raised.

Beltran immediately whirled around, suspicion in his eyes, but Burton threw up her hands.

"He just sprained it while we were fighting a runner," she said quickly, and the Captain relaxed.

"Get him fixed up," he said, and the other soldier nodded, waving for Santos to follow him.

"Come on, I got some cold packs in one of the first aid kits," he said, and led Santos away.

"Not to insinuate that you weren't following protocol," Beltran said to a still bristling Burton. "Come on, we have to set up camp. If you all don't mind giving us a hand, we could use a distraction while we set up the guns."

Farley nodded. "Do you have a more comprehensive map of the area?" He glanced around at his team. "And some spare ammo?"

The Captain led them over to a cluster of soldiers on the side of the runway. "Corporal, let the Sergeant here have a look at your printout," he said, and his subordinate nodded, stepping aside to reveal a few papers spread out on top of a toolbox. Beltran turned to one of the Privates. "Put together a care package for this team, they're in distraction duty."

"Yes, sir," the soldier said, and hurried off.

"Thank you, Captain," Barnes said.

Beltran nodded to them. "See you on the highway," he said, and then headed off to organize his troops.

"Sarge," Sawyer said as he sidled up next to Farley, "when I was scoping ahead, I think I saw something that would be perfect." He ran his finger along the 405 on the map, pointing to a few buildings on the airport side. "It's gotta be one of these."

The Sergeant cocked his head. "What did you see?"

"Right around here, one of these buildings, is a burger joint," Sawyer explained. "They'll have a kitchen…" he trailed off, letting the insinuation hang in the air.

Barnes grinned. "You want to blow up a burger joint?"

"I mean, that would attract some attention, right?" Sawyer asked sheepishly.

Farley nodded. "Definitely would," he agreed, and turned to the returning Private who'd been sent for ammo. "You wouldn't happen to have any explosives in that care package, would you?"

"Of course," the soldier replied with a grin. "Distraction duty pack, right here." He patted the duffel bag he held and passed it over.

The Sergeant took the bag and inclined his head. "Thanks, soldier."

Barnes checked their route as the team replenished their mags. "Shouldn't be too much resistance, it's a few blocks," he said.

"Here," Wilcox handed the duffel to Sawyer. "You hang onto the dynamite."

The sniper raised an eyebrow, taking it and slinging it over his shoulder. "Am I your pack horse?"

"Be a gentleman, hm?" Wilcox replied, batting his eyelashes.

Beltran's Corporal snorted a laugh and then schooled his expression to try to hide his mirth.

"Let the Captain know we'll be blowing up this burger joint," Farley said, pointing it out on the map. "We're heading out now."

"Yes, sir," the Corporal replied, and gave a salute.

The team headed out, taking the airport road across the river, guns at the ready.

"Man, I could go for a burger," Burton said as they approached the first intersection. "A big greasy double-decker with special sauce."

Wilcox grinned mischievously and opened his mouth.

"No," she immediately cut him off, holding up a finger. "Not *your* special sauce."

He shook his head. "You don't know what you're missing."

"I was always partial to bacon cheeseburgers," Barnes piped up.

Sawyer moaned with longing. "With pickles."

"No ketchup, though," Logan said. "Mustard and relish only."

"Terrorist!" Wilcox gaped at him. "Who doesn't like *ketchup*?"

"It's sugar-paste with a side of ass," Logan replied.

"Stay sharp, melee only," Farley cut in as they rounded the corner onto 3rd street, seeing some zombie stragglers spread out in the road. "Also, I might have to demote you, Logan. A burger without ketchup is a travesty."

Wilcox laughed. "Sawyer, give him the duffel," he said, "he's being demoted to pack bitch."

"He talks about jizzing on a burger and I'm the one getting demoted?" Logan scoffed.

Sawyer patted him on the shoulder. "If you've ever eaten at a burger joint staffed with teenagers," he said, "you've one hundred percent eaten jizz on a burger."

"Disgusting," Burton added with a shudder. "Teenage boys are the worst."

Barnes gave her the side-eye. "Like you never did anything gross when you were a teenager," he said, and then took a run at a ghoul ahead, stabbing his knife into its eye socket.

"I was pure as the mountain snow," Burton replied, giving a fake curtsey before ducking around a car to stab a zombie in the top of its skull.

"I call bullshit on that," Sawyer quipped as he kicked a creature in the chest, knocking it back, and then knelt to stab it in the face.

Farley jogged up to a trio of ghouls in the middle of the road, smashing the first one with the butt of his gun and sending it tumbling back into the one behind it. He lashed out with his knife to sever the head of the one still standing, and Logan quickly dispatched the two on the ground.

"What about fries?" Barnes asked as he caught up to them. "What do you dip your fries in, if you don't eat ketchup?"

Logan rolled his eyes. "Gravy," he replied. "Obviously."

"Gravy *and* ketchup," the Sergeant said as he viciously kicked a zombie in the face, caving its head in.

"Y'all are disgusting," Logan muttered, shaking his head.

They approached the intersection before the burger joint, and Farley and Barnes peered around the corner. There were a smattering of ghouls ambling around the parking lot, and the doors stood open.

"Sawyer, Wilcox, Burton, you get in and clear the place," the Sergeant instructed as he ducked back around to face them. "The rest of us will clear the parking lot and keep watch. Get the gas going, light the dynamite, and get the fuck outta there. We'll backtrack a block and take a side street to meet up with the troops heading for the 405."

The team nodded and then broke cover as one. The inside team ran past the parking lot ghouls, leaving them for the rest, and burst into the restaurant, guns at the ready. There were no patrons, but two zombies turned towards them from behind the counter, dressed in tattered fast-food uniforms.

"Would you like fries with that?" Wilcox quipped and fired two quick shots to dispatch both creatures.

"I got the gas," Sawyer said, sliding over the counter and heading into the back. "Get ready to run."

Gunfire peppered the parking lot outside, and Burton stood watch at the door as the rest of the team took out the ambling ghouls staggering around the drive-thru window.

Sawyer turned on all the burners, letting the gas hiss out, and dropped the dynamite by the door to the kitchen, unwinding the long fuse as he backed into the dining area. He knelt down just behind Burton, and pulled out his lighter, lighting the end.

"Let's go!" he cried, and the trio rushed outside.

"We're hot!" Wilcox declared, and the soldiers took off down the road the way they'd come.

A few zombies wandered out from between buildings, having been drawn by the gunfire, but they ran past them until they got to the intersection at the halfway point to the airport. Looking down the side street, they saw the tail end of the troops at the other end of the block heading for the 405.

Farley led his team at a light jog, and about halfway down the block, a *BOOM* shook the air, rattling all the windows on the street. A car alarm blared in the distance, just adding to the noise, and the Sergeant nodded to Sawyer.

"Good plan, Private," he commended.

His subordinate grinned. "Thanks, Sarge."

The now hundred-strong force of soldiers trekked to the 405, coming up on the wide highway now littered with bodies. Troops immediately set to building makeshift barricades out of the corpses, others getting the machine guns ready. There weren't any ghouls in the immediate vicinity, the bulk of what had been left from the mini-gun fire drawn to the burning burger joint.

Farley stepped up to the firing line, watching as the soldiers set up the 50 cals.

"This is much nicer than taking them out with fence posts and boat paddles," he said, and shared a laugh with the gunner before patting him on the shoulder. He turned and spotted Santos sitting in the grass, leg elevated. Another soldier took off his boot, revealing a massively swollen ankle.

"Ah, that's so much better," Santos groaned as the soldier activated a cold pack and wrapped it around his injured joint.

"You going to live, Private?" the Sergeant asked as he reached him.

Santos nodded jerkily. "Sure thing, Sarge," he replied. "Would be stupid to go down because of a tweaked ankle."

"We've been over this," Burton drawled as she approached with two bottles of water, handing one to the sitting Private. "You're not allowed to die until I'm bored of your company."

Santos chuckled as he unscrewed the cap. "I guess I'd better brush up on my conversation skills."

"Damn straight," she said, and bumped her water bottle against his.

Before long, the gunners began to take care of zombies heading towards camp, the bullets easily tearing them to shreds at a safe distance.

As the sun set, Captain Rocha and his team reached the camp, and he gave them instructions before seeking out Beltran. Farley spotted them and approached.

"Good job today, Sergeant," Rocha commended. "Thank you for your contribution."

Farley nodded. "No sweat, Captain," he replied. "Appreciate the assignment."

"You can head back to town and continue cleanup duty," Rocha said, jerking a thumb over his shoulder. "Once you and your men have had a little rest, of course."

The Sergeant's face fell. He didn't want to go back there. Using fence posts to clean up after the main teams had not been his idea of a good time, despite how he'd scolded Santos for saying so at the beginning of the day.

Beltran cleared his throat. "Actually, Captain, if it's alright with you," he began, "I'd like to keep Sergeant Farley and his team here with me. I have a mission that I think would suit them perfectly."

Rocha raised an eyebrow. "Oh?" he asked, and tilted his head at Farley, who looked up in excitement. "Would you prefer staying?"

"I mean…" the Sergeant trailed off with a shrug. "Should I try to look sad about not getting to go back to cleanup duty?"

The trio shared a laugh, and Beltran clapped him on the back. "Thank you," he said. "I have some plans that I think you could really help me out with."

"You got it, Captain," Farley replied with a grin.

Rocha nodded. "All right, I'll leave you to it," he said. "I need to report to Captain Kersey. Good job today, everyone."

"I'll find you in a bit," Beltran added.

The Sergeant saluted them, and then headed off, finding his team clustered around Santos, taking a chill in the grass. "Well, it looks like we're hanging out here for a while," Farley announced as he took a seat next to Barnes. "Beltran's got a mission for us."

"Fuck yeah!" Wilcox cried, pumping his fist into the air. "No cleanup!"

Sawyer grinned, leaning back and curling his hands behind his head. "That news was worth the hugs," he declared, and the team shared a laugh.

Farley shook his head and accepted one of the water bottles, taking a long swig and stretching out in the grass with his team for a well-deserved rest.

CHAPTER FIFTEEN

Captain Kersey took a thoughtful sip of his coffee, unable to shake the feeling of helplessness running deeply beneath the hope he was so afraid to let bubble up in his chest. Things seemed to be working, but it was dangerous to hope that everything was going to go according to plan.

Of course, a lot hadn't, so far, but it seemed most things were pulling through, regardless.

But at what cost? The soldiers knew what they were getting into, to be sure, but so many lives had been lost. *We follow our orders, to build this new world,* he reminded himself. They all had to do their part so that there would be a world for future generations.

He could easily picture it… the whole northwestern front, behind military barricades, families safe behind the walls, living their lives as best they could. He just hoped there were enough people left to save.

There was a knock at the door of his makeshift office, and it shook him out of his reverie. "Come in," he said hoarsely, and then cleared his throat.

"Hey there, Captain," David said, poking his head in. "I've got Captain Rocha with a report for you."

Kersey nodded, his chest feeling lighter already. "Good news, I hope," he said, and headed for the door.

"Well, he's alive, so that's a good sign," David replied, scribbling away on one of his clipboards. "I have other reports for you as well once you're done," he said as they reached the communications area.

Kersey nodded as he sat down at the radio. "Thanks, David," he said, and picked up the receiver. "Captain Rocha, this is Captain Kersey."

"Evening, Captain," Rocha replied.

Kersey looked at his half-empty mug of coffee and rubbed his forehead. "Evening, right," he murmured to himself, and then pushed the button. "Evening. How did the day go?"

"Despite our setbacks, surprisingly well," Rocha replied. "We're well on our way to clearing out Renton, and thanks to a team led by Sergeant Farley, we were able to secure the airport and the 405 for the southern blockade."

"Excellent news," Kersey said. "Keep up the good work, Captain. And be safe."

"You as well," Rocha replied.

The line went dead, and Kersey swivelled around in his chair. David stood there holding a fresh pot of coffee.

The Captain grinned and held out his cup, allowing his communications expert and fellow caffeine addict to fill it for him. He took a long sip of the hot brew and let out a sigh of pleasure.

"Well, what have you got for me?" he asked.

David filled a mug for himself and then set down his clipboard on the desk. "The northern flank is starting to gain ground, despite their setbacks," he began.

"Everything seems to be happening despite setbacks," Kersey murmured, shaking his head.

"Well, navigating the zombie apocalypse isn't exactly experienced territory," David replied with a dark smile. "I'd say we're doing pretty well, considering."

The Captain nodded. "Tell me about this horde in Tacoma," he said.

David headed over to his monitor, typing away to bring up a satellite image of the area. "The Olympia team has successfully taken over that area, and seems to be in a position to deal with the horde," he explained. "We're able to send in some Tomahawks to take care of the ones not on the interstate… but for the seventy or eighty thousand that *are*…"

Kersey shook his head. "We can't risk damaging the interstate," he finished. "We're going to have to figure out a plan of action." He stroked his chin. "How can we pull more of the zombies towards them away from Renton and the northern flanks?"

"What about air support?" David asked. "Send in some helicopters to pull them back,"

The Captain sighed. "I don't think we have the resources for that," he replied. "Word from the higher-ups always seems to be *no* when it comes to air support."

"I suppose nothing from the Renton airport will be useful unless we could graft some heavy guns onto the side," David mused. "Though that would be fun, I doubt we have the guns nor the ammo, let alone the tools."

Kersey nodded. "We'll likely have to go with decoy teams," he said, taking a sip of his brew. "But before I go delegating, I think it would be best to kick it up the chain of command to someone with better intel."

"Probably a good idea," David agreed, and scribbled on his clipboard.

"How is Copeland's team?" the Captain asked, leaning back in his chair.

The communications expert moved the map. "They have the bridge secure and are holding strong," he replied. "But there are concerns about hordes, big and small, heading their way."

"Have the reinforcements gotten there?" Kersey asked.

David nodded. "Yeah, and they're planning to push up into the next town to set up some traps and diversions," he replied, tilting his head back and forth. "But they're hoping for some more intel on the area so they really know what they're getting into."

"All right, get someone in touch with them so they can plan accordingly," the Captain replied. "How about Bretz?"

The communications expert shook his head, drawing his lip between his teeth. "Nobody's reached them yet," he replied slowly.

Kersey pushed the dark thoughts from his head and raised his chin, speaking quickly. "What's the news on the eastern front?"

"They're pushing towards the water still," David replied, moving the map once again and motioning to the area he knew the teams had been last. "They should be there by tomorrow. It's slow going through the neighborhoods with the lack of ammunition. The troops are starting to rely on whatever they can find to fight with."

The Captain pursed his lips and sighed. "That will slow things down significantly," he mused. "What's the holdup on the supply lines?"

"They're breaking down," David explained. "Just outside of Spokane there is a broken train that has the rails all tied up, so one of the shipments had to be unloaded. They're trying to move supplies by bus and truck, but both are in short supply, not to mention the shortage of gasoline."

Kersey took a deep breath. "We're going to have to do some scavenging, it seems," he said. "Get the next group of soldiers headed to the front lines to start searching every house for weapons and ammo, with every town they pass along the way." He motioned to the clipboard. "And relay that up the chain of command. Anything they can find will be helpful."

"Done," David murmured, scribbling away on his list.

"Okay, Mercer Island," the Captain began, leaning forward to lean his forearms on his knees. "How's it going?"

David pulled up the island on his screen. "It's totally secure, which is good news," he replied. "The bridge barricades are holding, but they're going to need supplies too if they're going to keep up with the diversions."

"Looks like the diversions are going well," Kersey stared at the significant dark botches of zombie hordes on both banks of the lake.

"Exceedingly well," David agreed.

"Get them what we can," the Captain said, and leaned back again, taking the last sip of his coffee.

David nodded, adding that to his list, and then crossing the room to grab the coffee pot again. He refilled their mugs and offered a tentative smile.

"You know, we're really getting through this thing," he said as he took a seat. "It's almost safe to start thinking about the future."

Kersey chuckled, shaking his head. "I was just thinking this morning about how nice it would be to safely think about the future."

"I can't stop imagining having a nice place to call home," David said wistfully. "A house packed to the tits with electronics. I could be the world's foremost authority on drones." He cocked his head. "Which should be easy, given there are only a handful of us left that can actually fly these things."

The Captain laughed. "That would be the life," he said. "Get you a nice big mansion and stuff it full of computers."

"I don't need a mansion," David replied with a smirk. "Okay, maybe I would for all the equipment I'd want to have. Turn the hoity-toity drawing room into a workshop."

Kersey leaned his chair back, lifting his feet to cross them on the desk. "If we could find one with a helipad," he continued, "you could have a whole army of drones ready to lift off when somebody shines the David Signal in the sky."

"Oh, there's an idea," he agreed, nodding like a bobblehead. "Post-apocalyptic techie superhero. I like that."

They shared a laugh and then sat in silence for a few moments, sipping their brew.

"What about you?" David finally asked. "What's your dream, for when this is all over?"

A wave of exhaustion washed over the Captain, and he scrubbed a hand down his face. "A good night's sleep," he replied. "Maybe a good week's sleep, all at once."

"Hook you up to a feeding tube?" David asked, grinning around his mug. "We could knock you out with a drug cocktail and keep you in a coma for a few months.

That might catch you up on at least some of the rest you've missed these last few weeks."

Kersey chuckled, swirling his coffee around in his mug. "Yeah, that would be bliss."

"Really, though," David pressed on, "what will you do?"

A million scenarios ran through the Captain's head.

Meeting a nice girl, maybe a badass retired soldier, someone who could keep up with him mentally and physically and understand what it's like to have gone through the things he'd seen in his life. Maybe they find a nice little villa on the coast, far away from the barricades and the fighting, a place that would be quiet and secluded. Maybe they settle down there, spending the days hanging out on the beach and the evenings reading books on the front porch while watching the sun go down. Maybe they get married, if there are still any officiants left somewhere, Bretz at his side, Kowalski cracking jokes behind him.

Maybe they have kids, when it's safe to do so, because maybe this whole thing works out and it becomes safe to do so. Maybe they raise beautiful, happy children by the ocean, teaching them all they need to know about the world, the new world and what it's going to be, away from the horror of rotted walking corpses that cannibalize your flesh.

But Kersey knew his life wasn't built on these maybes.

He took a deep breath. "The downside of being good at what you do," he said softly, "is that everybody wants you to do it again and again."

David swallowed hard, but nodded in understanding. "At least, Captain, you can do what you're good at knowing that you're bringing a safe life for the future of humanity."

Kersey chuckled softly and held up his mug for a cheers. "My life's work," he declared, "will be to find a giant spotlight big enough to write your name in the sky."

"I'll drink to that," his friend replied, clinking his mug. "To Super-David."

The Captain shook his head and smiled. "To Super-David."

END

Up Next: Salty Vietnam Vet Benny uses his piloting skills to deliver much needed supplies around the city in Seattle Pt. 7

DEAD AMERICA
THE NORTHWEST INVASION
BOOK 9
SEATTLE PART 7
BY DEREK SLATON
© 2020

CHAPTER ONE

Day Zero +26

Benny pulled his jacket over his shoulder, repositioning himself against the cheap sheetrock wall of the office to savor the last few moments of his nap. The sun would be up over the horizon soon, and the last several days had been exhausting. Every second he could have his eyes closed was precious.

The door to the building opened up, and two soldiers walked inside, jabbering loudly with one another.

Benny grumbled and shifted, trying to tune them out, and then finally sat up. "Hey assholes," he barked. "People trying to sleep in here. So take it outside unless you want to join the ranks of the unconscious."

The venom in the old man's voice made the two soldiers zip their lips and slowly back out of the room, closing the door behind them. This office had become an official napping room, so that the exhausted soldiers that needed some shut-eye between constant missions could get some rest.

"Ignorant fucks," he muttered, and let out a huff as he tried to get comfortable again. Alas, the damage had already been done. He was all riled up. He checked his watch. It was a little before seven. *Twenty minutes before sun up,* he thought bitterly. *Might as well get the blood flowing.*

He pulled himself up off of the ground, bones creaking from the uncomfortable bedding, which was really just a few random blankets tossed on the floor. What he wouldn't give for a good night's sleep in an actual bed.

With one of the few working transport helicopters, Benny had been constantly shuttling vital goods to the troops on the front lines of the war. This was the same job he'd had decades prior during Vietnam, and while he had to admit it was nice to not have to worry about return fire, it was still a drastic change from a month ago running aerial tours of the region from Spokane.

As he headed for the door of the napping room, he spotted a young soldier, no more than twenty, curled up under a desk. The kid shivered, hugging his knees, and Benny knelt down, laying his jacket over the kid like a blanket. He slipped out the door, shutting it as quietly as he could.

The airfield was still a hive of activity, just like it had been since the invasion began. The only major difference from the beginning of the invasion was the lack of front-line troops running around, as they'd mostly all moved up.

In their place were a couple hundred supply personnel, scrambling to unload trucks that had driven up from Spokane filled with goods.

The supply lines were rough, to say the least. The rail lines that had been bringing in ammo and rations from god knew where stopped in Spokane. Benny had heard rumours of a derailment, or something going wrong with the tracks, but it didn't really matter. The cold fact was that things had to be offloaded and put onto trucks, which slowed things to a crawl.

Everywhere Benny landed, the story was the same—soldiers from Privates all the way up to Captains begging and pleading with him to bring them more ammo, more weapons, more of anything they could use to fight off the dead.

Would be comical if it weren't so damned tragic, he thought as he walked through the airfield. *Experienced soldiers begging and pleading with a retired civilian for what they need… amazing it's come to this.*

Benny's eyes finally began to clear up, something that seemed to take longer and longer with each passing day. It was one of the many gifts that his sixties were giving to him. Able to focus, he spotted his helicopter in the middle hangar, receiving some work.

"There's my girl," he murmured. "Let's see how they're treating you."

His tour helicopter was large enough to fit ten full-grown adults, or at least it had been before the war. When the supply lines were faltering, a team of mechanics ripped out the seating to make room for more cargo. Benny really didn't mind it, since his aerial touring days were well behind him, but there was a part of him that was pained to see his baby torn apart like that.

"You boys treating her nice like a lady should be?" he drawled as he approached the mechanics.

Jerry smirked as he headed over in grease-stained coveralls, wiping his hands on a rag. "Oh yeah, treating her better than I treated my wife," he replied.

From underneath the helicopter, a muffled voice yelled, "Ex-wife!"

Jerry chuckled and glanced over his shoulder. "Yeah, well, this chopper isn't running around fucking the neighbors," he quipped, "so if course it's getting better treatment."

A chorus of laughter erupted throughout the mechanics in the hangar.

"Y'all make sure not to load me down too much," Benny declared as he watched a couple loading up wooden crates with a forklift. "I gotta get that baby off of the ground!"

Jerry clapped him on the shoulder with his now-clean hand. "Don't worry bud," he said, "we're keeping a close eye on it. These soldier boys like to go for broke, but we ain't gonna let them put you in danger."

The pilot smiled at him in thanks and then crossed his arms, turning back to his chopper. "So, how's she looking?"

"With as much flight time as she has on her, she's looking pretty good," Jerry replied. "Long term, we're going to have to source some engine parts to make sure she keeps purring, but for right now you're good to go."

Benny nodded. "So what am I hauling today?"

"Hell if I know," the mechanic admitted with a shrug. "That pencil-pusher David is around here somewhere, he's got the details."

The pilot raised an eyebrow. "Pencil-pusher?" he asked. "Come on now, don't be too hard on the kid. If we had the shit they have today when we were his age, we probably wouldn't have gone outside much either."

Jerry tilted his head back and forth and then finally put up a hand. "Yeah, I guess those drone things of his are pretty nifty," he begrudgingly said. "Could get into all sorts of shenanigans with those."

"I've heard stories about you," Benny accused with a wink, "pretty sure you've gotten into enough shenanigans without the need for technology."

They shared a hearty laugh and then turned as David skirted some toolboxes to get to them in the hangar.

"Looks like you two are in a good mood this morning," he declared, raising a can of some kind of sugary energy drink in a toast before taking a sip.

Jerry smirked. "Yeah, we were just brainstorming ideas on the kind of fun we could have with your drones there," he said.

"Well, once we survive this invasion," David replied, leaning in conspiratorially, "I'll break out some of the videos in my archive." He gave the mechanic a devious wink, and the two older men blinked at him.

"I'll be honest," Jerry said, putting up his hands, "I didn't think you had that in you."

The communications expert shrugged sheepishly. "Well, you know," he replied, "us *pencil-pushers* are a lot more devious than people like to give us credit for."

Benny gave the mechanic a playful slap on the back, and Jerry's cheeks pinked as he burst out laughing.

He shook his head. "All right, you got me," he said, wrinkling his nose in embarrassment. "I'll let you boys talk. Benny, you should be good to go in ten." He waved and headed over to the chopper to continue his pre-flight checks.

"So, what's on the menu today?" the pilot asked, back to business after his friend getting busted.

David took a long swig of his drink and smacked his lips. "I hope you got some rest, because we got a busy one for you," he said. "Two of the transports for the northern front are out of commission."

"Wait, what?" Benny's brow furrowed in worry. "What the hell happened?"

David put up one of his hands, palm out. "Don't worry, pilots are safe," he assured him quickly. "One of the landing zones got overrun while they were unloading, so they had to abandon it for the time being. They're getting a handle on the situation, but it could be the afternoon or even into the evening before they can resume. They're going to need supplies before that, though."

"Al right, I'll make that work," the pilot assured him. "Where's the landing zone?"

David cocked his head. "That one is still being determined," he admitted, and put up a finger, "but you have a stop before that." He pulled out a piece of paper from his pocket, and then turned around, spreading it out on the small desk behind them. "This is the Renton Airfield," he explained as he pointed to an airport just south of Mercer Island, southeast from downtown. "We were able to secure it yesterday and have a barricade set up on the interstate here to the east. There's a whole lot of trouble coming up the road towards them, but they need some heavy duty stuff if they're going to hold it."

"That what they loading up?" Benny asked.

David nodded. "Yep, fifty-cal rounds," he confirmed. "These things are worth their weight in gold, and it's going to be a good long while before we can get our hands on more of them, so treat them well. It's not like we can just go into the Super Center and pick up a few boxes of ammo."

"Which is a damn shame, really," the pilot replied with a sigh. "Could have had a lot of fun with that."

David raised an eyebrow. "I think we have different definitions of *fun*," he said dryly.

"I don't know," Benny drawled with a mischievous glint in his eye, "I'm looking forward to your archives."

They shared a laugh, and David took another long gulp of his drink.

"So, after I drop this stuff off," Benny asked, "where am I headed?"

David pointed to the top left corner of the map. "You need to head out to the fleet to the northwest," he explained. "Captain McCall will have your next supply run ready and waiting."

"Sounds like it's going to be a fun day," the pilot declared, and stretched his arms above his head. "On that note, you got anything for me?"

David nodded and pulled a tote bag from his backpack, handing it over.

Benny dug through it, checking all of the MREs, as well as a couple of packs of snack food. "All right, all right, looking good," he murmured, and then looked up. "Now what about my vodka?"

David's brow furrowed deep, pursing his lips in concern.

The pilot burst into laughter, clapping him on the shoulder. "Nah, I'm just fucking with you, boy," he admitted. "You know damn well I'm a bourbon man."

The communications expert shook his head, letting out a relieved chuckle, and reached into his pocket, revealing a silver flask and holding it out. "Not while flying," he added.

"Wouldn't dream of putting my baby in danger like that," Benny assured him, stuffing the flask into his pocket and patting it. "Saving it for the end of the day, or some other special occasion."

"Good man," David replied. "So, do you have everything you need?"

Benny nodded. "I'm good to go."

"All right, well," David said, jerking a thumb over his shoulder, "I got half a dozen other things I'm already behind on. I'll see you when you get back. Good luck out there."

They shared a nod, and the younger man headed out of the hangar to his next task. Benny reached into his tote bag and pulled out a slightly squished chocolate snack cake. He grinned and tore open the tasty treat.

With his mouth full of squishy cake, he mumbled, "Breakfast of champions."

CHAPTER TWO

Benny flew relatively low over the suburbs on the way to the airfield. The tree-covered neighborhoods did a good job of hiding the horror on the streets, though every now and then there were breaks in the trees.

He glanced down and saw asphalt littered with the dead. The glimpses were bad enough, but as he soared over a shopping center, a fuller picture emerged.

Hundreds of corpses, maybe even thousands, sprawled across the parking lot. Mowed down and left to bake in the sun.

Benny shook his head, unsure of how to even process this level of carnage. It was even more overwhelming knowing that this was happening all over the city.

So much life just fucking wasted, he thought bitterly. *It's a damn shame.*

He tried to focus on flying, pushing out memories of Vietnam, the same carnage of bodies sprawled across the ground, easily seen from a bird's-eye view.

But this isn't Vietnam, he reminded himself. *Those aren't people down there, at least not anymore. What's happening here is necessary, and I got a job to do.*

A few miles out from the airport, he spotted the front line of the military, pushing forward street by street. Even over the noise of the blades he could hear muffled gunfire, which hammered home just how prevalent it was on the ground.

He glanced over, seeing a massive firefight holding back a few hundred creatures. *If the front lines are this bad,* he thought, *what the hell is it like at the airport?*

He ascended, getting high enough to get a better lay of the land. He didn't have coordinates on the airport, so he had to rely on visual cues. As he rose higher, he spotted the interstate where the barricade was.

There were cars lined up, bumper-to-bumper, with several 50-cal machine-gun nests spread out across it. The nests were quiet, but several troops fired with standard assault rifles from the line, picking off zombies as they trickled towards the barricade.

Once the immediate threat was eliminated, several soldiers hopped over the line and got to work, picking up bodies and moving the thirty yards away from the line and stacking them up. Benny shook his head, thinking it was futile to create another corpse barrier, but he supposed that anything that could slow the zombies down even a little bit couldn't hurt.

Before looking for the airport, he flew down the interstate a little bit, just to see what was on the horizon. His stomach knotted and clenched, flipping end over end at the sight of a dense horde easily in the thousands heading a couple miles up the highway.

He immediately swooped around and searched for the airport. It took a few moments, but he finally located it, sitting on the edge of the water. It was a moderately sized airstrip, not big enough for 747s, but still bigger than the tiny regional airport like the one he'd just taken off from.

As he approached the strip, he spotted someone waving lights to get his attention. He hovered over them, watching, as they motioned to the south end of the runway. He gave the soldier a thumbs up and then moved in that direction. He landed gently and powered down the engine before hopping down to the ground.

As soon as his boots hit the ground, a few soldiers greeted him, the lead man holding out his hand to shake.

"Man, are you a sight for sore eyes," he declared. "I'm Sergeant Farley."

The pilot smiled and shook his hand. "Benny," he replied, "good to meet you."

Farley motioned to the men behind him to unload the cargo and then turned back to Benny. "Is everything for us?" he asked.

"As far as I know," Benny replied with a shrug. "Should be nothing but fifty-cal rounds. And it looks like you boys are about to need it."

The Sergeant's brow furrowed. "What are you talking about?" he asked.

"I flew down the interstate a bit," the pilot explained, pointing, "and you got a whole mess of those fuckers headed your way."

Farley's eyes widened. "How many we talking?"

"A lot higher than my dumb ass can count," Benny admitted, shaking his head.

The Sergeant immediately pulled out his walkie-talkie. "We have a massive wave headed our way, boys," he barked into the receiver. "Let's get that line secure as quickly as we can. Got more ammo headed up your way too. Make it happen."

"Anything I can do to help?" Benny asked.

Farley cocked his head. "Don't you have places to be?" he asked.

"I do," the pilot admitted, drawing out the word, "but if you can spot me some fuel, I'm sure I can find an excuse to be a little late."

The Sergeant cracked a smile and then reached out to grab the arm of one of the soldiers walking past to help with the unloading. "There's a fuel truck at the north end of the runway," he said quickly. "Go straight up and it's on the left, you can't miss it. Double time it up there and hurry back."

"Yes sir," the soldier replied with a nod, and took off running.

Farley turned back to his new friend. "How do you feel about bombing runs?"

Benny grinned. "As long as I'm the one doing the dropping and not the one receiving, I'm good with them," he replied.

"Good man," the Sergeant said, and then raised the radio to his lips again. "Corporal Barnes, do you copy?"

There were a few seconds of silence before a voice came back, "Little busy at the moment, Sarge, setting the stage for our unwelcome guests."

"I'll keep it brief, then," Farley assured him. "You want to come help me make some giant fire bombs to drop on our guests?"

"Hell yeah I do," Barnes replied immediately.

The Sergeant nodded. "Well, get your ass down here then," he demanded. "We don't have much time with the chopper."

"On my way," the Corporal replied.

Benny cocked his head. "So, what do you have in mind, Sergeant?"

Farley shoved his radio back into his pocket. "You ever make a molotov cocktail?"

"Only when my neighbors were being assholes," the pilot quipped.

The Sergeant smirked. "You ever make one out of five gallon water bottles?" he asked.

A devious grin broke out on Benny's face. "No," he admitted, "but looking forward to giving it a shot."

Farley motioned for the pilot to follow him, and the duo headed over to a building beside the hangar. The Sergeant led him inside, revealing a large kitchen and dining area, what once was an airport restaurant.

In the back, there were a few offices surrounding a common room, a large table in the center and a water cooler. Next to the cooler was a large rack holding numerous five gallon plastic water bottles.

Benny pulled one out, smacking the side a few times. "Not sure what kind of molotovs you were making," he drawled, "but mine weren't made of plastic."

"Just means we gotta get creative," Farley replied.

"That's an understatement," the pilot quipped. "What are you thinking?"

Farley pulled out a large knife, holding it up with a grin. Benny's eyebrows hit his hairline as he realized what the Sergeant was insinuating.

"You got a set of stones on you boy, I'll give you that," the pilot said, shaking his head. "Just know you're paying for any fire damage to my baby."

The Sergeant shrugged. "As my amateur daredevil cousin would say," he replied, "fire damage builds character."

"He sounds like quite the ladies' man," Benny said, crossing his arms.

Farley barked a laugh. "Well, he was a star on the carnival circuit for a few years," he explained, "so in his hick town he was."

"Knew I messed up by moving to the big city," Benny replied, snapping his fingers.

The Sergeant chuckled. "Come on, let's grab a few and get out there," he said. "Borrow some of that fuel before your chopper soaks it all up."

"You wanna run that plan by me again?" Barnes demanded, his eyes wide as saucers. "Because if I heard what I think I just heard, I may have to have you committed."

Farley and Benny stood next to the chopper, four of the five gallon plastic containers filled to the top with fuel. Several strips of cloth ran down the sides of the bottles, connected at the top.

The Sergeant shrugged, motioning with his knife. "Don't see what the big deal is," he said. "You just light the top, stab the side of it, and push it out of the chopper."

"And what do you think is gonna happen when the gas hits the open flame before it's out?" the Corporal demanded, crossing his arms.

The other two exchanged a glance, and the pilot spread his hands, palms up.

"As a wise man once said," he began with a grin, "fire damage builds character."

Barnes scrubbed his hands down his face. "Goddammit," he groaned, "if I have to hear one more pearl of wisdom from your daredevil bumpkin of a cousin…"

"You'll be alright," Benny assured him, patting his shoulder. "Now let's get loaded up, I have places to be."

The Corporal reluctantly climbed aboard, with Farley close behind. Benny fired up the helicopter, waiting for the blades to whip up to full speed before turning and giving a thumbs up to his passengers, who braced themselves for liftoff.

The chopper rose into the air, quickly gaining altitude while moving away from the airport. He made his way to the interstate and headed for the horde. Both Barnes and Farley moved to the front of the vehicle, looking out towards their destination.

The noise inside the vehicle was loud, but even with the noise Benny heard both Barnes and Farley exclaiming at the sight of the thick sea of zombies.

Tens of thousands of the rotted ghouls, packed densely on the interstate, all moving towards the checkpoint. As they grew closer, Benny began to hover, turning back to talk to the men. He had to yell, given the lack of headsets.

"So how the hell you wanna do this?" he bellowed.

Farley squinted, staring out the window as he contemplated. After a moment, he finally leaned in, waving them closer.

"We got four of these things," he said loudly, "so I'm thinking we go back about a hundred yards and drop a couple, one on each side of the interstate. Then we can move up the line another few hundred yards and do the same thing. We don't have enough to take them all out, but if we can create some breaks in the horde, it'll give us a chance to regroup between waves."

Benny nodded. "Sounds good to me, brother," he replied with a thumbs up. "I'll get us in position."

He flew over the horde, staying about fifty feet above the writhing mass. About a hundred yards deep, he hovered, giving his passengers a wave to let them know they were ready to go. As they fiddled with the makeshift bomb, he looked down at the horde.

There wasn't a speck of asphalt that he could see. It was wall-to-wall, shoulder-to-shoulder creatures. Every single one of them staring up at him, mouths open, screaming and moaning, grasping at the noise promising them a fresh meal.

Benny felt almost in a trance, transfixed on the creatures, studying them with dread gripping his chest. One was completely missing the side of its face, ear gone, cheek dangling by a thread.

Another was missing an arm, jagged bone sticking out about eight inches from the shoulder. Another one, fresher than the others but still rancid, displayed blood-soaked clothes around a multitude of deep bite marks. His whole body shuddered, and he shook his head, tearing his eyes away to look back at the maniac duo.

Barnes held onto the first bomb tightly as Farley guided it over the edge of the door. Then rested it gently on the landing rail, readying it to drop.

"You light it," the Sergeant yelled, "and I'll cut it!"

Barnes nodded and pulled out his lighter, setting the top bit of fabric on fire. In a matter of seconds, the flames raced through the fuel-soaked rag, creating half a dozen flaming strands on the container.

Farley jammed his knife into the plastic near the middle, a bit of fuel squirting out from the four-inch wide gap. Both men froze for a moment and then let out sighs of relief when it missed the flame.

The Sergeant nodded to his partner, and received one in return.

Farley ripped the blade from the container, and they immediately pushed it off the side. Fuel sprayed from the hole as it spun through the air, and about ten yards from the ground, finally caught, the whole thing going up in flames.

It exploded in a spectacular display of flaming liquid, coating dozens of creatures below.

Benny looked out and admired the success. Creatures catching fire and spreading it to other ones nearby. He glanced back at his passengers.

"Hang on, I got an idea!" he yelled, and began to lower the helicopter once he made sure they were holding on to something.

When the chopper hovered about fifteen feet above the outstretched zombies hands, the intensity of the wind coming off of the blades fanned the flames, spreading them to more zombies, creating easily a twenty-yard radius of crispified ghouls.

"Hell yeah!" Farley bellowed, pumping his fist into the air. "Good job! Let's move on to the next drop!"

Benny rose again, moving over to hover at the next spot while the duo got to work on a fresh bomb. He did his best to avoid transfixing on individual zombies again, but his eyes strayed downwards, pulling him into another trance full of dread.

Finally he snapped himself out of it again, staring straight ahead down the

interstate into the nearly impenetrable
mass of rotted flesh. He shook his head.

*We're going to need a lot more bombs
if this is going to work.*

CHAPTER FOUR

Benny landed the chopper on the airstrip. Barnes shook his hand a bit, still stinging from one of the flames that had leapt up and caught him as they pushed the final homemade bomb out the door.

"You gonna be okay, bubba?" Benny asked, brow furrowed.

Farley rolled his eyes. "Oh, he'll be fine," he drawled, "it's me you have to worry about. I'm going to have to hear about how I tried to set him on fire until the end of time."

"Damn right you are," Barnes agreed. He patted Benny on the back before hopping out of the chopper to run off and find some ointment for his minor burn.

Farley hung back, his expression sincere. "We really appreciate you taking the time to help us out," he said. "It's good to see civilians stepping up in our time of need."

"Civilian?" Benny scoffed. "Hell man, I've been flying these things since 'Nam. Did my part back then, and doing it now."

The Sergeant raised his chin with respect in his eyes and gave the pilot a salute. "Appreciate you even more, then," he said.

"My pleasure, Sergeant," Benny replied with a nod. "Anything else I can do to help, you just let me know."

Farley jerked his thumb over his shoulder. "Well, we made a dent in that horde headed our way, so I'm going to get busy making a few more of those bombs," he said. "So when you're done for the day, if you're bored, feel free to swing on by. We'll leave a light on for you."

"Consider it done," Benny agreed. "You boys be safe out there."

Farley smirked. "Eh, where's the fun in that?" he asked with a wink, and the two men bumped fists before the Sergeant hopped out.

Once he was clear, Benny took off and headed towards the ship. It was about eighty miles as the crow flies to the Salish Sea to the northwest of Seattle. The deep water separated the United States and Canada—or at least it did back when the invisible lines on maps mattered.

The fastest route was to fly right over downtown Seattle, which given that Benny was running behind schedule meant that was the route he wanted to take. He gained altitude to make sure that the buildings wouldn't be a threat, but also gave him a better view of the region.

It looked like a war zone.

I mean, it IS a war zone... he thought, but it didn't make it any less hard to see.

Plumes of smoke rose in all directions. It was hard to make out details, but he could see the edges of the front lines in some spots, masses of creatures in the road, all headed in one direction.

He flew over downtown, looking down at the roads and seeing them just jam-packed with ghouls. Just like the interstate, there was barely a spot of the street that didn't have a zombie on it. He clamped down on his dark thoughts, because these were future problems, and there was a lot more to get done before they could face this.

The rest of the flight was almost relaxing, something that was rare these days. Once he emerged from the Seattle metro area, it was nothing but undeveloped land, most of which was Olympic National Park. In the pre-apocalypse days, it had been a popular outdoor tourist destination. Now, it was among the last bastions of relaxation to be found.

As Benny flew over, there was a glint that peeked out from the top of a hill up ahead. He furrowed his brow, shaking his head. There weren't supposed to be any troops out there. He adjusted course and looked down, seeing a small community of people on the hill, several looking up at him and frantically waving their arms.

A collection of campers were in a circle, tightly giving them a safe-ish zone from any stragglers or wildlife that would come their way.

Even at fifty yards up, Benny could see the dirt and grime on these people, but most of all, the absolute elation on their faces to see an aircraft. He knew he didn't have time to land, which made guilt twist his guts, so he looked around for a solution.

There was a notebook beside his seat, and he grabbed it, scribbling out a quick note.

Military is here, help will be coming. May be a few days, but we're here and not leaving. Hang tight!

He looked around for something heavy to attach it to and finally reached for his food bag. He dug around, picking up a few MREs. He checked the labels until he found one that boasted *ham and egg omelette*.

"Yeah, that'll work," he said with a chuckle, and ripped the top off, stuffing the note inside. He lowered the chopper a little, about twenty yards off of the ground, and opened his window, holding his arm out to make sure that he wouldn't be dropping it on anyone's head.

He let go, and watched it hit the grass, and waited for one of the campers to run over and pick it up. A young-looking blonde woman pulled out the note, looked it over, and then gave him a thumbs up. Benny responded in kind, and then rose back up into the air, heading off towards his destination.

Good to know it's not just going to be military people who survive this, he thought to himself.

As soon as he reached the water's edge, Benny spotted the fleet of ships. There were dozens of them, all anchored just offshore. Several smaller boats shuttled men and material to the shore, taking control of some of the smaller waterfront tourist towns.

He headed out to his target ship, which was right at the head of the line. As he approached, he was waved in by someone on deck. After a successful landing on the helipad, he powered down and hopped out.

The deck crew descended immediately. Several people appeared carrying boxes, another with a fuel line, and mechanics swarmed the craft to check the engine. Before Benny could even take three steps, a soldier appeared at his side.

"Sir, Captain McCall would like to have a word with you," he said.

Benny nodded. "Yeah, that's not a surprise," he replied.

"He's in the ready room just inside that door," the soldier explained, pointing at a nondescript door a few feet away.

"Appreciate it," Benny said, tipping an invisible hat to the young man. He headed towards the door on deck, entering it and taking an immediate right to the ready room.

It looked like it could hold about twenty people and was covered wall-to-wall with maps. There were a few people on the outer edges of the room studying the pages and drawing on them, but Benny focused on the far end desk.

Captain McCall stood next to it, surrounded by several soldiers, but he waved them off when he noticed Benny approaching. "You all know what to do," he said brusquely, "now get to it."

"Yes, sir," the soldiers murmured, and split off in various directions.

"Benny, so good of you to join us," McCall said. "Beginning to wonder if you had just said to hell with it and found you an island retreat somewhere."

The pilot smirked. "And miss all this fun?" He waved a hand around. "Wouldn't dream of it."

"Look, I know you are ex-military and have been a civilian for decades now," the Captain said icily, "but there's no excuse for being nearly an hour late to pick up supplies. I expect better of the people under me, and you're no exception. So you need to shape up."

Benny ran his tongue over his teeth and cocked his head. "You know Captain, a month ago this would be where I would tell you to fuck off," he replied, emphasizing the last two words with such venom a few of the soldiers stopped what they were doing to gape at him. "However, I know you are under a lot of stress, especially considering we're down several transports at the moment. As a result, I'm going to let your condescending tone slide and let you get back to telling me what I need to do."

There was a moment of tense silence, and then the Captain opened his mouth to respond, but Benny leaned forward, narrowing his eyes.

"Oh, and just in case you thought I was taking a break to jerk myself off while daydreaming about your wife," he continued, "I was risking my ass helping those boys down at the Renton airport who

are about to be overrun by a whole
fuckload of those things. Hell, the only
time I wasn't actively helping to kill
those things was when I was flying out
here, taking a moment to drop a note to
some survivors in the hills who are going
to need some help here once we get this
shitshow under control." He broke away
from the desk, and walked right over to a
map of the area, snatching a marker from a
stunned soldier's hand. "That's about
where I saw them," he said as he circled
an area on the paper before handing back
the marker. "They're on top of a giant ass
hill, so you can't miss them."

"O-okay," the soldier stammered,
taking the marker back.

The annoyed pilot stalked back over
to the desk. "Now, I believe you were
about to tell me what suicide run you need
me to go on next?"

The room was deathly silent for a few
moments, and the Captain opened and closed
his mouth a few times before finally
making noise.

"I…" he stammered, clearing unsure of
how to handle Benny's outburst. "Um." He
cleared his throat. "We're loading you up
with some ammo and MREs. We're starting to
run low on both, but we have an urgent
need on our northern flank. Almost due

east of here is a town on a river called Burlington."

Benny nodded. "Heard some stories about Burlington from some of the people back at the airport to the east," he replied. "Sounds like those boys had a rough go of it."

"They did," McCall agreed, nodding, "and they've been in the shit since day one. We just reinforced them yesterday with five hundred more troops, but they need supplies in order to push ahead further." He paused, motioning to a page on his desk. "Satellite imagery shows a decent-sized horde headed their way, and they need to prepare, since those five hundred some-odd men are the only thing standing between our northern force and a full on second front war."

The pilot nodded. "I'll get the stuff up there and hurry back."

"Your contact on the ground is a…" the Captain began, shuffling through a few papers until he found the one he needed, "Sergeant Copeland. He's arranged a landing zone for you at the Super Center just south of the bridge."

Benny nodded again. "I'll be back, then," he said, and turned away.

"One more thing," McCall said, holding up a hand.

"Yeah?" the pilot asked.

"We need you back as quickly as possible, because there are more runs to make," the Captain said, and drummed his fingers on the desk for a beat. "That said, if the Sergeant needs something you can provide, take some time and help him out."

Benny nodded and walked out of the room, cracking a sly smile to himself outside at the verbal smack down he'd delivered to the pompous Captain.

Benny took off from the ship deck and glided over the open water. The sun was high enough in the eastern sky that it wasn't completely blinding him as he flew east. The glimmer of light on the water was scenic and beautiful, a welcome reprieve from the horror he'd come from in the city and what he was about to fly in to.

Okay, due east until I hit the interstate, then head north, he thought. *Shouldn't be too difficult.*

About ten minutes into the flight, he reached land, and immediately spotted signs of war. Several small groups of soldiers walked along the streets, clearing out stragglers while other secured buildings.

They must be desperate for ammo if they're already clearing out stores while the front lines are still fighting, he thought. *Just how fucked are we?* The thought made his stomach drop a bit, but he shook off the cloud of negativity threatening his mind and quickly located the interstate so he could make the turn north.

The highway was covered in bodies, no doubt from a march north by the reinforcements. He glanced to the side streets as he flew, but didn't see any movement.

At least they have this shit on lockdown up here, he thought. *Gotta be getting close.*

A few more minutes of flying and he spotted the bridge. There was a small army of soldiers on it, and in the street before it, but the details of the bridge were still too far out to see. He scanned the area and found the Super Center, finding his landing spot and gently setting the chopper down.

As the blades slowed, a large dark-skinned soldier walked up to him, and Benny's eyes lit up, recognizing the burly Sergeant from Spokane.

"I thought that name sounded familiar!" he exclaimed as he jumped down from the chopper. "How the hell are you, soldier?"

"Benny, my man!" Copeland replied, holding out his hand. "What are you doing up in these parts?"

The pilot shook excitedly, a goofy smile widening as he enjoyed reuniting with a familiar face. "Well, they told me you boys didn't know how to ration properly," he teased, "so they needed me to bring you some MREs and ammo."

"Is that what Captain McCall told you?" Copeland replied, rolling his eyes.

Benny wrinkled his nose. "So you're familiar with that uptight asswipe?"

"Our paths have crossed," the Sergeant replied with a chuckle.

"Well, boy, have I got a story for you," the pilot declared. "Come on and give me the tour, and I'll tell you while we walk."

Copeland nodded and let out a loud whistle. Several soldiers broke away from a nearby store and rushed over.

"I'm going to take my friend here up to the bridge," the Sergeant explained. "You men get this unloaded and sorted."

There was a chorus of *Yes, sir*, and Copeland put his arm around Benny's shoulders and led him towards the bridge.

"So, about that story," the Sergeant said, with the tone of a schoolgirl excited for gossip.

A few minutes later, the two men reached the bridge, walking around ammo reserves and men prepping spikes out of tree branches and broom handles.

"You didn't!" Copeland exclaimed, letting out a deep belly laugh.

Benny grinned. "I most certainly did."

"Oh man," the Sergeant said, wiping imaginary tears from his eyes, "I can't wait to be a civilian so I can tell him to fuck off."

"Well, if you want me to deliver a message," Benny replied, waggling his eyebrows, "all you gotta do is ask."

Copeland laughed again, shaking his head. "Good to know."

They reached the concrete barricade, which was manned by four armed guards. The pilot took a deep breath and let out a low whistle when he looked beyond it.

"That is a special level of fucked up there, Sergeant," he said.

Copeland crossed his arms. "The military trains us to improvise with what we have at our disposal," he replied with a shrug, "and that's exactly what we're doing."

Beyond the concrete barricade was a maze of corpses. Each wall was ten to fifteen yards wide and stacked three to four bodies high. It ran the entire length of the bridge, with about twenty in total.

"Come on, I'll give you a closer look," Copeland said, waving for his friend to follow him.

They hopped the concrete and walked out to the rotted maze. A few soldiers were working on the one closest to them. One man lifted two bodies stacked on top of each other, while another one jammed the dull end of a five-foot long stake into the two below. He used enough force to shove it through the first body and partially into the second one, giving it a good wiggle to make sure it was secure. He nodded to his partner, who lowered the other corpses back down, creating a sturdy trap. This wall had about a dozen spikes sticking out of it.

"How we looking, soldier?" Copeland asked.

"Sir, we have another couple of spikes to put on this barricade, and one more over there that needs some," one of the soldiers replied. "After that, we'll have the preliminary traps set. Once the boys in the back finish with their whittling, we'll add on more."

Copeland nodded. "Good work," he said. "Keep it up."

The two soldiers made noises in the affirmative and got back to work.

The Sergeant led Benny to the center of the road and turned to look down it.

"Between you and me," the pilot asked quietly, "how well do you think these are going to hold up?"

Copeland shook his head. "If some stragglers wander in, they'll work great," he replied. "If we get some of the horde they say is coming our way, then it might buy us some time. Minutes, but they'll be valuable. Plus, keeping the men busy with stuff like this keeps them out of their own heads, which is key when we're facing what we're facing."

"If it's anything like what they're facing down south," Benny said dryly, "you're going to need more than wooden spikes."

The Sergeant shrugged. "Base on what you brought us, it doesn't seem like we're high up on the priority list. So we're doing what we can. Which reminds me…" He pulled out his radio and began fiddling with the knob. "Sent a couple of my boys up to this little town to the northeast called Sedro-Woolley. It's a few miles off the interstate, but we're hoping we can pull some of the horde that way when they start getting close."

"Divide and conquer," Benny agreed, "hard to argue with a classic. Go ahead and do what you gotta do."

Copeland gave him a thumbs up as he raised the radio to his mouth. "Kowalski, it's Copeland," he said. "Do you copy?"

There were a few moments of silence, and his brow furrowed.

"Kowalski, it's Copeland," he said, more forcefully this time. "Can you stop slacking off and grab the radio?"

A moment later, the line opened, gunfire peppering the background. "Having a hell of a day over here, Sarge," Kowalski said.

Copeland sighed and shook his head. "What have you gotten yourselves into now?"

"Well, we were scouting like you said," the sniper replied, "and one thing led to another, and now we're surrounded by a few hundred of these fuckers."

The Sergeant took a deep breath. "Can you get out?" he asked.

"Of course we can," Kowalski scoffed. "Unless you mean get out alive, in which case there's zero chance. But we can certainly run out as zombies no problem."

Copeland put the radio to his forehead for a moment, closing his eyes. "Dammit," he muttered, and then brought the walkie-talkie back to his lips. "Okay, where are you?"

"Northeast corner of town, a few blocks up from a baseball field," Kowalski replied. "We're in a house-" Several rapid fire shots and some yelling cut him off. "Oh shit, Wade needs me," the sniper blurted.

"Just get to the attic and hang tight," Copeland replied quickly. "Help is on the way." He turned to Benny. "You got time to give a friend a lift?" he asked.

The pilot nodded. "Whatever you need, I'm game."

"Johnson, you copy?" the Sergeant asked.

"What you need, Sarge?" came the reply.

"Meet me at the Super Center," Copeland instructed. "Helicopter in the parking lot, we got an urgent errand to run."

Johnson grunted through the radio. "Oh lord, what did Kowalski do now?"

The Sergeant chuckled. "His usual stuff," he replied. "Double time it, because they're on the clock."

"On the way," Johnson assured him.

Copeland pocketed the radio and turned to Benny. "Sorry to cut the tour short," he said.

"You can just give me the aerial tour, then," the pilot replied, clapping him on the shoulder.

The Sergeant nodded as they headed back for the barricade. "Sounds good to me."

CHAPTER SIX

Benny piloted the helicopter of the
town of Burlington towards Sedro-Woolley,
which was just a few miles away. As he
rose high into the air, Copeland pointed
out some barricades they'd built in the
city. There were cars at almost every
intersection, creating pockets where
troops could station themselves to fight
off the dead.

"If we can break up that horde
enough, those pockets can hold them off,"
he explained. "At least for a while."

Benny eyed the roads. "Looks like you
got every car in town down there."

"Just about," Copeland replied with a
nod. "We started moving some up the
interstate a bit to slow 'em down, but
like everything else, it's a stopgap
measure."

The pilot shook his head with a sigh.
"It's a shame we can't just napalm them,"
he said.

"You and me both, brother," the
Sergeant replied. "You and me both."

They flew out of town, almost
immediately spotting Sedro-Woolley up
ahead.

"Can you do a flyover so we can see
where they're at?" Copeland asked.

Benny nodded and rose up to get a better view. Johnson leaned forward from behind them to look out through the front. The pilot quickly spotted the baseball field, and headed that way, and just a few blocks north of that was a house with hundreds of zombies surrounding it.

"Any chance you can get low enough that they can hop on from the roof?" Copeland asked.

Benny shook his head. "Too many power lines and trees," he explained. "I'd rather not crash this thing if I can help it."

"Not gonna argue with that," the Sergeant agreed. "Can you drop us off at the baseball field?"

Benny nodded. "Heading there now," he replied, and swooped in the direction of the baseball field. He lowered down on the infield, noting a few zombies on the other side of the fences, agitated by the noise.

"We won't be long," Copeland assured him.

Benny nodded. "I'm on channel twenty-two," he said as he checked his radio. "I'm gonna park this thing on the roof of that warehouse a few blocks over. I'll be ready to pick you boys up whenever you're good to go."

The Sergeant nodded, and they exchanged a fist bump before the two soldiers leapt out. Once they were clear, Benny took off and headed for his landing spot.

"So what's the plan, Sarge?" Johnson asked.

Copeland shook his head. "No clue," he admitted. "Let's just get up there and see what we see."

The duo walked towards the fence, a few zombies pressed up against it, wiggling their rotted fingers as they reached over the waist-high chain link. The soldiers didn't break stride as they pulled out their knives and approached them.

"Are we keeping a tally on how many times Kowalski gets into these sorts of situations?" Johnson asked as he lashed out, stabbing one of the ghouls in the forehead. "Because if I were a betting man, I'd say that by the end of all this, he's going to get some sort of record."

Copeland stabbed one through the eye and shrugged. "I mean, if you want to keep track, don't let me stop you," he replied. "Just put me down for twenty bucks on Kowalski getting stuck ten times before anybody else reaches five."

"I can work with that," Johnson agreed as he dispatched a burly zombie in the face. "Gonna have to give some high

odds to sucker in some of the people who
don't know him like we do."

The Sergeant chuckled. "Do what you
gotta do," he said, "just don't take money
from anybody above my head. Not sure I
want to explain that or why I keep sending
Kowalski on missions like this."

"What about Kersey?" Johnson asked, a
twinkle in his eye as he snapped a ghoul's
neck.

Copeland stabbed the final zombie in
the temple and paused. "He's a busy man,"
he replied slowly, "but I'll throw in
twenty on his behalf. I know he's good for
it, and he might get on me for not going
with a sure thing."

They chuckled as they hopped the
fence, casually stepping over the corpses
they'd just dropped. They picked up the
pace, beginning a light jog to the north.
The streets were clear, except for the
occasional body in the road.

"Guess Kowalski and Wade pulled
everything their way," Johnson mused.

Copeland nodded. "Let's just hope
there weren't too many of them," he
replied.

They moved off of the road and
started working their way through the
yards, heading up the last few blocks and
trying to stay out of sight. Eventually

they spotted zombies a couple of blocks up and moved cautiously, crouching.

When they reached the house across the street from their friends, they looked out at the zombies easily forty bodies deep from the house. They took cover behind the back corner to weigh their options.

Johnson shook his head. "Fucking Kowalski," he muttered, "never ceases to amaze me what that boy can get into."

"Come on, let's get inside and figure something out," Copeland said, and led the way to the back door. He tried the handle quietly, but it was locked.

Johnson smashed the window and reached in to unlock the deadbolt, opening the door and motioning for the Sergeant to enter with a flourish. They secured the door and did a quick sweep of the house, finding it blissfully empty.

They moved to the sitting room at the front of the house, peering out the big bay window overlooking the street.

The yard across from them was packed thick with ghouls, covering the entire grassy area and stretching back to the road. Looking closer, the front door appeared to be bowing under the pressure.

"That door isn't going to hold much longer," Copeland muttered, and pulled out his radio, raising it to his lips.

"Kowalski, we're in position," he said. "Where are you two?"

"We're up in the attic like you suggested," the sniper replied immediately. "We've punched a hole through the shingles, but haven't gone outside."

The Sergeant took a deep breath. "Either of you hurt?"

"Just our pride, Sarge," Kowalski replied, melancholy in his voice.

Copeland rolled his eyes. "Good, because you boys are going to have to haul ass in a minute."

"What's the plan?" the sniper asked.

The Sergeant squinted at the horde through the window. "We're going to figure out a way to pull them away from the house," he explained, "then you two are going to get to the chopper back at the baseball field."

"What about you?" Kowalski asked.

"Johnson and I will be alright," Copeland assured him. "We haven't killed anything today, so it'll help us hit our quota. You just be ready to move when we get the path clear."

"We'll be ready," the sniper replied firmly.

Copeland lowered the radio and looked at his companion. "All right," he said, "what's your big idea to draw their attention?"

"Me?!" Johnson gaped. "When did that chore fall to me?"

The Sergeant burst out laughing. "Don't worry, I got an idea," he said, raising a hand. "I'm going to head out there and pop off a few rounds, and lead as many of them away as I can." He jerked a thumb over his shoulder. "Just gonna run them around the block. Once I've pulled them away, you're gonna go out there and get on cleanup duty so those two knuckleheads can get out. I'll meet you three at the airfield soon after."

"Yeah, I can dig that plan," Johnson replied, nodding.

Copeland raised an eyebrow. "What, you aren't going to be all noble and volunteer for the dangerous part?"

"Shit Sarge, you've seen me run," his companion said sheepishly. "If I wanted to commit suicide, there are easier ways."

The Sergeant chuckled and patted Johnson on the shoulder. "Don't worry man, I wouldn't do that to you," he assured him. "Now get ready to move, I'll let Benny know what the deal is."

The Private nodded and readied his weapon as Copeland headed to the back of the house and slipped outside. He walked down a few houses to give himself a buffer, and then crouched, pulling out his walkie-talkie.

"Hey Benny, you copy?" he asked into the receiver.

"Haven't heard anything explode yet," the pilot drawled, "so going to go out on a limb and guess you haven't got your boys yet?"

Copeland chuckled. "Not yet, but we're about to," he said. "Going to need you to dust off in ten and head back to the baseball field to pick up three."

"Three?" Benny asked. "Sounds like we're missing one."

The Sergeant took a deep breath. "Only temporarily," he replied. "I'm the rabbit in this hunt, so I'm going to be late to the party and coming in hot. You just don't leave without me."

"Wouldn't dream of it," the pilot promised. "And I'll be there to pick up your squad. You be safe."

Copeland nodded. "Appreciate it," he said. "See you in a few." He shoved the radio back into his pocket and walked out to the road, three houses down from the horde.

He looked around, checking all the nooks and crannies nearby, but didn't spot any ghouls hanging out. They all seemed to be trying to get at Kowalski and Wade with their friends.

He checked his rifle before aiming it towards the horde. He picked a target and began firing, hitting several zombie heads in quick succession. The shot echoed throughout the empty neighborhood, drawing the attention of the ghouls.

Slowly but surely, they crept away from the house, shambling in his direction. About half of the creatures in the yard came after him, so he fired a few more shots to try to draw the rest out.

When the closest zombie came within ten yards of him, Copeland turned and started walking, pausing occasionally to shoot another ghoul to make sure they kept following him like the Pied Piper.

Johnson watched as the Sergeant led the bulk of them away, dismayed that there were still a dozen or so stragglers in the yard. "Damn loafers," he muttered under his breath.

He got up in a huff and strode out the front door, readying his knife. When he reached the road and looked, he spotted the back end of the horde a full block away. He contemplated using his gun, but then shook his head.

Only if I start getting overwhelmed, he thought. He walked up to the first zombie at the far end of the house and jammed his blade into the back of its skull. He whipped around and took on the next two, stabbing them in the face in quick succession. By the time their bodies hit the ground, the other nine had taken an interest in the noise, and worked their way towards him.

"Fuck it, I'm too old for this shit," Johnson declared, and raised his rifle. He quickly executed the rest of the creatures, one by one, dropping them expertly. When the front yard was nothing but unmoving corpses, he strode up to the front door and rang the doorbell.

Several moments passed before Kowalski opened the door, Wade beside him.

"Two men shacking up together is sinful!" Johnson bellowed in his best preacher voice. "You two motherfuckers need Jesus!"

The gore-covered duo stared at him, slowly shaking their heads at his antics.

"You done, Johnson?" Wade asked, voice tired.

The Private in question hooked a thumb into the top of his pants and shot them a lazy grin. "Depends, have you two repented?"

"Hell no, never will, Satan rules," Kowalski replied quickly. "Now can we get the fuck outta here already?"

Johnson sighed as if it were the worst thing in the world that they didn't find him funny. "Okay fine," he said "Come on, we got a chopper waiting."

"Wait, what about Copeland?" Wade asked, holding up a hand.

"He says he'll catch up," Johnson replied with a shrug.

Kowalski nodded and brushed past him on the front step. "Good enough for me," he said. "Let's move."

Copeland led the horde down the street, having reached four blocks away from the house. He'd stopped firing at that point, as any breakaways this far away wouldn't be a threat.

I know Johnson is slow, he thought with amusement, *but that should be enough time, even for him.*

He pulled out his walkie talkie and raised it to his mouth. "Benny, you pick up the boys yet?" he asked.

"Yeah, we're hanging out on second base waiting for you," the pilot replied. "Where you at?"

Copeland glanced over his shoulder again. "About four blocks east of where Kowalski was," he said. "I'm getting ready to make the turn and head back."

"Copy that, we'll be waiting," Benny assured him.

The Sergeant picked up the pace a bit, leaving the zombies behind and reaching the next intersection. *Just gotta make the turn, then double back and-*

He stopped short in the middle of the road at the sight of a small army of zombies. There were several dozen of them, and they turned towards him, rheumy eyes excited as they shambled towards a fresh meal.

"Damn," Copeland muttered under his breath, "looks like I'm going up another block."

He broke into a moderate sprint, heading up towards the next intersection, and more ghouls began to emerge from side streets, attracted to his fan club's moaning. He stopped in the middle of the road, looking around frantically for a solution.

He pulled out the radio and quickly raised it to his lips. "Benny, I'm in the shit," he blurted, "need some help."

"What do you need?" the pilot asked immediately.

Copeland scratched the back of his head. "Not going to be able to double back," he explained, "so just going to have to go north. Going to need a pickup, but I have no clue where."

"Just start heading north," Benny suggested, "we'll be able to find out."

"Ten-four," the Sergeant replied, and stuffed the walkie talkie back into his pocket. He moved north, into a yard next to him, and a few ghouls staggered out from the backyard.

Copeland didn't waste any time, raising his rifle and firing two quick shots in succession to drop them without breaking stride. He rushed through the yard and hopped the fence into the next one, only to be greeted by a couple dozen zombies pouring in from between the houses.

He knew the gunfire hadn't done him any favors on that front, and contemplated whether he should continue, but in any case the pack was too dense. He looked around and focused in on the back patio door, firing a few shots to shatter the glass.

He rushed over, barely beating the ghouls to the door, their hands grasping at air as he passed. He practically flew through the house, catching a glimpse of a corpse out of the corner of his eye down the hallway. But there was no time to pause, so he threw open the front door.

There were some stragglers in the front yard, and he dodged them, giving one a shove on the way by to send it tumbling to the ground When he reached the street, he looked back to see that there weren't any ghouls in his immediate vicinity, and took a quick breather to plot his path.

He moved into the next yard and then heard the relieving sound of a chopper overhead.

Copeland darted into the center of the grass in an open space and waved his hands frantically in the air. Benny hovered above, and Kowalski opened the door, motioning for the Sergeant to keep moving north.

He gave the sniper a thumbs up, and then continued his run, tearing down a couple more blocks while dodging the few zombies shambling around.

Soon he reached a large field, where Benny had set the chopper down in the center. Copeland hopped a fence and jogged up to the helicopter as Kowalski threw open the door.

"Damn Sarge, you had us worried there for a minute," he gushed.

The Sergeant shook his head, waving his hands back and forth in front of his face. "Oh no, we aren't doing that now," he declared. "The day you start worrying about me, is the day I submit my resignation."

The group laughed as he climbed aboard, and he reached into the front to pat Benny on the shoulder.

"Appreciate you pulling my chestnuts out of the fire there, bud," Copeland said with a smile.

The pilot raised an eyebrow. "Well, I still have to give McCall your… ahem… message," he replied. "Wouldn't have quite the impact if you weren't alive."

The Sergeant laughed as the engine revved up and the chopper lifted off,

headed back to Burlington before Benny's
next mission.

CHAPTER EIGHT

Benny flew back towards the south end
of town, towards Mercer Island. The
chopper had been refueled and restocked on
the ship, off to deliver vital goods to
the main diversion team. After coming over
the downtown area, he approached the
water's edge, seeing tens of thousands of
ghouls within a half mile of the shore,
attracted to the noise on the island.

"Whatever those boys are doing, it's
working like a charm," he murmured.

He flew out over the water and
spotted muzzle flashes coming from the
shoreline, spread out about every ten
yards or so. He looked around, finally
finding the shopping district to the
north, which was his landing zone.

As he flew over the stores, he
spotted a bright orange circle painted
onto one of the parking lots, with several
people standing around beside various
pickup trucks.

"Guess that's my stop," he mused, and
lowered his altitude.

He landed the chopper and powered it
down, sliding out of his seat and jumping
down to the ground. As soon as hit boots
hit the pavement, a small army of soldiers
rushed up to begin unloading. Benny nodded
in approval at their efficiency.

"You must be the new pilot," a Sergeant said as he approached with a Corporal in tow.

Benny nodded, offering his hand. "Yeah, a couple of other boys are out of action for the time being," he said, "so I'm picking up their slack. I'm Benny."

"It's appreciated," the Sergeant said as they shook. "I'm Sergeant Kipling, and this here is Corporal Herrera."

Herrera gave a curt nod as they shook hands as well. "We're burning through ammo quick, keeping those things across the way tied up."

"Looks like you're doing a good job though," Benny replied, motioning to the water, "because there are thousands of those things lined up wanting a piece of what you're serving up."

Kipling sighed. "Hope it's more than just thousands," he said. "We really need to be in the tens or even low hundreds, for this to be worthwhile."

"I mean, if you wanna go check for yourself," Benny offered, jerking a thumb over his shoulder, "I can give you a lift up."

The Sergeant shook his head, waving a hand. "Nah, it's all good," he replied, "not really anything we can change at this point."

"How much longer do you think you're gonna be on distraction duty?" the pilot asked.

Herrera shrugged. "No telling," he admitted. "Our troops are making a big push from the east, some of them even getting to the shoreline already."

"Speaking of which," Kipling cut in, raising a finger, "we do have another issue that could use your attention."

Benny nodded. "What do you need?"

"Why don't you come inside here, and I'll fill you in?" the Sergeant asked, and waved for him to follow.

The trio headed for a small Chinese restaurant in a strip mall. As they entered the building, Benny appraised several troops grabbing a bite, with a few soldiers in the back working the grill.

"You hungry?" Kipling asked. "Can we get you something?"

The pilot took a deep whiff, groaning at the scent of sizzling meat. "As long as it's not an MRE," he said, "I'll take whatever you got."

Kipling let out a sharp whistle, gaining the attention of the grill chefs. "Combo plate, right here!" he called.

The soldiers immediately sprung to action, pulling food off of the grill and putting it on a plate. One of them grabbed it and rushed it over, setting it on the table in front of Benny as they took a seat.

The pilot gaped at the fresh food in front of him, mouth watering at the sight and smell.

"One combo plate," the chef declared. "Everything is out of a can, but I have a few tricks up my sleeve. Hope you enjoy."

Benny grinned up at him. "Looks great," he said sincerely. "I appreciate it." He picked up his fork and dug in, moaning at the taste of hot spiced food.

Kipling pulled out a crudely drawn map of the island and surrounding areas, pointing to different spots on the map as he spoke. "Okay, we're here," he said. "To the south of us is Renton, where our boys have pushed forward and set up shop."

"Yep, I was down there earlier today," Benny replied through a mouthful of meat. "They got their hands full, that's for sure."

The Sergeant nodded. "I don't doubt it," he replied. "To the east, south of the I-ninety, some of the main force has reached the shore, however there has been some heavy resistance in spots so a significant portion of them are still half a mile back or so. North of the I-ninety is a completely different story."

"There are some densely populated areas in and around Bellevue," Herrera added, leaning forward on his elbows. "Which has really slowed things up. However, they've been pulling a lot of zombies from the downtown area their way, and it's straining the barricade on the bridge."

Kipling tapped on the area in question. "At the start of this, they blocked off the bridge with some trucks, and it worked okay for a while," he continued, "but the weight of twenty thousand zombies pushing against it is starting to create an opening. The higher ups are afraid that if it gets any larger, it could pose a threat to the advancement. So they've authorized a strafing run with the Apaches to thin out the herd."

Benny swallowed his mouthful and smacked his lips. "So, what can I do?"

"We have three men trapped on the top of those trucks, and they need an evac," Herrera replied. "If we can't get them off soon, they're going to be forced to take a dive into the water."

Kipling pursed his lips. "Which isn't an ideal situation, especially given that one of them is injured," he explained. "We've been bordered to arrange pickup for them, which in their mind means a water rescue. But if you're ballsy enough to land that thing of yours on a transport truck, I think it would have a better outcome for all involved."

Benny shoved another huge bite into his mouth, chuckling through the meat. "Normally it's a good strategy to call out the ballsiness of the troops to get them to endanger their lives," he said as he swallowed. "What you didn't account for, is that I'm a civilian." He pointed his fork at them and then back at himself.

The two soldiers nodded slowly, sharing a nervous glance.

"Lucky for you," the pilot continued, "I'm a crazy motherfucker so I'll do it just for the challenge." He let out a big belly laugh, and the soldiers joined in, shaking their heads.

Kipling leaned forward. "I really can't thank you enough."

"Thank me after I pull it off," Benny replied, shoving another forkful into his mouth.

"I'll do that," the Sergeant promised. "Now you take your time and finish your meal. Herrera here is going to ride along to help you out. He'll be waiting for you at the chopper."

The pilot nodded. "Good deal, Sergeant," he replied. "I'll have your boys safely back home in no time."

The soldiers smiled and got up, vacating the table to leave him to finish his meal in peace. As they disappeared out the door, Benny chuckled to himself and shook his head.

Didn't know this was on my bucket list, he thought, *but it sure as hell is now.*

Benny fired up the chopper, looking back to make sure Herrera was nice and situated in the back. After a moment, the Corporal gave him a thumbs up, and Benny returned it before taking off, quickly gaining altitude and heading to the north.

As they reached the top of the island, the pilot looked to the west, seeing the bridge in that direction was jam-packed with zombies.

There were a dozen or so men on the trucks there, giving a constant stream of fire to keep the horde at bay. From what he could tell, there was a good twenty yards of corpses on the bridge next to the truck.

The flight over the water was short, the target bridge quickly appearing on the horizon. Herrera moved up to the front of the helicopter, kneeling beside Benny. He tapped him on the shoulder and pointed to the east, where a large group of soldiers had managed to push through to the shoreline, setting up an encampment and gunner positions.

As they made it further up the coast they could see why, as throngs of zombies had pushed to the shore and worked their way towards them.

Benny and Herrera shared a look, silently hoping that those boys knew what they were doing.

The chopper rose up, a couple hundred yards above the bridge so the duo could get a proper lay of the land, and it was brutal. To the east, hundreds of zombies spread out on the bridge in a sea, most of which headed towards the noise of the invading force.

To the west was something straight out of a nightmare. Tens of thousands of zombies, pressed tightly together, surged forwards to try to maneuver past the barricade. The trucks started to shift, the gap between them now eight feet wide. The trickle became a steady stream.

As they grew closer, Benny spotted three men standing up on the back of the truck, waving at them.

"Get them to move back so I got room to work," the pilot instructed. "Not entirely sure exactly how this is gonna happen."

Herrera gave him a thumbs up and headed for the door as the chopper turned sideways so that he faced the troops. He waved to get their attention and then made an exaggerated motion for them to move back—way back.

They got the hint and clambered to the far end of the truck, near the center of the road. They were cautious, making sure they kept their footing on the truck that shifted back and forth due to the raging zombie river below.

Once they were clear, Benny inched the helicopter towards the truck, making sure to stay several feet above the top. It was a little touch and go, as the wind coming off the water made it difficult to hold it steady. After a few failed attempts, he shook his head.

He motioned for Herrera to come up to him, and then said, "Landing ain't gonna happen. But I can hover just above it and they can hop in." He held up a closed fist. "When I give you the signal, you get them over here quick."

"You got it," the Corporal replied, and got into position, ready to go.

Benny positioned the chopper over the truck, getting it as low as he possibly could. He managed to stabilize it about three feet from the top and then raised his fist to give the signal.

Herrera waved frantically for the men to start coming, and the soldiers moved as quickly as they could across the truck. The injured Private brought up the rear, and Herrera pulled him inside and slammed the door shut.

Benny lifted off, rising high and away from the flood of ghouls below, and then hovered for a moment, turning his head. "Everybody good?" he bellowed.

When he received an emphatic thumbs up from each of his passengers, the pilot smiled and faced front again, heading back for the parking lot. He touched down and powered off the engine, jumping out to help the boys.

He peered in and saw that one of the Privates was looking woozy. "Yo!" he barked to one of the soldiers behind him. "Let's get a medic over here!"

"Appreciate it," Private Hess said, "but we're good."

The injured soldier, Private Baker, offered a weak smile. "Not the first time we've been dinged up."

"I said, get a goddamn medic over here!" Benny demanded, and the man he'd been yelling at ran off.

"Again," Hess said, raising a hand, "appreciate the concern, but we're good."

The pilot wagged a finger at them. "You know, I had a guy back in 'Nam tell me the same thing," he said firmly. "I had just flown into a hotspot, taking fire on every side just to get his ass out of there. Got back to base and he said he was fine and didn't need a medic, even though he was bleeding from the head." He leaned in, brow furrowed. "And do you know what happened to him?"

"Umm," Baker replied slowly, "did he die?"

Benny shook his head. "Hell no, he didn't die, but do you know what he did when he got back to the States?" he asked. "He got into politics!" He threw up his hands. "So obviously there was some sort of brain damage done. Now do you want that to be you? Or do you want the doc here to make sure you didn't break that marble inside your skull?"

The three Privates exchanged awkward glances, not sure how to respond, but finally nodded at the brusque pilot.

"Yeah, a doc sounds good," the injured soldier agreed.

"Good, that's what I thought," Benny huffed, and backed up as the medic reached the chopper and climbed inside.

Herrera stepped up to him, shaking his head. "You're one hell of a pilot," he said.

"Just doing what I can," Benny replied.

"Well, after that speech, you should consider going into politics yourself," the Corporal teased. "That was quite persuasive."

The pilot clucked his tongue. "I'd rather stick my junk through a glory hole knowing there were zombies on the other side than be a politician," he declared.

Herrera burst out laughing.

"What, I'm serious," Benny replied, deadpan. "At least I'd still have my soul."

The Corporal clapped him on the shoulder. "That you would, buddy," he said. "That you would."

As they waited for the medic to check out the soldiers, Kipling approached and offered the duo a smile.

"Good job getting those guys outta trouble," he said.

Benny shrugged. "Just another day at the office," he quipped.

"Well, your day isn't over yet," the Sergeant continued. "Just got a call from Captain McCall. He wants you back at the ship pronto. Something's going down, but he didn't say what."

The pilot sighed. "That's always a good sign," he muttered. "Tell him I'm on the way." He watched the rescued Privates make their way down from the helicopter and crossed his arms.

Good god, what now?

CHAPTER TEN

Benny landed on deck and hopped out, immediately making a beeline for the ready room. A soldier stepped into his path and opened his mouth, but the pilot held up a hand.

"Yeah yeah, I know where he is," Benny said, waving him off. "Just get my baby loaded up, will ya?"

The soldier blinked at him for a moment, but then stepped out of the way and joined the others loading up gear and refueling.

Benny strolled into the ready room, the same vibe in the room of people still working on maps at the edges.

"Whatcha got for me now, Captain?" the pilot asked as he approached the desk.

McCall didn't look up from his papers, only whistling loudly, and within seconds, a soldier rushed over with a map, slamming it down on the table.

Benny's brow furrowed as he watched the frantic movements of the soldier pointing things out to the Captain. "McCall, what's going on?" he asked.

The Captain muttered something to the soldier, and once he was gone, he finally looked up at the pilot. "An hour ago, two thousand troops on the northern front got cut off from the main force." He spun the map around and pointed to an area to the northwest of the I-5 bridge that Corporal Bretz had partially blocked off earlier in the week. "This little area is known as Roosevelt, just a mile or so north of the I-5 bridge. It's a huge residential area with some significant shopping areas west of the interstate. The noise the main northern force is creating has riled up the zombies to the south, and they've been pouring over in droves. So we went to this group pushing to the south in an attempt to shore up defenses." He took a deep breath. "They went a little too hard, because they are now surrounded."

"Let me guess," Benny drawled, "they're out of supplies and need more?"

McCall nodded. "Yeah, and I'm afraid if they don't get it, we could lose everyone," he replied. "You're going to be landing in a hot zone, so I need to know if you're capable of doing that."

The pilot glared at him, ice in his gaze. "Bitch, I was landing in hot zones when your momma was still turning tricks in the Gas'n'Gulp parking lot to buy you baby formula," he growled. "The audacity to ask me if I'm capable of doing that. The fuck is wrong with you?"

The Captain held up his hands in surrender, palms out. "Okay, I'm sorry, nothing like that will ever come out of my mouth again," he promised. "Now, we're getting you loaded up. Do you need anything?"

"Yeah, I could use a sidearm," Benny replied. "Not that comfortable with anything bigger than that, but I'd like something to defend myself."

McCall nodded approvingly, and unbuckled his holster, removing his personal handgun and sliding it across the desk.

Benny blinked at the gesture and nodded in respect.

"Just so we're clear," the Captain continued, pointing a finger at him, "that's a loaner. Just want to show that I have confidence that you're coming back."

The pilot picked up the gun and inspected it before buckling the holster around his waist. "I'll treat her like she was my own."

"Thank you," McCall replied, and then pressed his palms against the desk. "Now if you want to coordinate with the Private over there, he'll get you set up with exactly where you need to go."

Benny nodded and headed over to the soldier in question, who stood reading reports and drawing on a satellite image of the area tacked to the wall.

"So, where am I going?" the pilot asked, putting his hands on his hips.

"Okay," the Private began, turning to him, "the troops have been able to set up a perimeter a couple blocks out from the football field here. This is going to be your landing zone." He pointed to a spot on the map. "Ideally, we're going to need to do a couple of runs, so touchdown, no pun intended."

Benny raised an eyebrow in incredulity at the joke, and the soldier blushed crimson, shaking his head.

"Sorry," he blurted, and cleared his throat. "Anyway, touchdown, they'll unload as quickly as they can, then get back here as fast as you can. Worst case scenario, the supplies we're sending can sustain them until reinforcements arrive, but the more they have the better."

"Understandable," Benny replied, "however, finding a football field in that area is going to be a bitch and a half. You got any other landmarks for me?"

The Private nodded. "Yes sir," he said, pointing to the map again. "There's a sizable lake a few blocks due west of the interstate. Find that then fly east and you can't miss the field."

"That'll work," the pilot replied. "I'll be back, and y'all just better be ready for me." He gave the soldier a nod and then headed out of the room, walking

with grizzled determination towards
another shitshow.

Benny piloted the chopper over the northern part of the city, scanning the horizon for the lake. The area below him was densely populated, packed full of homes and shopping centers. It was just the kind of place that the pilot would have considered nightmarish before the apocalypse, but doubly so now that the streets were packed with flesh-eating ghouls.

He looked to the north, spotting several of the roads populated with troops, most of which were slowly moving to the south. It was still a ways to go before they reached the water separating the northern area from the downtown part of Seattle.

A couple minutes of flight time later, he finally spotted a moderately sized body of water, no doubt home to some of the pricier real estate in the area.

"Okay, found the lake, just a little further to the football field," he murmured. "Now, where are you?"

Benny scanned the horizon east of the interstate, rising higher into the air to get a wider view. Finally, he laid eyes on it, right where the Private had said it would be.

"Bingo!" he cheered. "Let's go!"

He moved forward, the consistent pop of gunfire coming from below, even over the whizzing of the chopper blades. Below him was all-out warfare. Thousands of zombies descended on a four-block radius around the football field, slowly moving towards a wall of muzzle flashes.

"Keep holding them off boys, I got your ammo right here," Benny changed to himself, and descended quickly into the grass. He landed on the logo in the center of the field and powered down the blades.

He looked around, brow furrowing at the fact that no soldiers were coming to unload him.

"What the fuck?" he asked nobody in particular, and got out of the chopper. He looked around, confused. There was a torrent of gunfire nearby, but nobody was at the football field. "Something ain't right."

He drew his sidarm, readying it, and walked towards the main building at the western edge of the field. When he reached the gate, he opened it up and stepped into the parking lot. He spotted a figure beside a car, and his shoulders tensed when he realized they weren't standing like a live human.

Benny aimed his handgun at them, inching forward to get a better look. The legs twitched slightly, like a corpse reanimating putting him on edge. He took a deep breath and hopped around the side of the car, eyes widening as he spotted a pair of bloodied men in combat fatigues munching away at another dead soldier.

He steadied his aim, thankful that the ghouls hadn't taken notice of him yet. He fired once, striking one of the runners in the head, and adjusted his aim quickly as the second creature stood up to rush him. Benny was just quick enough, the bullet hitting the corpse in the forehead sending it tumbling to the ground.

The pilot stepped up to the dinner buffet on the ground, the soldier's chest torn wide open. Guts were strewn across the pavement, a gooey mess all around. Benny paused for a moment, his mind flicking through graphic flashbacks to years gone by. He finally shook himself out of it and put a round in the dead soldier's skull.

Man, fuck this, he thought frantically. *If they're behind the line, there's not a damn thing I can do about it.*

He clenched his jaw, trying to get his head on straight. He wanted to go back to the helicopter and get the hell out of dodge. It finally clicked that this was his only course of action, and he started moving back the way he'd come.

The trip was short lived, however. When he reached the gate to the field, he froze, eyes widening. On the other side, dozens of runners emerged, racing towards him at an alarming pace. He contemplated making a run for the chopper, but shook his head side to side.

"That's a fucking fantasy, if you ever heard one," he muttered to himself, rubbing his forehead. "Think man, think!"

He looked around frantically, trying to find somewhere to hide.

"Hey, mister, over here!" a woman called from a building across the street. "Hurry!"

Benny didn't have time for a second thought and broke into a run as fast as he could. As he reached the street, he looked down the road, spotting several more runners who turned their attention towards him.

"Don't look, just run!" the woman screamed.

Benny pumped his legs as hard as he could, racing towards the small business building across from the field. Two young Privates stood in the doorway, waving frantically at him to come in.

The runners made up ground quick, and his heart roared in his ears to drown out the sound of the undead footfalls hot on his heels.

One of the soldiers fired off several rounds from the doorway, striking the lead creatures in the chest, causing them to stumble. They weren't kill shots, but at least they bought Benny the precious seconds he needed to reach safety.

He flew past the soldier duo into the building, and they slammed the door, securing it. Seconds later, the zombies outside thrashed against it, desperate for the meal they'd lost.

Benny leaned over, gasping for air, heart hammering in his chest.

"Are you okay, mister?" the young female Private asked.

The pilot held up a finger as he caught his breath to signify he needed a second.

"Bartlett," the male soldier said, patting her on the shoulder, "why don't you get our new friend here some water." He watched her go and then grabbed a rolling chair from behind one of the desks and slid it over. "Here, have a seat. I'm Sellers, by the way."

Benny happily flopped back into the chair, leaning back and closing his eyes for a moment as his breathing steadied.

"Sorry it's not cold," Bartlett said as she held out a bottle of water to him.

Benny smiled and nodded, practically tearing the cap off and downing half of the bottle in a single gulp. "Ah, it's all right," he replied after the hearty swallow. "That hit the spot just the way it was."

"Glad I could help," the young blonde soldier replied with a smile.

"Now that you can speak again," Sellers continued, "you want to tell us what in the hell you're doing out here?"

The pilot nodded. "Name's Benny," he said, putting a hand against his chest. "I'm the helicopter pilot bringing you boys…" he paused, glancing at Bartlett, "ahem, I mean, bringing you troops some more ammo. Captain McCall said you were in some trouble, and goddamn was he not kidding."

"Yeah, it's been a shit-tastrophe ever since they ordered us forward," Sellers agreed. "We started having casualties on the second block, because we were moving too quickly."

Bartlett jerked a thumb over her shoulder. "And that was ten blocks ago," she added. "Maybe more."

"How did you get stuck here?" Benny asked, eyes widening. "Back at the ship, they said you had a multi-block perimeter."

Sellers scoffed. "Wishful thinking on somebody's part," he muttered. "We had a few good choke points for those things set up covering every direction, but all it takes is one of those getting overrun to set off a chain reaction."

"Runners," the pilot replied.

Both Privates nodded solemnly.

"Sellers and I were in a group to the east," Bartlett continued. "On the other side of the field. We heard constant fire all around us, but we couldn't figure out why."

The other soldier pulled up his own chair and sat down. "Then, all of a sudden, there was nothing coming from one side of us," he said. "At first, we got excited, thinking they had fended them off. But we were wrong." He lowered his gaze.

"Those things hit hard and fast, coming out of the neighborhood," Bartlett said, motioning wildly with her hands. "Beside us, in front of us, hell, some of them even got behind us."

Sellers leaned back in his chair with a huff. "After that, it was every man for himself," he explained. "There were fifty, sixty of us in that particular group. Bartlett and I managed to get across the field okay, but we don't have any idea what happened to the others."

"I saw some taking shelter in some houses, but they were fighting those things off while trying to get in," she said, and then swallowed hard. "I… I don't know if they made it."

Sellers motioned to the door. "We managed to get here and have been holed up ever since," he said. "Neither one of us has a radio, so all we can do is wait, and hope that somebody comes to get us."

Benny patted his belt, and then his stomach sank when he realized that the radio was still in the chopper. "Well, shit," he groaned. "I was all primed and ready to be the hero there, but it would appear as though I left my walkie talkie in the chopper."

"Well, it's the thought that counts," Bartlett replied with a soft smile.

The pilot shrugged. "I can tell you that the higher ups know y'all are in a heap of trouble," he said, "so they are sending a team in to relieve the pressure on you."

"So what do we do in the meantime?" Sellers asked, spreading his arms.

Benny smirked and reached into his shirt, pulling out his flask and wiggling it in the air. Sellers grinned ear-to-ear, but Bartlett frowned.

"What's wrong there, lil' lady?" the pilot asked.

She pursed her lips. "Never had a drink before."

"Well that settles it," Benny declared, holding out the flask. "You're first."

She reluctantly took it, unscrewing the cap and taking a whiff. She grimaced, and then shrugged, and took a big sip.

The other two laughed as she dissolved into a coughing fit.

"Oh god," she gasped, "it tastes like fire!"

Benny grinned as he took the flask back. "Don't worry, one day, sooner rather than later if you're lucky, that burn will be a welcome sensation," he declared, and raised the flask in a toast before taking a hearty sip.

Bartlett laughed and shook her head, and took a seat in their little circle to wait out the storm.

Three hours later, the trio lounged around the room, feet up, ankles crossed. The gunfire outside had become more sporadic in the last hour, but the banging on the door by the ghouls hadn't let up even for a minute.

"I really wish they would give it a rest," Sellers moaned. "You'd think by now they'd know they aren't getting in."

Benny shook his head. "Those fuckers are persistent," he replied. "If they think food is inside, they'll stand there for days on end to get it." He held up a finger. "On the plus side, their devotion to dinner is giving us a realistic chance at beating them."

"Could have fooled us," Bartlett retorted.

The pilot rocked the chair a little as he replied, "Yeah, you've had some setbacks, but we had setbacks in Spokane and got through it." He offered her a smile. "We'll get through this too."

"You were in Spokane?" Sellers asked.

Benny nodded. "Yep, they found me at the airport early on, and put my old ass back into service," he replied with a grin.

"Back into service?" Bartlett asked, eyes widening. "You served?"

He saluted her. "Yes, ma'am," he said. "Flew choppers in Vietnam. Wasn't exactly my first choice of a career path, but the military wasn't inclined to ask my opinion on the matter."

"How was it over there?" she asked, lowering her legs and leaning forward in her chair. "I mean, I've seen stuff on TV, and, you know, *Platoon* and *Full Metal Jacket*, but those don't really tell everything, you know?"

Benny chuckled. "Yeah, a bunch of pampered actors going back to their comfy trailers every night doesn't really tell everything," he agreed.

"Well fill us in then, what was it like over there?" Sellers asked. "It's not like we're going anywhere, anytime soon."

The pilot looked down, and then pulled out his flask, unscrewing the cap and taking a long sip. "Okay, I'll tell you a little to pass the time," he conceded, though his voice had lost its lustre. "Hopefully it'll get our minds off of the constant goddamn knocking. Not going to go too deep, though… I've blocked a lot of that shit out of my head over the years. Stuff nobody ever needed to see."

The two young soldiers nodded and focused on him intently. They'd seen some horrific things recently too, everyone had, and realized that talking about it wasn't going to be easy for many in the coming months or years.

"I was fortunate enough to not be on the front lines," Benny began, licking his lips. "At least not for any significant length of time. Just shuffling boys to the front and bringing the broken ones back for some care…" He paused, taking another sip. "Or burial. Even the ones that did come back unscathed didn't really come back. I could see it in their eyes, like they left themselves back in the jungle."

He looked up at the two soldiers, still a bit shell-shocked from the day, seeing the same look in their eyes as he'd seen in the Vietnam era troops. They were so young. He took a deep breath, changing tack.

"But the most memorable moment I had over there came when we were on leave," he said, brightening. "I forget which city we were in, hell, even if I remember it there's zero fucking chance I could pronounce it. There was a group of us pilots that ran together, and we'd go out drinking and causing a ruckus. We didn't see front line action, so we got our kicks starting trouble then running from the MPs. We figured worst case, we'd spend a night cooling off in the klink, which was usually quieter and more private than the barracks."

He chuckled to himself, and then took another sip, offering the flask to the kids, but they both shook their heads to decline.

"So, there were six of us at the bar," he continued, "about ten rounds deep when somebody made the suggestion that we should all go to a brothel."

Bartlett held up a hand. "That person was you, wasn't it?" she asked.

The pilot smirked. "I'm going to tell you the same thing I told the judge a few years back," he drawled. "I plead the fifth."

The soldiers laughed, loosening up a bit.

"So, as that mysterious unnamed person continued to push that particular idea," Benny continued, a mischievous glint in his eye, "the enthusiasm around the table was… how they say… waning. Until ole Charlie Webber said the phrase that I'm sure haunts him to this day." He raised his eyes to the ceiling and made his voice as high pitched as he could make it. "*Nah, I'm good, I want my first time to be special.*"

Both soldiers' eyes widened, and Bartlett clapped a hand over her mouth, causing Benny to laugh.

"That was the exact look we gave him, as well," he assured them, shaking his head. "It was like a light switch flipping. All of a sudden, this was the greatest idea ever conceived of by man. So we tell the bartender what our evening plans are, and how we need a 'special' time for our friend here." He raised his hands to do air-quotes for *special*. "Now, I don't know if this bartender hated us American boys, or if he was on the same page as us, but he sent us to a place none of us will ever forget. So we walk down a few blocks, making a turn into an alley and knocking on the back door of some place. This ratchety looking dude opened the door with a sawed-off shotgun in his hand, yelling in some language we didn't understand. He only stopped when I showed him the map on the bar coaster that the bartender drew for us. After that, this asshole became sunshine and rainbows."

"That's always a good sign," Bartlett quipped, sarcasm dripping from his tone. "Nothing concerning about that at all."

Benny let out a self-deprecating laugh, scratching the back of his head. "Well, when you're ten rounds deep, the only concerning thing in your mind is the thought that there won't be an eleventh round," he explained. "Anyway, we go into this place, and it's a seedy looking, velvet covered, interior design nightmare place. Of course, none of us were focused on that, only the ladies in skimpy sleepwear that started coming out of the back room to join us." He tilted his head back for a moment, rubbing his forehead. "While we were all enticed by the attention, this mean older looking woman came out. She was dressed to the nines, makeup and hair done up nice. Of course even with that, you could tell she had been there way too many years. She makes a beeline up to us, but stops by the doorman who whispers in her ear, causing her to get this devious grin on her face. The first words out of her mouth after that were '*Who's my special boy?*' We all immediately pointed to Charlie."

The soldiers let out horrified laughter.

Sellers covered his eyes with his hand and moaned, "Oh god, she didn't"

"Yep, she did," Benny confirmed, nodding sagely. "She walked right over to ole Charlie, grabbed him by the hand, and dragged him kicking and screaming to the back. All of that prime pu-" He choked back the word, glancing at Bartlett. "I mean… all of those lovely ladies that would have enjoyed an evening with Charlie, and he ended up with the warhorse. The rest of the night is kind of a blur. Last thing I remember is them bringing out a couple of bottles of something strong." He shook his head. "We must have found our way home, because we woke up in the barracks the next morning. Most of us spent the morning rubbing our heads to get the pounding to stop, and I'm pretty sure I was the only one to come back with any money left in my pockets."

Sellers leaned forward on his knees. "And Charlie?"

"He never spoke of that night to any of us," Benny replied, slapping his thigh. "But you could see it in his eyes. Something happened in that back room."

Bartlett chuckled, crossing her arms. "Well, he said he wanted his first time to be special," she said. "And you gave him that."

"Did you even listen to the story?" Sellers asked, turning to her with an incredulous look on his face.

She rolled her eyes. "I did, and I'm never going to forget it and I wasn't even there," she replied. "Pretty sure ole Charlie is never going to forget it either."

Benny barked a laugh and wagged a finger at her. "You're a live one," he said, "I like you."

The group shared another laugh and then froze when they heard the gunfire picking up outside. A moment later, the banging on the door ceased.

"Anybody else hear that?" Benny asked, pointing to the door.

His companions nodded, and he sighed with relief.

"Good, wasn't just my mind breaking, as usual," he said.

The trio rose to their feet and rushed to the window, peeking out. The zombies in the front of the building had rushed away, and they spotted them running towards a large group of soldiers in the street a couple of blocks up.

"Everybody down, now!" Benny yelled, and pulled his young companions away from the windows as gunfire erupted from outside.

It was sustained for a few moments, with a few strays piercing the windows and front wall of the building. When it died down, they peeled themselves off of the floor.

"Everybody good?" Benny asked, looking at each of them in turn. At their nod, he waved a hand for them to follow him. "Good, let's go greet our rescuers."

He led them outside, making sure to wave frantically as he emerged so that the soldiers down the street would know they were alive. The soldiers lowered their guns and waved back, heading their way.

"You three okay?" the lead soldier asked.

Benny chuckled darkly. "Yeah, just peachy," he replied. "How are y'all?"

The soldier blinked at him for a beat, and then stammered, "I'm… we're good, sir." He pointed to the two Privates. "You two, report to Sergeant Miller up the road a few blocks, he'll tell you where to go." He turned his gaze back to the pilot. "Sir, if you want to remain in the building, we'll have a transport team here in a couple of hours that will get you to safety."

"No can do son," Benny replied, raising his palms, "I got places to be."

The soldier straightened his shoulders. "Sir, with all due respect, that wasn't a request," he said firmly.

"And with all due respect, I don't give a fuck," Benny snapped, pointing a finger at him. "Now, I need you to get a few of your men here to come help me unload my chopper that's parked in the field out there, so I can get back to doing my fucking job, which is bringing you boys ammo and rations. You think you can handle that?"

The soldier blinked at him, flabbergasted, and then glanced over at the field, spotting the helicopter. "Is that what's in the chopper?" he asked. "Ammo and rations?"

"Yep," Benny replied, crossing his arms.

The soldier turned and whistled. "Four of you, on me!" he barked, and then motioned to the troops that rushed up. "You four…" He glanced at Bartlett and Sellers. "Hell, you six, go with the pilot and get the resupply unloaded. Move."

"Appreciate it, soldier," Benny said.

The soldier nodded. "My pleasure, sir," he replied politely, remorse laced in his tone. "Happy flying, and keep those supplies coming. We're going to need them."

"No doubt," Benny replied, and followed the six soldiers through the field.

It took a few minutes, but they managed to get all the supplies unloaded, and Benny climbed up into the helicopter.

"Sellers, Bartlett," he said, nodding to the young Privates. "Glad we got to spend some time together."

Sellers grinned. "Pleasure was ours, sir," he said.

"When we get this place pacified," the pilot continued, "don't be afraid to look me up. First round is on me."

Bartlett smirked. "If we hit round ten, then maybe we can get Sellers here his special night," she teased.

Benny barked a laugh and wagged his finger at her. "Love the live ones," he said, and winked at her. "Ten rounds it is. Now, y'all be safe out there." He hopped into the hot seat, firing up the chopper, and lifted off, giving a little wave to the soldiers on the ground before heading for the ship.

CHAPTER THIRTEEN

Benny landed on the deck, surprising
some of the soldiers. It took a moment
before they leapt into action and started
working on the chopper, but he hopped down
and strolled right past them, not saying a
word.

He walked into the ready room as
casual as a cat, and Captain McCall leapt
up from his desk.

"Good god man, are you okay?" he
demanded. "You've been gone for hours!"

Benny spread his arms and shrugged.
"Yeah, the landing site got overrun," he
explained, "and I had to wait to be
rescued." He unbuckled the gun holster,
but the Captain held up a hand to stop
him.

"Consider it yours for as long as you
need it," he insisted.

The pilot nodded and closed the
buckle again. "Thanks, although I could
probably use another mag," he said. "Had
to put it into action right after
landing."

McCall whistled sharply and pointed
to a soldier that darted over to them.
"Give the man your mags," he instructed.

The young soldier didn't even miss a
beat, just took out a few mags and handed

them over before rushing back to the wall to continue working.

"So," Benny drawled as he pocketed them, "what's the next mission of the day?"

The Captain motioned for him to follow and headed over to a map of downtown. "Welcome to downtown Seattle," he said. "If everything goes to plan by morning, we're going to be pushing on towards it to clear it out. Those strafing runs to the east were very effective, and the group that rescued you is going to be pushing across the bridge this evening. Which means it's time to get snipers in place."

Benny nodded, letting out a sigh of relief. "After the last few runs, I'm perfectly okay with staying a couple hundred yards off of the ground," he admitted.

"Then this mission has your name all over it," McCall replied. "Shouldn't be too difficult. You're going to have eight men to a trip." He pointed to various spots on the map as he spoke. "And we're just going to have you drop them off at these locations. Once you do, I'd like you to do some aerial recon for us of the immediate area."

"Aerial recon?" Benny asked. "Thought you had real time satellite uplinks?"

The Captain cocked his head. "We do," he replied, "but they're concentrated on the current front lines. You don't have to spend long on it, just get up there and see what you can see. If we're walking into a shitshow, it would be nice to know ahead of time."

"Captain, with the way this week is going," the pilot drawled, "is there really any question about whether or not it's a shitshow?"

McCall sighed and shook his head. "From your mouth to god's ears," he muttered, and then pointed to a nearby soldier. "He'll have your flight plan for you. Snipers are getting geared up and will meet you on the deck in ten." He turned away, but then raised a hand and turned back. "Oh, and I'll be on comm, so if there's a problem, just radio it in, and we'll mark it."

Benny nodded and grabbed his flight plan from the soldier on the way back out to the deck. The mechanics were still giving his helicopter some love, so he wandered over to the edge, looking out over the water.

The sun wasn't low, but it was certainly on the way down. It would be a couple of hours at most before he'd be night flying.

Yeah Benny, night flying ain't that bad, even on with as little sleep you've gotten this week, he thought to himself. *You could be on the ground pushing forward.*

He took a deep breath and thought about the dangerous spot these soldiers were in, especially kids like Sellers and Bartlett.

Benny flew the chopper towards downtown with eight snipers in tow. In the distance, plumes of smoke rose into the air.

Looks like someone is having some fun with molotov cocktails, he thought, smiling to himself. *Either that or someone found a flamethrower.*

When they got closer, he looked straight down on the streets, seeing them completely packed with ghouls. Shoulder-to-shoulder, they spread through the downtown core like rivers of death. One of the snipers, Rich, sat in the passenger seat, and adjusted his headset so he could converse with the pilot.

"There's a whole lotta heads in need of shooting down there," he declared.

Benny wrinkled his nose. "Given that we got off the ground," he drawled, "I'm fairly confident that you boys don't have enough ammo to make that happen."

"Just means you'll have to bring us some backup rounds," Rich replied with a smile.

The pilot inclined his head. "Only if I get to squeeze off a few rounds with your rifle there," he said mischievously. "Those fuckers are packed so tight, I'm bound to hit something."

"You got a deal," the sniper replied, giving him a thumbs up. "Most of our job is to distract them, so you won't be doing any harm."

Benny grinned. "I'm gonna hold you to that!" he declared and then looked around at the several target buildings coming into view. "You boys have a preference?" he asked. "You want the top of the world? Or something a little more down to earth?"

"Down to earth if you don't mind," Rich replied. "Less wind blowing in our faces and pushing our shots every which way. Let those slackers who didn't volunteer to go first deal with that."

Benny nodded. "You got it," he said, and chuckled at the surly sniper. He found the shortest building on his target list, a fifteen story hotel near the north of town. "Hang tight, we're coming in."

He picked his spot on the roof and lowered down perfectly, barely jostling his passengers. As soon as they touched down, the soldiers cracked open the door and filed out.

Before Rich slipped out, he gave Benny a fist bump. "We'll see you soon," he promised. "My gun will be ready for you to fire."

"Gonna be a blast," the pilot replied. "Y'all stay safe."

Rich jumped down and slammed the door shut, before moving back with his team. Benny lifted off to do his tour of the city, giving them a wave as he left. When he had a good view of the downtown area, he pulled out his radio and called back to the ship.

"Captain McCall, do you copy?" he asked.

A moment later, the Captain came back, "What you got for me, Benny?"

"Downtown is a total clusterfuck," Benny explained. "Roads are packed thick with those things, and it's going to be a bitch and a half to clear them out."

"We figured as much," McCall replied, "and we think we have a plan for that."

Benny's brow furrowed. "You *think* you have a plan?" he asked. "That's comforting to know."

"We've had to use up a lot of resources so far," the Captain explained, "so the initial plans are out the window. We gotta think on our feet."

Benny sighed. "Yeah, I'll buy that," he admitted. "I'm gonna head south and work my way back up the eastern side."

"Copy that," McCall replied.

He flew to the south end of town, seeing there was a lot of empty space. There were still thousands of ghouls on the streets, but they were spread out, unlike the traffic jam downtown.

"That island diversion is still holding strong," he murmured. He found the coastline and started moving up north, keeping an eye on the ground below.

Tons of zombies moved about, but nothing too concerning. The area around the I-90 bridge leading to Mercer Island was a bit crowded, but they were well equipped to handle that problem.

He raised the radio to his lips. "Captain, just passed the I-90 bridge," he said. "It's a bit crowded, but I'm pretty sure you already knew that."

"Yeah, those boys have it locked down pretty good," McCall replied, "so we're not too concerned."

"Okay, moving up to check out the northeast," Benny replied, and continued flying to the northeast portion of the bridge leading down. As he grew closer, concern tightened in his belly.

Not only were the streets packed with zombies, but even the grassy areas were covered. Thousands, tens of thousands, all packed together, moved northward. With so much gunfire, and being so far away from Mercer Island, every undead body and their brother was headed that way.

The pilot was about to call it in when he paused, flying over a large park a few blocks east of the interstate. It was less than a mile to the bridge that the northern group would be pushing down from. The entire park was packed, looking like an out of control zombie music festival.

His eyes widened, and he raised the radio to his mouth. "Captain, we may have a problem to the north," he said quickly.

"What do you see?" McCall asked.

Benny shook his head. "I'm at some park just south of the bridge, and this place is hopping," he replied. "There's probably ten, fifteen thousand zombies just about there in the open. It's going to be hell to push through them."

"Sadly, there isn't much we can do about it," the Captain said. "We have a limited supply of missiles, and they're not keen on using them just on packs of zombies. Has to be some pressing issue to break them out."

The pilot clucked his tongue. "What about the Apaches, then?" he asked. "Those mini-guns will clear them right out!"

"Same thing," McCall countered, though he at least sounded regretful. "Limited resources that they're holding in their back pocket."

Benny growled. "That's bullshit," he spat.

"For once I agree with you," the Captain said dryly. "But to somebody higher up, troops are easier to replace than weaponry, and unfortunately this just doesn't cut it."

The pilot fumed, clamping his mouth shut.

McCall sighed through the speaker. "I know you're pissed, believe me, I am too," he admitted. "But there's nothing we can do. Why don't you come on back to the ship and pick up another batch of shooters?"

Benny took a deep breath. "Captain, I have an idea," he said.

"I'm listening," McCall replied.

"Some Sergeant down at Renton airport jury-rigged some firebombs to clear out some of those things on the interstate," the pilot explained. "He said he was making a few more up. It might not clear them all out, but should put a dent in them. What do you say?"

There was a long pause, and then finally the Captain said, "I say go for it. But if anybody asks, you told me to go fuck myself and did it anyway."

Benny barked a laugh. "Don't worry," he said, "if it comes to that, I'll make it sound believable."

"I don't doubt it," McCall replied, chuckling. "I'll let the snipers know you'll be running behind. Be safe, and happy hunting."

Benny put the radio down and swooped towards the Renton airport, flying as fast as his bird would go.

Benny landed at the airport and quickly powered down, hopping out of the chopper before the blades finished spinning. A soldier approached him immediately.

"Where's Sergeant Farley?" Benny asked before the soldier could speak.

"I think he's around here somewhere," the Private replied.

The pilot nodded. "Take me to him, quickly," he urged, and the soldier nodded, motioning for the older man to follow.

They moved at a power walk, into one of the hangars, where Farley and Barnes stood around several oil drums.

"Sergeant Farley," the soldier called as they approached, "this man needs to speak with you."

Farley turned and spotted Benny, and his face lit up in a while. "I tell you what, you have impeccable timing!" he exclaimed. "We just got something special rigged up."

"Good, because we need it," the pilot replied, taking a deep breath.

Barnes' brow furrowed. "There another horde on the interstate?"

"We need to take something up to the northern group," Benny replied, shaking his head. "They're pushing towards downtown and they're in some trouble."

Farley smacked his hand down on one of the six oil drums in the center of the room. "Well, this will certainly do the trick!"

"This looks a little bigger than the other ones," Benny mused.

The Sergeant grinned. "Pack a hell of a bigger punch too," he declared. "Found a stash of jet fuel and filled these puppies up."

"Jet fuel?" the pilot asked, shocked and amused. "Here I was thinking we were just going to burn these things up. And here you are, ready to reduce them to liquid. I'm fucking in."

Barnes clapped his hands together. "So, what are we dealing with up there?"

"Ten, maybe fifteen thousand of those things in a park," Benny replied, jerking his thumb over his shoulder. "The northern force is pushing south over the bridge and these things are ready to meet them head on. If we can clear them out, or at least thin their numbers, they should be able to get a foothold on the right side of the bridge."

Farley nodded. "No time like the present," he said, and moved behind one of the drums. "Let's start wheeling these things out."

"How are we detonating them?" Benny asked. "Pretty sure flaming rags aren't going to cut it this time."

Barnes grinned and held up a block of plastic explosive. "Little C4 should do the trick."

"I would tell Captain McCall what we're doing," Benny drawled, putting a finger to his chin, "but from the looks of it, he's going to hear about it right after it happens, anyway."

The Sergeant held out his hand and tilted it back and forth. "Probably," he said. "Does your bird out there have an under attachment?"

"Yeah, got a hook with a remote release," the pilot replied, "why?"

Farley smirked. "Oh, you'll see."

The men laughed as the Sergeant motioned to some other soldiers to start moving the barrels outside.

Ten minutes later, the half-dozen barrels were on the runway, bundled together tightly on top of a heavy duty net. Once they were on there, they wrapped them up and prepped the whole shebang to be lifted off of the ground by the chopper.

"That is one big-ass bomb," Benny breathed as he stared at their handiwork.

Barnes crossed his arms, puffing out his chest. "I gotta tell you Sarge, that's a piece of work," he agreed.

"You got the detonator?" Farley asked.

Barnes held it up, a big grin on his face, rivalling a kid's at Christmas. "Ready to lay waste to some zombies."

"Then let's make it happen," the Sergeant replied. "Benny, you mind dropping us after?" he asked.

The pilot shook his head. "Not at all," he replied. "Just wouldn't be fair if you did all the work and didn't get to see it go off. Let's ride."

The trio got into the helicopter, and Benny fired it up, lifting up and hovering over the makeshift bomb. The grounds crew successfully attached it to the bottom, and he took off.

There was a bit of a drag on the chopper as it struggled for a moment to carry the weight, but once they got going, it was smooth sailing. The trip took a bit of extra time, and Barnes and Farley took in the bird's-eye view of the battlefield.

Even as the sun began to set in the west, they could still see the zombies stretched out from the coastline, plumes of smoke rising in the distance as god only knew what was burning.

"How would you like to be on that cleanup crew?" Farley asked, leaning in.

Barnes shook his head vigorously. "I'm quite content being on the demolition crew, thank you very much."

Farley laughed and smacked his partner on the back. The rest of the ride was spent in relative silence as they watched the zombie hordes below, growing in size in an almost mesmerizing fashion.

Finally they arrived at the park, hovering five hundred yards above the mass below. Benny waved for Farley to come closer.

"I know this is going to be a big one," the pilot began, "but realistically, how big are we talking? Just trying to figure out how far away we need to be, so we don't get caught up in it."

The Sergeant licked his lips nervously. "I'll be honest, never done anything this big," he admitted. "I'd say you can't go wrong going up to a thousand yards and then hauling ass after you drop the load."

"That detonator have a good enough range on it for that kind of escape?" Benny asked, inclining his head to Barnes.

"Oh yeah," Farley assured him, "it's rated for a mile, and with as heavy as that thing is, it won't take that long to hit the ground."

The pilot nodded. "All right, I'll get in position," he replied, and gave the Sergeant a thumbs up.

He rose into the air, hitting a thousand yards up, hovering over the center of the park. He looked down to make sure he was right in the middle.

Even if the wind catches it, that thing won't get outside of the park, he thought. *And even if it does, there's still going to be massive damage done.*

He turned and gave the boys a wave, and Barnes held up the detonator, flicking it on so that it was armed.

Benny took a deep breath, hitting the necessary switches on the console. Beneath the chopper, the *click* of the unlatching mechanism holding the bomb was loud. A moment later, it was free, tumbling to the ground below.

He immediately started moving forward as fast as the bird would go. Barnes kept a close eye on the bomb as it hurtled for the park, and just before it hit the grass, he pulled the trigger on the detonator.

The sound was deafening, the shock wave lurching the chopper forward. Benny struggled for control, keeping his breathing steady as he fought it, but quickly regained it. He breathed a sigh of relief as he looked out of his now-cracked windshield.

"Goddamn, that was a hell of a blast," he muttered, and then turned around so they could get a good view of things.

The sight was spectacular.

The bomb illuminated the dusky sky, the cloud of smoke rising above the height of the helicopter. They looked to the ground below, and it was a wasteland. Charred bodies, trees ripped from the root, nary a corpse still standing.

For a moment, they sat in amazement, triumph blooming in their chests.

The radio blipped, and Farley laughed. "Uh-oh Benny, looks like you're in trouble," he teased.

"Oh now, what are they going to do?" the pilot asked playfully, rolling his eyes. "Retire me to a comfy life of not flying into danger?"

The Sergeant cocked his head. "Shit, if they're going to do that, tell them it was all my idea," he offered.

Benny picked up the radio and raised it to his lips. "Had a feeling you might be calling," he said calmly.

"I was going to ask how the mission was going," McCall said, "but we heard that blast all the way out here. What in the hell did you do?"

The pilot smirked. "Have you ever seen a barrel of jet fuel detonate, Captain?"

"Can't say that I have," McCall admitted.

Benny grinned. "Well, now you can say that you've heard six of them detonate," he declared.

"Jesus Christ," McCall blurted, laughing. "Well, was it successful?"

The pilot nodded. "Oh yeah, leveled the entire park," he said, "and probably some of the nearby houses as well."

"Well, that's good, because I just got word that the northern force has moved across the bridge and are headed south as we speak," McCall replied.

Benny smiled. "That is good news, Captain," he said. "As soon as I drop off my two accomplices…" He paused, winking at Farley. "I mean… passengers, I'll be back to the ship to pick up the next load of snipers."

"I'll make sure they're ready," McCall said. "And Benny?"

The pilot's brow furrowed. "Yeah?"

"Good job out there," the Captain replied firmly.

Benny just smiled and put down the radio. "You boys ready to head back?" he asked.

"Whenever you are," Farley replied, patting him on the shoulder. "We're on your schedule."

The pilot nodded and continued to hover, taking one last look at the explosion site. It had been a long day, but he took pride in the amount of good he'd been able to accomplish. After that brief moment of enjoying the feeling, he maneuvered the helicopter to head back to Renton airport.

There was a lot more to get done before the assault on downtown was complete.

END

Up Next: A group of civilians risk their lives to warn the military of a deadly threat in Seattle Pt. 8

DEAD AMERICA
THE NORTHWEST INVASION
BOOK 10
SEATTLE PART 8
BY DEREK SLATON
© 2020

CHAPTER ONE

"Are you sure you want to bet all your chips?" Marcus raised an eyebrow, tapping the back of his fanned out cards. "Don't want you to go hungry, now."

Skylar's tongue darted out, and she wet her lips, smirking. "That sounds like a man afraid to call," she teased. "You'd have to dip into the sour cream and onion to match this bet."

Sporadic gunfire still echoed in the distance, a constant reminder that there was still hope in this shitshow.

"Okay," he said with a sigh, shoving the rest of the sour cream and onion chips into the center of the patio table. "I'll call."

"Read 'em and weep," she declared, laying down a full house.

Marcus groaned, picking up a rippled barbecue chip out of what was left of his pile and munching on it to soothe his loss. "I really thought you were bluffing," he admitted through a mouthful of fried potato.

"When will you ever learn?" Skylar replied, rolling her eyes. "We've been together four years and you still can't see through my poker face." She grabbed the cards and began to shuffle them idly, leaning back in her chair.

He chuckled. "Your poker face is what hooked me in in the first place, remember?" He took a small sip of the cold tea they'd managed to brew on the windowsill over the course of a few days. "You wiped the floor with those guys back in college."

"Oh my god, I forgot about that," she replied, laughing. "Jamie got so mad that night because he was trying to impress some sorority girl."

He shook his head. "And you were just cool as a cucumber as he threw a drunken temper tantrum," he said wistfully. "I'm pretty sure I fell in love with you on the spot."

"Is that why you asked me out that night?" She fluttered her eyelashes at him. "Because I can beat the boys at their silly games?"

He shook his head, reaching over to cover her hand with his. "No," he replied. "Because the silly games didn't affect you in the slightest."

"And that's why I said no to the silly drunk guy asking me out at a frat party," she replied with a twinkle in her eye.

Marcus put a hand to his chest. "That hurt," he admitted with an overdramatic pout.

"Hey," Skylar said, pointing a finger at him, "at least I wasn't a total snow queen. I told you to ask me again when you were sober. Because I didn't think you really meant it."

He grabbed her finger and brought it to his mouth, giving it an affectionate kiss. "But I *did* mean it," he said. "I just needed the booze to give me the courage to ask."

"Silly boy," she teased, and leaned in to peck him on the lips. Before she pulled away, she snatched one of his barbecue chips and shoved it in her mouth, leaning back in her chair with her prize.

"You fight so dirty," he moaned.

She winked playfully. "Don't you forget it, babe."

"You know, we should probably bag these up before they get stale and cook something real to eat," Marcus said with a sigh, smacking his thighs before he got to his feet. "If we have anything real left."

Skylar got up, slipping the deck of cards back into its cardboard case. "Pork and beans it is!" she declared.

They took a moment to look over the edge of the patio, watching the river of zombies fourteen stories down move towards the noise in the distance.

"You think eventually they'll just all clear out?" she wondered, running a hand through her long brown hair. "Just all of 'em, wander out towards the lake, and leave everything this close to the interstate empty?"

He shrugged. "I don't know…" he trailed off, looking out to the water. Their condo, the Lakeview high rise, stood tall at eighteen stories above South Lake Union, five blocks from the shore.

They'd spotted boats in Lake Union a few days prior and hadn't been sure if they were civilian or military. However, with all the gunfire happening, they were pretty sure it was the latter.

"I hope they can deal with it all so they can come get us," she mused as she gathered up all the chips and shoved them back into the large sealable bag they'd been keeping the last of their salty snacks in. "They're the military, they'll never run out of ammo, right?"

Marcus reached over and pulled her against him, curling an arm around her waist. "I'd hope that if they're sending boats in to fight them that they came prepared," he replied, and leaned in to plant a kiss on the top of her head. "Now, how about them beans?"

"Oh, am I cooking for you, Mister Man?" she asked, blinking up at him with a playfully defiant look on her face. "Send the woman to the kitchen? Should I go barefoot?"

He swatted her backside, sending her giggling in through the patio door. "You could wear nothing at all," he suggested, waggling his eyebrows.

"Oh yeah," she replied, rolling her eyes as she pulled a can out of the cupboard. "Super sexy, naked bean cooking."

He winked at her as he set up the little gas camping stove they'd been using since the apocalypse began. "Everything you do is sexy," he assured her.

She opened her mouth to retort something back, but before she could, an explosion rattled the windows.

"What the hell was that?!" Skylar cried, frantically looking out the patio door to see what had exploded in the distance.

Marcus headed for the front door of the condo. "I think it came from the other side," he said. "Let's check across the hall." He threw the door open and entered the condo across the way, which had been empty pre-apocalypse, even devoid of furniture.

The couple burst out onto the patio and clutched the railing, staring wide-eyed at the plume of smoke rising from Volunteer Park. Troops poured down the interstate, guns blazing.

"They're coming this way!" Skylar cried, pumping her fist into the air.

"Fuck yeah!" Marcus added, and wrapped his arms around her waist, swinging her around in a circle. They laughed and kissed, happiness radiating from them almost as if they weren't standing on a high-rise above a sea of walking corpses.

High on hope and adrenaline, they turned back towards the interstate, staring at the approaching army. Skylar was first to sober a bit, however, as she looked down at the glass siding of the patio. A jagged line zigzagged across it. She turned around, looking at the windows of the condo, cold dread sinking over her when she saw the weakened panes of glass.

"Marcus…" she said hoarsely, face rapidly losing color.

He turned around, goofy smile fading from his face, and his brow furrowed when he realized what she was looking at. "Shit," he breathed, his own expression sobering.

Their building had, at one time, been a convention hotel, before it had been repurposed into luxury condos five years prior. The convention center on the main floor had been modified into massive amenities, like a giant pool and a gym with courts for all manner of sports.

When people started getting sick, the whole convention center had become a makeshift rescue center for people, before anyone had known about blood type or infections or how the outbreak worked.

The high rise was sitting on top of a sprawling building full of thousands of flesh-eating zombies.

And now the windows were cracked.

"We need to talk to Jax," Marcus said firmly, and grabbed Skylar's hand.

The couple took off back into the condo and tore down the hallway together. They thundered down the stairs to the twelfth floor and then paused to take a look at the barricade they'd built. Couches and TV stands and recliners piled up to the ceiling, everything they'd been able to throw down there.

"How's it look?" Skylar whispered as Marcus leaned over the railing to check the activity below.

He tilted his head back and forth. There were dozens of zombies still down there on the other side, but at least they weren't pressing up against the barricade. "As good as it needs to look," he replied quietly, and then turned around to the stairwell door.

They headed down the hallway on the twelfth floor and found the condo they'd been looking for. Marcus turned the knob, finding it unlocked, and the duo burst inside.

Jax startled as they tore into his condo, looking up from his ham radio set up in the middle of the living room. He unlocked the brakes on his wheelchair and backed away from the table a touch, turning to face the fear-stricken duo.

"Can you hang on a sec, Lennox?" he asked, and set down the mouthpiece for his radio.

Marcus crossed the room to the patio door. Jax's condo, being on the east side, had been privy to the blast, and the glass door was completely shattered, shards littering the carpet.

"Are you okay?" Skylar asked, wringing her hands as she approached the wheelchair-bound man. "Did you see the explosion?"

He nodded. "Yeah, I'm okay, wasn't near the windows when it happened," he replied. "Any damage on your side?"

"No, but everything's cracked across the hall," Marcus replied, turning back from the patio. "Looks like the military's finally shown up, they're marching up the interstate. It looks like they blew up the park."

Jax's eyes lit up. "The cavalry's arrived, huh?"

"But the main floor…" Skylar trailed off, her voice cracking. "If those windows are broken…"

The wheelchair-bound man shook his head. "They won't be broken," he assured her. "The convention center probably has safety stuff, so not as fragile as ours." He tilted his head back and forth. "But… they could be weakened. I wouldn't want to bet on them holding with a thousand of those things banging on them."

"We need to warn them," Marcus said firmly, jerking a thumb over his shoulder in the general direction of their rescuers. "They're going to get overrun if the convention center can't hold."

Skylar swallowed hard. "But how?" She shook her head. "We haven't been able to go lower than this floor, there's too many of those things. Even if we could figure out how to get to the main floor, we don't know how packed it is down there. I don't think we could even get through there, let alone get outside and get to the interstate."

Marcus turned and stared out the broken door, chewing his bottom lip. "I don't think there's an efficient way to signal them from here, or even from the top floor," he mused. "I mean, we could let them know we're here, but I don't know how we could convey the probable danger."

"I can try to convince Lennox to go," Jax said, rubbing his chin. "He's not going to want to."

"Well, we'll have a bit of time to convince him," Marcus said, pointing through the door. "Looks like these boys are going to have their hands full for the next little bit."

Skylar approached him, sliding her arm into the crook of his elbow and holding on tight. A huge pack of zombies staggered up the interstate towards the army, and it wasn't long before gunfire cracked in the distance.

"I'm afraid to hope," she admitted quietly.

He leaned over and planted a kiss on top of her head affectionately. "Do you remember the last marathon we ran?" he asked, turning her away from the window to face him. "When the last week before, we saw Brad Perkins training?"

"Ugh, Brad fucking Perkins," she scoffed, rolling her eyes.

Marcus smiled, watching her shoulders relax a little as her mind flipped to her memories instead of their possible impending doom. "He was such a dick that day, and bragging about his speed," he reminded her. "Even though we already knew his stats."

"Everybody on social media knows his stats," she muttered. "I would have respected his accomplishments if he hadn't been such a jerk face."

"And you told me that you were afraid to hope to beat him," he said, giving her hand a reassuring squeeze.

She shook her head. "This isn't a good analogy, babe," she said. "He beat us that marathon."

"Yes, but a teenage girl threw a milkshake in his face when he did," Marcus reminded her with a smirk.

Skylar chuckled. "That was pretty satisfying."

"*And*, even though we didn't win, we still raised a ton of money for Kid's Wish," he added, cupping her cheek. "We did a lot of good that day. Do you see what I'm getting at?"

She sighed. "That even if we die horribly, our actions might still help people?" she asked.

"I mean, well…" he trailed off, wrinkling his nose. "I guess that's one interpretation. My point was that there could be unexpected victory despite things not going exactly according to plan."

She offered him a smile, leaning into his palm. "Thanks," she replied. "It does make me feel a bit more confident."

He wrapped her in a hug, resting his chin on her head as he watched Jax roll back over to the ham radio.

The wheelchair-bound man took a deep breath and picked up the receiver. "You still there, Lennox?" he asked.

"Yeah, bud, you okay?" came the strained reply.

"Yeah, I mean, as well as I can be, given the circumstances," Jax said. "We need your help."

"This is… no," Lennox said, voice breathy and panicked. "No, I can't help anyone. That explosion has my head spinning, I don't even know which way is up, man. What am I supposed to do to help anyone?"

Jax swallowed hard. "That explosion weakened all the windows in our building," he explained. "The convention center on the main floor has about a thousand of those things inside, and if they push hard enough, they're going to get out. We need to warn the military, or else they're going to get overrun. And that means no rescue for us."

"No, no," came the immediate reply. "I can't do that."

Jax shook his head. "But you can," he said calmly. "I know you can. You didn't think you could survive in the early days of all of this, but I knew you could, and guess what? You're still alive."

"I wouldn't have without you helping me," Lennox insisted. "I would have been fucked in the first twenty-four hours if you hadn't have guided me."

Jax nodded. "And I'm guiding you now, still," he replied. "I know you can do this."

There was a long pause, and then his friend finally asked, "What about the others? The other people you helped?"

The wheelchair-bound man lowered his gaze. "There's only one left, and he's too far away to make it in time," he explained. "Everyone else… everyone else is gone."

Lennox groaned in frustration through the radio, seeming to war with himself.

"I know it's difficult," Jax continued gently. "I can't even begin to understand what you're going through, what you've been going through since the start of all of this. But this is the only way to save lives. You're the only one who can help them."

Another long pause. "Okay," he finally said, eliciting triumphant smiles from the trio in the room. "I'll do it."

CHAPTER THREE

Lennox buried his face in his hands as the gunfire cracked in the distance. Images of bleeding and gutted bodies flicked through his mind, the screams of his comrades echoing in his brain like a chant of death. Muzzle flashes, explosions, the stench of shit and mud and copper mingling together in a heady cocktail of despair.

The explosion in the park had nearly sent him into a spiral, but instead of running to the closet, he'd run to the radio. He'd known that his one chance at a lifeline was Jax. The guy had been the guardian angel against his demons throughout this whole ordeal, not only having guided him home throughout the early days, but just being there for him as a friend, keeping him from falling into himself and becoming lost forever.

And now, now Jax was counting on *him*.

Pull your shit together, Lennox, he urged himself. *Lives are at stake… if you don't want these military boys to suffer, you have to help them.*

Steeling his resolve, he scrubbed his hands down his face and got to his feet. He looked around at his fortress, the house he'd barricaded himself in. The house that had protected him from those flesh-eating monsters outside.

"Okay," he muttered to himself, running his hands through his hair. "You're ten blocks south of the park. Gotta gear up and get the fuck moving."

He headed to his closet, the one holding all of his old gear. It was a particular closet that he hadn't opened in a long time. But it was time to face that fear and trepidation, now. Because this stuff would save his life.

He opened the cardboard box in the back and pulled out a leather holster with his service revolver and an extra mag. Behind it was a consumer grade assault rifle, with two extra mags, and he slung it over his shoulder. He sheathed his hunting knife, and snatched up a small LED flashlight, stuffing it into his pocket just in case.

Lastly, was his combat boots. He reached out slowly, hand shaking, gripping the boots between his fingers to lift them out. The toe still had a dark splotch of something—*blood, that's still blood on there*—but he shook his head as if he could shake the memories right out of it.

He laced up his boots and stood up, puffing out his chest to try to feel strong. He was out of shape. It had been a long time since he'd served, and with his

PTSD he hadn't kept up any kind of vigorous activity.

"No time like the present," he muttered. "Let's go do some cardio, Lennox."

He dug around in his front hall drawer until he found an old map of the area and spread it out on the small table. The streets were packed full of zombies, given all of the noise, but he had fourteen blocks to get through before he could reach the troops.

"If the park is blown out, it's probably safest to try to go through there," he mused, tapping his finger on Volunteer Park. He leaned over and peeked through two of the boards he'd nailed over the window next to the front door. There was a big enough slit that he could get a lay of the land, and his stomach knotted with dread and the sheer amount of ghouls heading up the street.

He was going to have to get creative.

He moved to the back of the house and peered out into the backyard. Luckily, there was nothing inside of his chest-high fence, which had thankfully held despite the hordes wandering around.

Lennox closed his eyes for a moment, taking a deep, steadying breath, and then cracked open the back door. He clenched his jaw at the cracking of gunfire in the distance. It was louder out here, and he reminded himself that it would just get louder and louder the closer he got.

He slipped outside, closing the door quietly behind him, creeping across the grass as stealthily as he could. His heart pounded in his chest, and he took a deep breath before peeking through the slats of the privacy fence.

You got a long way to go, Lennox, he thought to himself. *This isn't the time to get all freaked out. You got this.*

The groups of ghouls on the street here weren't as thick, spread out in packs of three or four. He waited for a considerable gap and then wrapped his fingers around the top of the fence. He grunted as he pulled himself up and over, landing on the other side with a louder *thud* than he'd anticipated.

Two nearby zombies turned to him, mouths open, but he simply ran past them. He was out of shape and not the fastest, but he was still faster than shambling corpses.

He made it to a front yard across the street, and then crouched behind a line of bushes, staying low as he continued to move up. The next few yards were clear, but up ahead he spotted two ghouls hanging out in a front flower garden, mystified by the knee-high fence surrounding them.

How'd you even get in there… he
wondered as he crept forward, drawing his
knife. He knew that he had to save his
guns for when he really needed them,
considering he didn't want to draw any
attention to himself. He stayed low,
pressing himself against the back of a
white picket fence as he moved towards his
target.

He pushed his way between two bushes,
and then leapt out, burying his knife into
the back of one zombie's head. He wrenched
it free and whipped to the side, stabbing
the second one in the temple, and then
ducked back into the bushes, waiting to
see if he'd attracted any attention.

He didn't hear any excited moans or
feet shuffling closer and chanced peeking
out at the street. He nodded to himself in
triumph, and surveyed the yards ahead.
They were all very open, and with the
zombies in the street getting thicker, he
wasn't sure he wanted to chance jumping
from tree trunk to tree trunk without
anywhere to retreat to.

He peered through the gap between
houses and realized the backyards didn't
have privacy fences. He'd been reluctant
to do all the backyards on his side
because he didn't think he'd make it
hopping every fence without being too
winded to complete his mission.

He moved down the gap and pressed himself against the back corner, peering out. The backyards were all linked in a big long row, with no fences backing into thick brush. It would be a gamble as to whether or not there were monsters in the trees, but it was a better gamble than the ones he knew were on the street.

Lennox took off like a shot. He stayed closer to the houses, keeping his eyes forward and every so often glancing over at the brush to make sure nothing was hurtling out at him.

He had the fleeting thought that the more the military fought, the higher likelihood there would be of fresh zombies that would be fast, faster than him. He shook it off. He couldn't worry about that right now. The troops would have tons more fast zombies if they got overrun by the ones breaking out of the convention center.

At the end of the row, he skidded to a stop, panting, pressing himself against the brick wall of the house. The zombie river continued on the main road, and he took a deep breath and sprinted across to the backyard ahead.

He darted through a kid's sandbox, and then nearly bowled back over into it as a pack of zombies poured out from between the houses. He knew he wouldn't be able to take them all. He backtracked, running along the side wall to the front yard. There was a dented van with flat tires in the driveway, and he ran behind it, catching his breath and hoping he wouldn't catch the attention of the street zombies.

The yards ahead were fairly open, and he cursed under his breath. He looked around frantically for something he could use as a distraction and noticed the open garage door nearby. Inside was a lawnmower, one of the self-propelling ones.

He chewed his lip. He could probably avoid notice getting in there to fire it up, but if it didn't work as he wanted it to, he'd be making a whole lot of noise that would give away his position without then diverting attention.

Think quick, think quick, he urged himself, weighing his options. As one of the backyard zombies stumbled into view, he realized he had to risk it.

Lennox tore for the garage, and quickly grabbed the rip cord for the lawnmower, giving it a quick jerk. The engine sputtered, but didn't come to life.

"Fuck, come on," he grunted, urging it to work. He pulled again, and nothing. Zombies in the street turned towards him excitedly. "Fuck, fuck, come ON!" he yelled, all semblance of stealth gone out the window.

He pulled again, and this time the lawnmower roared to life. He quickly pulled the lever and gave the mower a mighty push, sending it screaming down the driveway. It clipped a few zombies on the way by, and they turned in confusion towards the machine.

It hit the main stream, and then let out a loud whine as it couldn't go any further. Lennox took his opportunity as the ghouls turned towards it, reaching down and losing fingers to the spinning blades as the lawnmower fell over onto its side.

He knew it wouldn't last forever, so he took off like a shot, staying as close to the houses as he could, while the zombies concentrated on the cackling lawnmower.

The ghouls farther up seemed confused, unsure of whether to go towards the gunfire, the lawnmower, or pay attention to the blur running to their right. Lennox didn't pay attention to them. He had his eye on the prize, needing to take this a block at a time.

He managed to clear the second block, the wind whipping through his hair and heart pounding in his ears. Eight more to go.

CHAPTER FOUR

Four blocks from the park, Lennox
ducked into a child's wooden playhouse in
a backyard. He needed to take a breather,
and the zombies were thick everywhere. The
yard was surrounded by a waist-high chain
link fence, and before long ghouls pressed
up against it.

*How the hell do you know that I'm in
here?* He grunted. He didn't want to get
caught stuck in this little playhouse. It
was nice, for a playhouse, but there were
lots of open windows and he'd be zombie
chow for sure if he got surrounded.

He groaned as he crawled out of the
little house, swallowing hard at the sight
of ghouls all along the fences. *Shit,* he
thought, *shouldn't have stopped.*

He jogged across the yard, stepping
up onto the back porch and peering in the
sliding door. There was no movement
inside, so he tried opening it, but it was
locked.

"Of fucking course," he muttered, and
looked around. The patio set, though
overturned and splattered with blood,
looked relatively sturdy, with thick metal
chair legs. He picked one up and gave it a
mighty swing, cracking the glass of the
sliding door.

There was a sickening creak behind
him, and he glanced over his shoulder to
see the fence buckling beneath the weight
of the hungry ghouls. He took another
swing, and this time the glass gave way.
He shoved the chair forward, knocking out
any little pieces that could cut him on
the way in.

He jumped through the frame and
grabbed a hold of the massive refrigerator
beside him, dragging it over and shoving
it into place to block the door. He peered
around it, seeing ghouls tripping over the
chain link, pouring in from the
neighboring area.

Need to scope out the front… he
thought. *Need a plan of escape… this thing
won't hold for long.*

He turned around, and then
immediately threw his hands out as a
zombie snapped at his face.

Lennox screamed something
unintelligible, shock turning his brain to
mush as he struggled to keep the monster's
teeth away from his tender flesh. He
needed a weapon, to grab for something on
his person, but if he let go with one arm,
he was worried he wouldn't be able to hold
the corpse back.

"How are these things so damn
strong?!" he huffed and pushed as hard as
he could. He was able to shove the ghoul

back into the stove, and wrestled with it,
trying to bend it back far enough so he
could lock his arm and grab for his knife.

There was a thump at the sliding
door, and he looked frantically over his
shoulder, seeing a cluster of zombies
smacking into the glass. The fridge
shuddered, and his vigor renewed, a burst
of strength pouring through his arm as he
bent the zombie back under the fume hood.

He pulled his knife and plunged it
into the ghoul's face, tearing it free and
then darting through the kitchen towards
the front of the house. A zombie staggered
out of a door to the left, and he
instinctively kicked at it, knocking it
back with a firm boot to the chest.

He quickly glanced into the living
room to make sure nothing else was going
to come out at him, and then dove onto the
fallen ghoul, stabbing it in the forehead.

Lennox scrambled to his feet as the
fridge began to squeak against the
linoleum, and tore for the front door. He
peered out the front window, seeing
clusters of zombies milling about. None of
them were paying attention to the house,
but they were enough close to the door
that he wouldn't have an easy time running
through them.

He muttered obscenities under his
breath and whirled around at the sound of

a muffled *bang*. Down the hallway, arms began to flail around the side of the fridge. He knew he didn't have much time.

He looked up the stairs. If the banging was coming from there, that meant more ghouls upstairs. But if they were banging around, there was a good chance they were locked in a room. He glanced back at the front door. A zombie shambled close to it, and he shook his head. He knew it would be suicide to go out that way. But he couldn't waffle for much longer, with the horde pushing through the makeshift barricade at the back.

Lennox shook his head and ran up the stairs, taking them two at a time. He stopped on the landing, checking all the doors, and a *bang* came from the closed one on the left. He selected the bathroom, which was adjacent to the house next door, and slammed the door behind him, locking it for good measure.

"Okay, okay, what now?" He hurried to the small frosted-glass window and slid it open. It would be a tight squeeze, but he'd be able to make it through if he sucked in his gut. He punched out the screen and stuck his head out.

There were a few zombies wandering around in the grass below, but he wasn't keen on dropping all the way to the ground. He looked left and right, noting that just to the right of him was a little outcropping of roof that overhung a small room on the side of the house. Across from that was a tree, with decently strong looking branches, and then the roof of the bungalow next door.

He wasn't too excited by the prospect of being treed by zombies, or potentially being stuck on a roof surrounded by a sea of them. The bathroom door rattled on its hinges, wet *smacks* resonating, and he took a deep breath. There was no backtracking now.

At least if I can get across without detection, maybe there's less on the other side of the bungalow, he thought, and took a deep breath. The banging on the door intensified, and he shook his head.

He took his rifle from his shoulder and hung it out the window, giving it a light toss to the outcropping of roof. It hit on the butt and slid down the shingles. He watched in horror as it slipped off of the edge, and then his breath resumed as the strap caught on the eavestrough. It swung dangerously by half of the strap, and he shook his head. At least he had his other weapons, but the rifle was a nice little extra feeling of security in the world of flesh-eating monsters.

He put his hands on the window frame and wriggled his way through the opening. As expected, it was tight around his middle, and he cursed his lack of activity since his military years. PTSD and cheesies were good for nobody.

There was a moment of panic where he thought for sure he wouldn't make it through, and be forced to stay here, stuck as his legs got eaten on the other side. He couldn't even reach any of his weapons to shoot himself and spare the pain and agony.

"Fuck that," he grunted, and took a deep breath, flexing his abs as hard as he could and sucking in.

Lennox finally managed to budge, and struggle free of the window frame. He sat on it for a moment, legs hanging over the toilet, and tried to ignore the furious slamming on the bathroom door. The gap between the window and the roof wasn't small, and he needed to psych himself up.

Remember that raid where you were stuck in that flaming house, and you had to jump across to a flimsy old truck? He pulled his knees in, carefully planting his feet on the windowsill and hanging there in a crouch. *That was a way bigger jump than this. You did that, and you got four greenie Privates to do it. They'd make fun of you now old man, waffling over this piddly ass jump.*

He reached up and grabbed a hold of the top of the window frame, bending his knees and getting ready to spring.

The bathroom door gave a sickening *crunch* as he leapt, kicking off as hard as he could. He curled his legs up, willing them to catch the shingles, willing his body to fly far enough.

As soon as hit boots hit the roof, he immediately scrabbled for hand holds, not wanting to succumb to the same fate as his rifle. When he managed to steady himself, he stayed stock still, a tableau of relief on his hands and feet on the roof like a cat.

He took a few deep, shuddering breaths, and then there was a great *crack* from the bathroom and moans echoed through the window. Before long, rotted arms reached through the hole, and he clenched his jaw, marveling at how quickly he could have become their snack.

He leaned down and grabbed the strap of the rifle, somehow still hanging by the eavestrough, and pulled it up, slinging securely over his back once again.

Lennox turned, careful to steady his boots on the declined surface, and eyed the tree. The branches suddenly didn't look so sturdy now that he was faced with jumping to them, but he had no choice now.

He studied his points of entry, choosing a thick branch off shooting the trunk at an angle that was just right for a foothold. He rocked back and forth a few times, but before he could doubt himself he took a step and launched himself off of the shingles and into the tree.

Branches smacked him in the face, slowing his momentum, but his front foot managed to find its target. He slipped, arms flailing and grabbing whatever he could, and he managed to hang on, feet pressed against the trunk as he gripped bowing branches in his fists.

Hungry moans floated up to him, and though he knew it was a bad idea to look down, he did it anyway. He had quite the audience down there, and they were just waiting for him to fail so they could get their snack.

"Not today, fuckers," he grunted, and kicked up his leg until it was securely between the trunk and branch he'd originally been aiming for. He heaved himself up, swinging an arm to grab onto the trunk.

He pulled, groaning loudly as he managed to get his body wedged between the two branches.

What was that about a big jump?
Lennox stared across at the bungalow roof
and chewed his bottom lip for a moment.
This was a significantly bigger gap, and
he couldn't take a run at it. He looked
around to see if there were any other
sturdy branches he could use as a stepping
stone.

One jutted out from the trunk at an
angle, and he reached down to push on it,
testing its strength. He planted one of
his boots onto it, and gently swung over,
putting his body weight on it.

Okay, a little closer now, he
thought, but he couldn't go any further
out on that branch without it bowing too
much, potentially breaking. He looked down
at his audience again, and shook his head.
So much for doing this stealthily.

All he could do was hope to get
across the bungalow fast enough to find a
gap to jump down through.

"Is this trip over yet?" he muttered
and then rocked back and forth a bit to
wind up his leap.

He finally pushed off, raising his
feet again, and when the balls of his feet
connected with the edge of the bungalow,
he seemed to hang in the air for a moment,
nearly bowling back over into the sea of
death below.

He windmilled his arms wildly, managing to tip the scales just enough to fall forward, and dug his nails into one of the seams where the steel roof slats were bolted together. He hissed at the zing of pain in his fingers and managed to dig his toes into the eavestrough to alleviate the pressure on his fingernails.

He stayed like that for a moment, and then when he was sure he was secure, he reached over and grabbed one of the corner shingles, managing to get a good grip on the raised decorative pieces there. He made his way up to the top of the low roof and then swung around so he could climb down on the front corner opposite to him.

The road didn't look too packed, thankfully, and he hoped there was a good gap in the front yard. He made his way down to the edge as quickly as he could, before his audience found their way around the house, and leaned back as far as he could to take stock of the ground.

Miraculously, there were no ghouls below him, and before he could overthink it, he lowered his feet off of the edge until he dangled from the eavestrough by his hands.

The metal groaned, and he panicked, letting go before the trough could break free of the roof. A zing went up his legs as he landed, his body landing with a jolt. A few ghouls from the road turned in his direction, and he took off like a shot, tearing through front yards until he could barely breathe.

Two blocks away from the park, Lennox was exhausted. He had a stitch in his side, his feet ached, and it felt as if every breath were laced with pins and needles. He knew he was going to have to cross the street over to the left side, but wasn't sure how he was going to get through the ghouls.

They had gotten even thicker this close to the park, and he could smell the burnt rotted flesh on the air. He took a breather behind a row of garbage cans and contemplated his next move. The front door of the house next to him hung open, and he squinted to see if there was any movement inside. It didn't look like it, so he took off and barrelled up the front steps.

He shut the door behind him, and did a quick sweep of the main floor, finding nothing. He rushed to the kitchen and flung open the fridge, scanning for something to drink. There was a can of beer in the door, and he grabbed it, popping it open. He knew it wouldn't hydrate him, really, but at least it would wet his mouth a bit.

He took a few gulps and then set it down, grimacing at the taste of warm brew. He went back and peered out the front window, and took a deep breath.

"How the fuck am I gonna get across?" he muttered, scanning the area. He turned back to the kitchen and found the door leading out to the garage. He descended the few steps inside, looking around at the plethora of sports equipment and junk around.

He spotted something shiny in the corner, and pushed through some hockey nets to get to it. Leaned up against the wall was a curved chunk of fiberglass, looking like the detached hood of an old car. He lifted it, testing its weight, and then flipped it around, looking to see if there was anything to hold onto inside.

There were little bars welded to the inside, and he wasn't sure what they were for, but he wasn't about to look a gift horse in the mouth. He moved over to the garage door and peered outside.

"This is crazy. And stupid," he muttered to himself. "It needs to work. But there's not a good chance that it will." He cocked his head. "But what choice do you have?"

And how much are you going to argue with yourself out loud before you just go crazy? He took a deep breath and wrapped his hand around the door handle, giving it a twist to release it. *Here we go.*

He threw up the door and took off at a run, gripping the bars with white knuckles. The noise of the door opening attracted the attention of the ghouls in the immediate vicinity, and they turned towards him on the street.

Lennox let out a yell and smashed into the sea of zombies, smashing the hood into the lineup like a battering ram. He managed to keep up his momentum fairly well despite being so out of shape, knocking ghouls back with the curved fiberglass. Halfway through, he was concerned about the ones he left in his wake, but didn't want to waste any time looking behind him. The only way was forward, now.

When he broke through the other side, he threw the hood aside, and it hit the sidewalk with a loud *clang*. His shirt suddenly tightened around his throat, and he whipped sideways as a corpse managed to grab a fistful of his sleeve.

He jerked on it, but only succeeded in dragging his captor along into the grass. He fumbled with his knife, stabbing wildly, and managed to get it through the skull and wrench his arm free of the death grip.

He could smell the rotted breath of his enemies, they were too close. He ran. He didn't even know if it was the right direction in his panic, but the gunfire was closer and he thought he was running towards it.

Gun smoke and ash and blood and screams… stop it! He wrenched himself free of his memories, coming back to the present. *Lives are at stake, Lennox, keep your shit together!*

The park was only a block away. The scent of burnt rotten flesh wafted into his nose and he almost welcomed it. It kept him grounded, kept him present, chased away his old demons despite bringing new ones.

He came upon a waist-high chain-link fence and threw himself over it, finally chancing a glance behind him. Some zombies from the road approached, but not enough to be worried about the fence, so he slowed his pace a bit through the row of backyards to try to chill his racing heart.

The last yard separated him from the park by another waist-high fence, but he barely noticed it as he took in the carnage. What had once been a beautifully landscaped park was now a charred wasteland, complete with flaming zombies waiting to barbecue their fresh meal.

"Fuck me," Lennox breathed, and then shook his head. He had to get across the park to the north. And he was going to have to fight his way through.

The smoldering ghouls still wandering around were spaced out and slow, some of them falling here and there when their limbs succumbed to fire damage. He clutched his knife and drew his sidearm. There was no point attempting to be stealthy here. The gunfire was loud enough and the zone hot enough that extra gunshots wouldn't do much for his position.

He hopped the fence and moved at a quick walk, deliberate and strategic. He hopped over an unmoving black mass and slashed with his knife, severing a smoldering zombie's head like butter. A trio still on fire staggered towards him, and he popped off two quick shots to dispatch the closest ones, lunging forward to stab the third in the forehead.

Despite not being in combat for years, the training washed over him, taking control of his limbs, muscle memory taking the wheel as he moved through the park. He kicked a crispy corpse in the chest and leapt over another, stabbing another and dropping his shoulder to barrel through two barely standing ghouls like a linebacker.

He came out the other side of the park with a half a mag left in his gun, covered in soot and dust. He tore across the street, darting up a back alley behind some buildings towards the interstate. He let the adrenaline drive him, taking in deep lungfuls of air fresher than that of the burned-up park.

A zombie staggered out from behind a dumpster and he stabbed it up through the chin, piercing its brain and shoving it aside. The gunfire was so loud, so close, but he fought away the panic rising in his chest, desperately grasping onto his training, the adrenaline, the *mission*. This was his mission.

When he was in sight of the bridge, his jaw dropped. The military wasn't doing as well as he'd hoped. Troops fought a wave of zombies, and though many of them were firing from atop cars, enough were battling hand-to-hand that it was clear they definitely didn't have enough ammunition to go around.

What the fuck are you doing, marching in here unprepared… he thought, shaking his head. They were even more unprepared than they knew, and he had to tell them.

He wasn't sure how he was going to get over there, though. He had to get their attention somehow. There were too many ghouls between them. He jogged across a parking lot, trying to get a better vantage point, and saw that they'd set up a barricade of cars on the bridge, so that soldiers could fall back to safety and swap out with other troops. At least they had some kind of safe zone.

The telltale sound of helicopter blades cut the air, and his eyes widened as an Apache came into view. He opened his mouth to scream, scream at them to stop, but it was no use, nobody knew he was there.

He hit the ground, covering his head, as the chopper dropped another firebomb on the zombies, sending another shock wave through the area. The sound of shattering glass made Lennox's stomach sink into his toes.

He staggered to his feet as the helicopter swooped away, his body suddenly so tired, so exhausted, so done with this day.

No! The mission!

He studied the area. The bomb had gotten rid of quite a few zombies, but there were enough that he wouldn't be able to fight his way through to the barricade. He positioned himself at the edge of the parking lot, climbing up onto one of the cement dividers and waving his arms.

"Hey!" he screamed. "Hey! Over here!"

Nobody looked his way. The gunfire was too strong, the zombies too thick, the night too dark despite the solar-powered streetlights.

"Fuck," he muttered, and looked around frantically. Swaths of ghouls staggered into the parking lot behind him, and his heart rate picked up for what felt like the hundredth time that day. He clenched his jaw and pulled his rifle from his back, aiming at one of the cars near the barricade. He pulled the trigger, firing a few bullets into the door, and a few of the nearby soldiers froze, turning towards him.

He pulled out his flashlight and flashed it a few times, hoping like hell they would get the hint.

One of the soldiers gestured wildly, and a team of five began to battle in his direction, systematically taking out ghouls. Lennox jumped down from the cement pillar, rushing forward and taking out a few zombies from behind, lightening the load as the soldiers made their way to him.

"You bit?" one of the soldiers barked as they approached, and Lennox raised his arms.

"No, I need to talk to your higher-ups, *now*," he declared.

The soldier looked hesitant, but one of his teammates lunged past him to kick an approaching ghoul in the chest. "Come on!" he snapped. "We don't have time for this!"

Lennox scurried up to them, joining the team. He used his sidearm to help clear the way, and soon they were back at the barricade. He immediately clambered up on top, eyes wild, waving his gun around.

"You're all walking into a trap!" he yelled and then realized too late how much of a lunatic he must have looked like. As he stared down no less than eight gun barrels, he lowered his arms and holstered his sidearm. "Sorry, it's been a rough day."

A Sergeant approached, standing in between two of the aiming troops. "Who are you?" he asked, cocking a brow.

"Former Private Lennox Stadler, sir," he replied, putting out his hands. "I'm gonna come down, now." When his boots hit the asphalt, he tugged at his dog tags, pulling them out of his shirt.

"Sergeant Miller," the man in charge said, and motioned for his men to stand down. "What's this about a trap?"

Lennox took a deep breath. This was his mission. It was almost over. He'd done it. Jax had believed in him, and he'd made it here.

"The high-rise over there, it's on top of a convention center," he explained, turning to motion towards Jax's place. "There are a thousand of those things trapped inside, but they aren't gonna be for much longer with these bombs weakening the windows."

Miller immediately snatched a radio from his belt. "Captain Parker, do you copy?"

After a moment, a voice came back, "Copy, what's your status, Sergeant?"

Miller raised his chin, staring at the high rise. "There's a convention center just off the interstate we've just learned is full of a thousand of those things," he replied. "Windows are weak from the blasts, and if they get out, we'll be overrun. We're already fighting by the skin of our teeth out here, we'd be fucked with another wave of a thousand."

"One moment, Sergeant," Parker replied, and the line went silent for a time.

The hair on the back of Lennox's neck stood on end. He didn't have a good feeling about the look on the soldier's face. It was possible that he hadn't helped Jax after all, and dread began to build in his gut.

"Stand by, Sergeant," Parker came back, "we'll send back the Apache and destroy the building."

Lennox snarled. "No fucking way!" he cried. "My friends are in there!"

Miller fixed him with a steel glare. "We can't sacrifice our entire mission and put all of the troops at risk for a few people," he said firmly.

"Fuck that," Lennox snapped. "You can't just write them off. We need to get them out of there!"

The Sergeant stared down his nose at the fuming civilian. "Collateral damage is a byproduct of war," he said, waving him off. "An ex-soldier should know that."

"Those people are the reason that you have this information in the first place," Lennox shot back, pointing a finger at the condos. "They sent me out here to warn you because *they* wanted to save your lives. Without them you would all be fucking dead! You owe them!"

Miller clenched his jaw, clearly unimpressed with the tone, but his eyes betrayed his uncertainty on the matter. He turned away from Lennox and pulled out his radio again.

"Captain Parker, do you copy?" he asked, voice a little annoyed.

"What is it, Sergeant?" Parker replied immediately, voice equal in tone and measure.

Miller took a deep breath. "There are civilians in the high rise," he explained.

"How many?" the Captain asked.

Miller glanced at Lennox, who gritted his teeth.

"Three," he ground out, clenching his fists.

The Sergeant sighed. "Three, sir," he replied. "But-"

"We can't risk the mission for three civilians," Parker cut in. "Frankly, I'm appalled you even called back to tell me."

Miller held up a hand as Lennox growled his displeasure. "Sir, the civilians are the ones that got us this message," he explained. "Is there any way we can mount a rescue before we blow the building?"

There was a moment of silence, and finally the Captain sighed. "I take it they can't get out close to ground level?" he asked.

Lennox shook his head. "Everything below the twelfth floor is overrun," he said.

"That would be a negative, Captain," the Sergeant relayed through the radio.

"There will be a chopper on the roof to pick them up in one hour," Parker

replied. "If they're not there, they're
SOL."

Miller nodded. "Thank you, Captain,
I'll relay the message."

"Thank you," Lennox said, pressing
his palms together. "Thank you."

"Jax, come in!" Lennox's voice came through the radio, and Jax jerked in his chair, fumbling with the receiver. "Jax!"

Skylar and Marcus practically dove off of the couch they'd been curled up on, scrambling over to the radio desk.

"Lennox, did you reach them?" Jax asked, white-knuckling the radio while he waited for a response.

"I did," came the reply. "I'm standing here with the Sergeant right now, and he says thanks for the intel."

Jax punched the air with his fist, narrowly missing Marcus' face as he leaned over his shoulder. "That's great news!" he exclaimed, unaware of his near punch. "So what are they going to do?"

"Well," Lennox drew out the word, and then took a deep breath, "they're going to bomb the building. You guys need to get to the roof within the hour for pickup."

Skylar paled. "Wait, *what*?"

Jax shook his head vigorously. "The roof?" He scratched the back of his head. "Okay. Okay, thank you. We're going to get on that."

"See you soon, buddy," Lennox said.

Jax set down the receiver and maneuvered himself around to look at his shell-shocked companions. "Looks like we're getting out of here, finally."

"The roof, though," Skylar said. "I guess it makes sense that there's no other way. How the hell else would they be picking us up?"

Marcus chewed his lip for a moment. "Where's the roof access?"

Jax shook his head. "There's no direct roof access. The top level of the penthouse has a terrace," he explained. "That's where we have to get to."

"But the penthouse is overrun," Marcus argued.

Jax nodded. "It is," he replied, though they all knew that.

"What a shitty time for that rich asshole to have a company party," Skylar muttered, crossing her arms. "If he'd have waited a damn week then the upper floors wouldn't be full of those things."

Jax shook his head. "Too late to commiserate on that, now," he said. "Where is the barricade?"

"The stairs before the penthouse," Marcus replied. "The door was open, probably somebody trying to escape when the party guests started eating each other, so the top floors are full of those things."

Jax nodded. "So we need to fight our way up to the penthouse," he said slowly,

counting off on his fingers as he spoke,
"fight across it to the stairs, get up to
the top floor balcony, then get to the
stairs at the back to the roof terrace."
He swallowed hard. "You two need to—"

"No, no," Skylar cut in, waving her
hands back and forth in front of her face.
"We're not leaving you here."

He cocked his head, eyes as firm as
they could be. "I appreciate the
sentiment," he replied, "but I can't walk.
This isn't just a prop, you know."

"We'll carry you," Marcus replied
quickly. "We'll carry you up the flights
of stairs."

Jax shook his head, spreading his
arms. "While fighting zombies?" he
scoffed. "Or trying to be fast to outrun
them? You can't do that while hauling a
wheelchair around. Not to mention how
narrow the staircase is up to the
penthouse door."

"We're *not* leaving you here," Skylar
snapped. "So we're going to figure it the
fuck out."

"What have you got for weapons?"
Marcus asked. "We don't have anything at
our place other than kitchen knives."

Jax pursed his lips for a moment. "I
have a six-shot revolver," he admitted.
"In my bedroom closet. I've never fired it
before, though." He looked between the

two. "Either of you know your way around a gun?"

The couple shook their heads.

"My girl could outrun a bullet, but we've never fired one," Marcus said.

Jax shrugged. "I guess it's pretty straightforward," he replied. "I'll go get it for you guys. Probably good to have, just in case."

"Not *for us guys*," Skylar argued. "You're coming with us. You get the gun, I'll find some other hand-to-hand weapons, and babe, you figure out how we're taking Jax with us." She pointed to each of them in turn and then stalked off to the kitchen in a huff.

Marcus shook his head. "You'd better listen to her, man," he said with a smirk. "Sky always gets what she wants."

Jax swallowed hard and smiled sadly. "I'll keep that in mind." He wheeled his way off to the bedroom, past his bed, to the closet. He opened it up and rummaged around the shelf until he found the old shoebox with his gun.

There you are, old friend, he thought as he pulled it down and set it on his lap. He didn't open it right away. This box held so many memories for him, and none were pleasant.

The gun had been his father's, and his father's before him. He didn't even know why he'd accepted it from his mom when his father died. There was no love lost between Jax and his old man. It apparently had been too much for him to have a son that was 'half a man', as he loved to put it. At least his mother had never made him feel like less of a person with his disability, but even at a young age he'd been able to see it was hard on her, essentially raising a disabled son by herself because her husband was too thick-headed to be there for his family.

Jax sighed as he lifted the lid. The piece was old, but it was in immaculate condition. His father had kept it in perfect working order. He loved his guns, that man. Jax wondered if his father had ever put it to his own head, weighing the value of his life.

The wheelchair-bound man knew what that felt like. When his father had drank himself into an early grave, he'd blamed himself. Blamed his mother's depression on himself. Blamed so much on himself and his useless legs.

He remembered the feel of the cold steel, unforgiving against his warm flesh. He hadn't even had the courage to pull the hammer back. The saving thought had been picturing his mother's face, finding him dead of a gunshot wound to the skull.

That, and the fear. He hadn't *really* wanted to die. But it was a low moment.

He caressed the gun, debating whether to pick it up or not. *They won't make it very far with me. They won't make it out at all,* he thought. *I might be able to convince Marcus to leave me… but not Skylar. And there's not enough time to argue. They need to get to the roof, get up there and escape.*

He clenched his jaw. *What life is there for a cripple in the apocalypse?* He let out a dark laugh under his breath. *It's not like the zombies will give me handicap parking.*

"Hey buddy, I figured it out, I—" Marcus stopped short in the doorway, staring at his friend's guilty expression, hand resting on the gun in the box.

Jax blushed crimson, jerking his hand from the box like it was on fire.

Marcus took a deep, shuddering breath, and rushed over to him. He snatched the box from his friend's lap, putting the lid back on it, and then held up his other hand, a series of fabric strips in his hand.

"We figured out what we're doing," he said hoarsely, and then stared down his nose at the wheelchair-bound man, "and I'm not going to tell Skylar what you were about to do."

Jax opened his mouth to deny it, but snapped it shut again. He knew it was no use to try. He simply nodded.

"Thank you," he said quietly, and then straightened his shoulders. "What… what are we doing with these?" He reached out to touch one of the strips, realizing they were thick chunks of his living room curtain.

Marcus turned and waved for him to follow. "We're gonna make you into a backpack," he declared.

"A *backpack*?" Jax blurted, rolling his way out of the bedroom in disbelief.

Skylar emerged from the kitchen with a few butcher knives and a tenderizing mallet. "Well, we can make schnitzel out of those things at least," she announced, dropping the weapons on the coffee table with a clatter. "What have you got?"

"You remember those baby slings your sister used to make and sell on the internet?" Marcus asked, holding up one of the strips.

Her eyes widened. "Oh, the wrap carriers!" she exclaimed. "Good thinking!"

"I'm sorry," Jax cut in, raising his hand, "*baby* slings?"

Skylar nodded like a bobblehead. "Yeah, but you could use them for bigger kids too," she explained as she took the fabric from her boyfriend. "It's all about proper weight distribution. It'll help hold your legs up so you can piggyback on Marcus' back."

"Well…" Jax stammered, shaking his head. "I'm not light… I'll weigh you down too much."

Marcus rolled his eyes. "I know I don't look like much dude, but I can carry you up a few flights of stairs on my back," he said. "Skylar will have to do the bulk of the fighting, but we got this."

"You bet your ass we do," she added, and motioned to the floor in front of the wheelchair. "Kneel down, babe, it'll be easier to do this if you're closer to the floor."

Her boyfriend smirked at her, a wicked glint in his eye as he got down on the carpet, back facing Jax.

"Don't even, you dirtball," she scolded, swatting his shoulder as she reached out her hand to Jax. "Okay, so you wrap your arms around Marcus' shoulders, and I'll get you wrapped up like a snuggly bundle of joy."

He couldn't help but laugh at that, and reached forward, but paused. "Wait," he said, "how low is my ass going to be hanging here? I don't know if I'll be able to reach back far enough to kill anything that comes to take a bite."

"Hmm," Skylar mused, tapping her chin, and then raised a hand. "Hang on," she said, and dropped the fabric, running back to the kitchen. She emerged with a roll of duct tape in her hand, and rushed off to the bedroom, coming back to the two dumbfounded men with the comforter from the bed.

"What the…" Jax wondered, blinking at her.

"We're gonna make you into a burrito," she declared. "You'll be warm, but your ass will be safe."

Marcus laughed and shook his head, clapping Jax on the shoulder. "True MacGyver treatment today, my friend."

CHAPTER SEVEN

"How are you feeling?" Skylar asked as they entered the hallway, glancing back at Jax.

He held up his meat tenderizer, giving her a little salute with it. "Swaddled," he replied.

"My back is sweating already," Marcus added. "I can't imagine how warm you are in there."

They'd wrapped Jax in the comforter up to his armpits, and duct-taped it securely around him. Skylar had cut a slit up between his legs, and they taped the armor around his thighs so that everything hanging off of Marcus' back would be sufficiently padded.

He patted his marshmallow leg with the revolver, which they'd decided he would hang on to given his lack of mobility. "Toasty," he admitted, "but if it keeps me from being zombie food, I don't care if I'm running a fever after this."

Skylar smiled at him and adjusted her grip on the butcher knife she'd selected. "Good," she said. She was pretty proud of her handiwork with the fabric, having created a makeshift seat around Marcus' torso, held up by criss-crossing straps up and over his shoulders. She wouldn't be winning any safety awards anytime soon, but if they were able to pull this off and get Jax to safety on the roof unscathed, then she counted it as a win.

Marcus raised his two knives, having decided to don two since he had limited mobility. Skylar would be the one opening doors and such, so she needed a free hand.

"Let's do this," he said, and she nodded, taking a deep breath.

This was it. They had to make it through two floors of flesh-eating monsters in less than an hour in hopes of meeting a helicopter to get them out of here before the military bombed them.

Yeah, just another day in the apocalypse, she thought to herself, forcing the panic back down her throat. *We got this,* she urged herself, and led them down the hallway.

She opened the stairwell door as quietly as she could, and they slipped inside. The emergency lights still worked, albeit dimly, so they had a view of the silhouette of the barricade she and Marcus had built just before the landing on the penthouse floor.

She paused at the door to the fourteenth floor, chewing her lip for a moment. Time. Time was something they didn't have much of… but there was something she couldn't leave without.

"I just need to grab one thing," she whispered, and opened the door to their floor, ushering Marcus to follow her.

As she quietly closed the door behind her, he furrowed his brow.

"Babe, what are you doing?" he asked. "There's nothing in there that can help us."

She pressed her palms together, eyes begging. "I'm sorry, I'll be quick," she said, and ran down the hallway to their condo.

She slipped inside and went straight for the office, kneeling down in front of the bookshelf. On the bottom, next to a set of vintage Tolkein's, was a little wooden box. She flipped the latch and opened it, wrapping her hand around the silver coin inside.

It wasn't an actual coin, or at least not one used for currency. She ran a finger over the etched mountain drawing on the front and then flipped it over.

Skylar, my heart, my life, my world.

She clutched it in her palm, tears pricking the corners of her eyes. Her father had given her this when she was fourteen, when he was diagnosed with cancer. She'd been sure he would pull through, but he knew better, and as an adult she understood how naïve she'd been.

It was never easy to lose a parent, especially so young, and he'd gifted her the engraved coin as a reminder of his affection, even after he was gone. She'd carried it during every marathon. It was her lucky charm.

She kissed it and then stuffed it into her pocket, heading for the door. "Need your luck today, daddy," she whispered, and then slipped back out into the hallway.

"Find what you need?" Jax asked, his voice a little on edge.

Marcus looked down at her pocket, seeing the outline of the coin, and offered her a sad smile, reaching out to give her shoulder a reassuring squeeze. Skylar smiled back and then squared her shoulders.

"I'm ready," she replied. "Let's go."

She led them back to the stairwell, and they moved back in as soundlessly as they'd moved out. She took a deep breath as they crept up to the penthouse barricade.

The shuffling feet and moaning from above was enough to make Skylar's blood run cold, but she steeled her resolve and slid her knife into her belt, making sure it was secure. The last thing she needed was to drop her only weapon.

She grabbed onto a fancy-looking ornate chair, giving it a little wiggle to make sure if she removed it that the whole pile wouldn't fall down on them. When nothing else shifted, she tugged it free and set it aside. She moved up and did the same with a nightstand, pulling it down and passing it off to Marcus, who set it down a little harder than he'd meant to on the landing.

The resounding *smack* gave the zombies above something to get excited about, and moans erupted. They echoed down and down the stairwell, and soon hungry moans from below the bottom barricade responded, brethren calling back that they wanted a snack too.

Skylar swallowed hard and tugged on a coffee table they'd stood up on its end as a makeshift wall. A snarl sounded on the other side of it, and as she pulled it down, a ghoul on the other side reached over a tv stand, clawed fingers snatching at her.

She pulled her knife while propping the table against one shoulder, using it as a shield as she stabbed forward. She managed to catch the zombie in the eye socket, and wrenched the blade free. She was glad she'd aimed for soft tissue as the blade scraped against the skull on the way out. She wasn't sure the kitchen

knives would cut through bone, and she
didn't need to be missing at a crucial
moment or having her blade glance off of a
head.

Skylar aimed again, stabbing another
in the face, this time into the soft
rotted flesh of the ghoul's nose. As it
slumped down, the ones behind it got even
more excited and pressed against the
barricade.

"Sky…" Marcus hissed, stepping up
behind her.

She shook her head. "I don't think we
can pull this down without getting
overrun," she replied. "We'll have to
climb over." She pursed her lips, thinking
of how he was going to be able to do that
with his Jax-pack. "Or, I'll need to climb
over, and then once it's clear we can
dismantle the barricade."

"Here," he insisted, holding out his
second knife. "I'll take your spot and try
to get at them from here, distract them
while you get up top."

She nodded, glad that he hadn't taken
the time to argue with her. *That's why I
love you, babe,* she thought as she found a
foothold on a thick bookshelf. *You don't
waste time trying to talk me out of shit
when I know what I'm doing.* Time, time was
what they needed to make the most of, and
the danger of their situation didn't

really matter, considering if they didn't make it to the roof they'd get blown up anyway.

She balanced on her knees at the top of the pile, and Marcus did what he'd said he would, waving his knife wildly at the ghouls.

"Yeah, come get some, *bitches*," he snarled, and Skylar stifled a laugh. Her sweet Marcus using the word *bitches*? This truly was the end of days.

She inched her way over, as the bulk of the group clustered around her boyfriend. She'd hoped that she could just stab down from the top. But she wouldn't be able to reach.

Here we go, she thought. *Don't freak out, babe.* She studied the five ghouls and their positioning, and then took a deep breath, and jumped down to the floor.

Despite Marcus' cry of protest, he managed to stab a zombie in the face, cutting the count to four. "What are you doing?!" He bellowed, but she didn't answer because she didn't want the group to realize there was a fresh meal behind them.

Skylar grabbed a fistful of one's hair, jerking it back and reaching around to drive her blade into its temple. She dropped the body immediately as another turned towards her, snarling, and she lashed out without missing a beat, stabbing it in the eye.

"Hey! Right here!" Jax cried, Marcus' voice yelling something unintelligible. Both men flailed, but couldn't reach either of the two remaining ghouls as they turned to Skylar.

She eyed the railing of the top floor landing and made the quick decision to barrel forward. She darted to the right, and slammed her shoulder into one of the zombies, driving it back but not far enough.

She threw herself forward, shoving with her fists into its chest, but her momentum halted as the other one grabbed a fistful of her hair in a death grip. Her knives went clattering to the ground in her shock.

No no no… she thought frantically, but she couldn't give up. If these things killed her, then Marcus would be faced with a fresh fast zombie and it would be significantly harder for them to get out. If she was just bitten, then at least she could still get them to the roof.

She lurched to the side in an attempt to deflect a bite, figuring at least if it was on her arm instead of her throat it wouldn't be imminently fatal. She pushed hard against the ghoul at the railing, keeping its snapping jaws away from her face.

No bite came. She managed to glance back and saw that Marcus had a hold of the zombie's shirt—he couldn't reach it with the knife, but at least he was holding it at bay.

With renewed vigor, Skylar shoved forward again, her scalp screaming from the pull. This time she managed to tip the ghoul over the railing, and it hit the stairs below with a wet *crack*.

She reached up to grip the wrist of the zombie still twisted in her hair, trying to wrench it free. Just as she turned, she caught a glimmer of steel and a deafening *BOOM* resounded in the stairwell. Her ears rang, and she finally wrenched the rotted fingers from her hair as the corpse fell.

"Get this shit out of the way," Marcus grunted, pulling at the debris from the barricade.

Jax stayed stock still on his back, staring at the smoking gun in his hand in shock.

"Hang on babe, hang on," Skylar muttered as she pulled some of the furniture aside, shoving it into the corner and out of the way.

As soon as Marcus was clear, he was on her, holding her tightly as if he'd never let her go. "What the hell was that, huh?" he asked thickly. "You could have *died*, Jesus…" He buried his face into her hair.

"I'm sorry," Skylar murmured against Jax's arm, awkwardly caught in their embrace. "But it's okay, I'm okay. We've got to move." They parted, and she looked up at the gun-toting man. "Thank you." She blinked back tears, not wanting to think about how this all could have ended so fast.

"Of course," Jax replied hoarsely, and cleared his throat.

She knelt and picked up her knives, giving one back to Marcus.

"If there was time to switch," he said, shaking his head. "I'd be switching you, you little hellcat."

Skylar smirked, trying to bring some levity to the situation. "Don't pretend like it doesn't get you all hot watching me kick ass," she teased with a wink.

Marcus blew out an exasperated laugh and shook his head. He motioned to the penthouse door. "Let's do this, ass-kicker."

CHAPTER EIGHT

Miller barked out orders, sending soldiers to and fro on the lines to continue to take out zombies. They were almost finished with the current wave.

Lennox stood between two Privates, aiming downrange and taking down ghouls with utmost precision. He'd felt like lending his bullets to the cause was a must, especially considering this was their only hope of rescue. Jax had told him about the ships that came in on the lake, although Lennox had heard them he hadn't known where the gunfire was coming from.

Hope had been tentative that the military would be coming to save them. But of course, the military's focus wasn't to save a quartet of civilians. Their higher ups just wanted to clear the city.

Lennox tried not to be bitter about it. He knew how it was. The Sergeant took his orders from his Captain who took his orders from his General, and so on, all the way up to the President, if that's who was pulling the strings here. A full-on zombie apocalypse was a special situation, and it looked like they were clearing the city to hopefully build a safe place for humanity to survive.

Of course, that mission was damn important. And the soldier needed to press on, do everything they could, otherwise it would fail.

But on the other hand, if there were no civilians left to fill the damned safe place, then what the hell was the point of all this? One big giant military circle jerk?

Lennox shook his head, taking aim at another ghoul and dropping it. *There's got to be other survivors out there,* he thought. *Other communities, even. People to bring back here once it's done.* In any case, this particular Sergeant was the one who'd agreed to help his friends, so he was grateful for that.

Grateful that I'm persistent and mouthy, he thought to himself.

"Good job, boys," Miller barked as the last of the wave of zombies fell to the asphalt. "Orders are to sit tight here for a few until we can get that building down. Take a break, grab a bite. You boys on the barricade, keep watch for any activity."

"Yes, sir," one of the Corporals said with a firm nod.

"Lennox, you're to head to the back to wait for your friends," the Sergeant continued, pointing at him. "I appreciate the help, you're a hell of a shot."

Lennox nodded. He didn't want to acknowledge the praise. In truth, he knew he was good at shooting and killing. It was something that he'd spent years warring with inside of himself. He didn't want to be good at taking life.

At least with zombies, their lives were already claimed. It was a mercy, putting them down. That's how he had to frame it in his head to keep the demons at bay.

"How much longer do they have?" he asked as he walked alongside the Sergeant.

"Just under a half hour," Miller replied.

Lennox shook his head. He hoped to hell that they didn't run into too much trouble. Jax hadn't seemed thrilled about needing to get to the roof, and he wasn't sure if it was because there were zombies in the way, or just the fact that he was in a wheelchair. Maybe both.

"Do you know what the state of that building is, up top?" the Sergeant asked.

Lennox shook his head. "No," he replied. "I know Jax is on the twelfth floor, not sure about the other two, I think a few up from him? But I have no idea what the penthouse looks like. Hopefully nothing too bad. I know they had to barricade everything from Jax's floor down."

"Shouldn't be too bad to get up there, then," Miller replied.

"Yeah, stairs are real easy for a guy in a wheelchair," Lennox muttered.

The Sergeant's eyes widened a fraction, and then he shook his head. "Sorry," he said in a low voice, "I didn't realize."

"I know," came the reply. "He'll be okay. He's got two friends that can help him. If he was by himself he would have been boned, but I'm grateful to the others. I'm more hoping they're not having to fight through significant opposition. An hour is a good window, but if each of the floors is packed with those things…" He shook his head. It wasn't the time to be pessimistic. Jax had said he'd make it work.

You'd better, buddy, he prayed silently. *I want to see your face after all this.*

"Here we are," Miller said, motioning to a cluster of vehicles well behind the line. "Have a rest, someone will grab you some food and water." He clasped his hands in front of him. "Thank you, for the warning. For making it all the way out here. We would have been… well, you know."

Lennox nodded as he sat down, taking a load off. "You can thank Jax when he gets here safely," he said.

The Sergeant nodded and headed back to the barricade, leaving the tired man to close his eyes, leaning back against a large truck tire. *And you'd better get here safely, buddy.*

Jax watched with trepidation as Skylar reached for the doorknob, but froze at the sound of hands smacking the other side.

"Shit, of course," she muttered. The noise they'd made in the stairwell had been bound to attract attention.

As if on cue, there was a series of clatters from downstairs, and resounding hungry moans echoed in victory. The zombies had busted the barricade at the bottom.

"No going back now," Marcus said, and turned around to shove some of the furniture back in place to hopefully stem them from making it up to their landing. Jax held on tight, keeping himself from choking his friend, but still unused to the feeling of being suspended on his back. It was strange being wrapped up in the weird burrito seat.

Skylar turned to them. "Grab that coffee table," she said, pointing at the table she'd used as a shield when she was first stabbing zombies.

Marcus passed it over and then bent to heave a recliner down into the hole they'd made when they were climbing up. Jax tried to keep his breathing steady as his ride moved this way and that. He'd heard that when you were a passenger on a motorcycle, you had to just go with the lean, or else you could throw off the equilibrium of the vehicle. He tried to do that here, not too stiff but not too limp. Just go with the movement to make it easier on Marcus.

They turned back to Skylar, who was positioning the coffee table on its end next to the door.

"Okay, you brace the door, and don't let it open wider than the table," she instructed. "If there's only a few, I'll get them over the edge, and if there's a ton, we'll shut the door and re-evaluate. Deal?"

Jax shook his head, but Marcus just said, "Yep, let's do it," and stood behind the door, bracing himself as he wrapped his hand around the handle.

Jax held his breath. He wanted to ask, *what's the difference between a few and a ton?* He always had questions. But now wasn't the time. These two were saving his ass, when they could have left him behind to die. He wasn't about to start questioning their methods. Seeing Skylar grabbed by that zombie had turned his chest to ice—he'd thought for sure they were going to lose her.

He had the fleeting thought that he needed to learn to trust these two, because they went with their guts, and it seemed to work out. Plus, there were even more flesh-eating monsters coming up from the bottom, and he wasn't sure if that barricade was going to hold. The only way out was up, so taking stock over a coffee table would have to do.

"Go!" Skylar declared, and Marcus turned the knob.

The weight on the door was immediate, and he threw himself back against it, struggling to keep it closed enough that his girlfriend could keep the coffee table in place. She stabbed two ghouls in the face in quick succession, splattering gooey half-coagulated blood all over the place.

More arms reached through the gap, clawing for her face.

"How's it look?" Marcus grunted as he pressed against the door, feet planted firmly on the cement of the stairwell landing.

"Just two more," Skylar growled as she hacked and slashed, trying to knock the arms aside to get to the heads behind them.

Jax gripped his meat tenderizer and brought it down on one of the arms, snapping the elbow at an unnatural angle. The rotted hand hung limp and useless, unable to block her way, and she nodded at him in thanks.

He took out another arm. And then she managed to stab the one with functional limbs, dropping it with its brethren. He considered giving her the gun, but the noise would just draw more of them to the door, and they needed to at least try to get in without thirty ghouls right on top of them.

Speaking of ghouls on top of them, the stairwell zombies had reached the barricade, and furniture was shifting under their excitement. Jax swallowed hard. It wouldn't hold for long.

"Okay, open a little more," Skylar said as the last one fell, and she pushed inside, using the coffee table like a shield. "Stay quiet," she whispered.

Marcus leaned down, making Jax's stomach lurch, and shoved two of the bodies out of the way so they could secure the door behind them. He locked it, just in case, and Jax let out a deep breath he hadn't realized he'd been holding. One dangerous section down, two to go.

Well, three, if they counted the terrace, which he figured for the sake of realism, he should. Better to expect the worst, really.

Speaking of the worst, this penthouse had been a party. There were easily

twenty-five to thirty ghouls just on this
floor, let alone on the second. They would
need to get through them to the staircase
on the far end. At least the entire one
wall was glass from floor-to-ceiling, so
they could see by the light of the bright
moon.

He gripped the gun and mallet like a
lifeline. He had five bullets left, and he
had to make them count. He'd lucked out
being able to shoot that zombie at close
enough range it was impossible to miss,
but making noise was a last resort and
wouldn't be worth it if it wasn't a sure
shot.

Sweat dripped down the back of his
neck, from pure nervousness but also from
being duct-taped inside of a thick
comforter.

Skylar stepped forward slowly,
holding the table out in front of her,
keeping her footsteps flat and soundless.
It wasn't going to matter in a few
moments, as they were going to have to go
right through the center of the pack to
make it.

Something brushed against Jax, and
his brow furrowed. Was Marcus… he turned
his head, and his eyes widened when he
realized a zombie was gnawing at his lower
back. Thankfully the comforter was thick
enough, working in his favor, because the

teeth didn't pierce it, but it was
disconcerting, to say the least.

A low moan began deep in his throat,
and he patted Marcus' shoulder
frantically. He could try to smack it with
the meat tenderizer, but he didn't think
his arm would bend that way.

Marcus turned to look at him, but he
seemed reluctant to look away from Skylar,
who crept forward continually with her
shield.

"There's a… it's trying to eat my
back," Jax whispered as quietly as he
could into Marcus' ear.

His eyes widened, and he reached out
to tap Skylar on the shoulder. She paused
and glanced back at him, and he gently
maneuvered so that she had a full view of
the ghoul latched onto Jax's back.

He lashed out with her knife,
stabbing it in the temple, and gently
lowered the corpse to the floor so that it
wouldn't make too much noise.

"Uh," Jax murmured. It was too late.
The zombies inside were taking notice of
them. Skylar swallowed hard, and then
grabbed the coffee table, turning it
sideways.

"I'm just going to push through," she
said. "Stay close behind me, we'll just
shove our way through to the stairs."

Marcus nodded jerkily. "Okay, okay," he replied breathily, as if psyching himself up.

"Go!" Skylar hissed, and then darted forward.

Marcus took off, hot on her heels, and Jax gripped his weapons with white knuckles, eyes darting around everywhere to try to keep tabs on the ghouls. It was difficult, bouncing as he was, but as corpses flew left and right from the coffee table battering ram, others swarmed behind them.

He finally accepted his fate of not being able to fight, and just curled his head down, holding on to Marcus and trying to be as light of a backpack as possible. He could feel them on his back. He didn't know if it was hands or mouths, but he knew they were there, dragging at him. He wished fleetingly that he'd had one of the knives, so that if things got dicey, he could cut himself free and let the others save themselves, but realized that Marcus had probably engineered that on purpose.

He knew that Jax wouldn't pull the trigger on himself back there and risk being dead weight on Marcus' back, so he'd been given the gun and the meat tenderizer. There was no escape, all he could do was hold on and trust his friends, and hope that they didn't die because of him.

Eventually Skylar stopped, having to use her coffee table to bat zombies away from her. She shifted it over to one hand and slashed wildly with her knife with the other. Marcus stabbed a zombie in the face, kicking it in the chest to dislodge it from his blade, but his movements were slower, sluggish. He was either getting tired, having a hard time moving with his Jax-pack, or there were too many zombies weighing them down clutching to his back.

Or all three things.

Jax wanted to start swinging, but he was afraid that if Marcus moved too fast or in a direction he wasn't expecting, that he'd accidentally smack him in the face.

He reached back and swung behind him, trying to hit something, anything, but the ghouls were all lower than his area of reach.

Skylar let out a yell of frustration, and Marcus swung to see her swing the coffee table in a mighty arc, taking the head of a ghoul clean off. "Let's go!" she screamed, and tore for the staircase.

Marcus ran, his quick sprint shaking all but one of the ghouls, the corpse flailing around behind them as he took off. They reached the stairs, and thankfully there were none right at the top, so they barrelled up.

Or at least, Skylar did. Marcus struggled, grabbing the railing and trying to drag his way up the stairs.

"There's a zombie on my back!" Jax called to her, and she thundered back down the steps, kicking viciously at the barnacle corpse behind him.

It took two kicks, but the ghoul finally dislodged, falling down the stairs like a rag doll.

"Come on!" she urged, grabbing Marcus' free arm and helping him up the rest of the staircase. "We have to block them!" she huffed as the ghouls below began to crawl up the stairs.

Jax pointed to a sofa nearby that looked just about the right width to block it off. "There!" he cried.

Skylar ran around the back of it and shoved. Marcus grabbed the closest side and pulled, and between the two of them they heaved it to the staircase. The zombies were about halfway up now, and Marcus got out of the way, joining his girlfriend on the other side. They pushed until the couch got stuck at the mouth of the staircase.

"Harder!" she shrieked, and they gave it another good heave at the same time, stuffing the overly fluffy sofa into the gap, blocking the top half of the staircase. It worked like a plug, and perhaps wouldn't hold forever, but hopefully long enough for them to get to the terrace.

The home bar and rec room sprawled across half of the floor, the rest a glass wall looking out over the terrace proper. There was a pool and a decent amount of zombies milling about, or at least, they *had* been milling about. Now that they'd heard the commotion, they were turning and heading towards the open patio door.

"The stairs to the roof are out there, huh?" Marcus huffed, and Jax nodded.

"They sure are," he replied.

Skylar leaned against the wall for a moment. "Catch your breath, boys," she said. "We need another plan."

"We're going to need to take them all out," Skylar said, "otherwise if we get up there before the helicopter shows up, they'll follow us up."

Jax shook his head. "Unless we can lock a few in here," he pointed out.

"Maybe," Marcus added, chewing his bottom lip. "But the more come in here, the harder it's going to be for us to get out." He pushed the image of Skylar struggling in the death grip of a zombie from his mind. He had to focus. They were almost there.

He tightened his grip on his knives. He was tired. Sure, they'd run marathons together, but never wearing humans on their backs. It was definitely a workout. He had a feeling his back would be feeling this for a while once they made it out of here.

If we make it out of here… he thought, but then pushed that away too. They were going to make it. They had to.

"You okay back there?" he asked, and felt his friend shift on his shoulders as he nodded.

"Yeah, don't worry about me," Jax replied.

Skylar raised the coffee table shield and turned towards the patio. "We've got to do this, and now," she said, motioning to the door with her knife. Some of the zombies had reached the door.

One went *splash* into the pool, and Marcus cocked a brow. "If we can get them in the pool they'll be stuck," he suggested as he walked in step with her, readying his knives.

"Good call," she agreed. "Let's take them one at a time, at least as best we can."

He could hear the little tremble in her voice. He knew his girl. She was tough as nails, but was just as worried about him as he was about her.

"We got this," he said firmly, and she threw a smile over her shoulder at him.

"Yeah, we do," she agreed, and then rushed the door with renewed vigor.

Marcus hadn't expected that, and broke into a sprint to catch up to her. She stabbed one of the zombies and shoved the rest back through the door with the coffee table. It was just long enough to block the opening, but she had to keep her head back to avoid the gnashing teeth. She held it at neck height, giving him easy access to corpse eyeballs for skewering.

Skylar suddenly shrieked, and he looked down to see one of them crawling under the makeshift barrier, its legs gnawed to complete nothingness. It must have been one of the last to die, eaten by too many mouths. It held fast to her ankle, and she tried to kick at it, but was focused on holding the table up.

Marcus knelt, slamming his knife through the top of its skull. He tried to wrench it free, but it didn't come easily. He put his foot against its head to brace it, and gagged at the feeling of squish beneath his shoe. It didn't matter how long he spent fighting the dead, he couldn't imagine ever getting used to the putridity of rotted corpses.

There were two left on the other side of the table, and he popped back up, nearly losing his balance as Jax inadvertently sat backwards on the upswing. He corrected himself, but Marcus stumbled and bumped into Skylar.

It was enough to slide the coffee table from the doorframe, and she staggered forward as the table slipped. Marcus made a mad grab for her, but his hands caught nothing but air as she tumbled out of the patio door.

The coffee table bowled over the two zombies, and she reacted fast, rolling away to avoid getting bit in the face. Marcus darted forward, pressing down on the table with his foot to keep the two zombies pinned.

"Get them!" he cried as they thrashed and snarled. He didn't know how long he could hold them down for.

Skylar scrambled to her knees and lunged forward, stabbing each of them in turn, letting out a sigh of relief as they fell limp.

The relief was short-lived, however, as a ghoul staggered dangerously close to his kneeling girlfriend. Marcus threw himself over her, launching into the air, straight into the zombie's chest. Jax yelled in alarm as they flew through the air, straight into the pool.

The deep end, of course, they'd ended up in the deep end, with a thrashing corpse.

Marcus kicked away from it, knowing that breaching the water was more important than fighting the ghoul down here. He hoped that Jax had been able to take a deep breath, but he didn't want to keep him under the water too long.

He swam as hard as he could, feeling the weight of the comforter-wrapped man on his back. *This is going to be heavy as hell when I get out,* he thought bitterly. His momentum slowed significantly, and his lungs burned when he realized the corpse had grabbed a hold of his leg. *Can we catch a fucking break?!*

He kicked back as hard as he could, and then finally breached the water. Jax didn't make any noise behind him, and his heart raced as he struggled to swim for the side of the pool. Skylar was a few feet away, battling a duo of zombies with all she was worth, blood flying everywhere as she slashed with the knife, removing limbs that dropped to the patio with wet *smacks*.

Marcus' fingers brushed the edge of the pool, but he didn't quite get a grip. *Dammit, dammit, I'm so damn HEAVY…* he thought frantically, splashing wildly. He kicked again with his free leg at the zombie's arm holding him back, but he couldn't get enough momentum with the resistance of the water.

He finally grasped the edge of the pool with his fingertips, and pulled as hard as he could, hoping to hell that he could keep a grip on the rough cement. There was a mighty *splash,* and he saw Skylar tearing over to him, having shoved a zombie into the shallow end.

She skidded to a stop, nearly falling over when she reached Marcus, dropping her knife and grabbing his arm with both hands.

"Is Jax okay?!" he demanded as she pulled him up.

She grunted as she heaved him out onto the cement, grabbing his shoulders to help them out. "I don't know," she huffed, "his eyes are closed."

Fuck fuck fuck, he thought frantically as he struggled to get out of the water. "Thing's got my leg," he gasped.

Skylar leaned down after he was halfway out, and pried the corpse's fingers from her lover's ankle. Marcus kicked free, scrambling out of the pool, dripping on his hands and knees, Jax completely limp dead weight on his back.

"Can you give him mouth-to-mouth?" he asked breathlessly. "In this position?"

Skylar swallowed hard, and he could see the cogs turning in her head, wondering the same things he was. If Jax was dead, should they just cut him loose? Could they revive him? Would they have to cut him out of the backpack to revive him? Or more importantly…

"No time," she snapped, and wrapped her hands around his bicep to help him to his feet.

Marcus glanced in the direction she was looking, seeing a quartet of zombies approaching along the side of the pool.

He took a deep breath, putting a foot underneath him and pushing up to a standing. The sopping comforter plus Jax' slack form made this difficult, but he made it. Once he was wavering on his feet, Skylar pulled on his arm towards the staircase.

"We can't leave any walking around," he argued.

She shook her head. "We need to get Jax to the upper level," she insisted. "If they're bottlenecked on the staircase, I can just keep kicking them down and stabbing them."

Marcus' heart leapt into his throat. "That's a dangerous plan," he said.

"It's our only option," she snapped, and practically dragged him along with them. "Come on."

They tore for the stairs. A duo of zombies stood at the bottom of it. But she let go of Marcus and didn't break stride, lowering her shoulder and smacking right into one of them. The ghoul flailed its arms as it went sailing over the edge of the eighteen-story building.

Marcus braced himself as the other zombie staggered towards him, realizing that he'd left his knives in the pool. With the limp fingers hanging down his chest, he was sure the meat tenderizer and revolver were down there as well.

Skylar whirled around, a blood-spattered angel of death, and drove her blade into the ghoul's temple before it could reach him. "Come on!" she yelled and waved for him to move up the stairs.

Marcus grabbed the railings, using his arms to pull himself up as much as his legs. Adrenaline coursed through him, the only thing propelling him through the utter exhaustion weighing him down.

He glanced over his shoulder halfway up, looking down at Skylar as she grabbed both railings, swinging her legs out to boot a pursuing ghoul in the chest. There were only five left, and they fell over each other like bowling pins as she kicked it down the stairs.

"Go!" she yelled, looking back at him.

Marcus didn't want to leave her, but he knew he needed to take care of Jax. The longer they waited, the less effective CPR would be to try to revive him. He hoped the guy had just passed out from shock or something, and that he hadn't inhaled a bunch of water.

He reached the top of the stairs, and his blood ran cold. Eight zombies turned to face him, mouths open, arms outstretched.

"Fuck me," he breathed, his heart sinking. He had no weapons. There was a possibly dead man strapped to his back, soaking wet. The love of his life was fighting undead monsters downstairs.

Marcus took a second to be overwhelmed by his thoughts, and then frantically began working at the knots in the fabric. In any case, he didn't need to have Jax strapped to him anymore. He'd set him down and try to hold the zombies at bay until Skylar could get up there with her knife.

Of course, the fabric had been pulled tight, and now it was wet, and his fingers were wet, and the creatures grew closer and closer. He let out a frustrated scream as he fumbled with the knots, and hopelessness began to creep in.

Skylar burst up the stairs, eyes wild and hair askew, knife crimson, as well as most of the rest of her. Marcus stared at her, mind reeling. He needed her to cut Jax loose. But there was no time. And he knew, deep in the pit of his stomach, that she was going to run for those zombies. The sadness in her eyes told him that she was sorry.

Don't do it, he thought, and he wanted to say it out loud, but he knew that if the roles were reversed, he would fight the zombies too. He would try to buy her as much time as he could.

She moved then, to take off at a sprint, and then froze at a most unreal sound.

Helicopter blades. And then the *whirrrr* of a mini-gun.

Marcus ran for Skylar then, his legs suddenly made of rocket fuel, and crashed into her, knocking the two of them off to the side as the chopper peppered the zombies with bullets. He didn't know if they would have been in the line of fire or not, but he'd reacted instinctually.

She yelled something, but he couldn't hear it over the roar of the gun. When it finally stopped, the chopper lowered down onto the roof, and the two of them sat up, Marcus struggling with Jax still sopping wet and draped over him.

They stared at the vehicle in shock, both blinking as if in disbelief that they'd been saved, really and truly.

A few soldiers jumped down, waving maniacally to them.

Skylar leapt to action first, pulling on Marcus' arm to help him to his feet. The adrenaline seemed to leach out of him then, sapped by their impending rescue, his body suddenly realizing that it didn't need to push anymore, didn't need to desperately try to survive.

One of the soldiers furrowed his brow. "What's wrong with buddy?" he asked, motioning to Jax.

"They fell in the pool," Skylar explained, and turned, sliding her knife under one of the fabric straps around Marcus' shoulder. She grunted as the knife failed to easily cut through the thick curtain fabric, and another soldier came forward with his own knife to help.

Marcus staggered forward as Jax fell free, his body feeling like jelly as the weight left him. Skylar caught him, clutching his shoulders like she never wanted to let go, but he patted her arm gently.

"I'm okay," he huffed, "help Jax."

She nodded and moved over to the still man's side.

"Is he bit?" one of the soldiers asked. "Why was he strapped to you?"

"He uses a wheelchair," Skylar replied, "and we didn't know how else to get him all the way up the stairs. He's not bit."

Marcus turned around, watching as the soldier put his fingers to Jax's throat.

Please be alive, please… he thought, a mantra in his head to whatever deity could have possibly let the apocalypse happen to the world.

The soldier began doing chest compressions, and Skylar swallowed hard, beginning to work at the duct tape with her knife to at least free him from the thick wet comforter.

IS HE ALIVE?! Marcus wanted to yell.

Skylar managed to rip all the duct tape open, releasing the wet comforter so the soldier could get a better compression. They waited with bated breath for something, anything.

Marcus clenched his jaw. They came all this way, carried him all this way. He saved him from blowing his brains out downstairs, just to die here, beneath their rescue helicopter.

Jax coughed and sputtered, his body spasming.

"Oh, thank fuck," Skylar gushed, leaning over him to slick his hair back from his forehead. "Jax?"

"Okay, get him into the chopper," one of the soldiers said, waving at them maniacally. "We don't have much time." He knelt and wrapped a hand around Marcus' bicep, helping him up into the vehicle.

Skylar and the soldier who'd saved Jax lifted him, carrying him to the door where two more soldiers helped pull him aboard. As soon as she clambered up, Skylar curled up against Marcus, sliding her arms around his neck and pulling him against her chest.

"We made it," she said, her lips a hair's breadth from his ear.

All he could do was nod against her, pressing his forehead into her throat, relishing in the feel of her pulse. She

was alive. They were alive. They'd made
it.

CHAPTER ELEVEN

The helicopter flew to the north, landing near the interstate, well back from the front line of the barricade. As soon as it touched down, soldiers appeared from all directions to help the civilians down to the ground.

Jax couldn't believe he was alive. As two soldiers gently lifted him down and set him into a rolling office chair somebody had provided, he looked around at the world, taking in a painful, ragged breath. He didn't know what had happened when he hit the water, whether the shock had knocked him out or what, but he was damned grateful that Marcus hadn't just left him in that pool.

Or let him shoot himself. Or any of the other ways he could have been abandoned to die that day.

"Thank you," he said hoarsely, and the soldier smiled at him, patting his shoulder before climbing back up into the chopper.

As it lifted off, the telltale whistle of missiles cut through the air, and the trio of survivors stared as their home was effectively flattened.

"It would have been quick, at least," Marcus said darkly.

Jax couldn't help but laugh. He didn't know what else to do. Before long, his wheezing giggles caught fire, and the couple standing behind him joined in, the three of them busting a gut and causing more than a few soldiers to eye them, concerned.

"I can't believe we made it through that," Skylar finally gasped, holding her stomach. "I just can't believe it."

Marcus shook his head. "*I* can," he declared, kissing her temple. "Because we had you."

"I am so getting laid tonight," she joked.

He wavered on his feet. "Maybe after I sleep for a good seven days straight, love."

"Here," a soldier said, shoving another rolling chair behind Marcus. "You look like you're about to topple over. Let's have a look at you."

"Are you the medic?" he asked, and motioned to Jax. "I think you should check out our buddy here first, he almost drowned."

The soldier turned to Jax and knelt down, setting down a metal box. "Sorry we didn't have a wheelchair for you," he said, shaking his head. "The guys radioed us to see if we could find one, but all we had were a few office chairs. We'll try to find something as fast as possible for you."

"Man, honestly, I don't care if I have to ride a rocking horse," Jax replied, eyes wide. "I'm just happy to be alive right now."

The medic chuckled. "Fair enough."

"Jax!" Lennox bellowed, rushing over. "Man!" He leaned down to give his friend a tight hug.

Jax laughed, patting him on the back. "Good to see you, face to face," he said as Lennox stood back up. "Sorry, I'm still damp."

"You smell like rotten chlorine," Lennox said brightly. "Do a triathlon to get to the roof?"

"Pretty much," Jax replied, swallowing hard and wincing at the burn in his throat.

Lennox held out a bottle of water. "Here, shit, sorry," he gushed, unscrewing the cap. He turned to Skylar and Marcus, pulling out another bottle from the side pocket of his pants. "It's warm, but does the trick."

"Thanks," Skylar said, accepting the bottle and opening it. She held it down to her boyfriend first, but he waved at her to go. She rolled her eyes. "Oh no, no, after you," she teased, and took a swig before forcing it into his hands.

"Skylar and Marcus, right?" Lennox prompted, cocking his head at them.

She offered a smile. "Yes, and you must be Lennox," she replied. "It's nice to properly thank you, in the flesh, for saving our lives."

"Well, it was Jax that gave me the push to get out here and do it," he replied, shoving his hands into his pockets. "And if it weren't for him I wouldn't have made it this far into the apocalypse, so I s'pose everything just comes full circle, huh?"

Marcus raised his bottle. "Damn right it does," he declared.

Skylar let out a deep *whoosh* of breath. "You know, I loved that condo," she admitted, "but I am so glad to be on the ground."

"Agreed," Jax added, taking another sip of water as the medic patted his knee.

The soldier moved over to Marcus. "Looks like you all escaped with a few bumps and bruises," he declared as he checked them over. "Nothing a little rest won't fix."

"Rest sounds good," Skylar replied, giving her boyfriend's shoulder a squeeze.

The medic stood up and gave them a nod. "You deserve it," he replied. "Thank you, the four of you, for getting us the intel on the convention center. You saved a lot of lives today."

The quartet murmured responses, and Jax scratched the back of his head. There was a lot of thanks going around, and a lot to be grateful for.

"There will be a transport here for you soon," the soldier told them, and picked up his kit. "Take it easy, you four." He turned and headed back to the front lines. "Now, we press on to downtown."

END

Up Next: As the military closes in on downtown, a small team of soldiers undertake a daring mission to help win the war in Seattle Pt. 9

DEAD AMERICA
THE NORTHWEST INVASION
BOOK 11
SEATTLE PART 9
BY DEREK SLATON
© 2020

CHAPTER ONE

Day Zero +27

To the east of the I-5 laid a neighborhood just north of Volunteer Park. Battles raged all along the roads, gunfire cracking in every direction.

"How much longer until dawn?" Private Bartlett asked as she held her gun at the ready.

The densely populated area was a mix of high-priced apartments and upscale businesses, and had been home to a large number of young professionals who'd spent their days commuting to their high rise office jobs.

"Still another hour," Private Sellers replied, checking his watch.

Bartlett sighed. "Dammit."

Post apocalypse, the area had become a nightmarish collection of zombies, darkened corridors, and danger. This, of course, was made worse by lack of sunlight.

The two soldiers stood in an intersection with their squad of ten, two blocks to the east of the interstate, surrounded by residential housing. The next street had a couple of stores and some solar powered streetlights, but the trees at the far end blocked the majority of the light.

Their mission was to keep a firing line and a keen eye to the west. They didn't have any sort of barricade, which made the whole situation more nerve-wracking, just taking a knee in the middle of the road.

"Make sure the flanks are covered," Sellers reminded the troops. "We don't want any surprises."

Corporal Korver rolled his eyes, looking down his nose at the young Private. "Relax kid," he drawled, "we cleared the yards already."

"Our last squad thought that too," Bartlett snapped. "Then a runner got loose."

Sellers narrowed his eyes. "There's a reason we're with you now, instead of still with them," he added.

Korver paused at the pain in their voices and clenched his jaw. While nothing official had come down the line, he'd heard from some of the others that there were significant losses among the southern force the day before. The last thing he wanted was for rumors to spread around to the others.

"Potts, Benton," he declared, "pick a side and cover it."

The two Privates moved to the left and ride side respectively, taking a knee and keeping a close, intense watch on the houses to each side.

All of a sudden Private Galindo fired off several shots from his assault rifle, startling the whole team into high alert.

When he stopped, chest heaving, Korver turned and smacked him on the arm.

"Galindo, what the hell, man?" he demanded.

The Private's eyes were wide. "I saw movement down the street."

"Really?" the Corporal asked, skepticism evident in his tone. "Where? Why don't you point it out to the rest of us since you can see in the fucking dark?"

Galindo strained his eyes, trying to get a read on the area where he shot, but couldn't see anything. "Well…" he trailed off, dragging out the word. "I don't see it anymore."

"Probably because it wasn't there to begin with," Korver snapped, pointing a finger at him. "In case you forgot, we don't have more ammo coming, and we have a long-ass day ahead of us. So unless you want to start fighting hand to hand with those undead bastards, I would suggest you wait for the target to get real close. You don't have to hit them at a distance, they aren't shooting back at us."

The Private nodded begrudgingly, wincing at the verbal beat down. He checked his ammo reserves, wrinkling his nose when he found only two full mags remaining.

"Now, everybody," the Corporal declared, "keep your eyes peeled for movement. We're past the choke point bridge, so we're going to get hit with everything coming from downtown."

As if on cue, the gunfire coming from the east kicked up, only a block away. It was intense fire, sounding like hundreds of rounds being squeezed off in rapid succession. The group stiffened, muscles tense, and several of them turned their aim towards the noise.

"Stay steady, everyone," Korver warned, and they waited with bated breath.

The firing continued for several moments, and then quickly died down, which did nothing to ease the tension in the troops. They remained motionless and silent, straining their ears and eyes, waiting for any sign of the enemy.

Eerie moans began to float towards them from the south, and the Privates turned that way, taking aim into the darkness.

"Nobody fire until you're a hundred percent sure you can hit the target," Korver said firmly, still facing the east.

After several moments of tense waiting, zombies appeared beneath the streetlight at the next intersection, fifty to sixty yards away. At first it was just a trickle, a few small groups of three or four, but by the time those groups had crossed the beam of light, there were dozens coming up behind them.

The soldiers held fast, the ghouls too far away to shoot.

"Corporal," Galindo murmured to his superior, staying as quiet as he could, "hundred or so down the street headed our way."

Korver nodded. "Heard," he replied, voice low.

The firing to the east had completely stopped, and a full minute went by of nobody saying anything, the only sound the shuffling and groaning of the approaching monsters.

"Twenty seconds and we gotta start shooting," Galindo whispered, "or we're going to get overrun."

"Heard," the Corporal repeated.

As the soldiers prepared, a set of footsteps came up the road, moving rapidly. Korver strained his ears even harder, hearing some heavy breathing, huffing and puffing. It was too dark to see what it was, runner or human, so he squared his shoulders as it grew closer.

"Nobody fires unless I do," the Corporal said quietly. When there was no response, he clucked his tongue and asked firmly, "Is that clear?"

There was a quiet chorus of *yes, sir*, and Korver gripped his assault rifle tightly, preparing to unload if he needed to. A few seconds later, the footsteps sounded deadly close, soon followed by wheezing.

"Don't shoot, just run!" the person yelled, voice hoarse from overexertion.

A male soldier emerged from the darkness, weaponless and covered from head to toe in blood. His eyes were wild, terrified, and as he reached the line, he shoved the Corporal aside and kept tearing past them.

Korver tried to reach out to slow him down. "Hey—"

"Run! Run!" the soldier cried, batting him away. He vanished into the darkness on the other side, and the soldiers whipped back to where he'd come from as more footsteps smacked the pavement.

Korver raised his weapon again, prompting the rest of his team facing that direction to do the same.

"As soon as you see one, start shooting," he commanded. "Can't let runners get a foothold!"

The soldiers prepared, muscles tense as the hungry snarls and pounding feet grew louder.

"Going hot," Galindo warned.

The Corporal nodded. "Do it," he replied.

The Private took aim and fired, prompting the other troops facing south to do the same. Their gunshots were calm and collected, each of them strategically picking targets and dropping them, one by one.

They kept the slow-moving creatures at bay, the closest still standing about twenty yards away, but the crowd was thicker the deeper they looked.

A moment later, a runner came into the light from the east. There wasn't much to illuminate it, but they could make out the fast moving ghoul. Korver fired first, sending three-round bursts downrange. The first batch ripped into the zombie's chest, tearing through its tattered crimson fatigues. One round from the second burst found its target, cracking through the bridge of the monster's nose, sending it flopping backwards onto the pavement with a wet smack.

As soon as it hit the ground, a dozen more appeared to take its place, racing quickly towards the living and breathing lunch in the middle of the intersection.

"Open fire, open fire!" Korver screamed in panic.

The soldiers next to him unleashed a torrent of bullets, everyone shooting in three-round bursts. Most of the shots either missed the bodies completely, or hit harmlessly on torsos and shoulders.

As the runners grew closer, the soldiers were able to adjust their aim, hitting a few in the head, but several troops resorted to panic fire as the threat grew bigger and bigger.

One ghoul reached a few yards of Sellers, but both he and Bartlett focused their guns and fired simultaneously, both bullets punching it in the forehead just before it reached him. The creature lurched forward, sliding on the pavement, and coming to a stop just at his feet.

"Watch it, Potts!" Korver barked, and she stood up from her kneel, retreating while firing into a trio of runners on the left side of the road.

She was able to hit the leader in the head, but the other shots found throats instead, and the other two took their opening to leap on her.

The zombies attacked viciously, spraying blood every which way. Potts screamed, her agony palpable as flesh tore from her body.

"Keep firing!" the Corporal screamed at Sellers and Bartlett, and broke from his position. He emptied the rest of his mag into the feasting zombies, taking them out and plunging a bullet into the now gurgling soldier's forehead to stop her from suffering and reanimating.

He didn't take a moment to grieve, couldn't waste any precious moments, and simply smacked in another magazine and turned back towards the runners still bearing down on their position. He could make out half a dozen through the darkness, but he didn't want to assume there weren't more.

Meanwhile, Galindo and his team picked up their firing rate, the zombies from the south still growing in number.

"Last mag!" Galindo yelled, slapping in a fresh mag to continue firing. The others in his group continued, and then Private Benton suddenly turned to the west, unloading bullets in that direction.

"Contact west!" he screamed. He ripped off a couple of shots towards the yard between some houses. He hit a zombie in the head, dropping it, but more emerged from the shadows.

Galindo's team struggled to hold back the horde, the ghouls at the front edge having come within fifteen yards of them.

"We're going to get overrun, Corporal!" Galindo cried.

Korver, Sellers, and Bartlett continued to fire on the runners, working in three-round bursts, and another one dropped. As soon as it flopped backwards, five more joined the handful of others rushing towards their position.

The Corporal grunted in frustration. "Move to the west!" he barked.

The trio began to retreat while still firing. Galindo and Barr stood up from their knees and moved back while the three still on the eastern side of the formation continued shooting to the south horde.

Korver whipped around, joining Benton in pushing to the west, hitting targets in the yard while leading the group towards the alley between the houses.

"We're moving!" Galindo bellowed, and he and Barr joined Sellers and Bartlett in firing towards the runners, hitting a few of them.

Privates Marin and Waller leapt to their feet, the latter grabbing Private Parra by the arm to pull him up.

Parra looked to the east, his eyes widening at how close the runners were getting. He jerked his arm free and fired, but his aim was off. Rather than retreat, he adjusted his aim and fired again, but missed.

The military ghoul rushed him, and he froze in terror. By the time he snapped out of it, the zombie was on top of him, ripping at his throat.

Marin screamed and rushed to his aid, grabbing the ghoul by the back of its clothes. He managed to get it off of Parra, but his hand slipped on the blood-soaked fabric as the ghoul got free, whirling around and launching into his gut, teeth first.

Marin wailed and pulled his handgun, shooting the zombie through the top of its head.

Waller stood stunned, seeing his friends bleeding and wounded from zombie bites, sealing their fates.

"Waller, move!" Galindo bellowed, bringing up the rear of the retreat.

The grieving Private raised his rifle, aiming at his bleeding friend.

Marin immediately threw his hands up, palms out. "Waller, no, no!" he begged frantically. "Let me keep fighting, let me —"

Waller pulled the trigger, hitting his friend in the forehead. He immediately let out an agonized scream, angry at the situation. He whirled to face the west, stomping after his team, and then froze as Galindo raised his rifle, aiming past him.

Waller whipped back around, but it was too late. The monster that used to be Parra scrambled to its feet and launched itself through the air, tackling him and biting into his bicep. Waller groaned and hissed in pain, punching the zombie in the head to try to dislodge it.

Galindo chewed his lower lip and then fired a three-round burst, hitting both Parra and Waller in the top of the head, leaving them both limp on the road. Before he could think too hard about it, he turned and rushed after the remains of his team at the far end of the alley.

"Where are the others?" Korver asked, but the Private just shook his head, not needing to vocalize what had happened.

"Where are we going, Corporal?" Sellers asked, eyes wide.

Korver rubbed his forehead. Down to six, including himself. Just six. "Not sure yet," he admitted.

"There's an apartment building on the next block," Benton suggested. "That should provide us enough cover until this horde passes."

The Corporal shook his head. "No, we have to move south."

"South?" Galindo gaped at him. "You saw how many of those things were there. And hell, that doesn't include the runners." He shook his head wildly. "That's suicide!"

Korver narrowed his eyes. "We have orders to hold this line and that's exactly what we're going to do," he said firmly. "If we don't, then we're going to get wiped out on this side of the water."

"What about the zombies that overran the line to the east?" Galindo demanded. "You want to take them out too?"

Korver nodded. "If we can."

"I think there's a storefront near the far end of the block to the south," Bartlett piped up, holding up a hand. "We might be able to fend them off in there if we can get to it."

Sellers nodded. "I saw it too."

"Gotta admit," Benton added quietly, "I like the idea of being inside more than being exposed out here."

Bartlett nodded emphatically. "And we might be able to draw over some zombies from the next street up as well."

As Korver contemplated the Privates all trying to convince him, Galindo turned and fired several shots down the alley at a few zombies stumbling into it.

"Fuck it," he grunted. "Anywhere is better than here."

"Let's move," Korver finally agreed, and led the team out of the alley and into a grassy area separating the two rows of buildings. The group raced down the area, aiming down the alleys as they crossed to make sure there were no surprises inside.

When they reached the end of the row, standing outside a mid-sized single story building, Korver immediately went to work on the lock. Galindo and Barr aimed back to the north, popping off a few shots at zombies that had followed them back down.

"Well, at least we know they'll follow us wherever we go," Galindo muttered.

"We got a runner," Barr said, whipping behind them.

Galindo clenched his jaw. "Make that two," he said. "Sellers, Benton, get in here."

The two Privates stepped up and readied their weapons, but he shook his head.

"We'll handle shooting them," Galindo said.

Sellers furrowed his brow. "What do you want us to do?" he asked.

The runners passed the slow-moving zombies, still about thirty yards away.

"If we miss," Galindo said, "you need to hold them at bay."

Sellers and Benton shared a concerned look.

Barr shook her head. "Just get low and grab them," she explained. "We're only going to need a second to finish them."

"Damn well better," Benton muttered.

Galindo and Barr tracked their targets with their barrels as they grew closer. They waited until they were within ten yards before pulling the trigger.

Barr's shot pierced the zombie's forehead, sending it tumbling back to the ground in a heap. Galindo's shot was a dull *click* instead of a loud *boom*.

"Fuck," he said flatly.

Sellers dove forward, dropping to one knee, and lashed out with his fists, catching the zombie by the belt and shirt. The momentum sent it tumbling over him, but Sellers anticipated it and twisted, smacking it into the ground. He used every ounce of his strength to hold it down, and Galindo pulled his handgun to execute the beast at point-blank range.

"Appreciate the assist," he said.

Sellers clenched his fists as he got to his feet. "Next time you want me to risk my life," he growled, "make goddamn sure there's a bullet in the chamber."

Galindo opened his mouth to argue, but closed it again. He'd fucked up, and his teammate was absolutely right.

"Got the door," Korver called, stepping aside, "let's move!"

The six soldiers burst into the store, the Corporal brought up the rear to secure the door. Sellers, Bartlett, and Galindo pushed through the store, which turned out to be a trendy clothing boutique, clearing it quickly. When they reached the front, they stopped, staring out the front windows, which were nestled into a waist-high wooden wall.

"Mother of god," Sellers breathed, "that's a lot of zombies."

As they waited on the others they stared at the sea of ghouls outside, slowly shambling past them to the north.

"And that's just the ones we can see," Bartlett murmured. "God only knows how many of them have already gone past."

Benton and Barr walked up, joining the others overlooking the street, gawking at the view.

"Command, this is quadrant three," Korver barked into his radio. "Over."

There were a few moments of silence, and the Corporal turned to look out the window as well.

"Command," he tried again, "this is quadrant three, do you copy?"

"We have you," somebody replied, "what's your status?"

Korver let out a sigh of relief and then shook his head. "Position was overrun, have taken shelter one block south," he explained. "Preparing to engage the enemy. Be advised that the team at quadrant four was taken out."

"Do you have a count?" came the reply.

The Corporal sucked in a deep breath. "Ten, give or take."

"No exact count?" command asked, sounding indignant.

Korver sighed. "Negative," he replied. "However, a survivor from that squad ran through our position, so it's likely he pulled the runners in our direction."

"Noted," command replied. "We are sending reinforcements to your position. The line is being pushed north too much for comfort, so your orders are to take as many as you can out, and hold them there."

The Corporal rubbed his forehead. "ETA on reinforcements?" he asked.

"Thirty minutes," came the reply.

Korver nodded. "Understood," he said. "Korver out." He pocketed the radio and stepped up to the window, looking both ways to the north and south. "Looks like a few dozen of those things have gotten past this point, but it's still too dark to see the south past the intersection."

"How do you want to play it?" Galindo asked.

The Corporal looked around the room as he contemplated, seeing nothing but clothing racks. He stepped over to the nearest one and threw the overpriced dresses on the floor. He grabbed the rack and shook it a bit, testing the sturdy piece of metal that stretched about six feet.

"Benton, give me a hand with this," he said, and when the Private approached, they picked it up and moved it over to the front door, pushing it up against it. "Door is sturdy enough, solid wood," Korver mused. "But those things can break through if they bunch up. Benton, Barr, start looking around for heavy things to shore this up. Bartlett, Sellers, start finding us some weapons that don't require ammo."

Galindo cocked his head. "What about me?"

The Corporal raised a hand. "We're going to build us a barricade."

In a matter of ten minutes, Korver and Galindo had moved most of the heavy clothing racks over to the windows, and adjusted the heights of them to form an extension of the wooden wall. With the added metal, the barricade came chest high, meaning the zombies would still have a tough time reaching through.

"That's some quality work there, Corporal," Galindo said as he stepped back, swiping his palms together.

Korver nodded. "It'll do it a pinch," he replied. "At least I hope it will."

Sellers and Bartlett came out of the back room carrying armfuls of metal posts that had been designed to snap onto the racks that were now pressed against the walls. They dropped them onto the ground, the loud metallic *clang* echoing throughout the room.

"This is all we could find," Sellers declared.

Korver picked up one, feeling the heft in his hand. "Got some solid weight to it," he murmured. He inspected the end, seeing that it was empty but had a spot for something to be inserted. "A shame we don't have the blade attachments for it," he joked.

Bartlett smiled wryly and reached into her pocket, pulling out a six-inch long insert. The extended portion was considerably thinner, with a couple of metal notches on it where clothes would hang. She stepped over and slid it into the end of the post with a sharp *click*.

"It's not a spike," she said, "but it's solid metal and thin enough that we should be able to punch through the skull."

Korver inspected it and nodded approvingly. "I think you might be right there…" he trailed off, and turned back to the window, which now had the attention of a hundred or so zombies. They'd been filing over with each bump and clang of the barricade building procedures. "Hope you're ready for a workout, because we have a hell of a crowd waiting on us."

Benton and Barr emerged from the back storeroom carrying a heavy case, struggling to get it to the front. When they got there, they dropped it on top of the rack base by the door, joining several other various objects.

"Don't know how well that's going to hold up, but it's what we got," Benton declared.

As if on cue, one of the windows cracked under the pressure from the zombies.

"Looks like we're going to find out," Korver said, holding up his metal rod. "Get your weapons and get in position."

Everyone picked up one of the rods, and Bartlett passed out the extended puncture tips. As they did this, the window on the far right shattered, and rotted arms reached inside. The jagged glass ripped through their limbs, but they didn't seem to care, being as dead and hungry as they were.

Bartlett and Sellers rushed over and began jamming their weapons right into zombie heads. It took them a few tries to find the right angle, but soon Sellers was able to deliver a kill shot, punching right through the decrepit forehead of a ghoul.

"Put the bar on the metal racks and just thrust forward," he called. "Don't worry about aiming, you'll hit something!"

Bartlett nodded and rested her own bar on the rack, and shoved it forward with all of her might. Despite her tiny frame, the thrust went between two creatures and embedded into the eye socket of a skull in the second row.

"There you go," Sellers said with a grin. "Now just do that a couple hundred more times!"

She shot him a playful middle finger and then geared up for another thrust.

On the other side of the room, the other four soldiers had taken up positions at their windows.

Tired of waiting, Korver readied his weapon. "Break the glass, let's get killing!" he bellowed, and thrust through, shattering the window and driving the rod right into a rotted skull.

The rest of the team followed suit, beginning their assault on the ghouls outside.

The fighting was tense, the creatures reaching through as far as they could and nearly grabbing hold of the soldiers trying to keep them at bay. One monster managed to grip Galindo's weapon, and he let out a roar, shaking it back and forth.

"Motherfucker," he yelled, "give me my spear back!"

He finally wrestled it free of the death grip, and slammed it through the zombie's eye socket, letting out a victory shout before continuing his assault.

As the minutes ticked by, zombies dropped by the dozens. Some soldiers began to tire out, needing a breather to rest their thrusting arms. As they dropped their limbs to give them a rest, Korver continued to dispatch ghouls with precision and speed.

"Keep pushing!" he yelled. "This ain't break time, bitches!"

The pep talk fired up the group, and they went back at it, pushing hard. Bartlett turned and saw the front door hinges starting to warp, and then the to one snapped free of the wall.

"The door!" she screamed. "Get the door!"

Galindo was closest, and glanced over, eyes widening as he dropped his weapon. He threw his full weight into the door as the latch cracked open. Even with his full body weight and the makeshift door jamb, the zombies were too powerful, and the door inched open.

"Need a hand over here!" he bellowed as rotted arms began to reach through the gap, flailing around for food.

Barlett dropped her rod and rushed over to the door, drawing her handgun. She inched as close as she could to the opening, aiming through the crack and firing. She shot quickly but deliberately, dropping every head she could get a clean view of.

But even with the reduced stress, the door continued to creep open.

"Benton!" Bartlett screamed.

The Private beside Korver rushed over to help with the door. He threw himself beside Galindo, helping to hold it at bay.

Bartlett continued to shoot, while the other three held their own at the windows.

"Shit, they're starting to get too high!" Sellers cried, and one of the zombies managed to flip over to the inside, having used its dead brethren as a stepping stone. Rather than take the chance, he pulled his handgun and fired one round into the back of its head before resuming his stabbing through the window with the rod.

The others were soon facing similar problems with zombies tumbling inside. Soon enough, the thud of metal to skull was replaced wholly with handgun fire.

Korver's blood rushed in his ears, the bleakness of the situation setting in, and looked out towards the back of the horde to see if they'd even made a dent. To his surprise, the ghouls at the back were wandering in the other direction, and then a few dropped dead.

"Reinforcements are here!" he cried. "Keep fighting!"

The group summoned an extra bit of strength, changing their strategy from kills to one of outright defense. They used the rods to shove zombies back outside rather than wait for them to get close enough to kill, hoping to stave off the horde long enough for the soldiers outside to take care of them.

The gunfire outside intensified, and the small team held the ghouls at bay as soldiers moved in a single line, shoulder to shoulder, marching towards the store and wiping out all the zombies. As the crowd thinned, several soldiers with machetes stepped up and went to work, slicing and dicing rotted flesh.

As the ghouls moved away from the doors and windows of the store, the group inside began to relax. They sagged, breathing heavily, trying to steady their pounding hearts.

"You okay?" Sellers asked, putting a hand on Bartlett's shoulder.

She nodded and checked her handgun, finding the mag empty. "Yeah, I'm good," she replied. "Not looking forward to fighting hand to hand the rest of the day, but I'm good."

He patted her on the back, and they leaned against the wall to catch their breath.

Korver approached the door and motioned for Galindo and Benton to help him move the barricade out of the way. They shoved everything aside, and when it was clear, he pulled aside the busted door, leading the team outside into the street.

It was total carnage in front of the shop. The bodies by the windows were piled several high, dark blood pooling beneath the corpses. Rotted limp corpses were strewn everywhere, limbs sticking out every which way.

A large man in protective gear walked up to them as the special forces team waltzed through the mess, making sure all the ghouls were dead and dispatched.

"Your team okay?" he asked as he removed his mask.

Korver nodded. "We're down four, but the rest of us are okay," he replied.

"I'm sorry for your losses…" the soldier paused expectantly.

"Corporal Korver," he offered.

"Korver, okay," he nodded firmly. "I'm Sergeant Bauer." He looked around, appraising the piles of corpses around the store. "Looks like despite your losses, your team managed to do some damage."

The Corporal nodded. "That we did, sir," he replied.

"Is your team operational?" Bauer asked.

Korver inclined his head back and forth. Despite their exhaustion, he knew they'd be in tip-top in short order.

"Physically we are," he explained. "But we're real short on ammunition."

Bauer nodded. "I can help with that," he replied, and squeezed a small radio receiver on his vest. "Need an ammo resupply on my position ASAP." He turned to the Corporal. "Is there anything else you need?"

"Wouldn't turn down a hot meal," Korver replied with a small smile.

Bauer laughed and shook his head. "Good try, Corporal," he said, wagging a finger. "Afraid that's not in the cards for any of us for the time being. Got a lot of work ahead of us before that happens."

As he finished his sentence, there was a gigantic explosion in the distance, startling Korver and his team. Bauer didn't even blink an eye as they all looked to the south, the sky lighting up from the flames.

"What the hell was that?" the Corporal breathed.

The Sergeant grinned. "Bringing the fight to the enemy, Corporal," he explained, spreading his arms. "Which is what I need your team to do. Let's step inside for a minute."

He waved for them to follow him into the store and headed towards the back counter. He pulled out a piece of paper from his pocket and spread it out on the flat surface. It was a satellite view of the area, and he pointed to it as he spoke.

"Okay, we're here, just south of the water," he began. "We have a force twenty thousand strong marching down the interstate and headed straight for the center of downtown. Now, we have sniper teams set up on several downtown rooftops to act as distractions, but we need another, which is where your team comes in." He tapped on the paper. "Your target is Freeway Park, approximately two and a half miles south of us. It's perfectly situated on the interstate, with the ten story building overlooking it. We have reports of a massive horde moving up the interstate, and we need to slow it down."

Korver blinked at the page. "I'm glad you have faith in us," he said slowly, "but there's only six of us. How are we supposed to distract a horde large enough to threaten our main force?"

"You're the tip of the spear," Bauer explained. "We have another, larger team moving in from the east, but they are hours out. Your job is to get there and set the stage so they can just waltz in and start firing. We're going to be cutting it close as it is, so anything you can do is going to help out. Questions?"

The Corporal cocked his head. "If this horde is such a threat," he drawled, "then why aren't they using the Apache's to just mini-gun them into goo?"

"Because they aren't densely packed enough yet," the Sergeant replied, shaking his head. "There is a finite amount of ammo, so they are being very selective about their strafing runs. If you can help get them packed up enough, they'll be able to take them out."

Benton leaned forward on the counter, studying the map. "Why not just let the main force take care of it?" he asked.

"Simple logistics," Bauer explained. "Twenty thousand troops don't do much good when you can only get fifty to the line at a time. Plus, all it would take is a few runners getting a foothold, and it would be chaos." He paused as the Private nodded in agreement. "There's a lot to get done," he prompted. "Any other questions?"

Galindo raised his hand. "Yeah, what happened to the team that was originally supposed to do this?" he asked.

"Pretty sure you met them earlier when some of them ran up on your position," Bauer replied. "Now it's next man up."

Galindo stared at him with wide eyes, not even masking the horror on his face. This was about to be a bad situation, and the team that had been equipped for it had already fallen.

Bauer held up a hand and then pressed her finger to his ear to listen to a message coming into his ear bud. He nodded and lowered his hand.

"Okay, your supplies will be here in five," he said. "It'll also have your contact info for the eastern support team so you can coordinate their arrival. You have a map of the area?"

Korver nodded, patting his vest pocket. "Yes, sir."

"Good," the Sergeant replied. "Be safe, move quick, and I'll see you when this is over."

The Corporal nodded as Bauer put his helmet back on and stepped out onto the street, leaving the six soldiers alone. None of them said a word, standing in somber silence for a few moments to contemplate what they were about to walk into.

As the sun came up, the group headed to the south. The streets were littered with the dead, chopped, shot, and mangled beyond recognition. To the southwest, the plume of smoke from the building detonation continued to hang in the air. The troops were careful to step around the dead, just in case any of them were still hanging on to their putrid existence.

"Man, those special forces guys really know how to fuck stuff up," Galindo murmured as he sidestepped a particularly disassembled zombie.

Barr shook her head. "Yeah, not sure why we're the ones being sent on a suicide mission when they are much better equipped to handle it," he added.

"Probably because we're expendable grunts and they're not," Sellers quipped.

Bartlett rolled her eyes. "Thanks buddy," she drawled, "always one for the uplifting banter."

"Just calling it like I see it," he replied with a shrug. "Just like chess, you don't send your queen rushing behind enemy lines. That's the pawn's job."

She shook her head. "Again, so uplifting," she replied.

"Look at the bright side," Benton cut in, "at least we're out here enjoying the sun. We could be cooped up in a shack, surrounded by thousands of those things."

"Day's still young," Korver said dryly.

The team let out a bit of a chuckle, each and every one of them trying to keep their spirits up and their minds off of the incredible danger they were about to be in.

At the end of the road, Korver pulled out his map. He studied it, noting some developed areas running right along the interstate, with a park a few blocks to the east of it.

"What do you think?" he asked. "Fight our way through civilization? Or take a stroll through the park?"

Galindo raised his hand. "Park all day long, Corporal," he said firmly.

The rest of the troops nodded and voiced their approval for that plan.

"Park it is," Korver said, folding up the map and putting it back into his pocket.

He led the group east a few blocks, finding the beginning of the park. They were cautious in the parking lot as there were a few cars there, which meant at one point there'd been patrons at the park.

The Corporal stopped them at the entrance and let out a whistle. A few moments later, a handful of creatures

stumbled out of the woods, shambling by
the cars in their direction.

"Conserve your ammo," he instructed.

Galindo, Sellers, and Benton stepped
up, drawing their knives. They waltzed
over to the zombies and quickly dispatched
them with direct headshots, dropping the
corpses to the pavement. Once the
immediate threat was dealt with, they took
up defensive positions just in case more
ghouls arrived.

After a moment, with no more of their
friends showing up, Korver took point and
led the team through the first set of
trees. When they reached the opening, they
all stopped short, staring wide-eyed at
the devastation before them.

"What the hell happened here?"
Sellers breathed.

They stared at the complete
destruction ahead. Bodies and their
severed limbs covered the entire area.
Trees had been completely uprooted or just
outright destroyed. Blood and guts covered
the ground as far as the eye could see.
The only exception to the unmoving carnage
was a handful of zombies at the far end of
the park, emerging from the opposite tree
line.

Galindo clapped his hands together
with excitement. "Oh shit!" he exclaimed.
"You remember yesterday when I said I

heard something big, and all of you said I
was crazy?" He pumped a fist into the air,
and didn't wait for a response before
continuing, "This must have been it!
Because if this wasn't a bomb of epic
proportions, then I don't know what the
hell it was."

"In our defense," Barr replied,
holding up a hand, "who knew this would be
the one time you weren't full of shit."

A chuckle rippled through the group,
and then Korver straightened his
shoulders.

"Watch your step through here," he
said firmly. "These things may look dead,
but they may still be kicking. A bite to
the ankle is just as deadly as a bite to
the jugular."

The troops nodded and began the move
across the devastated park. They
cautiously stepped over charred bodies,
making sure not to get too close. Sellers
let out a high-pitched scream and leapt a
couple feet back, knife high in the air.

"You alright there, bud?" Bartlett
asked, eyebrow raised in amusement.

He nodded, pointing to where he'd
been standing. "Got a live one, there."

Bartlett moved over slowly and leaned
over to have a look at the mangled corpse.
The blast had blown off the bulk of its
body, leaving only the top foot of its

torso and head. When it seemed to realize a meal was near, it gnashed its teeth in a fruitless attempt to get a bite.

"Put it out of its misery and let's keep moving," Korver instructed.

Barlett turned and playfully motioned to Sellers. "Might as well get your revenge," she offered.

He shook his head and knelt, jamming his blade into the top of the ghoul's head.

The group continued moving and stopped about thirty yards away from the zombies coming out of the woods. There were a dozen of them, spread out several yards apart from each other.

"Teams of two," the Corporal instructed, "let's knock them out."

Everyone drew their knives and paired off, moving in a wide arc towards the line of ghouls. It was a textbook demolition of the dead, forceful kicks knocking the front line to the ground before moving on with head strikes on the back line. Each duo made quick work of the zombies in their path.

When they reached the end of the park, they paused next to a large tree so that Korver could consult his map.

"So, where we headed?" Galindo asked and leaned against the trunk, crossing his arms.

The Corporal pursed his lips for a moment. "Well, no real good options here," he mused. "It's solid civilization for the next mile or so until we get to the park. The stuff near the interstate looks more like storefronts, with more residential stuff to the east."

"I vote residential," Sellers put in, raising his hand. "Lot more open spaces."

Barlett nodded in agreement. "And fewer cars for them to hide under," she pointed out. "With any luck, Sellers here won't scream like an eight year old girl."

"You aren't going to let me live that one down, are you?" he asked, rubbing his forehead.

She smirked at him. "Not for a long time."

"All right," Korver cut in. "Residential it is." Before he could move, his radio chirped, and he sighed. "Surely this is good news," he deadpanned, and raised the radio to his lips. "This is Corporal Korver."

"Corporal, this is Captain Clay," a distinguished voice sounded on the other end. "I believe you are the one clearing the path to Freeway Park for my boys."

Korver nodded. "Yes, sir," he said. "We are en route to it as we speak. Making good time."

"That's good to hear," Clay replied, "however I need you to divert course. A situation has arisen."

The Corporal sighed before clicking the radio button. "Sir, my orders are to take the Freeway Park building so you can come in and hold the horde at bay," he explained. "I don't know what they told you about us, but we're only half a dozen strong."

"I appreciate the fact that this is putting you in a difficult spot," the Captain replied, "but there's more information that you aren't aware of."

Korver nodded. "Of course, Captain," he said quickly, "please continue."

"The bulk of my forces are bogged down less than half a mile from the eastern bridge," Clay explained. "At first, we thought we could push through, but we have been swarmed. We're in a fast spot, but it's going to take too much time for us to fully break out. When this became evident, I sent an advance team of fifty to make a play for the target at Freeway Park." He paused for a beat. "Corporal, I lost contact with them fifteen minutes ago. To put this bluntly, unless you want to tackle the interstate horde on your own, I'm going to need you to mount a bit of a rescue operation."

Korver dropped the radio down by his side, making a deep noise of disgust. It was a stretch for the team to be doing this mission in the first place, and now they'd have to go into full-on rescue mode. He looked around at his team, seeing the same discouraged looks on all of their faces.

"What do you think?" he asked.

Galindo looked around at everyone and then cleared his throat. "I think I speak for everyone when I say this is a shit sandwich," he declared. "But under the circumstances, I think we're going to have to choke it down."

Korver sighed and raised the radio to his lips. "Captain, where are they?" he asked.

"There's a small college about a mile east of the park," Clay replied. "Last I heard, my men were retreating into the residence hall. The leader of the group, Sergeant Salinas, was in a stairwell firing his weapon. Last thing I heard was him screaming, "they're everywhere!" Only sounds after that were moans." He paused, clearing his throat. "I don't know how many are left, or if any of them are. All I know is that they are the only reinforcements you're going to get before nightfall, which will probably be too late to do much good."

The Corporal took a deep breath. "We'll get your men, Captain," he promised. "Or, at the very least, give it all we've got."

"You have my thanks, Corporal," Clay said sincerely. "Good luck."

Korver put the radio away and pulled out his map. Everyone clustered around, and he pointed to the park.

"Okay, we're here," he murmured, "at the park."

Galindo clucked his tongue. "What's left of it, at any rate," he quipped.

"Here is our target by the interstate," Korver continued, following with his finger. "Now we just have to figure out where the hell the college is."

Everyone leaned over the map, the Corporal slowly moving his finger east of the target.

"Wait, that's gotta be it," Bartlett said, reaching over to point at a few blank areas to the east. "Those have to be sports fields, right?"

Sellers nodded, staring at the area. "I think she's right," he agreed. "Everything else in the area is completely developed."

"I don't see any other potentials, so that's my vote unless anyone has a viable objection," Korver said. He glanced over at Galindo.

The Private shrugged, shaking his head. "Hell, we're going to be walking into trouble no matter where we go," he said. "Does the specific location really matter that much?"

"Let's get moving," Korver said, folding up the paper and putting it back in his pocket, "it's going to be a hell of a hike."

The bulk of the team sat in the living room of a house, everybody but Benton, who stayed low and out of sight. Korver studied the map, seeing they were still a mile and a half away from what they thought was the college.

Barlett peeked out the front window and saw a few dozen zombies in the front yard, just milling about aimlessly, completely unaware that fresh food was right near them. She chuckled under her breath.

"What's so funny?" Barr asked.

She shook her head. "Sorry, I'm just finding it humorous that there was a time in my life when I actually enjoyed hide and seek," she explained.

Barr laughed, rubbing her forehead. "Yeah, the apocalypse does suck the fun out of a lot of this stuff, doesn't it?" she asked.

"Could be worse?" Sellers suggested.

Barr raised an eyebrow. "How?"

"We could be outside playing tag instead," came the reply.

Bartlett and Barr nodded in approval, sharing a shudder.

"Man, what is taking Benton so long?" Galindo muttered. "He should have had those things moved already."

Korver cocked his head. "Why don't you go upstairs and help him out, then?"

Galindo sighed. "Should have just kept my big mouth shut," he muttered under his breath, and got up in a huff. He walked up the stairs to the back bedroom, spotting his companion standing by an open window with a stack of hardcover books. "What's the deal?" he demanded. "Does it really take you that long to cause a diversion?"

"Fuck you, man," Benton snapped, pursing his lips. "You come try to hit that shed with a book. See how well you do."

His comrade took it as a personal challenge, and waltzed up to him, snatching a book from his hand. He licked his thumb and playfully flipped through it, a smug expression on his face.

"Looks like a real page turner," he said dryly. "Now, where am I throwing this?"

Benton smirked and pointed to the neighbor's backyard, a good thirty yards away from the house. Galindo looked out, seeing the collection of books scattered throughout the yard. All trace of smugness fell from his face, dissipating like smoke.

"Well hotshot," Benton said, waving his hand like a game show host, "have at it."

Galindo nodded, psyching himself up for the throw. He motioned for his companion to back up.

"All right, get out of the way," he drawled. "Let me show you how it's done."

Benton stepped out of the way, crossing his arms, eyebrows raised skeptically.

Galindo moved back to get a running start. He raised the book, did a few practice heaves, and then darted forward. He picked up momentum and swung his arm with everything he had. Unfortunately for him, he let go a little too late, and the book smacked into the window frame, barely clearing the threshold and landing on the roof.

Benton bit back his laughter, keeping a straight face as he approached the window. He put a hand to his forehead, as if looking far into the distance.

"Holy shit," he declared, "I think you completely cleared it! I don't see it at all!" He dropped his hand and looked out the window. "Oh, wait… it went four feet."

Galindo rolled his eyes, clapping his hands sarcastically. "Yeah yeah," he drawled. "It's a tough throw. Now, how the hell are we going to hit it?"

Benton tilted his head back and forth as he appraised the steep incline of the roof. "I think one of us is going to have to go out on the ledge while the other holds on so they don't fall off," he said.

Galindo raised an eyebrow incredulously and then waved him forward. "Well, I don't want you thinking I stole your idea," he said, shaking his head, "so the honor is yours."

"Normally I would have a witty comeback to explain why you are such a pussy," Benton replied, holding up a finger, "but I've seen you throw. So if we want to leave this house anytime soon, I'm going to have to do the throwing."

Galindo grimaced, finding it physically painful to not quip back hard at his friend. But he held fast, knowing he could jeopardize his safe spot inside the house.

"All right," he finally said, "I'm ready when you are."

Benton nodded and picked up a stack of books, setting them on the windowsill. He stuck a leg through the hole, keeping a tight grip on the window frame.

"Get a good hold of me," he instructed, "and I'll start chucking."

Galindo reached out and grabbed his companion's belt firmly from the back. He made sure he had a good grip and then nodded. Benton picked up a book, making sure his stance was secure. He reared back and lobbed the book over his head.

It sailed in a high arc, landing a few feet short of the metal shed. He grunted and then adjusted his aim, throwing the book with everything he had.

The second one finally hit the roof of the shed with a loud *smack*, piercing through the quiet moans that filled the air. Galindo quickly helped him back inside, and the two of them watched with bated breath as the zombies from the front yard shambled towards the shed.

"Nice throw," Galindo admitted.

Benton grinned. "Thanks," he replied. "Come on, let's get downstairs."

They headed down, finding the rest of the team getting geared up.

"You boys finally hit the target?" Barr teased.

Galindo nodded. "Yeah, he had a hell of a throw," he commended.

"Good for you," Barr said dryly. "Now get your shit because we're on the move."

The two soldiers grabbed their gear as the group waited by the front door for the zombies to leave the front yard. They scanned the neighborhood, seeing that it was mostly empty, just a few stragglers down the road a bit.

When the coast was clear, Korver opened the door quietly, leading them outside in single file. The soldiers followed, as quickly and quietly as they could.

The Corporal thought that the bomb from the night before in the park was what was to blame for the neighborhood being so eerily empty, and it also could mean trouble ahead, like the eye of a hurricane. Before he could even finish the thought, his fear was soon realized.

A steady stream of deliberate gunfire echoed towards them, and the team of six stopped, not wanting to attract any attention to themselves. The shots weren't panicked, just several shots in a steady stream.

Korver motioned for the group to get closer together, so they could move as a single unit. They reached the next block, and the gunfire intensified. The Corporal ducked down beside a house and peered across the street.

There were dozens of zombies, all moving in the same direction towards the house. Korver waved for Galindo to sidle up beside him.

"What do you think?" the Private whispered. "Civilian?"

The Corporal shook his head. "More likely a diversion spot," he whispered back. "Regardless, it's putting a crimp in our plans."

"What are you thinking?" Galindo asked quietly.

Korver chewed his lip for a moment. "The college is another mile or so due south of here," he explained, "so I don't want to go too far to the east, but we might not have a choice."

"Vehicle?" Galindo suggested.

The Corporal shook his head. "Too risky, too noisy," he replied. "We gotta stay quiet."

As they contemplated, there was a scuffle from the back of the group. They turned and saw Bartlett fighting with half a dozen zombies that had wandered around the corner. She let out a soft yelp as one of them grabbed her arm.

She wrenched it free, narrowly avoiding the gnashing teeth and losing a chunk of flesh to a man-eating corpse.

Sellers, Barr, and Benton leapt into action. Sellers rushed forward, lowering his shoulder to plow right through the group, not stopping until he was all the way through and several of them were on the ground. Benton and Barr quickly followed him, stabbing the fallen ghouls in the head.

Galindo reached over and grabbed Bartlett's shoulder, forcing her to look at him. "You okay?" he asked.

She inspected her arm, finding no bites. She nodded shakily, and he helped her up. They watched the other three finish off the last few zombies, and the trio sauntered over, Sellers in the rear.

He suddenly stopped short, eyes going wide, and took off at a run, skidding behind cover next to the Corporal. "There's fifty of those fuckers headed our way," he hissed, "we gotta get inside."

Korver thought for a moment, looking across the street to see that the zombies headed towards the noise were starting to get backed up, staying in the yards instead of moving ahead. He cocked his head, the thought dawning on him that those creatures may be the pack of the pack.

"If we go inside now, we may never get out," he murmured. "Look."

Sellers peeked out and cursed under his breath, but nodded in agreement. "Well, we can't stay here," he replied.

The Corporal waved for everyone to huddle in. "Okay," he whispered, "we're moving quickly and quietly. Two blocks to the east. If we get separated, rendezvous in the backyard of the third house on the left after the second intersection." He waited for everyone to nod and then raised his hand. "Move."

The group leapt up and ran to the east, away from the gunfire. Two houses up, Korver darted in between two houses as several zombies emerged from the next one up. As he made the turn, he came face to face with a duo of ghouls.

He grabbed one by its bloodied and tattered shirt, and drove it into the backyard, shoving it to the ground. Galindo threw down the other next to it. They turned quickly towards the east, not wasting any time killing the creatures. They made it across a few backyards, but on the last house on the block there was a privacy fence that stood six feet high.

Korver stopped and turned back to the north to get around it. When they reached the edge, they saw dozens of zombies heading through the intersection, spread out and moving at a steady clip.

"We gotta push through them," he murmured.

Galindo stared at the horde, chewing his lip in thought. He spotted a few rolling dumpsters on the next block and pointed them out. "Looks like it was trash day," he said.

The Corporal looked and nodded in approval, waving for the rest to cluster in. "Okay," he said quietly, "we're going

to have to push through a group of these
things. They're going to give chase,
there's no question about it. When we get
across, everybody grab a trash can as they
go by."

The other four soldiers exchanged
glances of confusion.

"Just trust me," Korver continued,
"grab one and bring it along. Hell, grab
two if you can manage it." He turned to
Galindo. "How do you feel about covering
our retreat?"

The Private wrinkled his nose.
"Depends," he replied. "How would you feel
if I got eaten while covering your
retreat?"

"I don't know," the Corporal replied,
a playful twinkle in his eye, "I might
shed a tear." He raised a finger. "*Might*."

Galindo cracked a smile. "Well, I'll
see if I can spare you that terrible
fate," he replied.

Korver nodded and motioned for
everybody to follow him, moving as quickly
as they could. Galindo held back, taking
up the rear position.

The Corporal was first to the
intersection, making a point to smack into
the first zombie he encountered,
delivering a forceful shoulder strike and
sending the surprised ghoul flailing to
the asphalt. He repeated this with another

one halfway across the road, sending it to the ground as well. When he glanced up the road, there were a hundred or so of the monsters, all of which far more interested in the meals on legs than the noise in the distance.

The group ducked and dodged outstretched rotten hands as they reached the other side. Korver led the five of them up, everybody grabbing trash cans and rolling them behind.

Galindo stopped ten yards deep into the street, pulling his knife and waiting for the zombies to start coming his way. "All right, come on, who's first?" he barked.

A few zombies were ahead of the others, staggering towards him. Galindo leapt into action, smacking one of them in the head with his blade and shoving it back into the others. Rather than go in for the kill, he kept his distance to keep the attention of more zombies coming his way.

An elderly-looking zombie with a tattered flower dress staggered towards him, and he stabbed it in the forehead, dispatching it quickly and kicking it back into its brethren. Another in a business suit made a lunge for him, and he cracked it with his elbow, reeling around and stabbing it in the temple. As he readied to strike again, there was a loud whistle from fifty yards behind him.

Galindo quickly turned tail and ran, quickly catching up to the others. As he grew close, he appraised the makeshift barricade made entirely of rolling trash cans. He stopped just short of it, having had some time as the zombies were slow moving, and inspected his team's handiwork. The cans lay on their side, stretching from one side of the road to the other, layered two deep. He nudged one with his foot, moving it slightly.

"Great craftsmanship," he said, letting out a low whistle.

Korver shrugged. "It isn't perfect," he admitted, "but it'll slow them down."

"How?" Galindo cocked his head.

Barr grinned. "Why don't you hop over and find out?"

He attempted to step over, and found that it was more difficult than he thought, as the can came up to his knees. Finally he gave it a hop, the leg landing between the two lines, and stumbled over to the other side. Sellers and Benton caught him before he face planted.

"We only have to buy enough time to get out of their sight," Bartlett explained. "If your gracefulness is any indication, it'll do just fine."

Galindo shook his head and headed past them towards the next street, hiding his blush. "Come on, let's get moving," he said tersely.

The rest of the team chuckled and followed him.

Nearly an hour had passed as the group slowly worked their way south. The constant stops to cause diversions and stay out of sight was time consuming, but it was a lot more pleasant than starting a battle that could have quickly escalated into something they couldn't win.

They took a breather inside a small business that overlooked one of the sports fields they'd seen on the satellite image. There was a huge college sign across the street, letting them know they were in the right place. There were dozens of zombies on the sports fields, with more roaming the buildings between.

"Now the only question is," Barr mused as she studied the area, "where is the residence hall?"

Benton leaned forward, squinting. "Looks like there are only a dozen buildings or so," he said. "Shouldn't be that hard to find."

"Yeah, nothing says easy like looking for an address while fighting off hordes of zombies," Barr retorted, rolling her eyes.

Benton scoffed. "I didn't say the whole thing would be easy," he shot back, "but finding the building out of twelve shouldn't be overwhelming."

"Bullshit," Barr snapped. "*Shouldn't be too hard* is the same as saying it's easy."

As the two soldiers bickered, Bartlett got up from the couch and walked into the kitchen with purpose, causing the others to pause and wonder what she was doing.

"Hey, you okay?" Sellers asked.

She didn't answer, just disappeared inside, and the trio followed her.

"Hey, you'll have to forgive us," Benton gushed as he rushed inside, "we fight quite a bit."

Bartlett shook her head. "Not why I came in here," she assured him, "but thanks for the concern." She dug through a small table in the corner of the kitchen, filled with knick-knacks and whatnot on the top. Finally she pulled out a phone book, holding it up for them to see.

Benton raised an eyebrow. "Glad you were able to find us another bludgeon to use against those things," he said, appraising the large and heavy book.

"I think we'll find what's inside to be more useful," she replied, and slammed it down on the kitchen table, kicking up a cloud of dust.

"Oh," Benton said lamely, clearly embarrassed he hadn't made the connection.

She opened it and pored through it, before finding an entry under the college name that read *Residence Hall.* Just to the side of it was the address, *1422 Mayfair Drive.*

"We may not know what the building looks like," she said, "but we know where it is. It's not much, but I figure it's better than going in completely blind."

The other three chuckled a bit, nodding in approval.

"That's a hell of a find, Bartlett," Benton admitted.

Sellers nodded with a grin. "Especially given the fact you are way too young to have used a phonebook in your life," he added.

"I spent summers at my grandmother's house," she said defensively, "and she would have me look up the number to the pizza place after she burnt dinner."

The group chuckled and headed back out into the living room.

"Hey Corporal, you're not going to believe this find," Barr declared.

Bartlett carried the phone book to Korver, pointing out the address.

"Quality work there, Private," Korver said. "Now, we just have to figure out where that road is, and we'll be in business. Let's gear up."

The group readied their weapons before moving over to the front window to plot their course.

"The sports fields on either side of the buildings look like they could be trouble," the Corporal mused.

Barr cocked her head. "Looks like most of the fencing is still in place," she added, "so that should help contain a lot of them."

"Still, it's something we're going to have to keep any eye on," Galindo put in. "Last thing we need is an unexpected mob."

Korver nodded, pursing his lips. "I think our best bet is to go straight down the main road leading to the heart of campus," he suggested. "That gives us a street on either side for a retreat, if need be."

"How big does the campus look on the map?" Sellers asked.

The Corporal pulled out the piece of paper and looked at it, using his fingers as makeshift measuring tools. "It's hard to tell with as pulled out as the view is," he murmured, "but it's at least twice as big as the sports fields. So three, maybe four blocks?"

"Corporal, I hope I'm not overstepping my bounds…" Bartlett began slowly. "But I think we should check out the street names running north and south before venturing onto campus."

Korver nodded. "That's a good idea," he agreed. "Last thing we want is to get four blocks deep only to realize the street we need is on our left. In that case, when we break out of here, we get into groups of two." He pointed at the soldiers as he spoke. "Sellers and Bartlett, you check the road on the left. Barr and Galindo, you get the right. Meet back at the top of the center street. If you encounter zombies, it's either melee or avoidance. No gunfire until absolutely necessary. Everybody clear?"

There was a round of *"clear"*, and then he nodded firmly.

"Let's move out," Korver said, and the group left the house, rushing across the street and over a large parking lot headed towards campus.

There were a smattering of zombies in the lot, but they were easy enough to avoid. The troops gave them forceful shoves, sending them to the ground. They rushed to opposite streets, branching off to check the names on the signs.

They reconvened at the top of the center street, and Korver turned to them.

"Find what we're looking for?" he asked.

Galindo shook his head. "No Mayfair Drive," he replied.

"Same here," Sellers added.

"Let's get moving to the south, then," the Corporal instructed, and waved for them to follow.

The troops moved, slowing as they approached the first intersection. They headed for the western building, inching up towards the road. As they grew closer, Korver looked up to check the street names.

"Fuck," he muttered under his breath. No Mayfair.

The Corporal motioned for the group to stay back, and he looked around the corner. There were a few dozen ghouls down the street, hanging around the entrance to the sports field. Just at the end of the road, he could see that the gate was open, and several more dozen ghouls littered the field.

He glanced the other way, seeing that the street was virtually empty save for a few creatures the next block up. He turned back around.

"West could be trouble," he said quietly, "the gate to the field is open and there's a party going on. We need to get across the intersection, quick."

Galindo raised an eyebrow. "Any trouble in the other direction?"

"Pretty clear, nothing to worry about," Korver replied, shaking his head. "Forget single file, we need to cross shoulder to shoulder, minimize our exposure. Let's get across."

The team lined up, stretching halfway across the road. Korver silently counted them down, then started across. They stayed as low as they could, moving quickly while trying to keep their steps light. They reached the other side and pasted themselves against the western wall. Korver worked his way back to the corner to see if they'd attracted any attention.

A few zombies shuffled their way, almost looking confused.

Come on, he silently prayed, *you didn't see anything. You know you didn't see anything.*

His positive thinking paid off, and two zombies near the back bumped into each other and swatted at one another, moaning loudly. The handful of creatures in the front turned back their way, staggering off.

The Corporal breathed a deep sigh of relief and then turned to give the team a thumbs up. They moved to the next block, pausing again at the intersection. Korver looked up and spotted the welcome sign: *Mayfair Drive.* He looked to the west, seeing only a smattering of ghouls, then to the east where there were a few hundred or so congregating around a single building.

He backed up, motioning for the others to look quickly before clustering around him to talk plans.

"Can't see the building numbers from here," Galindo said quietly, "but I'm going to guess that's our place."

Barr shook her head in disbelief. "No way we're fighting through all of them."

"I agree," Korver said. "We're going to have to get a diversion going." He looked around and then honed in on Bartlett and Sellers. "I know this is a shit detail, but we need those things out of the way. Can you two handle it?"

The duo exchanged a fist bump with each other and nodded.

"We'll make it happen, Corporal," Sellers promised.

Korver nodded. "Good," he said. "This street is pretty clear, and it looks like it runs into the tail end of the field. You should be able to lure them down and escape around it. If you get good enough distance between you, retreat back to the house and we'll meet you there once we get the survivors out."

"What are we going to do?" Galindo asked.

Korver pointed to the building on the other side of the street. It was a small cafe with the side door dangling open.

The Private rolled his eyes. "Oh good, get a quick snack before launching a suicide run," he joked. "Love it."

"You two get moving," the Corporal said, motioning to Sellers and Bartlett. "Be safe."

They nodded as the others headed over to the cafe, drawing all the shades shut and securing the door.

"Well, how do you want to do this?" Bartlett asked, turning to her partner.

Sellers peered down the street to the horde. "They're pretty densely packed," he mused. "Shouldn't take more than a few shots to get them pulling in our direction." He looked towards the field, staring at the four zombies a couple blocks up, spread out fairly well. "I tell you what, if you want to handle getting them moving, I'll take out the ones in our way to the field."

"How much lead time do you need?" Bartlett asked.

He shrugged. "Give me two minutes, and start firing," he said.

She nodded and both of them readied their weapons. He was the first out of hiding, staying close to the wall to minimize exposure. He started with a brisk walk, keeping his footsteps light, before breaking into a full sprint on the next block.

The first zombie he encountered barely had time to turn around before getting a knife to the skull. He quickly tossed it aside and walked over to the next one, which had begun shambling in his direction.

"Three more, easy," he murmured, and lunged over to deal with the stragglers.

Meanwhile, Bartlett came out of hiding, slowly walking up towards the zombie mass in front of the building. As she grew closer, she appraised the massive group, stretching back twenty yards from the double door entrance.

Bartlett took a few deep breaths, tamping down the fear, and prepared to fire. She aimed towards the center of the mass, centering on a gnarly mop of blood-splattered blonde. She fired single bursts. She didn't pay attention to whether she was hitting anything, despite taking down a few corpses it wouldn't really matter in the grand scheme of the horde.

After the second shot, dozens of ghouls turned towards her, moaning and shambling in her direction, arms outstretched. By the fifth shot, most of the horde had her in their rheumy sights.

By the tenth shot, she was the most popular girl to ever set foot on campus.

The front line of the horde reached twenty yards from her, and she jumped up, looking over their heads to make sure most of the creatures had pulled away from the door. Knowing she couldn't do much else, she retreated down the street, moving at a pace equal to the ghouls so they didn't lose interest.

As she walked, she watched Sellers deftly take out a few zombies with his knife, stabbing skulls and tossing corpses aside. A few more staggered out from a side street, and he dispatched them easily before turning back towards his partner.

"Damn, looks like you got their attention," he declared.

Bartlett raised her forefinger and pinky, shooting him a *rock on*. "That's an understatement," she replied smoothly. "And just like the crackhead at the gas station, I'd like to keep my distance from them, so let's get moving."

The duo began their stroll towards the field, and when they reached the grass, they stared out at the landscape. There were dozens of zombies, easily in the low hundreds, spread out across the green space, some of which were coming their way.

Both soldiers stiffened, but relaxed a touch when they realized the fencing was still up and intact.

"So, how soon until we start running?" Sellers asked.

Bartlett glanced over her shoulder at the horde, gauging them about fifteen yards away from the edge of the grass."I say as soon as the first footsteps off the pavement, we haul ass."

"Wanna place a friendly wager on who makes it to the house first?" Sellers asked, waggling his eyebrows.

She barked a laugh. "I've seen you run," she scoffed. "Just wouldn't feel right taking money from a cripple."

He simply smirked as they waited, and as soon as the first ghoul stepped foot on the grass, they took off like a shot towards the rally point.

The four soldiers prepared to leave the cafe, as Galindo crammed a fistful of chips in his mouth. Barr laughed, shaking her head at the mangy soldier.

"Okay, looks like Bartlett was able to get most of them away from the door," Korver murmured, watching out the window as the last few stragglers wandered past. "Chances are there are going to be more in the lobby. Take them out silently, but be prepared to be loud if need be."

Galindo tried to talk, but it came out muffled and he choked on his mouthful of fried potato, spitting crumbs all over himself.

"I think what my mis-mannered friend here is saying," Barr piped up, patting Galindo on the back, "is that we should be on the lookout for runners as well."

The Corporal nodded. "Potentially a lot of them, too," he agreed. "The Captain said he sent a group of fifty this way, so it could be all kinds of trouble in there. If things get too hot, retreat and secure the front door. I don't want to abandon anybody, but we aren't in a position to take on that kind of threat."

The soldiers nodded in agreement, and Korver turned back to the window. The route to the building was clear, so he raised his hand, waving for everyone else to join him.

The quartet filed out onto the side street, knives at the ready, looking towards the fields to make sure that the zombies headed in that direction were far enough away, most of the way down the block. With the distraction safely working, they moved swiftly and quietly towards the housing complex.

The building was on the corner of the next block, still with half a dozen zombies milling about, most of which were pressed up against the building, smacking on the side. Korver pointed to Galindo and Benton to cover the left side, and the four of them leapt into action.

The soldiers rushed the ghouls, jamming blades into the backs of their skulls all along the walls, dropping the corpses before any of them could even turn around to see what was coming. In a matter of seconds, they were zombie free, at least on the outside.

The Corporal approached the door carefully and stepped into the lobby. It was a large space, covering most of the first floor. The front windows provided a decent amount of light, allowing them to see completely across the room.

It looked like a war had gone down in there, blood and corpses covering every inch of space. Bullet holes riddled the walls and furniture, some even in the ceiling. There was some movement at the far end of the room, and Korver knelt down, smacking his knife on the marble floor.

A high-pitched *ting* reverberated through the room, and a dozen zombies emerged from the shadows. Two of them broke free of the group at a full sprint in crimson soaked military fatigues.

"Runner!" the Corporal cried. "Galindo!"

The two of them dropped their knives and readied their rifles, tracking the movement of the ghouls as they grew closer. At ten yards, they opened fire, both of them finding the target and dropping both runners immediately.

"Benton, get that door secure," Korver barked. "Rest of you, on me, let's clean this up."

The three soldiers approached with their knives out, heading for the ten zombies shambling towards them. As they got close, Galindo stepped over to the side, picking up a lightweight wooden chair and tossing it hard, hitting several of them and knocking seven of them to the ground like bowling pins.

"Looks like a tough spare to pick up there, bud," Barr quipped.

Galindo grinned and held up his knife. "Don't worry, I got this," he declared, and leapt into action. He went after the two still standing, quickly taking them down. Barr lunged and took out the ones of the ground, easy pickings.

Korver took out the last one standing and rejoined the duo, the room secure in a matter of moments.

"What in the hell were they doing over here?" Galindo asked, looking around.

The group headed over to where the ghouls had been, spotting the door for the stairs, which was shut and covered in blood.

Korver took a deep breath. "Okay, let's see what we're dealing with," he said, and approached the stairwell door. He gently pushed it open, peeking inside through the crack.

Within seconds, several decayed fingers grabbed the door, trying to pull it open.

"Oh shit!" the Corporal cried.

Galindo and Benton grabbed the door release and yanked it towards them, and Barr pulled out her handgun and started firing through the crack. One by one, she was able to drop a few zombies, causing the hands to fall away. Once it was down to three sets, the boys were able to pull the door tight on them, the rotted fingers wiggling away against the door frame.

"Knife!" Korver barked.

Barr pulled out her blade and ran it down the frame, severing finger after finger until they were able to pull the door completely shut. Once it was secure, they backed off, staring on as the creatures inside pounded on it.

"Pretty safe to say we aren't taking the stairs," Galindo muttered.

Benton pursed his lips. "How the hell we getting up, then?" he asked.

"Elevator?" Galindo suggested.

Barr shook her head. "There's no power," she countered. "And even if there was, it would be a death trap."

"I'm not saying hitch a ride in the elevator," he shot back, rolling his eyes. "I'm saying let's use the shaft. We should be able to get on top of it and get the next floor door open."

Benton shrugged. "I've heard worse ideas."

"Only because you've spent so much time with Galindo," Barr pointed out.

"Facts," Benton agreed.

Korver shook his head. "Still, I think it's our only option," he said. "Let's find it."

The group fanned out over the lobby, and finally Barr let out a shout. "Got it!" she called.

The four troops converged on the elevator. Galindo pulled out his knife and wedged it between the doors, prying it open. When it cracked apart, Barr and Benton grabbed and started pulling. As they did, Korver kept his gun at the ready for any surprises.

As the doors slid open, they stared down at the horrific scene before them. Four civilians lay dead on the floor of the elevator, covered in bite marks. One person, who looked to have been a middle-aged man, had a hole in the side of his head, a handgun laying next to him. The troops shook their heads.

"Not sure exactly what happened here," Galindo mused, "but goddamn, it's nothing good."

Korver took a deep breath. "This isn't going to be pleasant," he said, "but we gotta pull them out."

The soldiers begrudgingly started grabbing bodies and pulled them out of the elevator, clearing a path for themselves.

"Galindo, grab that chair over there," the Corporal instructed.

Galindo grabbed a hard plastic high-backed chair, setting it in the middle of the elevator. Korver hopped up onto it and started working on the roof hatch. It took him a moment with the knife, but he was able to pry it open.

"Give me a hand up here," he grunted as he wrapped his hands around the open hole. As Galindo got ready, Korver turned to the other two. "Once he's up, get the chair out of the way, because we might be coming down real quick."

They climbed up one at a time, and Barr moved the chair out of the way immediately. Korver and Galindo knelt in front of the second floor door, getting it pried open enough to dig their fingers in.

Before they pulled, the Corporal turned to his partner. "If there are more than three of those things on the other side of this door, I want you to go down first," he said firmly. "That clear?"

Galindo nodded, and then they heaved the doors open all the way. They jumped back, just in case of a threat, but nothing was there. They cautiously stepped forward, peering into the hallway, and then climbing up onto the second floor and looking around.

The hallway was empty, clean, and appeared to have been spared any bloodshed or battle, which was confusing to both soldiers.

"Either those guys never made it this far, or they somehow managed to avoid

every zombie and got to safety," Galindo
murmured.

Korver shook his head. "My guess is
the former," he said dryly. "Still, let's
work our way down the hall and see if
anybody is home."

Each of them took a side, heading
down the hallway, inspecting each door and
giving it a knock. When they got to each
end, there was no response from anywhere.
They doubled back to the elevator.

"Third floor?" Korver asked.

Galindo nodded. "Looks like," he
agreed with a shrug, "but how the hell are
we doing this?"

The Corporal let out a sharp whistle,
and Barr's head poked up through the top
of the elevator.

"Get up here," Korver instructed, "we
need some help."

The two soldiers clambered up, and
all four reconvened on top of the elevator
car. Galindo reached over to the elevator
cable and climbed up like a pro. The three
soldiers at the bottom grabbed it and
pulled the heavy cable towards the door
side, so that he could reach. It took all
three of them to keep it steady.

"Okay, when I get this door open, you
be ready to let go," Galindo reminded
them.

Korver nodded. "Got it."

The Private wrapped his legs around the cable, securing himself enough around the stiff cord so he could start working on the door with his knife. He managed to get the blade in and pried it open a bit. He took a deep breath before pulling it fully open.

As the doors gave way, he saw pools of blood, as well as corpses on the ground. Nothing jumped out at him, so he gave the others a thumbs up and then grabbed the edge, pulling himself up into the third floor hallway.

He drew his handgun immediately and whipped to the right at the sound of banging. There were a dozen zombies about twenty yards away down the hall, all congregating around one door. He clenched his jaw and leaned back into the elevator shaft.

"Dozen hostiles," he whispered, "going to need some help."

He continued to aim at the zombies tensely as Korver made the climb up to the door. It took the Corporal a few moments, but he finally hauled himself into the hallway. He looked at the situation and then motioned through the door for the other two to stay put.

"You feel comfortable shooting at this range?" Korver whispered.

Galindo nodded. "Yeah, I'm good," he murmured back.

"Let's light 'em up, then," the Corporal said.

They aimed, picking their targets, and then after a quiet countdown, squeezed their triggers simultaneously. Two zombies immediately dropped, and the bulk of them turned their attention towards the fresh meat in the hallway.

As they began to move, three runners in combat fatigues burst through, tearing towards them. The soldiers fired, having trouble finding their targets right away until finding foreheads.

Galindo took aim at the final runner, but missed, hitting it in the jaw.

"Move back!" Korver barked, and as the Private darted out of the way, the Corporal dropped into a crouch, waiting for the ghoul to reach him. When it did, he swung his arms up, catching the zombie under the armpits and shoving it into the elevator shaft, head first.

The ghoul's head gave a sickening *crack* as it hit the far wall, and then the body plummeted to the car below with a sharp *crunch*.

"Hell of a move there, Corporal," Galindo breathed.

Korver shrugged. "Wasn't my first choice, but it worked," he replied. "Come on, let's clean it up."

They resumed firing, quickly taking out the remaining zombies in the hallway. With the situation clear, the Corporal leaned back into the elevator.

"We're going to check out the door," he said. "You two hang right."

At their nods, he led Galindo towards the room that the zombies had been so interested in. The Private grinned and did a playful *shave and a haircut* knock, and a moment later, the lock clicked.

The door opened, revealing a blood-soaked soldier, pallid and eyes wide. His face broke out into a giant smile when he saw the two soldiers standing there.

"Oh, thank you," he croaked. "We didn't think anybody would ever come."

"What's your name, soldier?" Korver asked.

The young man stood up straight. "I'm Private Casey," he replied, and then motioned to two men inside, sitting on dorm beds snacking on some junk food left behind by the previous residents. "This is Private Ibarra, and Private Hartman."

"Gentlemen," Korver continued, "I'm Corporal Korver, and this is Private Galindo. Captain Clay sent us to rescue your team so we can push on to Freeway Park. Did anybody else make it?"

Casey swallowed hard and shook his head.

"Nah man," Hartman said, standing up from the bed. "We're it."

Galindo's eyes widened. "Christ," he breathed. "I thought there were fifty of you. What the hell happened?"

"Shit hit the fan," Hartman replied, tossing an empty chip bag on the floor. "That's what happened."

Korver nodded. "We'll have plenty of time to hear the whole story once we get to Freeway Park," he said firmly. "Let's get a move on."

The three Privates grabbed their gear, and Ibarra picked up a large duffel bag, slinging it over his shoulder.

"What you got there?" Galindo asked, raising an eyebrow.

Ibarra grinned. "Party favors." He gave him a playful wink and headed past him towards the elevator.

Galindo smiled. "This should be fun," he quipped.

The group reached the shaft and everyone worked their way down to the bottom, one by one. The newcomers introduced themselves to Benton and Barr, and the newly formed group headed back out into the lobby.

Korver led the way to the front door and peered out front. There were a few dozen zombies staggering about, attracted by the gunfire, just enough to make life difficult.

"There another way out of here?" he asked, turning back to the rescued soldiers.

Ibarra jerked a thumb over his shoulder. "Back entrance to an alley," he replied, "but not sure we want to go that way."

"Why not?" the Corporal asked.

"Fenced-in area leading to the street…" Hartman trailed off, shaking his head, "and not all of us made it inside."

The others exchanged a look, nodding in understanding. Runners.

"We could always just shoot out one of the windows and go that route," Galindo suggested. "Not like we have to worry about being sued for property damage or anything."

Barr shook her head. "Noise is going to attract those things in our direction," she replied. "Unless you want to stay behind and distract them while we make our getaway."

"Not high up on my list of things to do," Galindo admitted. He held up a finger. "Wait, Ibarra, you got any party favors that could help us out here?"

His new companion grinned and unzipped the duffel bag. "Thought you'd never ask." He pulled out a small block of C4 with a detonator.

"Isn't that a bit overkill?" Benton asked.

Ibarra shook his head. "Nah, overkill would be leveling the building. I'm just gonna…" he paused and smirked, "do a bit of rearranging."

Korver chuckled and waved to him. "Get it set up," he instructed.

Ibarra headed for the front reception desk, securing the explosive to the front wall facing the doors, and then attached the detonator. "We're good," he declared as he joined the group.

Korver led them to the side street window and shot it out. The group quickly jumped out, one at a time, and they took off running to the north towards the rally point.

Zombies staggered after them, arms outstretched, and a block up, the Corporal nodded.

"Hit it," he said, and Ibarra smashed the detonator, sending an impressive shockwave through the air, shattering glass in several buildings.

Benton poked at his ear, shaking his head. "I thought you were just rearranging?" he asked.

"Job was a little bigger than I thought," Ibarra admitted sheepishly.

Benton laughed, and clapped him on the back, and the soldiers picked up the pace to head back to the rendezvous.

The group of nine set up in some bushes across the way from Freeway Park. The target building, a ten story structure that overlooked the interstate, was two hundred yards away. There was a four-lane frontage road, an on ramp, and a large parking lot standing between them and the front door, as well as fifty or so zombies.

On the interstate, which ran straight at the building before curving around it, there were thousands of ghouls, spread out with a few yards between each of them, most shambling slowly to the north, where there was faint gunfire in the distance.

"Great," Galindo muttered, "so now what?"

Barr shrugged. "We get inside and get to where we need to get to," she replied.

"Interstate's raised a bite," Bartlett mused, "so probably the third or fourth floor should give us a good vantage point."

Galindo threw up his hands. "Again, that's great, but then what?" he asked. "These three guys are the only reinforcements we have. There are thousands of those things on the interstate. How are we supposed to do anything to them?"

"One thing at a time," Korver cut in. "Let's get in there and secure, first."

Galindo begrudgingly nodded his head.

"So, how are we getting in?" Sellers piped up.

Barr cocked her head. "Those Things are spread out pretty good," she pointed out. "I say we just plow through right to the front door."

"And if it's locked?" Galindo asked.

She tapped her gun. "I got the key."

Casey pulled out a pair of binoculars and looked towards the building, scanning the area until he spotted an underground parking lot. "Might have a better option," he said, and handed the binoculars over to Korver, pointing.

The Corporal looked and saw that only one of the doors appeared to be open, and there weren't too many zombies around the entrance. "Parking garage, huh?"

"Would make sense," Hartman agreed, "those stairwell doors would most likely be unlocked. And I'm guessing it's not too crowded if you're suggesting it."

Ibarra nodded. "I like that better than a suicide run to the front door."

"Any objections?" Korver asked.

Galindo raised his hand, and the Corporal looked around.

"Good, let's move," he said, and the Private scowled, lowering his hand.

"Hold that thought, Corporal," Ibarra said quietly.

Korver's brow furrowed in annoyance, but closed his mouth when the Private pulled out another block of C4 and set it by a tree.

"Once we get inside," Ibarra said as he stood up, "wouldn't hurt to have something else for them to focus on."

The Corporal nodded. "Good call."

After the bomb was set, the group headed out, running straight for the building while fanned out and staggered, five in the front line, four in the back. The run wasn't a straight shot, several zombies attempting to stagger into their path. They didn't bother to go for the kill, simply shoving them out of the way to keep moving.

After some ducking and diving, the group reached the parking garage, which went under the building. Korver and Galindo squeezed off a few rounds to pick off the zombies by the entrance. The group ducked inside, the lead two pulling out flashlights and aiming with their guns.

They did a quick sweep of the lot, seeing a handful of vehicles as well as a few zombies, quickly dispatching them with bullets to the face.

"Get that door shut and get our distraction going," Korver called.

The others turned their attention to the door, while the Corporal and Galindo cleared the room. THe gunfire echoed against the concrete walls as they pulled down the door, watching as the few dozen zombies caught up to them.

Ibarra hit the detonator, and the explosion rattled the building. A few moments passed, and they looked outside, watching as the bulk of the zombies wandered off towards it.

"Come on, let's get upstairs," Korver suggested.

They found the stairwell that led up, and the Corporal took great care to open it extra slowly, learning from the last time. Thankfully, this stairwell was empty.

The group worked their way up floor by floor, checking to make sure that each door was secured. When they finally reached the fourth, they stopped and clustered around.

"Let's get in and clear the floor," Korver said. "We'll figure out our next move after that. Teams of two, move hard, move fast."

He turned as the group nodded, and threw open the door, allowing them all to pour inside. They broke off into duos, rushing through the cubicle farm in the center of a large open area. It was dark,

with the only light coming from the
exterior windows, but it was bright enough
to show movement.

"Contact, contact!" erupted from a
few soldiers, and then gunfire echoed in
the room.

Bullets ripped through the dozen or
so ghouls in the open area, dropping them
quickly. Korver came in once everything
was silent and surveyed the situation,
watching as the rest of the teams quickly
cleared the offices against the walls.

After a minute, there was no more
noise, and sporadic yells of "Clear!" He
walked to the front window, facing the
interstate. Soon, all nine of them stood
there, staring silently at the sight
before them.

The building faced a long, straight
stretch of highway, and from their view,
they could see tens of thousands of
zombies stretched as far as the eye could
see. Several on ramps on either side of
the road acted as bottlenecks for more
ghouls joining the main horde. The
creatures were still spaced out fairly
well, three to four yards apart in most
cases, with the occasional cluster.

"Goddamn," Galindo breathed, "there
is nothing good going on here."

Barr shook her head emphatically. "How are the nine of us supposed to bunch these things up?"

"You got anything in that big bag there, Ibarra?" Sellers asked, turning to the Private beside him.

Ibarra wrinkled his nose. "I have some explosives, but nothing that's going to do much good without a massive amount of sustained firepower supporting it."

"Which we don't have," Bartlett cut in dryly.

Galindo nodded, rubbing his forehead. "I have maybe forty bullets left."

"Same," Barr added.

"I'm a little higher," Benton piped up, "but it's kind of a moot point. We'd need thousands just to group them up, let alone hold their interest."

Korver took a deep breath. "I'm open to suggestions," he declared. "At the moment, the best plan I can come up with is to break the glass and start yelling like a bridesmaid at a Vegas bachelorette party. Which I'm going to assume isn't going to be much of a success."

"I don't know," Galindo drawled, "I think the humor value alone on that puts it in the must try category."

Bartlett cocked her head. "Ibarra, you have anything else in that bag besides explosives?" he asked.

He walked over to the desk, swiped everything off of it and set the duffel down. "Knock yourself out," he said, stepping back and waving her over.

Bartlett unzipped it and started pulling out the contents.

Sellers gaped from over her shoulder. "You didn't think a fifty-cal was worth mentioning?" he demanded.

"I got one strand of bullets," Ibarra said, shaking his head, "so no, it's not gonna do a whole lot."

"What happened to the rest of the ammo?" Benton asked.

Casey lowered his gaze. "The guys carrying it didn't make it."

"Well why didn't you say something when we were at the dorms?" Barr asked, crossing her arms. "Maybe we could have made a play for it!"

Hartman shook his head. "They were in the stairwell."

There was a moment of tense silence, and then Galindo sighed.

"Okay, so we have a hundred rounds of fifty-cal ammo," he said. "That's something at least."

Bartlett turned to the Corporal. "How much time do the Apaches need to get here?"

"I don't know," he replied, and pulled out his radio. "I'll find out." He

headed off to call command, and Sellers
raised an eyebrow.

"Oh god," he said as he eyed
Bartlett, "you have an idea, don't you?"

Galindo's brow furrowed. "Wait,
that's a bad thing?' he asked.

"Depends on who you ask," Bartlett
replied.

"Yes" Sellers declared.

She shook her head. "Don't ask him."

"So what's the idea, girl?" Barr
asked, leaning on the desk.

Bartlett licked her lips. "When we
came in, there were a few SUVs in the lot
downstairs," she began. "We get a few of
those, drive them onto the interstate,
create a blockade, then use the fifty-cal
to carve us out a hole big enough to get
out. Get a little cover from the shooters
up here, and it could work."

The group simply stared at her,
blinking.

"Told ya," Sellers said dryly.

Barr pushed off of the desk, shaking
her head. "That's um… bold," she said.

"I appreciate you thinking outside
the box and all," Hartman said slowly,
"but those cars aren't going to last very
long with that size of a crowd. They'll
push through pretty quickly."

"Depending on what Corporal Korver has to say," Bartlett replied, "it may be all we need."

Everybody turned and looked towards him as he finished up with the radio, turning towards them. He stopped in his tracks, suddenly curious as to why everyone was staring at him.

"Um, what?" he asked.

Galindo shrugged. "Oh nothing," he drawled, "just waiting to see if we have to go on yet another suicide mission or not."

"How long on the helicopters?" Bartlett asked.

Korver turned towards her. "Airfield to site flight time is fourteen minutes," he replied. "However, if we can give them a small window, they can be on us in three."

Galindo sighed. "Goddammit," he muttered under his breath.

"Did I miss something?" Korver asked, brow furrowing.

"Come on over, Corporal," Sellers groaned. "Bartlett has an idea."

"You're out of your goddamn mind, Bartlett…" Korver said, shaking his head. "I like it." He waved everyone over to the window. "Okay, here's the plan," he began, motioning as he spoke. "Three vehicles, SUVs or trucks, whatever we can find down there. Use that exit ramp on the left and block off as much of the road as possible. Two man teams, one focuses on drawing the zombies in. One person targets the zombies on the left, the other two doing what they can to draw the ones from the other side of the road in. The other three will need to get things set up to escape. That means the fifty-cal."

"I can also rig up the rest of the C4," Ibarra added, "get is small enough that you can throw it out to clear the way in case things get too hairy."

Galindo grimaced. "That sounds a little risky, doesn't it?' he asked.

"Don't worry, I'll make them small enough that they won't kill you," Ibarra assured him. "Your ears will probably be ringing for a week, but you'll live."

Korver nodded. "You hold the line as long as possible," he instructed. "That noise is going to draw those things from every direction and pull more in from the surface streets. With as fast as they're moving, if we can hold them for ten minutes, it'll be dense enough for a strike."

"We going off the clock for this one?" Galindo asked.

The Corporal shook his head. "Ten minutes is the ideal," he replied. "But as soon as the fifty-cal team calls it, then the mission is over. I'm not willing to sacrifice anyone for the sake of this. They'll just have to live with what we can do. It's an important mission, but anyone dying to buy an extra few seconds isn't going to change a whole lot."

The other soldiers nodded in appreciation.

"So who are the teams?" Galindo asked.

Korver thought for a moment before responding. He didn't want to choose who to send down, considering they might not be coming back.

"Any volunteers to make the run?' he asked.

Every hand in the room shot up without hesitation, and the Corporal smiled.

"Proud of everyone in this room," he said sincerely. "But we still need to leave some people behind to cover."

Casey raised his hand. "I think Ibarra should stay up here."

"Fuck you," Ibarra snapped, "I can fight."

His friend nodded. "I'm not saying you can't," he assured him. "But you're the only one who can get those explosives just right. If those things start coming back down the interstate in big numbers, you might have to rig something up on the fly."

Ibarra wrinkled his nose, but nodded begrudgingly. "In that case, I want Hartman and Sellers to stay up here with me," he said, pointing between the two soldiers. "Both of you look like you have good arms, so you can get that shit out to the masses."

"I can live with that," Korver agreed. "Any objections?" When nobody said anything, he clapped his hands together. "Good. Let's get down to the garage and get our rides."

Fifteen minutes later, the ground team had three large SUVs started up and ready to go. They were big behemoths, with sunroofs for that extra bit of protection to fire from.

Casey and Barr got into one with the 50-cal. Korver and Benton took another, and Galindo and Barlett took the third.

Ibarra stood between the vehicles. "So who is going to be my bomber?" he asked.

"Right here," Korver called, and held his arm out the window.

Ibarra approached him and handed over a small bag. The Corporal looked inside and found six small blocks of C4, each with its own remote detonator on it.

"These things are going to pack a bit of a wallop," the Private explained, "so you can spread them out a bit. My suggestion is to run a trail down the exit ramp, so you can get back to the building." He held up the detonator trigger. "This thing is set to proper frequency, and when you hit it, all of them are going to go off. So for the love of god, don't have anything on you when you pull it."

Korver nodded. "Note," he replied. "What about the ones you're going to throw out?"

"Different frequency," Ibarra assured him. "So you don't have to worry about it."

The Corporal cocked his head. "I'm going to keep an eye on you from the road," he said. "If you see we're about to get overwhelmed from those things retreating, give me a signal."

"Consider it done," Ibarra replied.

Korver grabbed his radio and held it out to him. "Frequency is dialed in," he said. "As soon as we head out, call in the

Apaches. I've given them the time window, so they'll be ready."

"I'll handle it," Ibarra assured him.

Korver nodded and smacked Benton on the shoulder. "Let's get this done."

The Private hit the horn a few times, prompting Sellers and Hartman to approach the garage door. They looked outside, and gave a hand signal of *four*, letting the drivers know how many zombies were right outside.

They threw open the door, and as soon as the light poured in, Benton hit the gas. He tore out of the garage, smacking into the four zombies, sending them flying. The two other vehicles were close behind, with the three of them quickly making the turn towards the interstate.

Dozens of zombies spread out across the frontage road and parking lot, all of which immediately turned their attention towards the roaring vehicles.

The on ramp was a quarter mile away, and they reached it quickly. There were a couple dozen ghouls staggering around, several of which were easily smacked aside as Benton led the convoy up.

The interstate, however, was a different story, with hundreds of corpses in the immediate area, thousands more stretching in both directions. The majority at least was on the other side of the center barrier. The noise from the engines and squealing tires drew the attention of most of them.

"Go south ten yards and park it," Korver instructed.

Benton smashed through several zombies, clearing a path through the hundred or so that were within twenty or so yards of the vehicles. He reached the concrete median and slowed down before crashing into it, crushing several ghouls right against it.

"Smooth parking job, there," the Corporal drawled.

Benton shrugged. "It worked, didn't it?"

Korver didn't respond, simply leapt out of the vehicle and raised his assault rifle. He picked targets close to him and started firing, dropping several in a matter of seconds. As he did this, the other two SUVs pulled up behind Benton, getting as close as they could. As soon as they stopped, Casey and Galindo jumped out of their passenger seats and opened fire.

The fighting on the bridge was intense, with three soldiers unloading every shot they had to clear the immediate area. Thirty zombies dropped within a minute, creating a buffer zone for Casey and Galindo.

"I'll cover," Korver barked, "get the fifty-cal up!"

The duo grabbed the machine gun out of the back and immediately started setting it up. While they did this, Korver continued firing with his rifle, keeping the ten yard buffer zone side.

Past that, however, hundreds of zombies slowly wandered back towards them, thickening up the mass.

"Better hurry it up!" Korver barked.

As he held the line for the duo, the other three soldiers in the SUVs popped up from the sunroofs and began firing. Bartlett, in the outer vehicle, shot at the zombies trying to walk around her. THe three vehicles were able to block off most of the road, but there was a good eight yards in the final lane and shoulder where they could pass on her side.

She sprayed in three-round bursts, dropping several of them by the SUV, and keeping the others occupied by focusing on her. She turned to the southern force, which was overwhelming. She paused for a moment, in awe of the horrifying sight of thousands of ghouls all headed her way.

"Keep shooting!" Barr screamed.

Bartlett snapped out of her reverie and joined the other two in firing. Barr, in the middle vehicle, split her time between the ghouls on their side and helping Benton attract a crowd on the other side of the median. Within minutes, there were easily a thousand ghouls on the other side, pressing against the concrete and attempting to get at the soldiers.

Finally, Galindo and Casey got the fifty-cal set up, loading in their single strand of a hundred rounds.

"We're hot!" the former bellowed, and Korver rushed back behind them.

They opened fire, the bullets shredding the creatures within a few yards of them, ripping their bodies in half and sending limbs flying everywhere. They squeezed off about thirty rounds, spraying the immediate area and creating a good thirty yard buffer. The zombies, for the most part, weren't dead, but they were cut in two, making them a non-threat for the time being.

"Casey, you got this?" Korver asked, and received a thumbs up. "Good. Galindo, on me. We gotta get our retreat set."

The duo ran back towards the on ramp, where a few dozen ghouls roamed up. They stopped at the top and fired, picking their targets carefully and efficiently and dropping them.

The Corporal pulled out some of the explosives and set one in the middle of the road before moving up another fifteen yards and setting another. They looked down to the bottom of the ramp, seeing about a hundred zombies massing together, slowly moving their way.

"This is going to be tight," Galindo said, shaking his head. "What's our time?"

Korver looked at his watch. "We still need seven minutes."

The Private shook his head again, knowing it was a long shot. He fired again as Korver started lobbing C4 down the on ramp.

As the battle raged below, Ibarra, Sellers, and Hartman stood on the fourth floor, keeping an eye on things. The first two overlooked the fighting force, seeing that they were keeping the southern zombies at bay, and creating a traffic jam on the ones coming from the north.

"They're getting a hell of a crowd down there," Sellers commented.

Ibarra looked at his watch, seeing they were five minutes in. "Still have five more minutes to go, too."

"Hope they can hold out that long," Sellers said.

"Ibarra!" Hartman yelled. "You need to see this!"

Ibarra clapped Sellers on the shoulder. "Stay here, keep watch," he said, and rushed over to the side window running parallel with the interstate. As he reached it, he spotted a couple thousand zombies headed back towards the noise.

"They're in trouble," Hartman said.

Ibarra pulled out his handgun. "Let's buy them some time, then," he declared, and fired into the glass, demolishing the window.

He grabbed a ball of explosive, armed it, and chucked it as hard as he could towards the horde. They watched as it vanished into the middle of the pack.

"I'd cover your ears," he warned, and then pulled out a detonator, hitting the trigger.

The blast was forceful, sending dozens of ghouls into the air, and knocking easily a couple hundred to the ground. A hundred or so near the front weren't affected, but at least the rest of them were slowed.

"Let me know when they get moving again," he said, and handed over a block of C4. "If I'm tied up, arm it and chuck it, and I'll detonate it when you're ready."

Hartman nodded, and Ibarra went back over to the front window to watch the battle raging below.

Meanwhile, on the ground, Bartlett continued firing at the zombies trying to get around the edge of the vehicle. Several managed to do so.

"Barr!" she cried. "I need help!"

Barr spotted the zombies coming around and immediately hopped out of the SUV. She quickly raised her weapon and began firing, clearing out the handful of creatures that had come around. Casey looked back, completely unaware that there were zombies coming up on his rear.

"Thanks," he said, eyes wide at his unknowing danger.

Barr nodded and moved back towards her vehicle, when she noticed it beginning to move. The tires squealed a bit as they slid across the road.

"Jesus christ," she breathed, "they're going to push through."

She let out a loud two-finger whistle, getting the attention of Benton, who was concentrating on the zombies on the other side of the barricade. He turned and saw the SUV shifting and immediately started getting out of his.

"Bartlett, we gotta move!" Barr cried, and the Private in question crawled out of her vehicle as it began to slide as well.

The three soldiers convened beside Casey, who opened up his fifty-cal on some more zombies coming up. Korver and Galindo came running back from the on ramp.

"Why are you out of position?" the Corporal demanded.

Barr pointed to the SUVs, which were sliding even more now, a few arms sticking through the gaps that grew larger by the second.

"Shit," Korver growled, and immediately looked up to the window, waving his arms frantically to get the attention of Ibarra. After a few seconds, he saw a flashlight blinking on and off. "We got two minutes to get the fuck out, let's move!" he barked.

The six soldiers ran towards the on ramp, dozens of zombies pouring around the side of the SUV blockade. Several of the troops began firing, holding them at bay as they moved off of the road.

Korver pulled out the detonator and got it ready. "Fire in the hole!" he yelled and hit the trigger.

The soldiers were momentarily staggered as the blast hit them, blinking and shaking their heads. Looking down the on ramp, the explosions had reduced the ghouls there to red paste.

They ran as hard as they could, avoiding limbs and trying not to slip on the slick pavement. When they reached the bottom of the ramp, there were about fifty zombies standing in between them and the garage.

"Light 'em up!" Korver cried, and the group formed a firing line, moving swiftly.

The soldiers fired as they went, creating a path for them to run through. As they tore towards the garage, the *chop-chop* of the Apache helicopters cut the air overhead. A few seconds later, the *whirrrr* of multiple mini-guns spun up, unleashing a flood of bullets onto the interstate above. A few explosions from the SUVs being decimated added to the cacophony.

"Get to the garage!" Korver screamed, leading the team across the street to the building, taking out several zombies with his gun as they went. He was the first to reach the door and immediately lifted it up.

Galindo and Benton reached it next and helped him get it high enough for everyone to slide underneath. Once everyone was clear, they let it slam to the ground before the zombies could catch up to them.

"That was one hell of a run," Galindo said, swiping his palms together.

The Corporal clapped him on the back as he caught his breath. "Yeah, let's never do that again," he said.

"No argument there," Galindo agreed.

Korver dusted himself off. "Everybody okay?"

"Ears are ringing like a motherfucker," Barr admitted, "but other than that, I'm good."

The rest of the group nodded, muttering in the affirmative.

"Come on, let's get upstairs and see how it looks," Korver said, and led the group trudging up the stairs to the fourth floor, muscles exhausted. "Ibarra, what's the situation?" the Corporal asked when they entered the cubicle farm.

"Wholesale slaughter," the Private replied brightly.

The nine troops stood at the window, all of them marveling at the sight. Thousands of zombies lay on the interstate, a heaping mass of rotted flesh, coating the road for several hundred yards. The only real sign of movement was the fires burning from the exploded SUVs.

Korver looked further down the road, seeing more ghouls coming up from the downtown area. They took a few steps onto the corpses and ended up slipping over, the uneven terrain of carnage difficult for them to navigate.

"Isn't perfect," Galindo mused, "but should be enough to hold them off until reinforcements arrive."

The group continued to stare off in silence. Each of them took pride in

completing their mission, but wore heavy
shoulders at the price paid to make it
happen.

Most of the group had found a place amongst the cubicles to curl up for a nap. All but Korver and Galindo, who sat by the window overlooking the highway. The car fires had long since burned out, but several fires raged around the city, illuminating the night sky. The additional moonlight gave them a good view of the carnage below.

A few hundred zombies had managed to navigate the killing fields, stumbling and slipping the entire way. There were thousands lined up behind them, most of which just stood around, not bothering to push the issue.

"Think we should call in another airstrike?" Galindo asked.

Korver shook his head. "Nah, the situation is pretty solidified down there," he replied. "Somebody has bound to be in a worse situation than us out there."

"That's true," the Private agreed. After a few moments of silence, he asked, "You think we're really going to be able to set up shop here in Seattle?"

The Corporal paused, pursing his lips for a moment. "I think we're going to take it over," he said slowly. "Judging by where the fires are, it looks like they're almost to the water."

"I know that," Galindo replied, shaking his head. "What I mean is, do you think we'll be able to make it work?"

Korver shrugged. "Honestly, I don't know," he admitted. "There are so many variables to think about. Power, food, clean water. All that shit is way above my pay grade. I'm just here to kill zombies and occasionally do some heavy lifting."

The Private chuckled. "Well, you did a hell of a job today, Corporal," he said.

"Tell that to Potts, Parra, Waller, and Marin," Korver replied, voice cold as ice.

Galindo chewed his lip for a moment, taking a beat to remember his dead comrades. "You got the rest of us through, though," he finally said. "Couldn't have done it without you."

"Yeah…" Korver drew out the word, but wouldn't look at his companion. "Maybe."

Before Galindo could reply, the Corporal's radio came to life.

"Corporal Korver, this is Captain lay, do you copy?" the Captain came through.

Galindo rolled his eyes. "Better late than never, I suppose," he muttered.

"Right?" Korver agreed and then raised the radio to his lips. "Copy, Captain. What's your twenty?"

"We're a block away from the target building," Clay replied. "Wanted to get input on the best entry point."

The Corporal scratched his head. "East side of the building, there is an underground parking garage," he explained. "The gate to the left is unlocked, just have to pull it up and get inside. We'll meet you down there."

"See you in a second," the Captain said.

Korver sighed and got to his feet. "All right, let's be the welcoming committee."

They made their way down to the garage. As they exited the stairwell, soldiers were pouring in by the hundreds.

"We're looking for Captain Clay," the Corporal said to a nearby soldier.

The Private saluted him. "Right this way, sir," he said, and escorted them to the Captain who was by the door, barking out orders. Sporadic gunfire cracked outside.

"Let's get a move on, men!" Clay cried. "Get inside and secure this door!"

"Captain, these men are looking for you," the soldier said.

The Captain turned away from the door and extended his hand. "You must be Corporal Korver," he said. "Good to finally meet you."

Korver shook his hand and nodded. "Likewise," he said. "This is my right hand man, Galindo."

"What's the situation here?" Clay asked.

The Corporal jerked a thumb over his shoulder. "Interstate is blocked off, at least for the time being," he explained. "We were able to get enough of them packed together for an Apache run, and the bodies on the ground have made it difficult for the others to press on."

"And how secure are we in here?' the Captain asked.

"Fourth floor is secure," Korver said. "Rest of the building is unknown. We blocked off the stairwell doors, but that's all we had the firepower for."

Clay turned towards his troops. "Sergeant Sierra," he yelled, "front and center!"

A young rough and tumble man rushed up, stopping just short of them. "Yes, sir?"

"I need you to assemble half a dozen teams of ten," the Captain instructed. "We need to sweep this building floor by floor, and clear it of any threat. The fourth floor is already secure, so leave it be. I expect this to be done within the hour. After that, we need to get firing positions set up in every direction."

"Yes, sir!" Sierra declared.

Clay nodded. "Get a move on," he said.

The Sergeant rushed off, yelling out for various Corporals to fall in.

"Show me the battlefield," the Captain said, motioning for Korver and Galindo to lead him up.

The trio headed up to the fourth floor, leaving the troops in the garage to do their own thing like a well-oiled machine. When they reached the window, Clay looked out, appraising the carnage on the interstate and the lack of any major push by the zombies on the far side.

"That is some damn fine work, Corporal," he declared.

Korver nodded. "Thank you, sir."

"Limited resources and you completed the mission," the Captain continued. "Not sure if we could have done it any better if we had made it here on time."

The Corporal nodded again. "Appreciate that, sir," he said. "Now, what can we do to help?"

Clay admired the man with a smile. "Even after the day you've had, you're ready to keep pushing," he said, and glanced around at the exhausted team napping, completely unaware of what was happening in the room. "You and your troops are to get some sleep. If I see you before zero-eight hundred, I'll put you on latrine duty for a month."

Korver cracked a smile before saluting. The Captain saluted back and shook his hand once again.

"Get some rest, Corporal," he said. "We'll take it from here."

As he vanished into the stairwell, the two soldiers breathed a sigh of relief.

"That is one order I will do gladly," Galindo declared, and patted his friend on the back. "Get some rest, friend," he said.

"You too," Korver replied, and turned back to the window, giving the war zone one last look as his companion went to find a place to crash.

It was a lot to take in, a lot to process. Finally, he let out a big sigh, and laid down on the ground, ready to put the horrors of the day out of his mind.

There would be a lot more work to be done in the morning.

END

Up Next: With the battle won Captain Kersey joins the President and his team to discuss what comes next in Seattle Pt. 10.

DEAD AMERICA
THE NORTHWEST INVASION
BOOK 12
SEATTLE PART 10
BY DEREK SLATON
© 2020

CHAPTER ONE

Day Zero +28

The sun had been up for a few hours now, though Captain Kersey and David Frazier wouldn't have known it, since they were hunkered down in the windowless communications room at the Cle Elum airport.

Multiple radios surrounded the two with several soldiers monitoring them, relaying orders and up to the minute information to troops in the field. For the last thirty hours, the Captain had been a fixture in this room, poring over every bit of information that came in. David, his communications expert, updated the giant war room map sitting on a table at the back.

Kersey was surprisingly alert despite having been up for days, only catching short fifteen-minute catnaps here and there. But this was the final push towards victory, and even though the Seattle mission was essentially on autopilot at this point, he couldn't pull himself away.

"Failed building containment heard," one of the soldiers said into his headset, "what's your current location?" He paused to listen, and Kersey watched his pencil scribble across his notepad. "Four story building, section forty-seven to the south of the I-ninety. Confirmed. Size of force?" the soldier asked. After a beat, he repeated, "Forty outside, unknown number inside. Slow-moving breach. Stand by."

The soldier turned to David, who stood at the ready over the map. He'd perked up at the notice of containment failure and already had his finger over the target. He trailed down to a marked spot just south of the building.

"Containment breach solution," he said.

The soldier nodded. "Go."

"Sweep team thirty-two are in the area on store purges," David replied. "Redeploy some to deal with it."

"Heard," the soldier replied with a nod, and turned back to his unit, dialing up the sweep team to issue their new instructions.

David kept his ears open, listening hard for certain words as the soldiers spoke to the troops in the field. *Breach, overrun, runners*—all three of those words brought a sense of urgency, and he had to react quickly.

One word, however, brought not only relief, but a sense of joy.

"Barricade formed on the I-five south of airport," another soldier declared.

David grinned. "Which airport?" he asked.

"International," the soldier replied.

The communications expert couldn't stop smiling as he took his bright red marker and drew a line across the interstate to the south of the airport, connecting a previous solid red line from the water of Elliott Bay all the way to the Renton airport. The latter had been the main hub of the southern barricade for days now, and their position was only strengthening.

"Kersey, come take a look at this," David said, waving him over.

The Captain got up out of his chair and walked over, leaning over the table. David pointed to the bright red line running along the entire southern border of Seattle. It joined another at the northern portion of the map. Little green plastic army men stood all along the eastern waterfront in between, creating a massive safe zone.

"Is that confirmed?" Kersey asked, eyes widening.

His companion nodded. "Triple confirmed," he replied. "I even sent one of my drone pilots up so I could fly the length of it. It's solid."

"Resistance from the south?" the Captain asked, afraid of the hope blooming in his chest.

"Minimal," David replied. "The southern teams pushing up from Olympia pulled a lot of them their way, so barring some unforeseen circumstance, the southern flank is secure."

Kersey let out a huge sigh of relief, nodding and scratching the back of his head. The main portion of the battle was approaching conclusion, and he allowed himself to embrace hope. It wasn't over yet, but it was getting there.

"How are the teams pushing west looking?" he asked.

David reached down and picked up one of the little army men that had been positioned at the western coast. "Well, as you can see by my state-of-the-art place holders, they have almost completely cleared the streets within the interior of the safe zone," he explained. "We have a couple hundred scouts constantly patrolling the area to make sure we don't have any jailbreaks, and a hundred sweep teams taking out high priority targets. Store and weak looking structures, stuff like that. So far, the trouble has been minimal, with the group we just dealt with being the worst we've had in a while."

Kersey stared at the map in silence for several moments, everything imaginable running through his head. Soldiers wiping out zombies, a clear city, civilians able to walk around without worrying about certain death.

"David," he said slowly, "have we actually pulled this off?"

His companion nodded, putting a hand to his forehead. "I think we have, Captain."

The two men laughed, shaking their heads, partially in relief and part disbelief that they'd come to this.

"I'm sorry to interrupt, Captain," a soldier said from behind them, clearing his throat.

Kersey turned to him, motioning for him to continue. "No, please do," he assured him. "What do you have for us?"

"Just got word that they cleared out the horde in front of the stadium by the Coast Guard base," the soldier replied.

David punched a victory fist into the air. "Liberated the first VIP camp, that's amazing!" he cried.

"Now we just have to hope the people inside are useful to the litany of new issues we're going to be facing," Kersey replied, turning back to the table.

"I've been talking with Whitney and John from the President's team about that," David said, "and they seem confident that Captain Galvan did a better job than most."

The Captain cocked his head playfully. "Talking with Whitney and John, huh?" he asked. "You trying to take my place with the planning?"

"Nothing like that," David replied, chuckling. "Just idle chatter, spit balling when we need a break from the mind-numbing invasion planning."

Kersey clapped him on the back. "I'm just fucking with you," he assured his friend. "Although if you do have any bright ideas on how we can turn this war zone into a home, I'm not going to turn them down."

"Funny you mention that," David replied, holding up a finger. He headed for his desk and pulled out a giant binder. He held it out and dropped the heavy tome onto the desk with a loud *thud*. "I have had a few thoughts."

The Captain stared at the thick book, eyes wide. "Mother of god man," he breathed, "when did you have time to work on all that?"

"Well, only the last few pages are my ideas," his friend replied, smirking. "The rest of this behemoth is the info you're going to need for the next strategy meeting."

Kersey shook his head. "I was getting ready to say—"

"Pardon me Captain," the soldier piped up again, "but General Stephens is on the line for you."

"Speak of the devil," David quipped.

Kersey pointed to him. "Get that binder ready," he instructed. "I think we're about to take a trip." He headed over to the radio and picked up a headset. "General Stephens."

"Captain Kersey," Stephens greeted, "how are you holding up, my friend?"

Kersey chuckled. "Been running on fumes for the better part of a week now," he admitted, "but still kicking."

"Uh oh," the General replied playfully, "don't tell me you're back to your old sleep schedule?"

The Captain laughed. "You mean going full throttle with the occasional fifteen minute power blackout?" he asked. "Yep, that's me at the moment."

"Oh, to be young and full of energy again," Stephens replied wistfully. "I remember those days."

Kersey shook his head. "I remember those days as well," he agreed. "Been a while since either of those things applied to me."

"Well, if you're anything like me," the General said, "the last week has aged you ten years, so you might be right."

The Captain nodded and pulled up his chair, falling back into it with a sigh. "Ain't that the truth," he agreed.

"So, how are things looking on your side of the battle?" Stephens asked.

Kersey reached for his mug of lukewarm coffee. "We've been in the war room for the last thirty hours or so, keeping track of everything," he reported. "As of right now, it looks like we have ourselves a solid, safe foothold here in Seattle."

"That's what my people are telling me as well," the General replied. "In fact, I just heard we've pushed through to the Coast Guard base by the stadium. Seeing as how you played a huge role in making this happen, I wanted to invite you out to the official liberation of the fortress."

Kersey glanced over at David as he took a large gulp of coffee, and his friend nodded approvingly at him. "Absolutely General," he said into the radio, "it would be my pleasure."

"Outstanding," Stephens replied. "I have a helicopter on standby that I can send out your way from the ships and pick you up."

Before the Captain could respond, he noticed David wildly waving his arms. "One second, General," he said, and then turned back to his friend. "What is it?"

"Benny landed a couple of hours ago," David said with a smirk. "He might get a kick out of meeting a General."

Kersey barked a laugh, shaking his head as he raised the receiver to his lips. "Actually General, I have a ride already here," he said. "Where would you like us to meet you?"

"The Coast Guard base on Elliott Bay would be just fine," Stephens replied. "I'll let them know to expect your arrival."

The Captain nodded, swallowing the last sip of rapidly cooling brew. "Look forward to it," he said. "We'll be heading out shortly."

"Guess I should get moving too," the General said. "Enjoy the fly-in, Captain. You've earned it."

"Yes, sir," Kersey replied, and set down the receiver. He beamed with pride, taking a deep breath and allowing himself to enjoy the fruits of all of their hard work. He turned to David, who stood behind him, already holding the giant binder.

"I'll go wake Benny up," he said.

The Captain nodded and held up his empty mug. "Might want to have some coffee in hand before doing that," he suggested. "He seems to be feisty when he doesn't have his fuel."

"Tell me about it," David replied, rolling his eyes. "I had the unfortunate task of getting him up a couple of days ago, and I swear it looked like he was trying to stab me. Like he legit tried to pull something from his waist and thrust it forward." He shook his head. "I didn't take it personally, because I thought he was just reacting to a bad dream or something, but the more I think about it…"

Kersey paused. "Yeah… we should probably get some bourbon as well before waking him up," he said, and the duo shared a chuckle before heading out of the comm room.

CHAPTER TWO

Benny piloted the chopper towards the battle zone, Kersey in the passenger seat and David sitting in the back. As they approached the easternmost battlefield, the Captain gazed down at the carnage.

There were a few small fires burning themselves out, as well as numerous troops in the road, doing patrols and shuffling gear around. Several trucks stood outside of a shopping center, soldiers loading up goods from inside.

"They're not wasting any time, are they?" Kersey asked into his headset.

Benny shook his head. "Naw, they sure aren't, Captain," he replied. "I swear, half the loads I ran yesterday they pulled right out of the stores and put it right into my baby here."

"I can believe it," Kersey agreed. "Our meager stack at the airport was wiped out pretty quick. I know we weren't high up on the totem pole, with most of the stuff going to the front lines, but didn't expect it to go that quick." He peered out at the I-90 bridge that connected with Mercer Island. "You doing okay on fuel?" he asked.

The pilot nodded. "Oh yeah, we're good," he replied. "Why, you wanna take a detour?"

"Can you fly me along the southern border?" the Captain asked. "I just want to see for myself what it looks like."

"You got it," Benny said, and adjusted course, sending the chopper south to cut across Mercer Island.

Kersey looked down and watched a line of trucks moving across the I-90 bridge towards the interior of the safe zone. There were tons of troops moving to the west as well, abandoning the island. As he focused his attention on the far side of the water, his eyes widened at the sight.

Tens of thousands of zombies lay dead, stretching for hundreds of yards back from the water. Pile after pile, rotted crimson flesh stacked high, limbs splayed everywhere.

"Looks like the island diversion worked to plan," he said.

Benny nodded. "That's an understatement," he replied. "I talked to a couple of boys who were with the team coming up behind those things. Said it was like shooting fish in a barrel. Just had to walk up and plug them in the back of the head, one by one."

Kersey smirked to himself, happy that his suggestion had paid off with dividends. As they reached the south of the island, the Renton airport came into view.

"And if you will look straight ahead, you'll see the Renton Airport, home to some of the most ingenious fighting men this country has to offer," Benny declared in his best faux-airline pilot voice. "One Sergeant Farley had the bright idea to combine jet fuel and high explosives, creating one of the biggest bombs I've ever had the pleasure of dropping."

The Captain blinked at him. "Wait, was that the Volunteer Park bomb?"

"The very same," Benny replied with a grin.

Kersey laughed, shaking his head. "I'm pretty sure I heard that one back at the airport."

"That may be," the pilot replied, "but you probably didn't hear the smaller five gallon molotovs we dropped on the interstate horde down there."

The Captain looked down and spotted a couple hundred yards of dead bodies on the interstate, charred to a crisp. Benny lowered the chopper down so they could get a good look at just how far the carnage stretched.

Far in the distance, Kersey noticed a smattering of zombies, a group no bigger of fifty or so. "Even with all that, they're still coming," he said with a sigh.

"Chances are we'll be clearing those fuckers out for months," Benny replied. "But their numbers aren't anywhere big enough to break through."

The Captain nodded, pursing his lips. "Hope you're right, buddy," he murmured. "Hope you're right."

Benny turned the chopper around and flew back to the main line, flying along it so his passengers could get a good look.

At every single street there was a fortified barricade. Most of the time it was made from cars they'd appropriated from local neighborhoods, but every so often there was a larger vehicle like a dump truck, with some chain link fencing stretched across the roads.

Kersey chuckled as he appraised the flimsy fencing. "Yeah, we might need to pencil in some more concrete barriers, there," he said.

"Just add it to the shopping list," Benny said brightly, "and we'll get around to it." He flew a little further down the line before making the turn north towards the Coast Guard Base.

Just in the few miles from the line to the base, there was a wide variety of activity around. Several groups had already pushed to the water, others still several blocks away, engaged in skirmishes with the dead.

In a few cases, groups broke away from the coast and moved back in to reinforce their comrades who were in harm's way.

Closer to the Coast Guard base, the stadium loomed in the distance just on the other side of it. For the last mile or so, there wasn't a zombie in sight on the street, just a huge military presence with tens of thousands of troops roaming the street and clearing the buildings closest to it.

"Man, they're making a hell of a lot of progress here," Benny said. "When I flew over yesterday, they were still a ways off from the water, and now they're half a mile deep in clearing things out entirely!"

Kersey grinned. "Well, they're bringing in heavy hitters like you, buddy," he declared. "Can't take any chances, after all."

The pilot chuckled and shook his head, happy for the playful banter with a familiar passenger. He focused on the base, noting a spot close to the main building that was clear.

"Not sure if I'm supposed to land here or not," he admitted, "but fuck it. What are they going to do, stop me?"

Kersey laughed. "I got your back," he promised. "Have at it."

Benny lowered the chopper to the ground, and almost immediately a young soldier came running over, waving his hands in the air frantically.

"Whoa, whoa!" the soldier screamed as Kersey's boots hit the pavement. "You can't land that here!"

The Captain raised his hands. "Relax soldier," he said calmly, "we're expected."

"And who are you?" the soldier demanded.

"I'm Captain Kersey," came the reply.

The young man's eyes went wide as saucers, face white as a sheet. "Oh my god, sir," he babbled, waving his hands back and forth in front of his face, "I'm so sorry." He scrubbed his fingers down his cheeks. "I'm so sorry, sir, really-"

"Hey, hey, relax," Kersey cut in, taking pity on him. "Take a deep breath."

The soldier finally bit back his rambling and lowered his arms.

"Do you know where General Stephens is?" the Captain asked.

"Oh yeah, I can take you to him," the soldier gushed, nodding furiously. "Please, follow me."

David and Benny approached from behind.

"Captain," the pilot piped up, "you
do what you need to do. I'm going to see
about scaring up some fuel for my baby
here." He jerked a thumb over his shoulder
at the big bird.

Kersey nodded. "If anybody gives you
any shit," he said, pointing a finger,
"you tell them to come talk to me and the
General."

"Love the benefits of having friends
in high places," Benny declared with a
happy sigh, miming tucking his thumbs into
pretend suspender straps.

Kersey and David chuckled, then
followed the young soldier across the
base. The place was a flurry of activity,
troops setting up barricades, fencing, and
machine gun nests.

"Looks like this is where the
military is going to call home," David
mused. "At least for the time being."

Kersey nodded. "Makes sense," he
agreed. "If things go to shit, they can
just go straight to the water."

The soldier led them into the main
building, and waved them towards the
staircase. "Just gotta go up to the second
floor," he said.

"Lead on," Kersey said, side-stepping
a few soldiers carrying large pieces of
wood to fortify the windows. The hum of
power drills and banging of hammers was

loud as the troops reinforced the interior of the building, turning it into a hardened position.

The second floor was a lot quieter. There were just a handful of soldiers and civilians walking about, with a few offices set up with detailed maps and radio equipment.

"Looks like they don't care about fortifying this floor," David commented as they walked.

Kersey shrugged. "Guess they figure if they lose the first floor, anything on the second would just be delaying the inevitable," he mused.

"Better to be eaten than starve to death, I suppose," David said. "Not that I'm very eager to prove that theory."

The soldier led them down a hallway to a back office. General Stephens sat behind a desk, reading over reports in several binders strewn across the surface.

The soldier knocked on the doorframe. "Excuse me, General Stephens," he said gently. "These men say they're here to see you."

Stephens looked up, his serious expression brightening instantly. "Well, well, well," he said with a grin, "look what the cat dragged in." He got up from his seat and approached the door as the duo entered, holding out his hand.

"Been a while, General," Kersey said as they shook vigorously.

Stephens nodded. "You're telling me," he replied. "Last time I saw you back in Kansas, you were just a lowly Sergeant. Now look at you. Standing here as a Captain and dispensing advice to the President."

"Not bad for a grunt, huh?" Kersey replied, and they shared a laugh.

The General wagged a finger at him. "Don't sell yourself short, my friend," he demanded. "You have done your country proud these last few weeks. Hell, you've done the whole damn human race proud."

"Let's not go too crazy here, General," the Captain replied, scratching the back of his head in embarrassment.

Stephens raised his chin. "I'm being quite serious," he declared. "Thanks to your hard work and ingenuity, we now have a foothold to rebuild this country, and the world. Communications are sketchy with other nations, but none of what we're hearing is good. But there will be plenty of time to discuss that." He waved a hand. "Come, have a seat."

"Excuse me, General?" the soldier by the door piped up as Kersey and David sat in front of the desk. "Is there anything you need from me, sir?"

Stephens glanced at Kersey as he took his own seat.

The Captain turned towards the door. "Can you make sure my pilot, Benny, gets whatever he needs?"

"Absolutely, sir," the soldier replied, nodding sharply.

David raised a hand. "And if you could scare up some coffee, I don't think any of us would complain," he added.

The soldier's brow furrowed, as if confused at how to respond to a civilian request. He glanced at the General for help.

Stephens smirked. "You heard the man," he said, "see if you can find us some coffee. I heard a rumor that they were rigging something up in the break room downstairs."

The soldier nodded and hurried away.

Once gone, the General held out his hand towards David. "Sir, I don't believe we've met," he said politely. "If the Captain here is bringing a civilian into a meeting with me, I'm going to assume you bring something to the table other than the ability to order drinks."

"My name is David Frazier, sir," the communications expert replied, shaking Stephens' hand. "I joined up with the good Captain here back in Spokane, and have been with him ever since, coordinating not only the local drone surveillance, but compiling all of the battlefield data." He held up the giant binder and set it on the desk.

Stephens pulled it over to him and flipped through it, nodding approvingly. "Appears to be some damn fine work," he said. "If you ever want to move up to working with a General, my stuff could use an upgrade."

"General, are you really trying to poach my communications expert?" Kersey asked playfully, cocking his head.

Stephens smiled. "Of course not, Captain," he replied, folding his arms in front of him. "You forget, I'm a General. If I wanted your communications expert here, I would just assign you to an out of state mission."

"Been there once already," Kersey replied with a chuckle.

Stephens grinned. "Victim of your own success, I'm afraid," he replied. "Oh!" He held up a finger. "Speaking of successes, I have a surprise for you." He picked up a walkie talkie from the desk and held it to his lips.

Kersey and David exchanged an intrigued glance, the former shrugging with no clue what the surprise could be.

"Mary, can you send in my guest, please?" Stephens asked into the radio. He set the device down and nodded to the Captain. "You're gonna like this."

A moment later, there was another knock on the doorframe, and they turned around, laying eyes on Corporal Bretz.

"Holy shit!" Kersey cried, launching himself out of his chair. "How are you doing, man?"

Bretz's face broke out into a lopsided grin. "Little sunburned from hanging out on top of a truck for the better part of the week, but other than that, not too bad," he replied.

"A week on top of a truck?" David blurted, eyes wide. "Damn, how did you pass the time?"

The Corporal deadpanned. "Trashy romance novels."

The other three burst out laughing, but he didn't even crack a smile.

"No, seriously," he continued when they were finished, "trashy romance novels. Some of the guys that helped us procure the trucks thought it would be a laugh to put those in our care packages."

Kersey wiped imaginary tears from his eyes. "If you need me to have someone court-martialed for that offense, you just let me know," he said, patting his friend on the shoulder.

"Actually, some of them were quite entertaining," Bretz admitted, laughing.

The Captain turned to Stephens, brow furrowing in playful concern. "General, have you had this man checked out thoroughly for head trauma?" he asked.

Bretz knocked on his own head. "With a skull this thick, I don't think they'd be able to get an accurate reading."

There were laughs all around as the two men took seats across from the desk, clapping each other on the back.

The soldier returned with a tray of mugs. "Here you go, General," he said, focusing on keeping his hands steady. "I got enough for everybo… dy…" he trailed off as he noticed Bretz, and his eyes widened in panic.

"It's okay man," the Corporal said, waving his hand flippantly. "I've already had my fill for the day."

The soldier looked relieved, shoulders slumping, and passed out the steaming mugs before scurrying out of the room.

"So, tell me Kersey," Stephens said, wrapping his hand around his cup, "how was the flight in? All I've seen are reports on how it looks out there."

The Captain leaned back in his chair. "To put it mildly, we're going to need one hell of a cleanup crew," he admitted, circling his coffee under his nose. "Our

troops have done a hell of a job out
there."

"And they're continuing to do so,"
David added. "Those barricades to the
south look fierce."

Kersey chuckled after taking a sip of
coffee. "Not sure using a beat-up sedan as
a barricade can be considered fierce, but
they do have a solid line formed," he
said. "Not to mention, on the interstate
there's a pile of bodies half a mile long.
No hordes are going to penetrate that
line."

"Good to know my reports appear to be
accurate," Stephens replied, nodding. "Our
troops are doing some good work."

The Captain smiled. "That they are,
General," he replied, "that they are."

"General," David piped up, raising
his hand, "any idea how we are looking
around the base here?"

Stephens shook his head. "Haven't
seen firsthand," he admitted. "But from
what some of the soldiers who helped get
me set up here were telling me, they are
going full tilt boogie on clearing this
area out. Every building, every nook and
cranny, cleared in triplicate. This base
is going to be more secure than Fort
Knox."

"Well, more secure than Fort Knox used to be," Bretz cut in. "Has anybody checked on that place recently?"

The General chuckled. "No, but I'll put out an A.P.B. on Goldfinger if it'll make you feel better," he said. His radio beeped as the others shared a laugh. "Excuse me a moment," he said, and picked up the radio. "Yes, Mary?"

"General, I've just been informed they are working on the entrance to the stadium," the woman on the other end said. "You are being requested to join them."

Stephens nodded. "Tell them I'm on the way," he replied.

"Yes, sir," she replied. "Oh, and I let the President's team know that there is going to be a delay due to this. They happily rescheduled for an hour from now."

The General smiled. "You're the best, Mary," he said, and then put the radio down. "What do you say, boys? You want to come check out one of our stadium fortresses?"

"Absolutely," Kersey replied, taking a gulp of his brew and getting to his feet.

Stephens nodded as he stood up from his office chair. "And afterwards, we get another in-depth meeting with the President to find out what other insane task we get to tackle next," he said with a soft groan.

"Silver lining through," Kersey countered. "You could be one of those civilians who just gets to kick back and enjoy the fruits of our labor."

David held up his hand. "Yeah, where do I sign up for that one?"

The quartet shared a chuckle as the General led them out of the building and into the parking lot. A young soldier stood outside of an SUV and stepped forward as they arrived.

"General Stephens," the young man greeted, "I'll be your driver to the stadium."

Stephens' brow furrowed. "Driver?" he asked. "The stadium is just on the other side of the road there. I think we can manage."

"Sir, I have my orders to drive you there personally," the soldier insisted.

Stephens cocked his head. "Did the President give you those orders?"

"Um…" the soldier stammered. "No sir."

Stephens leaned in a little closer. "What about another General?"

"Uh… no, sir," the soldier replied, starting to sweat now. "It was my Captain."

"You know how military ranks work, don't you, son?" Stephens asked.

The soldier nodded jerkily. "Yes, sir."

"Good," the General replied, clapping his hands, "so I'm going to give you new orders. You are to report back to your Captain that the General says he doesn't need a goddamn babysitter to go across the street. And make sure you emphasize the *goddamn*, because I really want it to resonate."

The soldier gaped at him for a moment. "Um… okay," he stammered. "I mean, yes, sir."

"Run along, now," Stephens demanded, waving him off.

"Yes sir," the soldier squeaked, and turned away, then back. "Oh, and the keys are in the ignition," he added, and then scurried off.

"Gentlemen, our chariot awaits," Stephens said, and motioned them forward with a flourish.

The four men piled into the SUV, and the General fiddled with his seat, moving it into the proper position before flipping on the air conditioning.

"You boys getting air back there?" he asked, glancing in the rearview.

Both Bretz and David made noises in the affirmative, and Stephens grinned.

"All right, let's ride then," he declared, and then hit the gas.

He peeled out, screeching the tires as he picked up speed. Kersey chuckled at the genuine look of pleasure on his face as he sped across the lot.

They crossed the interstate underpass, and the stadium came into view in the distance. Several snowplows moved limp corpses to the far corners of the lot, clearing the path and setting them up to be disposed of. Heavy machines grabbed stacks of dead zombies and dropped them into garbage trucks that were standing by.

"That…" David shook his head, gagging. "That is a horrific sight I probably could have lived without seeing."

Bretz took a deep breath. "It's going to be a hell of a messy job cleaning this town up," he said. "Millions of bodies, and that's on top of battle zones, blood-soaked locations, and a whole hell of a lot more nastiness spread out."

"Good to see a week in the sun didn't damper your positive outlook on life," David said dryly.

The Corporal shrugged. "Just calling it like I see it," he replied. "We can only hope that some of the VIPs they rescued for the stadium were crime scene cleanup crews."

They pulled up in front of the stadium, where a couple of soldiers were in the midst of using an industrial strength blowtorch to cut through the front locks. The quartet got out of the vehicle and headed over, several soldiers stopping to salute the General and Captain as they approached.

After a moment, the Sergeant on site appeared. "General, I'm Sergeant Weiss, thank you for coming, sir," he said, saluting. "We almost have this door open."

"Any word from inside?" Stephens asked.

"Yes, sir," Weiss replied. "The Captain on site…" He checked his notepad. "A Captain Galvan is ready to meet you."

Stephens nodded. "Good," he replied, and then looked around with an eyebrow raised. "Do we not have any medical teams on standby? These people have been locked up for a month, they might need some assistance."

"Yes, sir," the Sergeant replied, "I have two med teams en route as we speak. Transportation is a bit lacking, so it's taking longer than expected."

Stephens nodded. "Very good," he said, "thank you."

Weiss headed off and the four men stood about twenty yards away from the stadium door. The blow torch soldiers finally cut through the lock, allowing them to swing open the doors. When they did, they revealed half a dozen soldiers standing there, with one older gentleman at the front of the line.

"General Stephens," he greeted, stepping forward and saluting with his soldiers behind him, "I am Captain Galvan. The Seattle Fortress is ready for your inspection, sir."

Stephens returned the salute and then extended his hand. "No need for an inspection, Captain," he assured him as they shook. "However, we'll gladly take a guided tour, if you don't mind."

Galvin smiled. "It would be my pleasure, sir," he said. "Right this way."

Galvan led the General and others into the stadium, walking across the outer hallway and into the field portion of the stadium. He pointed to the south along the rim where almost all of the seats had been ripped out of the upper deck and replaced with greenhouses.

Several people on the field played touch football, while others threw around a frisbee and a baseball. There was even a yoga class in the visitor's end zone.

"Welcome to the field, gentlemen," Galvan announced. "As you can see, we have kept the majority of it as clear as possible so that the residents here have a place to work out or just relax. Not everybody is a gym rat, so I wanted to make it a priority that people had space."

David pointed to the end zone. "Is that a yoga class?"

"Yes it is," Galvan replied with a smile. "Please feel free to join if you like. Becky is a great teacher, and she loves breaking in new people."

David chuckled, waving a hand in front of his face. "Appreciate the offer, but I strain muscles standing up too quickly," he admitted. "So I'll take a rain check."

"Looks like you are doing a good job of keeping them fit, Captain," Stephens piped up.

Galvan nodded. "Not just fit, sir, but we put a premium on entertainment, as well," he explained. "We dedicated a small generator to the film room and would run movies for the kids, as well as football games for the adults on Sundays, just like they were pre-apocalypse. Even had a few teachers come in with some of the VIPs, so we had them run some fun classes like creative writing. The mixed media art class was a big hit from what I hear."

"If you don't mind me asking, Captain," Bretz cut in slowly, "why would you spend so many resources on entertainment?"

Galvin clasped his hands behind his back as they walked. "Well, my father was a prison warden," he began. "He told me that one of the smartest things he did was to expand the library and activities for the prisoners. The fighting and acting out dropped significantly after he did that. You see, when you're locked up, you don't really have a lot to look forward to, which puts people on edge or makes them just outright lose hope," he explained. "Neither of which is an ideal situation when you can't leave the building. While I know this isn't a prison, some people could very well have viewed it as such, so I took his advice to heart. The more we could keep people focused on anything other than the dire situation we were in, the smoother this ride would go."

David smiled. "Your father sounds like a good man," he said.

"Nah, he was an alcoholic hardass who thought beating the kids with a belt was raising us right," Galvan replied firmly, shaking his head. "But good advice is good advice."

David's eyes widened, and he looked a little embarrassed, and Bretz smacked him on the shoulder playfully as they continued following the Captain.

"If you'll give your attention to the upper deck there, you can see our greenhouse farm," Galvan continued, seemingly unperturbed. "The sunlight in these parts isn't the greatest this time of year, so it's been a real struggle to grow much of anything."

Bretz shrugged. "I'm not the biggest farmer in the world, but it's only been a month," he said. "Even in the best cases, you should still be a couple weeks out from harvest, right?"

"While you are correct on that," the Captain replied, "we were losing a significant portion of the seedlings before they could even begin to grow. In all honesty, if Seattle wasn't picked to play host to the invasion, I doubt very seriously we would have lasted the winter."

Stephens held up a hand. "David, make a note," he said. "We need to bring up the greenhouse issue with the President. If they're having issues with it, other cities might be as well."

"Consider it done, sir," David replied, scribbling on the back of one of the pages in the binder. "I actually speak with Whitney and John on a regular basis, and they're handling the majority of the logistics for supplies. I can let them know, if you like."

Stephens smiled. "Captain Kersey trusts you, which means I trust you," he said sincerely. "See that it's done."

"Yes, sir," David replied.

Kersey turned to the Captain. "What kind of population do you have here?" he asked.

"Two thousand, one hundred and forty-two," Galvan replied proudly. "I'm sorry, forty-three," he amended, shaking his head. "Had someone give birth to a bouncing baby boy a couple of days ago."

"And morale?" Kersey asked.

Galvan shrugged. "About as good as can be expected with that many people living in a stadium eating MREs and stale leftover concession stand food," he replied.

"How is your VIP list?" Stephens asked.

Galvan waved to a soldier nearby, who came running over with a large notebook, holding it out for the General.

"In there you'll find a list of every VIP, as well as civilian family member, and soldier," the Captain explained. "All listing their skill sets. We have a wide variety of people. Doctors, mechanics, a few gunsmiths. Even have a couple of honest to god blacksmiths."

Bretz's eyes nearly bugged out of his head. "Where in the world did you find blacksmiths in Seattle?" he asked.

"As luck would have it, there was a renaissance fair setting up when this hit," Galvan replied. "I figured with the lack of power and supplies, having some people skilled in old school ways might be worthwhile to have."

The Corporal nodded in appreciation. "Good way of thinking about it."

The General thumbed through the notebook and then handed it to David before looking at his watch. "David, please look this over before the meeting with the President," he instructed. "Might need to call on you for some information."

The communications expert blanched, blinking at him. "You… you want me in the meeting with the President?" He gaped.

"Outside of Captain Kersey here," Stephens explained, "I'm guessing you know more about our current situation than anyone else. Plus, they're on the other side of the country, so there's not a damn thing they can do about my decision to have you in the room, now is there?"

David couldn't help but smirk at the plucky General. "No sir, I guess there's not," he admitted.

"Captain Galvan, I'm afraid I'm going to have to leave you to it," Stephens said, turning back to him. "We have another meeting to attend. Is there anything I can do for you?"

Galvan shook his head. "No sir, I believe we're all set here," he said with a smile, and then slowly raised a finger. "Although, I do have one request."

"Let's hear it," Stephens said.

"My people here are a little hesitant to rush back out into the world," the Captain explained. "Especially with a week's worth of fighting going on within earshot. If it's all the same to you, I would like permission to allow them to stay in the stadium for the next few days, at least until the constant gunfire has died down for a bit."

Stephens nodded. "I think that would be best, Captain," he agreed. "In fact, I'm not sure what the housing plan even is, yet. Frankly, I'm not sure anybody has thought that far ahead."

"Well, if you need a place to bed down for the night," Galvan replied, "I'll set you up in one of the VIP suites."

The General chuckled, shaking his head. "Almost afraid to ask what that consists of."

"We renovated the corporate skyboxes and turned them into getaway cabins," the Captain explained. "Use it as a reward for when people went above and beyond around the stadium."

Stephens smiled. "I'll keep that in mind," he replied. "Thank you, Captain." He turned back to his companions and rolled a hand above his head. "Well boys, shake a leg. Can't keep the President waiting."

Kersey and Stephens sat at a small desk with a satellite phone sitting in the center of it. David and Bretz sat just behind them, against the wall. Mary entered with a tray of bottled water and set it down on the desk.

"Sorry it's not chilled," she said.

David chuckled. "Not your fault these slackers haven't gotten the power back on, yet," he said playfully. "It's been a whole forty-five minutes since they took over the city, I think they're getting lazy, don't you?" He gave her a wink and she laughed, waving her hand at him.

"Be careful there David," Kersey teased, "last time I made a joke, the General here put me on a train and sent my ass halfway across the country."

Stephens stared cooly at the communications expert. "I'll do it again, too."

David started to laugh, but it fizzled out when he realized the General was still deadpanned. "Oh…" he stammered. "Uh… I'm sorry…"

Kersey and Stephens couldn't hold back any longer, and burst into laughter, as David's face went crimson, and he shook his head in relief.

"It's good to know you can still go into 'put the fear of god into them' mode at the drop of a hat," Kersey gasped through gales of giggles.

Stephens caught his breath and clapped his friend on the back. "Pretty sure it's in the promotion requirements to be a General."

"If not, it really should be," the Captain replied, shaking his head.

The phone in the center of the table clicked on and a friendly male voice greeted them. "General Stephens, are you there?"

"We are," Stephens replied, getting comfortable in his chair as he unscrewed the cap of one of the water bottles.

"Please hold for the President," the man said. There were a few clicks, and then he continued, "Mister President, I have General Stephens."

"Thank you," President Williams said. "General Stephens, how are you getting set up in your new office?"

The General swallowed a swig of water before replying, "Very nicely sir, thank you. Have a nice view of Elliott Bay, and some enterprising young soldier figured out a way to get the coffee maker going, so life is good."

"Fresh coffee and a view?" Williams replied. "So how does it feel to have a better situation than the President?"

Stephens laughed. "Don't tell me they didn't stock up the pantry before all this went down, sir," he joked.

"There's still some coffee left, but supplies are a little lower than I would prefer," the President replied. "Contemplating sending General Adams here out on a store run."

There was some laughter through the line, and then Adams added, "There will be a shopping request sheet by the front vault door."

"If it's any consolation General," Stephens piped up, "we are fresh out of creamer. So we're roughing it out here."

Adams chuckled. "That wouldn't affect me, because I take my coffee like I take my women," he replied. "Cold and bitter."

There was more laughter on the line.

"As much as we would love to unpack General Adams' coffee comment," Williams cut in, sighing through his own mirth, "we do have a lot to get to today."

There was a smattering of *Yes, sir* throughout the line.

"General Stephens, on my side of the line I have General Adams, Whitney Hill, and John Teeter," the President continued.

Stephens leaned forward in his chair. "Good morning, everyone," he greeted. "I'm joined by Captain Kersey. Listening in to the call is Corporal Bretz and civilian David Frazier."

"Pardon the interruption," Adams cut in, "but should we have a civilian not in the Presidential Bunker on this call? We know the people in this room aren't talking to anybody."

"General, I've been working with David closely over the last couple of weeks," Whitney piped up, "closely coordinating troop movements and supplies. He's a valuable resource."

Kersey nodded, leaning in. "And to be frank, he probably knows more about the inner workings of the logistics than anybody else in this room," he added. "Myself included."

"All right," Adams said quickly, "I withdraw my objection. Let's move on."

Williams cleared his throat. "So, if it's okay with the rest of you, I'd like to start with the big picture. How are we looking in Seattle?" There were a few moments of silence, and then he clucked his tongue. "Please, don't everybody start talking at once," he joked.

There was some laughter on both sides, and then Whitney piped up, "Okay, I'll kick things off. Our stronghold in

Seattle is protected by water to the west, and our forces who marched in through the east. Our two big concern areas were to the north and south." There was a shuffling paper and then a click. "Now I know that you can't see our screen over the phone, so I'll give it the best description I can for you. At the beginning of the invasion, we had a real concern about a significant number of zombies coming down from Vancouver. After receiving permission from those in the Canadian government, at least those we could locate, we launched a strike on the main bridges leading south of the city. As you can see by the satellite imagery, this was a wise move. There are an estimated hundred and fifty to two hundred thousand zombies that have found their way to the water's edge, drawn by the noise."

"Pardon the interruption," Williams cut in, "but can they really hear our bombs going off that far north?"

"Indirectly they can," John answered. "Think of it like standing on a football field and there's someone every twenty yards. One person in the end zone yells something out, which is repeated by everyone down the line. The last person didn't hear the first person yell, but he knows that he did. Similar situation here. Although there's a good chance our

missiles taking out the bridges account
for a lot of the mass."

"Point taken," the President replied.
"Please, Miss Hill, continue."

"Thank you, Mister President,"
Whitney said, and cleared her throat.
"Now, even though the worst of our fears
weren't realized, we have still faced a
significant, albeit manageable, threat.
Stretching around fifty miles on the
interstate are an estimated twenty
thousand zombies. They are slowly working
their way towards our northernmost
barricade in Burlington."

"What are we doing to mitigate this?"
Williams asked.

"Over the last couple of days, we
have been able to move up a couple
thousand troops to that position," Whitney
continued, "and have begun doing hit-and-
run operations to thin their numbers."

The President made a small noise of
confusion. "Hit and run operations?"

"Yes, sir," she replied. "Setting
fire traps, using abandoned cars as
makeshift IEDs, things of that nature.
We're still expecting several thousand to
eventually reach the barricades on the
bridge, but those numbers are very
manageable." There was another click as
she changed the screen they were watching
on the other end. "Shifting to the south,

we have successfully set up a barricade running from the water all the way across through the residential areas east of Renton. The airport is secure, and we have reinforcements being moved in via the water to back them up. On the interstate, we have several heavy machine gun lines set up, and a buffer of several hundred yards."

"What kind of buffer?" Williams asked.

She paused. "Corpses."

There was a short silence, and then he continued, "Seems a little morbid, don't you think?"

"Morbid? Yes," Whitney confirmed. "Effective? Absolutely. Those things have problems traversing uneven terrain, and thanks to some aerial strikes there is a whole lot of uneven terrain impeding their advancement."

"Would enough of a force be able to push through it?" Adams piped up.

"Possibly," she replied, "but their numbers have been split thanks to our Olympia crew." There was another click, and then she continued, "A few days ago, we beached a ship to the west of Olympia. Those couple thousand troops were able to establish a beachhead and push forward to Olympia. Since then, they have launched numerous operations to draw the enemy in their direction, which has helped the northern group secure the line."

"Any word on how that group is faring?" Williams asked.

John cleared his throat. "Yes, my team spoke with them this morning," he replied. "The majority of the troops are set up in defensive positions to hold the attention of the crowds. They do have a few roving teams that are still active and bringing in more zombies, but they're unsure of how long they'll be able to keep that up."

"Are they in any immediate danger?" the President asked, and then immediately continued, "Sorry, let me rephrase, as everybody outside is in immediate danger with those things." He took a deep breath. "Are they in need of immediate assistance? Or can they sit tight for a few days before we send in a rescue team to relieve them?"

"By all accounts, they are set up for a few days," John replied. "They're secure, and they have plenty of rations to ride it out."

"Okay, good," Williams said. "General Stephens, if you wouldn't mind making this a priority once the situation becomes more stable in the safe zone? I don't want to leave those troops exposed any longer than necessary."

Stephens nodded. "Yes, sir," he replied, and took a sip of his water.

"Miss Hill," Adams piped up, "has there been any update on the Portland horde? I know there were concerns about that group on the interstate coming north."

"Yes," she replied, and there were more shuffling papers as she continued, "our diversion tactics worked well. Virtually every zombie on the interstate started moving south after our bombing run."

"That is fantastic news," Adams commended.

"Well, it is fantastic news for our southern flank," Whitney agreed. "However, we saw something of a concern on our last scan." More clicks. "One of my team members noticed this, and they are confident that this wasn't there before the strike."

There was a long pause, and then Williams said, "Forgive me Miss Hill, but I'm having a difficult time understanding what I'm seeing here."

"We did too at first," she replied. "Our working hypothesis is that these metal contraptions on the road were able to take out a significant number of zombies. As you can see, there is a radius around each device that is clear of corpses. They appear to be lawnmowers with metal rods welded to them like helicopter blades."

"So what's your takeaway on that?" the President asked.

"We believe that there were survivors in this area that were forced out due to our bombing run," Whitney replied.

Everyone on both sides of the call fell silent.

"I was under the impression we weren't targeting civilians with this strike," Williams finally said.

"Mister President," John spoke up slowly, "we used every bit of intelligence we had to do our best to aim away from the populated areas, or what we assumed were populated areas. The surrounding area is heavily wooded, so it's entirely possible that we missed a settlement. TO be blunt, without direct contact or eyes on the ground, we wouldn't have any idea they were there."

Williams sighed heavily. "Okay, I understand," he murmured, and then cleared his throat. "General Stephens I hate to continue to add to your workload, but can you please add sending assistance to Portland when you have a chance?"

"Yes, sir," Stephens replied, nodding. "Once we get Olympia squared away, I will send a team down there to investigate."

"Thank you, General," Williams replied. "Okay, is there anything else with the broad strokes? Or can we get into the nitty gritty of the safe zone?" There was a moment of silence, and then he continued, "All right, moving on. Does anybody have an update on clearing the buildings within the safe zone?"

"General Stephens, does anybody on your end have a figure on this?" John asked. "I know that we have had teams operating since the beginning of this, but with the ebbs and flow of battle, I imagine some teams were repurposed during the assault."

Stephens turned in his chair and smiled. "I believe David is going to be the best one to answer this question."

The man in question stared at him with wide eyes, like a deer caught in headlights. Bretz smacked him on the back and pointed to the desk.

David scurried forward, white-knuckling the binder, and Kersey got up, offering his chair. He sat down beside Bretz, just as David fumbled the binder, sending it down onto the desk with a loud *SMACK*.

"Oh my god, I'm so sorry about that, Mister President," he said hoarsely.

Williams chuckled. "It's all right son," he replied. "Take your time and get settled."

"Thank you, sir," David gushed, and then took a deep breath, poring through some pages before finally clearing his throat. "Okay, during our push west, we had roughly a thousand troops that were tasked solely with structure clearing. Most of the time they were used when the main force came across a breach." His voice became calmer, more businesslike as he fell into the zone of reporting information. "If the building could be patched up securely, they did that, but more often than not they had to clear it. As you can imagine, this is a slow, tedious task. Right now in the safe zone, we have teams of scouts souring the area, keeping watch for breaches so these teams can move in. I think we can all agree that the last thing we need are runners showing up in the safe zone."

There was a chorus of emphatic noises in the affirmative.

"David, do you have a timeline on how long it's going to take to completely clear these things out?" Williams asked.

The communications expert shook his head. "That's impossible to say at this point, sir," he replied honestly.

"Please son, humor me," the President said gently. "Give me your best guess. I promise I won't hold you to it."

David chewed his lip. "Okay, um…" he said, tilting his head back and forth. "For the immediate downtown area, say one mile out from the Coast Guard base, we're looking at a few weeks. From north to south, barrier lines stretching completely across the occupied area? Months."

"Months?!" Williams exclaimed. "How is that possible? We just marched through over a million of those things in the span of a week. Now you're telling me it's going to be months before we get the structures cleared out?"

David winced, but nodded. "In order to do it safely, yes sir."

"Would you care to go into a little more detail there?" the President asked. "Because I'm still not fully understanding why it could take that long."

"Gladly, sir," the communications expert replied, forcing his voice to stay steady. "In talking with Captain Kersey, Miss Hill, and John, we determined that the safest way to clear a structure was to have triple redundancy."

"Triple redundancy?" Williams asked dryly.

"That's correct, sir," David replied quickly. "Let me give you an example. On a

standard two-story family home, we would
have a clear team of six. These six, in
teams of two, would move in and sweep the
house of hostiles. For safety reasons,
just outside of the exits would be another
team of six, covering every way that a
runner could escape. Out at the street
would be another team in a vehicle, ready
to strike. Now this team would have the
ability to cover more than one house at a
time, since their main job would be to
alert everyone else in the unlikely event
of a runner, but they would still need to
be there."

"That seems like a bit of overkill,
don't you think?" Williams asked,
skepticism evident in his tone.

Kersey leaned forward in his seat,
lacing his fingers together in front of
him. "Mister President, Captain Kersey
here," he cut in. "If anything, we aren't
being cautious enough. Runners are an
extremely dangerous problem, and if some
of them got loose within the safe zone, it
could be catastrophic. I understand fully
that it's time consuming and uses a lot of
manpower, but to be frank, we've spilled
an enormous amount of blood just to get to
this point. It would be a shame to have
all that go to waste because we didn't go
the extra mile with safety."

There was a moment of silence before Williams replied, "I understand that point of view. It's easy for me to question the validity of these safety procedures when I'm locked up safely in a vault," he admitted. "You do what you feel you need to do to execute the mission successfully and safely."

"Thank you, sir," Kersey replied, and leaned back in his seat.

"If someone on your tea wouldn't mind," Williams continued, "please provide us with daily updates on the progress."

The Captain nodded, picking up his bottle of water and unscrewing the cap. "Absolutely sir," he said, "we will keep you in the loop."

"Moving on," the President said, "I just thought of a question on this topic that brings up another more pressing question. What is our current force size? I was just wondering if we could allocate more troops to the structure clearings and it dawned on me that I have no idea what our force strength is."

There was a long pause, and Kersey raised an eyebrow. "David, I hate to do this to you," he said with a chuckle, "but you probably have the most up to date information."

David nodded, flipping through his binder to several pages with handwritten figures on it. "Okay, I need to preface this before I start diving into the numbers," he began, running his finger across the page. "My small team of four and I have been trying to process this data in real time along a thousand other variables that…" He paused, chewing his lip. "I'm sorry, but this is going to come off as callous, but I honestly don't mean it as such."

"It's okay," Stephens said. "You just lay out the facts. Nobody is going to hold it against you."

David nodded and took a deep breath. "The other variables were things like troop movements, and reacting to real time threats, so they were more important than compiling the deaths," he said, wrinkling his nose at his choice of words. "Please understand that every death hurts, and every time I had to take a report, I felt it, but there simply wasn't time to mourn. We had to keep moving forward."

"Son, I've been in battle, as have several other people on this call," Adams assured him. "We understand that mentality completely. We've been there."

David's shoulders relaxed a little. "Thank you, General," he said, and took a deep breath. "Okay, on to the numbers. When this operation started, we had approximately a hundred and sixty-five thousand troops, and another twenty-five to thirty thousand on the ships. To make life easy, let's call it one-ninety. Now, communication has been spotty with some teams, and there has been a lot of chaos in some of these battles, especially when runners break free. But as of right now, our best guess as far as casualties go, is somewhere between fifteen and twenty percent."

There was a long pause, the horror palpable on both sides of the call.

"Son, I don't mean to discount your numbers," Williams said slowly, "but are you a hundred percent sure on that?"

David licked his lips. "I'll admit Mister President, there is a fair amount of assumptions and guesswork in these numbers," he replied. "But I erred on the side of caution when compiling these. Confirmed dead was easy enough to add, but there were a lot of teams that simply lost contact. On rare occasions it was equipment malfunctions, but most of the time it was because whoever had the radio in the group fell in battle. In these cases, I implemented a twenty-five percent rule."

"Would you care to expand on that?" Williams asked.

David nodded. "Certainly, sir," he replied politely. "If there were, let's say, eight people in a squad, and they fell off of the radar, I used the twenty-five percent rule and assumed that two of the were KIA. We heard more than enough stories over the previous week of positions that were completely overrun, only for survivors to find a place to lay low, or they made it to another squad. Sadly though, based on the number of runner reports we've processed, my twenty-five percent rule may be wildly optimistic."

Stephens scribbled away at a piece of scrap paper and then raised his hand. "So, using some rough calculations," he spoke up, "our best case scenario is that we have a hundred and fifty to a hundred and sixty thousand troops here. Now keep in mind, this doesn't include those involved with the caravan project, or the ones that are still stationed overseas. But this is what we have to work with in the safe zone."

"That's going to be a lot of mouths to feed long term," Adams piped up, "not to mention getting them sheltered. There's only so many nights they can spend outside."

"And that doesn't even include the civilians," John added.

"Do we have an accurate number on them, yet?" Williams asked.

"My team was compiling those numbers before the meeting," Whitney replied. "If we can break for just a moment, I can confer with them and get you that answer."

There was a shuffling of papers, and the President said, "Okay, let's reconvene in ten."

"Corporal Bretz, are you still in the room?" Williams asked, leaning forward and resting his arms on the conference room table. There was a shuffle through the speaker in the center.

"Yes Mister President, I'm here," Bretz replied, sounding confused.

Williams inclined his head to his companion to his right. "General Adams here just informed me that you were the leader of that truck caravan group that tried to block off the northern interstate when this whole thing kicked off," he said.

"Yes sir, that's correct," the Corporal replied.

"Well son, I got one question for you," Williams declared. "How in the hell do you walk around with balls that big?"

Laughter erupted in the room and over the speaker, and then Bretz finally said, "Well sir, when you've had them as long as I have, you just kind of get used to them."

"You did a hell of a job out there," the President said. "Not a lot of people would have volunteered for a job like that."

"Quite frankly sir, it needed doing," Bretz replied, "and my team and I gave it our best shot."

Williams nodded, lacing his fingers on the table. "When you talk to your team," he said, "will you please give them my personal thanks? Their actions saved a lot of lives and made it a lot easier for our troops to march west."

"I'll do that, sir," the Corporal replied.

Whitney entered the room, arms full of clipboards and random stacks of papers. "Sorry about the delay, everyone," she said as she took her seat, frantically organizing all of her sheets. "I just wanted to make sure I had the right numbers."

"No problem Miss Hill," Williams said, motioning to her. "Please, proceed when you're ready."

She plucked the right paper out of her pile, and then pulled a USB drive out of her pocket, heading for the television against the wall and plugging it into the back. She picked up her remote and pulled up an image.

The screen came to life, showing a satellite view of the downtown Seattle area that stretched out in a fifty-mile radius. There were a hundred or so red dots on it, with a high concentration around the edges.

"The dots on this image represent roughly where we have located survivors," Whitney explained. "A fair number of them are individuals who managed to barricade themselves inside their homes or businesses, and had enough resources to ride this thing out. Some are small clusters of people who did the same. In a few cases, like the dots in the park area to the west of town, we have located small communities of people who have been roughing it in the wild for the last month."

Adams leaned forward as he studied the screen. "And we've brought these people in already?"

"Only the ones we've come across while pushing west," Whitney replied, shaking her head. "Some of our helicopter pilots have spotted the wilderness communities, and have delivered messages that we'll be getting to them soon."

Williams nodded, raising a hand. "Do we have an estimate on how many civilians?" he asked.

"Like everything else these days, it's just an educated guess," she replied, "but we're looking at the five to seven thousand range."

The room fell silent at the words.

Kersey cleared his throat on the other end. "Five to seven thousand survivors, in a town of four million," he said slowly. "I don't even know what to say to that."

"Miss Hill," Stephens asked, "is it possible there are other civilians we haven't located yet?"

Whitney nodded, turning towards the speaker. "Yes," she said, "but none of us on my team feels like it's going to bump the numbers up all that much."

"Has any effort been made to locate survivors in smaller communities?" Adams asked, brow furrowing. "Fewer people could mean a better chance at survival."

She clasped her hands in front of her. "It is on our list sir," she confirmed, "and I have one person on my team whose sole mission is to scope out these locations and figure out a game plan to reach them. However, we have a lot more pressing issues to deal with before bringing more people into the fold. The two most important being housing and supplies."

"Out of those two, the housing aspect is going to be the easiest," John piped up, tapping on a notepad in front of him. "We have located every downtown hotel and condo building, and have made that our top priority to clear out first. The weather is already cooling, and it's not going to be too much longer before sleeping outside isn't an option."

Williams nodded, cocking his head. "Do we have a timeline on getting enough beds for everyone?"

"Short term, we should have enough beds on a rotating basis within a week," John replied. "That's going with a twelve hours on, twelve hours off shift schedule. Although, that's not going to be the best conditions."

The President's brow furrowed. "What do you mean?"

"The water in these buildings may or may not work," John explained, "and if it does, they certainly don't have hot water. We don't have staff or a way to keep these rooms clean. And to veer into a gruesome yet necessary problem, a lot of people died in these rooms… and I don't mean they passed in their sleep." He shook his head. "Until we get in there and see what we're dealing with, I won't have an accurate timeline on getting things up to snuff."

Williams sighed. "Are there any other options?" he asked, spreading his arms. "Moving some troops out to the suburbs where we've cleared it out?"

"The troops on the front lines at the barricades are already taking care of that for themselves," John replied with a nod.

"They have enough houses to pick from that I don't think it'll be an issue for them. It's not viable to have the interior troops that are working out from the Coast Guard base to commute to the suburbs for rest. Because fuel, like everything else, is going to be a major issue in procuring."

Williams drummed his fingers on the conference table. "Guess this is as good a time as any to start discussing our supply situation," he prompted.

"Pardon me, Mister President," David said earnestly from the other end of the phone, "but I do have a bit to add to the sleeping arrangements before we move on."

Williams motioned to the speaker and then shook his head when he remembered the young man couldn't see him. "By all means, David," he said.

"When the invasion first began, we put together scavenging teams that specifically targeted stores that had food as well as ammunition," the communications expert began. "Most of the time, the ammunition was in sporting goods stores. Just about every single one of these places is going to have a robust camping section, especially in this area of the country. While it's not going to be enough to give everyone winterized protection, we should be able to cobble together several thousand tents and sleeping bags."

John nodded thoughtfully. "David, if you can send me over an inventory list and where it's at, I'll start coordinating with the transport teams to get them where they need to go," he suggested.

"You'll have it as soon as we're done here," David replied.

John scribbled on his notepad. "Thank you."

"So let's talk supplies," Williams said, clasping his hands together. "I know there is a lot to get to, so let's focus on the basics first, then we can move on from there. Off the top of my head, the three most important are food, water, and warmth. Who wants to start us out?"

"I will, sir," Stephens said through the speaker. "Our MRE situation is pretty dire. Even going to two meals a day, we will deplete our stock within the week. Once those are gone, then they're gone for good, because we don't have the production capacity to make more."

Williams pursed his lips. "What about local sources of food?" he asked.

"I do have some reports from my scavenging teams on the grocery stories, just need to…" David trailed off, and there was the shuffling of papers through the phone. "Found it. Okay, so my teams were more concerned with ammo than food, but they have inventoried a dozen grocery stores, so this will give us a rough idea of what we can expect. The fresh product is all but gone, especially since the power went out. The potatoes should be fine, but that's going to be about it as far as the fresh food goes."

"And how is the non-fresh situation looking?" Stephens asked.

"Canned goods like beans and soups will be fine," David replied. "As will dried pasta and ramen."

"Living off ramen," Kersey cut in, "it's like college all over again."

There was some light chuckling on the other end, and even the President joined in, rubbing his forehead.

"Or adult life, if you're like me," David quipped. "But I digress. Luckily we're in a heavily populated area, so most of these stores are going to be well stocked. On top of that, virtually every house, apartment, and restaurant is going to have a stockpile of goods that we can procure."

Williams took a deep breath. "David, give me your best guess," he said. "Just on canned and dried goods, how long can we sustain nearly two hundred thousand people?"

There was a long pause, and then David cleared his throat. "Based on the numbers I'm seeing and doing a whole lot of guesswork when it comes to what we're going to find in restaurants and homes…" More shuffling papers. "If we go with a strict rationing, I'm taking fifteen hundred calories a day diets, we might be able to stretch it six months."

Adams balked, shaking his head. "Fifteen hundred calories a day?" he demanded. "That's not even going to keep our troops at their current weight, especially given their exertions."

"I understand that, General," David replied quickly. "And if we need to up the calorie count on a limited basis to those doing the most work, I'm sure that can be arranged. But every day we're above that fifteen hundred calorie average, it's one less day we have on the calendar to get a sustainable source of food."

Adams crossed his arms, but then nodded begrudgingly.

Williams waited to make sure he had nothing else to say and then looked around the room. "Does anybody have any idea what needs to be done to create a sustainable source of food for the community?" he asked.

"In the short term, we need to get as many greenhouses up and operational as we can," Kersey spoke up. "I'm not a farmer, but from what I understand, it can take three to four months to start harvesting. That's cutting it close."

"There are more than enough hardware stores in the region that we should have the raw material to make that happen," David added.

"We just have to make sure we pick the correct areas to build them in, as they're going to need sunlight," Kersey continued. "The stadium fortress was having issues with their setup because the sun doesn't get very high in the sky this time of year."

John nodded, scratching his chin thoughtfully. "I know generator usage isn't going to be practical given the fuel situation, but what about bike powered generators?" he suggested. "We literally have an army of fit human beings, we should be able to power lights, shouldn't we?"

"I think it would be more practical to use that manpower to take over the power stations and get them up and running," Kersey countered, "but we can get into that once we're done with the supply issues."

John raised a palm, conceding. "Agreed," he said.

"What about local farms?" Williams suggested. "Surely there have to be some farmers up there."

"Planting season has passed, and won't be around until March," David explained, "which is right around the time we'll be running out of food."

Whitney crossed over to her seat and scribbled on her notepad. "I'll have my team do sweeps of the area to locate the farms," she said. "At the very least, we can spend the next few months preparing for planting season."

"I have a question," Adams cut in, raising a hand. "Do we have anybody that knows a damn thing about farming? It's one thing to plant some tomatoes in the backyard, but it's another thing entirely to create a sustainable food source for two hundred thousand people."

"Based on my experience, General, there are a lot of people from the heartland who are in the military," Kersey replied. "I'd be willing to bet that some of them grew up on farms."

The President leaned forward. "General Stephens, as soon as this meeting is concluded, I want you to start pulling anybody with farming experience off of the line and keep them protected," he declared. "To put it bluntly, we can give

anybody a weapon to fight, but specialized
people are going to be hard to come by."

"Yes sir," Stephens replied, "I will
start pulling them immediately."

There was another shuffle of papers
through the phone speaker, and then David
said, "We may not be totally in the dark
after all. I just looked at the census
that Captain Galvan gave us when we opened
up the stadium, and it looks like there
are half a dozen farming families safely
within the walls."

Williams nodded. "General Stephens,
let's build off of that," he suggested.
"Have the troops you locate coordinate
with the farmers, so we can get some food
growing."

"Yes, sir," Stephens replied.

Whitney held up her palm. "David,
before we move on," she said quickly, "can
you get me a copy of that list? I won't
need names, I just need to know how many
of what we have at our disposal."

"You got it," David replied.

Williams nodded appreciatively at
her. "Please keep us up to date on the
progress of the greenhouses and farms," he
said to the phone. "But for now, let's
move on to the next major concern. Fresh
water."

"We have located several water
treatment facilities, including some close

to downtown," Whitney reported, running a finger down her list. "These places are mostly automated, so it's just going to be a matter of getting the power back on to get them operational again."

Adams took a deep breath. "Even so, we're still going to need people who know how to operate these things," he reminded her, "as well as keeping the pipes clear so the water keeps flowing."

"If I might add," Kersey piped up, "in addition to the fresh drinking water, I think it would be nice to have a functioning restroom situation. Because to put it bluntly, two hundred thousand people can create a whole lot of shit. Not going to take long for the stench to become overwhelming."

"I don't know Captain," Stephens countered, "might be a welcome change from the stench of death in the air."

John shook his head, stifling a smile. "Without debating the merits of which smells worse, this does bring up another point," he said. "What are we going to do with the millions of dead bodies? Just leaving them be will create a whole host of problems aside from the stench."

"They were loading them into dump trucks from outside the stadium," David replied, "but I don't think that's going to be a viable solution for the city given the fuel situation."

Adams nodded. "That's a good point, but let's table the fuel situation for the moment," he said. "Realistically, what can be done with that many bodies?"

"Sadly, the only two viable options are mass graves and burning," Kersey said, "and with our fuel situation I don't think burning is going to be possible."

Williams pursed his lips for a moment. "David, please add two things to your list," he finally said. "Please collect every shovel and manual digging instrument you can find, and coordinate with Miss Hill's team about the best spots for mass graves."

There was a thick silence, as the overwhelming thought of burying the entire town of Seattle sank over everyone like a stone.

"I'll get it done, sir," David finally said, voice a touch hoarse.

The President pressed his palms down on the conference table. "Okay, on to the next major issue," he said, blowing out a deep breath. "How are the military supplies looking? I know the MRE situation isn't good, but how are we looking elsewhere?"

"The fuel situation is dire, to say the least," Stephens replied. "The consumer grade vehicles can utilize local gas stations and stay operational, at least for a while, but when it comes to aviation, we're in trouble."

Adams' brow furrowed. "Exactly how bad are we talking, Stephens?" he asked.

"With what we have on the ships and airports we control," the General replied, "we have about forty hours of flight time for our helicopters remaining, a little less if we're transporting something heavy. The planes are even worse, with about twenty hours of flight time remaining on those."

Williams looked to Whitney. "Is it possible to take over some other airports in the region?"

"We have a list of small regional airports," she replied with a nod, "but for the most part, we'll burn as much fuel getting to them as we'll find there. In my opinion, we should leave them be so that if we have to do longer runs to Portland or beyond, we'll have a spot to refuel and extend our range."

"I agree with Miss Hill," Stephens said. "Having the ability to stretch our range is a lot more valuable than having a couple more tanks of gas here."

Williams shook his head. "What about the oil fields in Canada?' he asked.

"Wasn't that one of the main reasons we picked Seattle as an invasion point?"

"We are coordinating with the Canadian government to secure the fields and get workers up there again," John confirmed. "We also have our eye on processing facilities on the US/Canada border that we can utilize. The problem there is, we still have a significant zombie infestation problem that will need to be dealt with."

The President shrugged. "Well, we certainly have the manpower to handle that," he said, looking around. "Don't we?"

"Manpower?" Stephens replied. "Absolutely. Ammunition is going to be an issue, however."

Williams pursed his lips. "How big of an issue?"

"We expended a lot of rounds to secure the city," Stephens explained. "We've allocated a significant number of rounds to the soldiers manning the lines. Essentially two bullets for every suspected zombie they may encounter."

Adams leaned forward. "What are the reserves looking like?" he asked.

"Undistributed rounds?" Stephens replied, dragging out the word for a moment as he thought. "If we're lucky, maybe half a million rounds, with ten percent of that being for the heavy weapons."

John rubbed his forehead. "Not sure how much damage we're going to be able to do with every soldier getting three and a half rounds apiece," he said dryly.

"David," Whitney spoke up, "how are the stores looking for ammunition?"

"Ninety-five percent is consumer grade stuff," the communications expert replied. "Nine mil, shotgun shells, and enough twenty-two ammo to fill the stadium."

"A twenty-two isn't going to have much stopping power," Kersey admitted, "but in the right hands it could be a viable weapon."

Adams shook his head. "Still not ideal to be sending our troops into a massive confrontation with," he said gruffly.

Williams looked around the room, eyes searching. "So, what can be done about this?" he asked.

"First thing we need to do is collect every spent casing we can come across," Whitney replied. "There should be hand loaders and raw materials in gun shops and elsewhere. It's not going to be a huge score, but bullets are going to be scarce. We need to salvage every single one we can."

"We should also add distribution warehouses to our list of places to check," David added. "The internet delivery ones probably won't have anything, but the big box stores just might."

John nodded, pointing his pencil at the speaker. "Should probably check there for food and other goods as well."

"Miss Hill," David said, "if your team can get us a list of potential targets, I'll get teams sent out there."

She nodded, scribbling on her notepad. "I'll send over what I can."

Williams nodded and took a deep breath. "So, what else can we do on the ammunition front?" he asked. "Because while salvaging and scrounging for rounds is good, we're going to need something bigger."

"Mister President, I do have a plan for this," Stephens piped up, "but I need a little more time to work on it before presenting it, just to make sure it's viable. Can we schedule a short meeting this evening to discuss it?"

Williams blinked and shrugged. "Of course, General," he replied, and then looked down at his list of topics. "So let's move on to… power. Who has something on this?"

"Sir, my team has located every power plant serving the greater Seattle area," Whitney replied. "Every one of them, save one, is a hydro plant. Assuming the person in charge of the stadium was smart enough to protect some power plant workers, it shouldn't be a big deal to get the lights back on in a reasonable amount of time."

"According to the ledger," David added, "there are a dozen people with power plant experience."

Whitney smiled and motioned to the phone. "Well, there you go," she said.

Williams nodded. "If everything is hydro except one, what's the last remaining plant?" he asked.

"Nuclear," Whitney replied, and the tension was palpable.

After a few beats, Williams asked, "Is it in any danger of melting down?"

John shook his head. "Unlikely," he replied calmly. "These plants have multiple failsafes that keep them secure in case of a catastrophic event, such as them going unmanned during a zombie apocalypse. That said, these failsafes do have an expiration date, usually within six to eight weeks, and every day past that puts them in danger."

"Where is this one located?" Williams asked.

Whitney tapped her pencil on her notepad. "To the west of Olympia," she replied. "Reports on the ground say that the area is partially secured, so hopefully within the next few days, we can get people in there to look it over."

"Please, just for my own mental wellbeing, make this a priority," Williams said, holding up both of his palms. "We already have a zombie infestation, the last thing we need is to go all fifties monster movie and have radioactive zombies as well."

There was some light chuckling, though more than a few of his comrades couldn't help but picture the devastation a nuclear meltdown could cause.

"Yes Mister President," Stephens replied, "I'll make that a priority."

Adams crossed his arms. "This does bring up another question, though," he said. "What about the other nuclear plants around the country?"

"There are a total of fifty-eight plants nationwide," John replied.

Williams blinked at him, chewing his lower lip. "What's the likelihood that we can reach them all and shut them down before they risk going into meltdown?" he asked.

"Honestly sir, not good," John admitted. "We might have the manpower on the ground thanks to the caravan groups, but they're not going to have the experts on hand to shut them down."

"Is it possible for the power plant experts to draw them up a plan?" Kersey asked. "Like a guide to shutting them down safely?"

John shook his head thoughtfully. "I'll be honest, I have no idea," he admitted.

"I'll have Captain Galvan convene a meeting with them right after we're done here," Stephens suggested. "We can address it at this evening's meeting."

Williams pressed his palms together. "Time is of the essence, General," he said. "Why don't we take five so that you can go ahead and relay that message to him? That way they'll have an answer for you by the time you get over there."

"As you wish, Mister President," Stephens replied.

Williams nodded and leaned back in his chair. "Okay, reconvene in five."

CHAPTER SIX

"Okay, is everyone back on the line?" Williams asked through the speaker.

Stephens nodded, swallowing a sip of water. "Yes, Mister President," he replied. "We're all here."

"Good, let's continue," Williams said, and there was a shuffle of papers through the phone. "Now that we've covered supplies and basic necessities, I want to hear about our military capabilities. What is the current status of our force?"

Stephens and Kersey shared a pointed look, and then the General said, "Mister President, I don't really know how else to put it other than… it's a complete and total clusterfuck."

"By all means General," Williams said dryly, "don't feel like you have to sugarcoat it for me."

Stephens sighed. "My apologies Mister President," he said, rubbing his forehead. "But that is a one hundred percent accurate statement. Our forces are a complete mess, and there's no real easy way to fix it."

"While I believe your assessment," Williams said slowly, "would you humor me and walk me through it?"

The General took a deep breath, clasping his hands on the table in front

of him. "Of course," he replied. "The
Texas Virus, or whatever the official name
is, targeted everyone with A-type blood.
So right off the bat, we lost forty
percent of our fighting force. It was
indiscriminate, taking out Privates all
the way up to Generals, and everything in
between. On top of that, we have lost tens
of thousands in battle, even before we
invaded Seattle." He shook his head.
"Securing the small towns in Kansas and
the debacle at Kansas City hit us hard. We
also had a fair number of defections as
well, people who weren't exactly thrilled
with our retreat strategy. Combine all
that with the incredibly fast speed this
hit us with, and our command structure is
a complete mess." He sighed. "On top of
that, there are a fair number of those in
command positions who aren't suited for
this type of warfare. They have spent
their entire careers facing a completely
different kind of enemy, and some just
haven't adjusted to this kind of warfare.
As a result, some perished in battle, and
others have had their command relieved
because their unwillingness to change
tactics got people killed."

"That doesn't sound ideal," Williams
commented, sounding tired.

Stephens shook his head. "It isn't,
but there's more," he continued. "At the

moment, we don't have access to personnel
records, so we don't know who was in line
for a promotion or not. We've also had a
fair number of discharged vets joining the
ranks again, because if there ever was an
all hands on deck moment, it's this one.
If they could document their prior rank,
we just went ahead and reinstated them at
that rank. Those who couldn't were
relegated to Private status… though of
course that did open the door to
cosplayers."

"I'm sorry, *cosplayers*?" Williams
asked, voice mystified.

Kersey leaned forward. "Yes, Mister
President," he said. "Are you familiar
with comic book conventions? Where people
would dress up as their favorite super
hero? That's cosplaying."

"Yes Captain, I'm tracking now,"
Williams replied flippantly. "So, some
people out there took this opportunity to
live out their military fantasies. These
people showed up in combat fatigues with a
rifle, and you let them in?"

Stephens took a deep breath.
"Frankly, we needed guns, and people to
use them," he explained. "There were some
we suspected of being cosplayers, so we
had people watch them carefully."

"Have there been any incidents
involving this group?" Williams asked.

The General tilted his head back and forth. "Some," he admitted, "but not more than the normal rate of incidents among enlisted men."

"Still…" the President said, drawing out the word. "I would like you to keep an eye on it if you wouldn't mind. On that point, Miss Hill, do we have access to the military database?"

"I believe we do, Mister President," Whitney replied.

"I know that we have a lot on our plates, with some issues like food and preventing a nuclear meltdown taking precedent," Williams said, and paused to wait for everyone's light chuckling. "However, we need to do a full census of the military. Find out who we have, cross check it with the military database, and get the structure of our military back in order."

Kersey nodded, leaning forward. "If I might add to that," he cut in, "I think we should do a census of everyone, civilians included. We not only need to know who's here, but we need to know what they can do. We're not just setting up a military stronghold, we are actively rebuilding society. As a result, we're going to need everything a society has. From emergency services all the way down to cooks. To be blunt, grunts are a dime a dozen, but someone who knows how to properly prepare a steak is a rarity and should be treated like royalty."

"Now we just need to get some cattle farmers to raise us some animals," Adams added.

Stephens laughed. "And a butcher to carve it up properly," he said.

"And a truck driver to get it from point A to point B," Whitney added, chuckling.

"And a mechanic to make sure the truck works properly," John added through his own laughter.

David shook his head with a grin. "And an AC repair man to make sure the truck is properly cooled."

The laughter died out, the cold reality of the situation sinking in. The structures of civilization had survived the assault, but the inner workings of society had crumbled to death and gore, and nothing was going to be as easy as one step. Just having a steak contained so many steps.

"General Stephens," Williams said finally, clearing his throat, "it would appear as though you have one hell of a massive undertaking on your hands. I would suggest appointing someone, civilian or military, to head up this portion of the operation."

"Might I suggest Captain Galvan?" John piped up. "By all accounts, he worked very well with the civilian administrator of the Seattle stadium, so this would just be an expansion of his duties from the last month."

Stephens and Kersey both nodded emphatically at each other.

"I have absolutely no objection to that whatsoever," the General agreed. "I can speak to him about the job after we wrap up here."

"If you and John feel like he's up to the job, consider it his," Williams confirmed.

Stephens nodded. "I'll give you an update this evening."

"Thank you, General," Williams replied. "Before we move on to the next topic, I have a question for Captain Kersey."

Kersey's brow furrowed. "Yes, Mister President?" he asked.

"Captain, in light of your actions in Spokane and Seattle," Williams began, "and the fact that our command structure has been decimated and is in desperate need of people experienced in this kind of warfare, how would you feel about being a General?"

The room fell silent, and Kersey stared at Stephens, blinking rapidly and then glancing to Bretz, who grinned widely.

Kersey opened his mouth and then closed it again, at a loss for words. He finally managed to find his voice, stammering, "Wow, Mister President…" He let out a deep *whoosh* of breath. "That is the most humbling offer that has ever been extended my way."

"Well son, you have a mind for this kind of warfare," Williams explained, "and we need people like you in decision-making positions. Now I fully realize this would probably set a record for fastest promotion from Sergeant to General, but I think we can all agree these aren't ordinary times."

Kersey stared down into his lap for a moment, and then looked to Stephens, who smiled and gave him a thumbs up. He licked his lips and then cleared his throat.

"First off," Kersey began hoarsely, "thank you for thinking so highly of me, sir. I joined the military because I wanted to make a difference for the people of this nation. With what you just said, I feel like my decision was justified. That said, I would love to." He took a deep breath. "However, for the moment, I must decline."

Bretz let out a small noise of surprise, and Stephens's eyes widened.

"May I ask why, Captain?" Williams asked, clearly confused.

Kersey swallowed hard. "Well, sir, for as long as I can remember, every time General Stephens here says he's working on a plan, I go ahead and pencil myself in for some new PTSD."

Everyone laughed, on both sides of the call, and he shook his head, smiling to himself.

"In all seriousness though," he continued, sobering, "I feel like I can do more good in the field than in a war room, especially now that we have Seattle secured."

"Captain, it takes one hell of a man to turn down a promotion like this, and especially turn it down in favor of going back out into harm's way," Williams commended. "Not only do you have my utmost respect, you also have my promise that as long as I'm in charge of this country, my offer stands."

Kersey nodded firmly. "Thank you, Mister President," he said sincerely. "And depending on what General Stephens runs by me after the meeting, I may have a different answer for you this evening."

Williams burst into laughter, backed up by the others.

"Well, getting back on track," he finally said, "now that we have this foothold, how do we bring new people into the fold? How do we let them know we're here?"

"Traditional media isn't going to work," Whitney pointed out, "because even if we somehow got them up and running, nobody is going to be tuning in."

"We can certainly let our caravan teams know," John cut in, "and they can spread it directly."

"I like that idea…" Whitney mused. "But it's not exactly feasible to expect survivors in Georgia or Florida to make a cross-country journey to a safe zone."

"I don't know," John replied, "we run out of coffee in here, and I'll consider it."

"I think we all would," she agreed with a chuckle.

Kersey cocked his head. "What if we made it so people don't have to make it all the way here on their own?" he asked. "I mean, we control the rail lines from here to North Platte, Nebraska, don't we? It wouldn't take many men to set up a secure area for people to rest until the train came back."

Stephens nodded, pointing at him. "The depot at North Platte still had plenty of fuel," he said. "We could keep a single line running back and forth for months."

"I like that idea," Williams said. "Let's start game planning it. Figure out what it would take to make it happen. It's not a huge priority, but I would like it on the list."

Stephens scribbled on his scrap paper. "Consider it done, sir," he said.

"But come on people," Williams declared, "let's think outside the box, here. How else can we spread the word about Seattle?"

David stood up from his seat and stood next to the table, leaning towards the phone. "I have an idea, sir," he said. "It's not the most efficient, but it pays dividends in the long run."

"All right, let's hear it," the President replied.

"Well, a lot of survivalists use ham radio to chat with one another, and there's a good chance that some of the survivor communities have access to one as well," David explained. "It's going to be tedious, but we can send out messages to every frequency, and continue trying until we reach people. If we manage to find a few, then they can spread it to the others they know. We can also set up a dedicated frequency where people can tune in to get up to date information. This isn't going to yield instant results, but long term, it should work."

"That's what I'm talking about," Williams replied. "How do you propose we go about implementing this?"

David shrugged. "First off, we need to locate ham radios," he said.

"Talk with Captain Galvan in the stadium," Whitney piped up. "I'm pretty certain they have a setup already."

He smiled. "Thank you, I'll do that," he said.

There was a moment of silence, and then David took his seat again.

"Okay," Williams finally spoke up, "doesn't seem like there are any other ideas, but I think we have enough to get started on. I believe everybody has their immediate tasks, but I want to take a moment to brainstorm about the next phase of rebuilding society and what we might need to focus on. Never know when you might have a brilliant idea, so might as well get ourselves thinking on it. So how wants to start us out?"

"I think once we get through the next few months and get ourselves on solid footing," John began, "we're going to have to think about bringing back in a normal economy. Having an emergency community-based approach to things is fine for a while, but it won't take long for people to want to be rewarded for going above and beyond what's asked of them. So we need to be thinking of how to bring in some form of currency."

"Why wouldn't the dollar work?" the President asked. "It's served us well for a couple of centuries, now."

"Because there is way too much of it out there, just ripe for the picking," John explained. "The last thing we want is to have adventurous types leaving the safe zone to rob a bank in Portland and flood our economy with bills. We need to create something from scratch so that we can control it to make sure things don't go haywire."

Williams grunted softly. "That's an understandable concern," he mused. "As much as it would pain me to be the President that presided over the demise of the dollar, we have to do what's best for the community. So what else?"

"I think when we get the results of the census," Whitney cut in, "if there are people in the military with special skills, they need to be allowed to leave service to pursue that."

"I was under the impression we were already going to reassign vital personnel to civilian roles," Adams replied gruffly.

"For stuff like farming and doctors, absolutely," Whitney explained. "I'm talking about secondary things, like carpentry or mechanics. Things that aren't going to make or break the community, but certainly things that will increase the livability of it. We should also help those who want to set up storefronts so that we can really get a thriving economy going again. The last thing we want is to force people into jobs they hate and control every aspect of it. That's only going to last for so long, and having that would potentially alienate the civilians who come here. We need this place to feel like a home, not a military-occupied war zone."

"Excellent points, Miss Hill," Williams commended. "Anybody else?"

Kersey cleared his throat. "We need to put someone in charge of entertainment," he suggested.

Adams barked a laugh, and then quickly cut himself off when he realized nobody else joined in. "Apologies, I thought that was a joke," he admitted.

"I'm very serious about this, General," the Captain insisted. "We're going to need things to keep everyone's mind off of the massive pile of work that needs to be done, as well as the danger that is going to be at our doorsteps for years to come. We're going to need a team of curators to bring in every bit of media that we can find while going through businesses and homes. CDs, movies, video games, books, board games, anything and everything that can be entertaining. On top of that, we should also think about what Captain Galvan did in the stadium, instituting community classes like Yoga and art projects. Not only does it keep people occupied, but it brings them closer together."

"Another good point, future General Kersey," Williams said.

The Captain rolled his eyes and chuckled to himself as Bretz patted him on the shoulder teasingly.

"I think we have more than enough to go on for the time being," Williams declared. "Let's break and reconvene at zero-seven hundred Seattle time. Does that work for everyone?"

There was a murmuring of the affirmative from both sides of the call.

"Fantastic," the President said. "Let's start working on the most pressing issues, and General Stephens, I'll look forward to hearing your plan for our ammunition problem."

Stephens nodded sharply. "I'll do my best not to disappoint you, sir."

The line went dead, and the quartet sat in silence for a moment.

Finally, Kersey turned in his seat and cocked his head, smirking at Stephens. "Okay, you want to clue me in to what I'm going to be doing instead of sitting in a cushy office like you?"

The General barked a laugh, and leaned back in his chair, a playful grin on his face. "Tell me Kersey, have you ever been to Idaho?"

"Idaho?" Kersey stammered, shaking his head, eyes wide. "What in the almighty hell is in Idaho that can't be found here?"

Stephens held out his hand. "Bretz, can you hand me that magazine on the shelf next to you, there?" he asked.

The Corporal looked behind him and found a magazine on the shelf with a buxom blonde on the cover, holding a machine gun way too large for her body. He handed it over, and Stephens tossed it on the table.

Kersey raised an eyebrow. "I mean, if *she's* there I'll take the next flight out," he joked.

"You and me both, soldier," Stephens agreed. "But flip to page forty-seven."

The Captain opened the magazine, licking his thumb and flipping through the pages. He reached the right one and began to read out loud. "How Boise, Idaho, became one of the biggest gun manufacturing towns in the world." He dropped the book, staring at the General with wide eyes. "Seriously?"

"Absolutely!" Stephens exclaimed excitedly. "They have over a dozen major manufacturers there, all set up and ready to roll. Machines, as well as raw material. Now, at some point we'll have to replenish the raw materials, but having the manufacturing capability would go a long way towards sustaining our military."

Kersey couldn't help but chuckle to himself. "So? What do you want me to do?" he asked, spreading his arms.

Before Stephens could answer, Bretz stood up and stepped next to his Captain. "What do you want *us* to do?" he corrected.

Kersey nodded at him with a smile.

"I need you to assemble a team and parachute into Boise," Stephens continued. "Figure out what the situation on the ground is, make contact with the locals if there are any, and secure the factories."

The Captain laughed. "Oh, is that all?" he asked, sarcasm evident in his tone. "How many are you sending me in with? Four hundred? Five hundred?"

"Ten," Stephens replied, deadpan. "Including you."

Kersey rubbed his forehead, a horror laugh escaping his throat. "You want ten of us to drop in a secure a dozen sites?"

"Why only ten of us?" Bretz asked in disbelief.

Stephens shook his head. "Because that's all the fuel we can spare for the airplane," he explained. "So unless someone wants to hang onto the wing—"

"Kowalski," Kersey and Bretz blurted at the same time, and the General chuckled.

"Please don't put Kowalski on the wing," he pleaded, pressing his palms together. "Don't dare him to do it either, because I know he will."

"Okay…" Bretz said petulantly, and Kersey feigned a pout.

When they were done with their little show, Kersey asked, "So, when can we expect reinforcements?"

"Realistically?" Stephens took a deep breath. "Ten to fifteen days."

Bretz crossed his arms. "Oh, is that all?"

"They're going to have to come via surface roads," Stephens replied. "And there's not exactly a direct route they'll be able to take. Plus, and this may sound harsh, if the plants have been gutted, burned down, or there are other complications, we need to know that so we don't waste our extremely limited resources on this excursion."

Kersey nodded, leaning back in his chair. "That makes sense," he admitted.

"So, I guess if the situation on the ground looks bad," Bretz drawled, "we'll just hitchhike back?"

The Captain smirked. "Or, we could vacation Boise," he suggested playfully.

"I hear it's nice in about six months after the winter goes away."

"Don't worry," Stephens said, putting up his hands, "I'll have a plan in place for extraction if things go south."

Kersey smacked his knees, letting out a deep breath. "Well, already regretting not taking your job, General," he declared, and they shared a laugh as he got to his feet. "But seeing as how this is our mission now, when do we leave?"

"Twenty-four hours," Stephens replied. "I know you've been sleeping like shit this week, so we're going to set your tea up with rooms at the hotel just across from the stadium so you can get rested."

Kersey nodded. "All right, I'll go assemble my team," he replied.

The General raised an eyebrow. "You know, you can just tell me who you want and I'll get them here, right?" he asked.

"We're about to embark on yet another suicide mission," the Captain explained. "I feel like it's my duty to inform my lucky participants in person."

Stephens nodded in appreciation. "I understand," he said. "In the meantime, I'll make sure you have everything you could possibly need for your load out."

"Appreciate that, General," Kersey said, and headed for the door. Before he left, he turned to David, who'd stepped aside with his stack of papers. "David, it's been a genuine pleasure working with you these last few weeks," he said, extending his hand.

The communications expert shook and smiled. "Likewise, Captain," he replied. "It has been awe-inspiring to watch you work."

"I wouldn't go quite that far," Kersey replied, chuckling. "I will say, however, that I admire the fact that you are sticking on a heading up the community outreach program, among other things."

David shrugged. "This is my home now too," he pointed out. "So I gotta do what I can to make it succeed."

"You don't let the General here give you any shit, you hear?" Kersey said, waving a hand at a smirking Stephens.

David grinned. "You come back from Idaho in one piece, you hear?" he replied.

Kersey gave him a nod and led Bretz from the room, headed for Benny's chopper.

"Well David," Stephens declared, "I guess you have officially been passed off to me. Are you ready to get started building your radio network?"

The communications expert nodded, practically vibrating with excitement. "Absolutely, sir," he replied. "Let's get to it."

CHAPTER EIGHT

Kersey looked down at the scout and sweeper teams below the helicopter as Benny flew them north towards Burlington.

"Man, this shit is gonna go on for years, ain't it?" the pilot asked.

Kersey nodded. "Afraid so, buddy," he admitted. "But this kind of action up here shouldn't last more than a few weeks."

"Then the real fun begins, right?" Benny asked.

The Captain laughed. "I think we have different definitions of fun," he said dryly.

"So, where you boys off to next?" the pilot asked. "Or is it top secret and all that jazz?"

Kersey chuckled, a mischievous twinkle in his eye. "Not sure who you would tell," he said, "but let's be honest, do you really think people would take you as a credible source?"

"Depends on the topic," Benny shot back playfully. "If I'm dispensing knowledge about military operations? Probably not. If I'm letting them know which run-down diner waitress will give them a Blue Plate Special in the walk-in freezer if you tip 'em right? Then probably so."

Kersey burst out laughing. "Why do I get the feeling that you've led an interesting life, buddy?" he asked.

"Oh, I've got some stories that will haunt your dreams, Captain," Benny assured him.

Kersey shook his head. "I have no doubt that you do," he agreed. "But to get back to less disturbing topics… we're going to be heading out to Idaho. Boise, to be specific."

"Well hell," the pilot burst out, "I lived in Boise for a while after the war!"

The Captain blinked at him in shock. "You don't strike me as the Idaho type," he admitted. "The 'I'd bang a ho' type, but not Idaho."

"You're right about both," Benny replied, laughing.

"So how in the hell did you end up there?" Kersey asked.

The pilot shrugged. "Man, it was right after getting back from the war," he replied. "Made the near fatal mistake of falling for the first woman who paid me any attention. Couple months into things, she convinced me to pick up and move to Boise so she could pursue her dreams of being a farmer or rancher or something she was woefully unqualified to do. Apparently she thought growing a pot plant in her closet made her a farmer."

"Come on now," Kersey cut in playfully, "growing pot in your closet is a skill, after all."

Benny nodded. "Wholeheartedly agree," he admitted, "but if you smoked what she was growing you would know she didn't have that skill."

"So what happened?" Kersey asked.

The pilot took a deep breath. "Well, we got out there, and of course I was the only one with money, so it was my name on the apartment lease," he began. "To her credit, she managed to find a job on a farm pretty quick. Unfortunately, she lasted about three days before saying it wasn't for her. A week later, she hopped a bus and headed home, leaving me with a year long lease."

"You know you can break those, right?" Kersey asked, raising an eyebrow.

Benny rolled his eyes. "Oh of course I know," he replied, "but it was a great excuse to make her lazy ass catch a bus than go back with her."

"Sounds like you made the right call, man," Kersey said, and they shared a laugh.

The bridge fortifications approaching Burlington came into view, having been improved with elevator gunner nests on either side made out of painter's scaffolding. Benny hovered over the Super

Center and set the chopper down in the middle of the lot.

As the blades slowed, Sergeant Copeland approached the bird.

"Copeland!" Benny exclaimed as he hopped to the ground.

The Sergeant offered him a wide grin. "Hey buddy," he said, "wasn't expecting a resupply today."

"Well, I had some special cargo that I felt needed to be delivered personally," Benny explained, and stepped aside as the other two came around the chopper.

Copeland shook his head. "Aw hell, here comes trouble," he declared.

"You don't know the half of it," Kersey admitted with a grin, and they shook hands.

"Come on, we got a nice little relaxation spot set up," the Sergeant offered, waving for them to follow him. "You want me to call anybody else up here?"

Before Kersey could respond, somebody yelled from the front of the Super Center.

"Holy shit, is that Captain Kersey, live and in the flesh?!" Kowalski called.

The Captain laughed and shook his head. "I think Kowalski is going to be more than enough," he said.

The sniper approached, a spring in his step as he appraised the duo. "And

Bretz!" he exclaimed. "You're looking pretty good there, got a nice tan going on. Which is impressive given the cloud covered days. How long did you have to bake to get that kind of color?"

"Longer than I'd like to admit," Bretz replied dryly.

"You might as well join us Kowalski," Copeland suggested, "the good Captain here is bringing us some new trouble to get into."

The five men headed into the Super Center, where several soldiers were walking about and hanging around. Some snacked on junk food, others lounged around on makeshift cots between the registers.

"Hey, if the two of you are here," Kowalski asked without turning around, "then what kind of trouble is Baker and Mason getting into?"

Kersey and Bretz shared a concerned glance, and the Captain cleared his throat. "Baker got himself a bit of a concussion, so he's resting up," he said thickly. "Mason…"

There was an awkward silence, and Kowalski stopped walking, turning around. He swallowed hard, shaking his head. "That's a damn shame, man," he said quietly, in a rare moment of seriousness. "Mason was a good kid."

"Yeah, he was," Kersey agreed.

Copeland gave them a moment of silence and then waved for them to follow him. "Come on, we're almost there," he said.

They entered an area at the back of the store that looked like a summer backyard cookout. There were several tables and outdoor lounge chairs spread out in a circle, with a charcoal grill in the middle. A soldier stood there, grilling up some canned meat with a smile.

"Hey Sergeant," he greeted, "just about got these done if you're looking for a hot meal. Bread's a little stale, but it's still good."

Copeland nodded and held out his hand for the tongs. "Appreciate it, soldier," he said. "I can cover it from here, why don't you go take ten? We have some things to discuss."

The soldier nodded, handing over the tongs and inclining his head towards the Captain before sauntering off towards the front of the store.

"Anybody for some canned meat burgers?" Copeland asked, checking the patties and flipping them.

Everyone nodded and took seats around the patio table, and Kowalski took up a stack of plates, passing out the burgers as Copeland removed them from the grill.

"Okay, Captain," Copeland finally said as he sat down with his own plate, "lay it on us. What sort of suicide mission are we going on this time?"

Kersey took a bite of his sandwich, holding up a finger as he chewed and swallowed. "How do you boys feel about conquering Boise, Idaho?" he finally asked.

Copeland raised an eyebrow. "Conquer Boise?" he asked. "How many of us are they sending?"

"Ten," the Captain replied, and then dove back into his sandwich.

"Yeah, that should probably be plenty," Kowalski quipped, leaning back in his chair.

The group laughed, and then Copeland finally rubbed his forehead.

"You serious?" he asked

Kersey nodded. "Yep, serious on both counts," he confirmed. "There's a huge ammo shortage, and General Stephens discovered that Boise is one of the gun manufacturing capitals of the world. Our job is to go in, secure the factories, make contact with local survivors—"

"If there are any," Kowalski interrupted through a mouthful of fried meat and bread.

Bretz clapped his friend on the back. "You know our luck Kowalski," he declared, "there's going to be survivors."

The sniper swallowed. "Hopefully they're friendly this time," he added.

"Again, you know our luck," Bretz replied, rolling his eyes.

"Reinforcements?" Copeland asked.

Kersey swallowed his last bite of food. "Coming on the ground," he replied, "so realistically two weeks out."

"At least we'll get a two-week vacation from the rebuild," the Sergeant pointed out.

Kowalski raised a hand. "Can we make it three weeks?" he asked. "I really don't want to be around for the corpse removal phase of things. My job is to put them down, not pick them back up."

"It's rare that I agree with Kowalski," Copeland began, jerking a thumb at the sniper, "but I'm with him."

"So when do we leave?" Kowalski asked.

Kersey sat back in his chair. "We fly out tomorrow afternoon," he explained. "General Stephens has us set up in a hotel near the stadium, so we can get properly rested."

"I'm totally ordering room service," the sniper declared.

"Hell man, I just want to sleep for twelve hours in a soft bed and not be disturbed," Copeland moaned, but then raised a hand. "Wait. We get our own rooms, right?" he asked.

Kersey chuckled. "Don't worry," he said, "if we don't, I'll make sure Kowalski bunks with someone else."

"Gotta be my sniping buddy Wade," Kowalski said, raising a fist. "Room service and picking off zombies from the top floor. Now that sounds relaxing."

"Speaking of Wade," Copeland cut in, "you know who you want to be on this little excursion?"

Kersey nodded. "I've been giving it some thought," he said. "Need people I know can work under pressure… well, and Kowalski."

The group laughed, and the sniper playfully gave his Captain a middle finger before shoving the rest of his sandwich into his mouth.

"I figure the four of us," Kersey continued, "plus Johnson if he can be spared from the barricade here."

Copeland nodded. "I can arrange it," he said. "So who else are you thinking?"

"Wade has to be on the team for sure!" Kowalski cried, near choking as he struggled to swallow his giant mouthful. He coughed and smashed his fist into his chest, finally clearing his airway before continuing, "Can't be the only sniper in the group."

"Looks like we have a vote for Wade," Copeland said. "I'd like to bring along Dawson, Mack, and Moss."

Kersey nodded. "That gets us to nine."

Bretz raised a hand. "I don't think Baker would forgive us if we left him behind for cleanup duty," he suggested.

"Last I heard he was still in the infirmary," the Captain replied, brow furrowing.

"Don't worry, I'm sure I can break him out," the Corporal said.

Kersey chuckled. "Just make sure to leave survivors," he replied. "We're kind of short-handed."

"No promises," Bretz said with a grin.

The group chuckled and sat around in a rare moment of silence, enjoying the relaxation before the chaos that lay ahead.

END

Up Next: The action shifts to El Paso as the massive zombie horde marches towards the unsuspecting survivors in the El Paso: Creeping Death series.

www.ingramcontent.com/pod-product-compliance
Lightning Source LLC
Chambersburg PA
CBHW060740210726

48292CB00012B/29